MAYOR GOOD BOY

GOES HOLLYWOOD

ALSO BY DAVE SCHEIDT AND MIRANDA HARMON

Mayor Good Boy

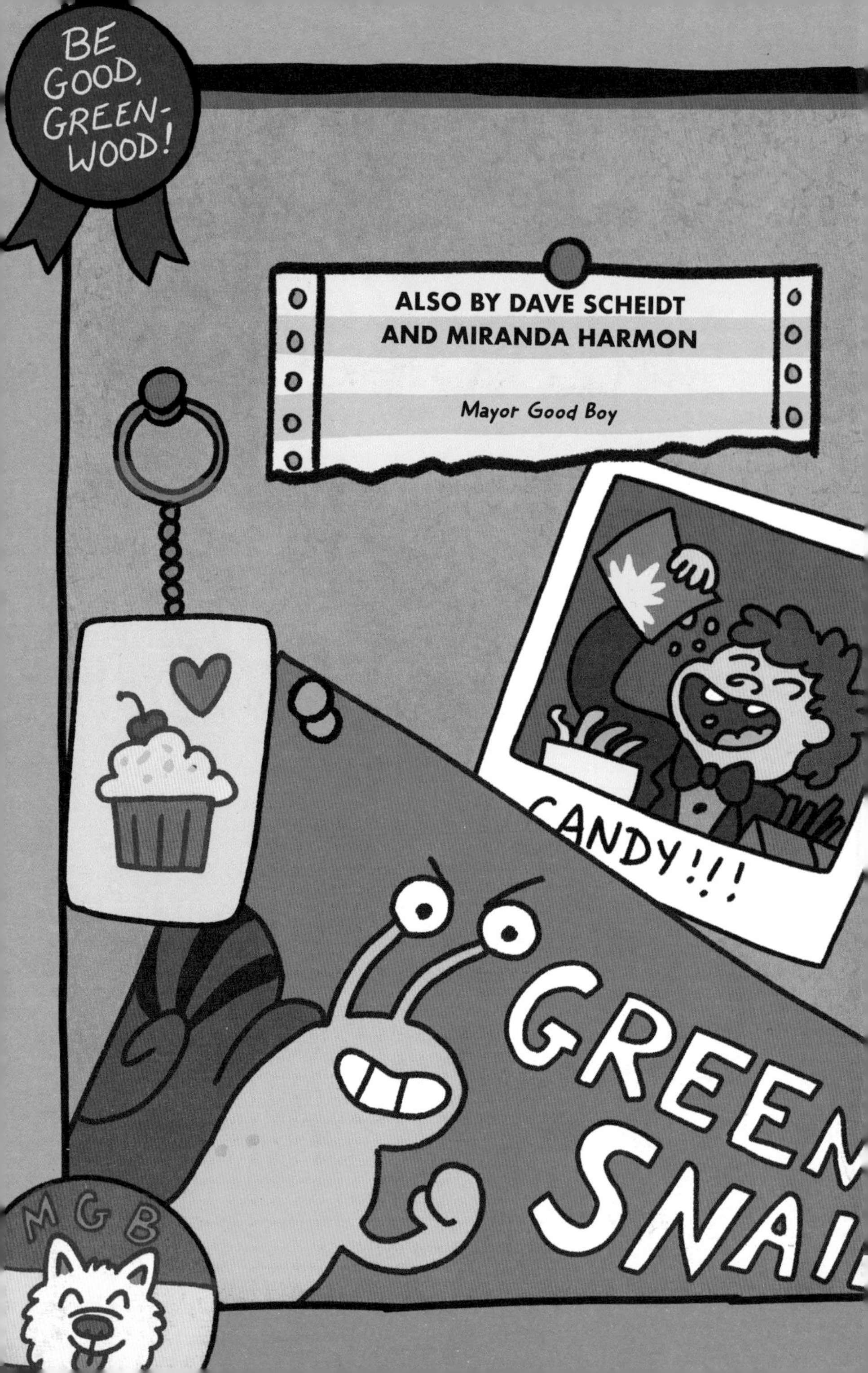
BE GOOD, GREENWOOD!
CANDY!!!
MGB

MAYOR GOOD BOY

GOES Hollywood

Written by Dave Scheidt
Illustrated by Miranda Harmon
Colored by Lyle Lynde

RH GRAPHIC
NEW YORK

ADMIT
ONE

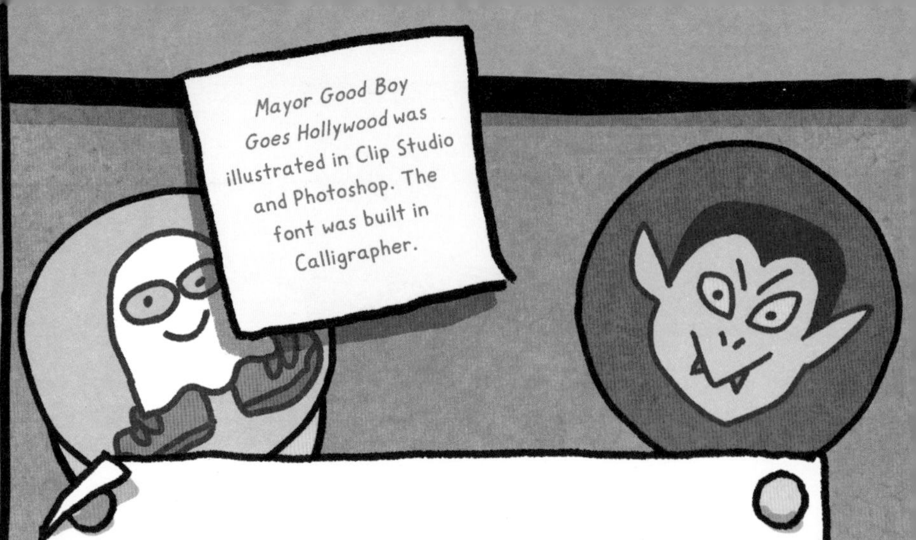
Mayor Good Boy Goes Hollywood was illustrated in Clip Studio and Photoshop. The font was built in Calligrapher.

This is a work of fiction. Names, characters, places, and incidents either are the product of the author's imagination or are used fictitiously. Any resemblance to actual persons, living or dead, events, or locales is entirely coincidental.

 Published in the United States by RH Graphic, an imprint of Random House Children's Books, a division of Penguin Random House LLC, New York.

RH Graphic with the book design is a trademark of Penguin Random House LLC.

Visit us on the web! RHKidsGraphic.com • @RHKidsGraphic

Educators and librarians, for a variety of teaching tools, visit us at RHTeachersLibrarians.com

Library of Congress Cataloging-in-Publication Data is available upon request.
ISBN 978-0-593-12489-5 (hardcover) — ISBN 978-0-593-12545-8 (library binding)
ISBN 978-0-593-12490-1 (ebook)

Designed by Patrick Crotty
Colored by Lyle Lynde

MANUFACTURED IN CHINA
10 9 8 7 6 5 4 3 2 1
First Edition

RH GRAPHIC
A comic on every bookshelf.

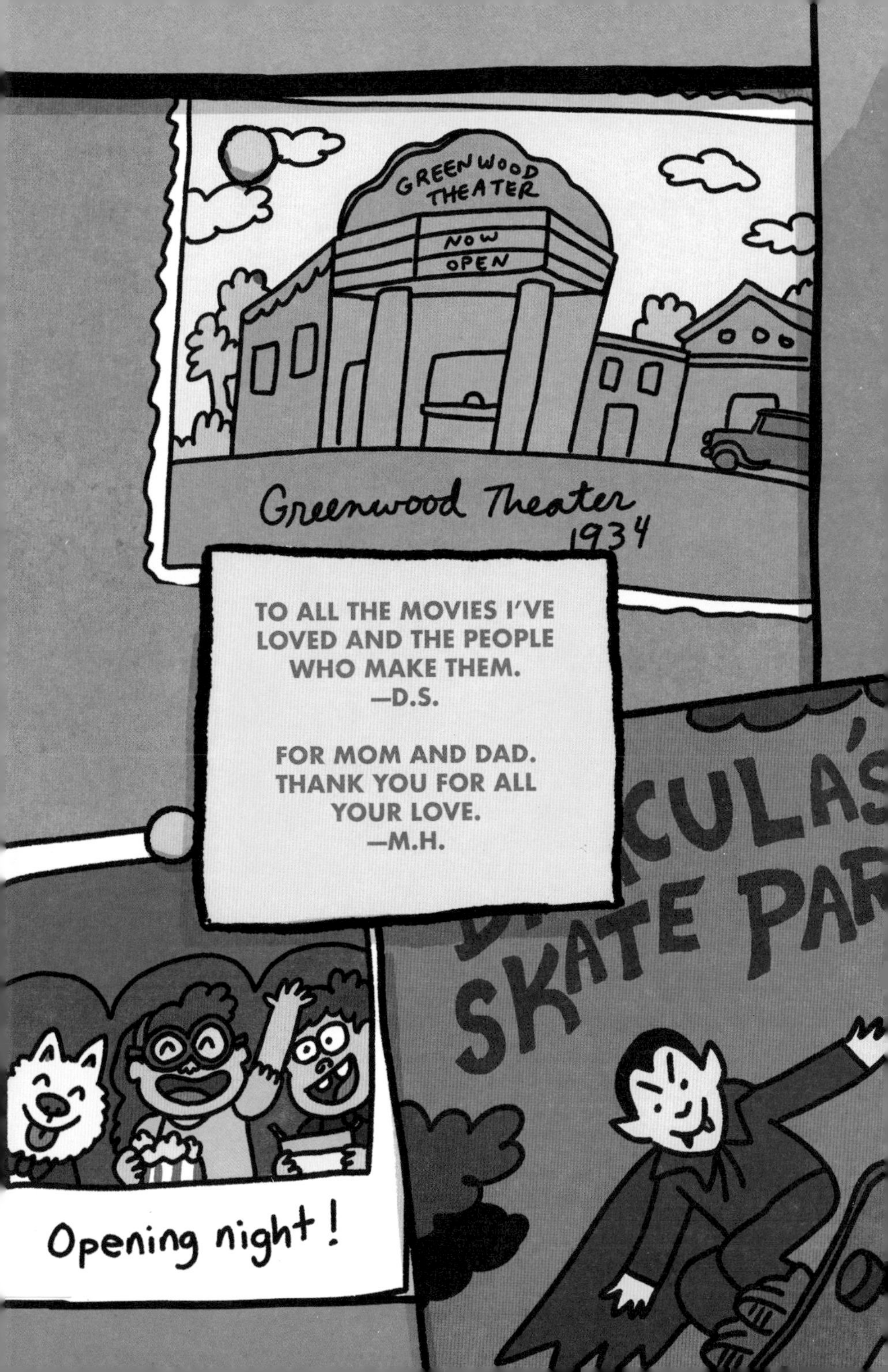
GREENWOOD THEATER
NOW OPEN
Greenwood Theater 1934
SKATE
Opening night!

TO ALL THE MOVIES I'VE LOVED AND THE PEOPLE WHO MAKE THEM.
—D.S.

FOR MOM AND DAD. THANK YOU FOR ALL YOUR LOVE.
—M.H.

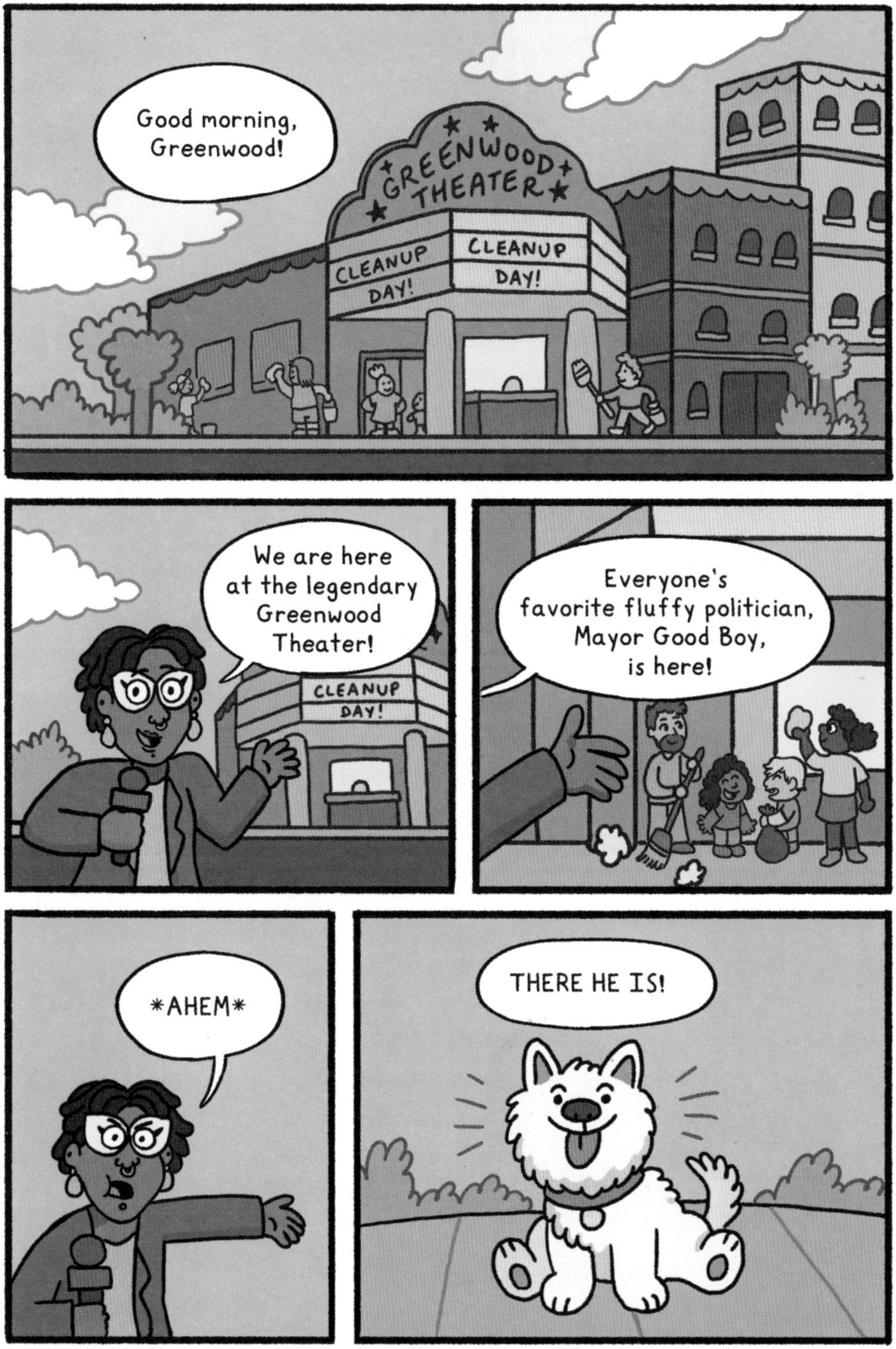
Good morning, Greenwood!
GREENWOOD THEATER
CLEANUP DAY!
CLEANUP DAY!
We are here at the legendary Greenwood Theater!
CLEANUP DAY!
Everyone's favorite fluffy politician, Mayor Good Boy, is here!
AHEM
THERE HE IS!

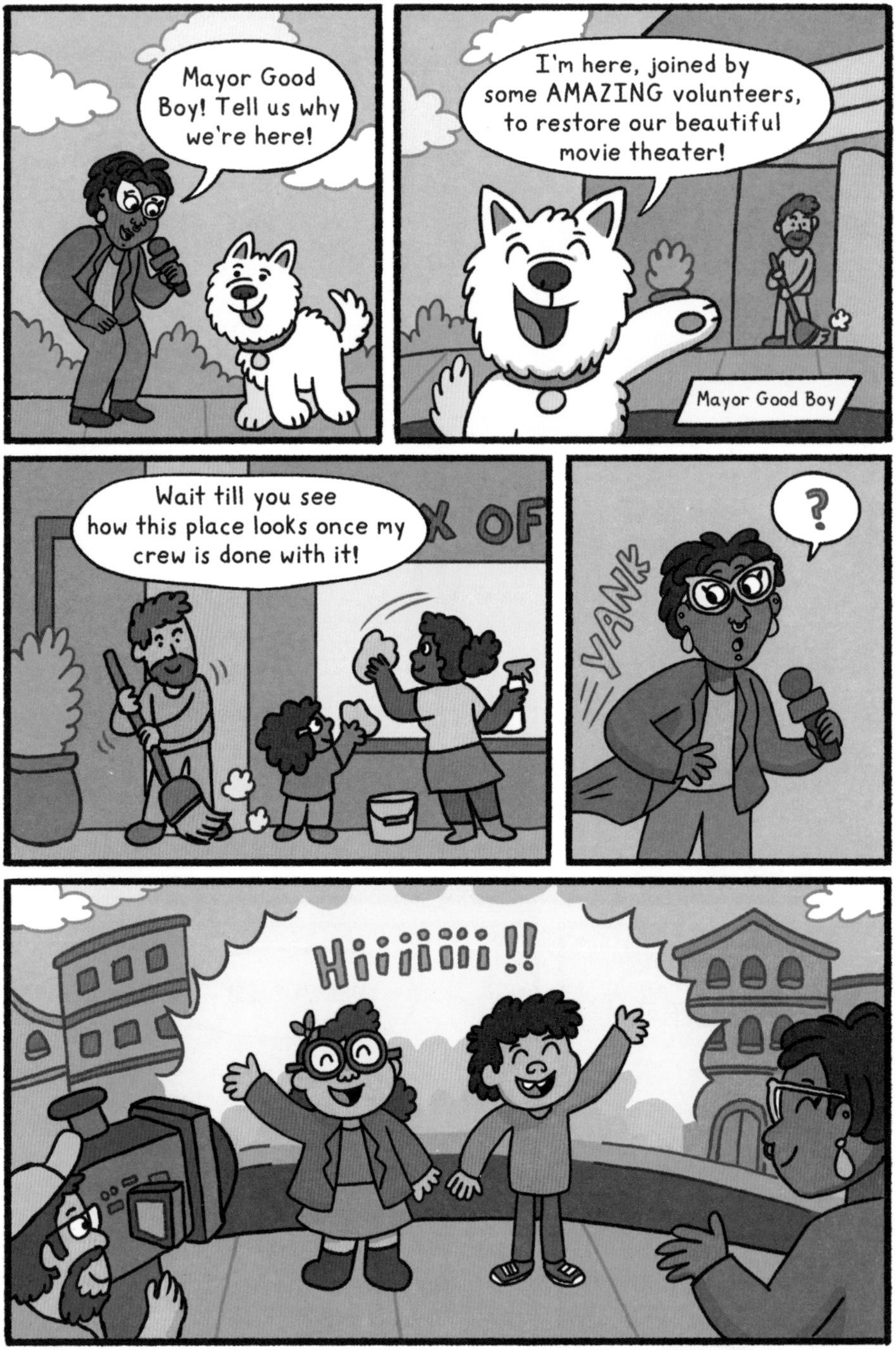
Mayor Good Boy! Tell us why we're here!
I'm here, joined by some AMAZING volunteers, to restore our beautiful movie theater!
Mayor Good Boy
Wait till you see how this place looks once my crew is done with it!
X OF
YANK
?
Hiiiiiii !!

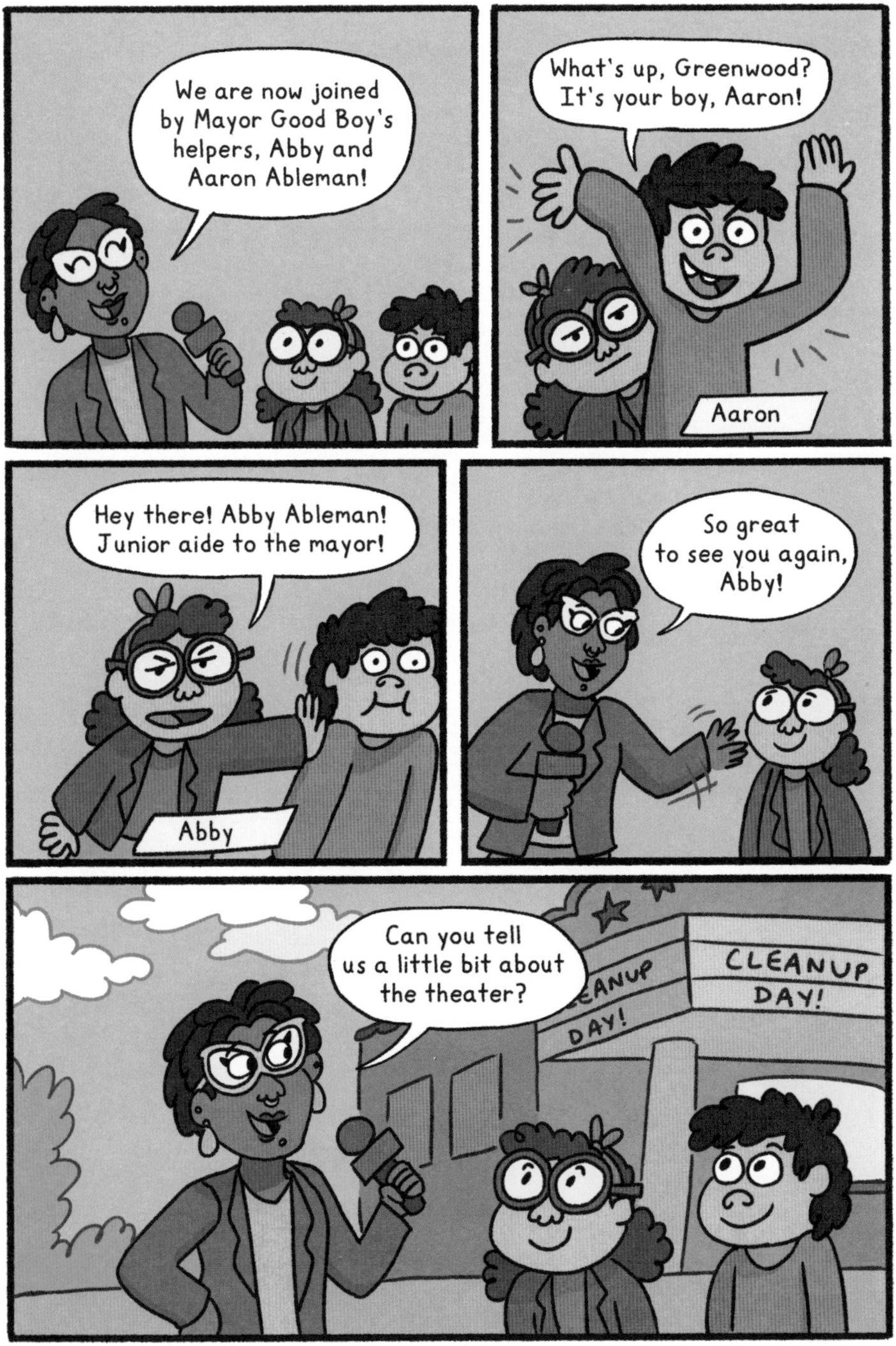
We are now joined by Mayor Good Boy's helpers, Abby and Aaron Ableman!
What's up, Greenwood? It's your boy, Aaron!
Aaron
Hey there! Abby Ableman! Junior aide to the mayor!
Abby
So great to see you again, Abby!
Can you tell us a little bit about the theater?
CLEANUP DAY!
CLEANUP DAY!

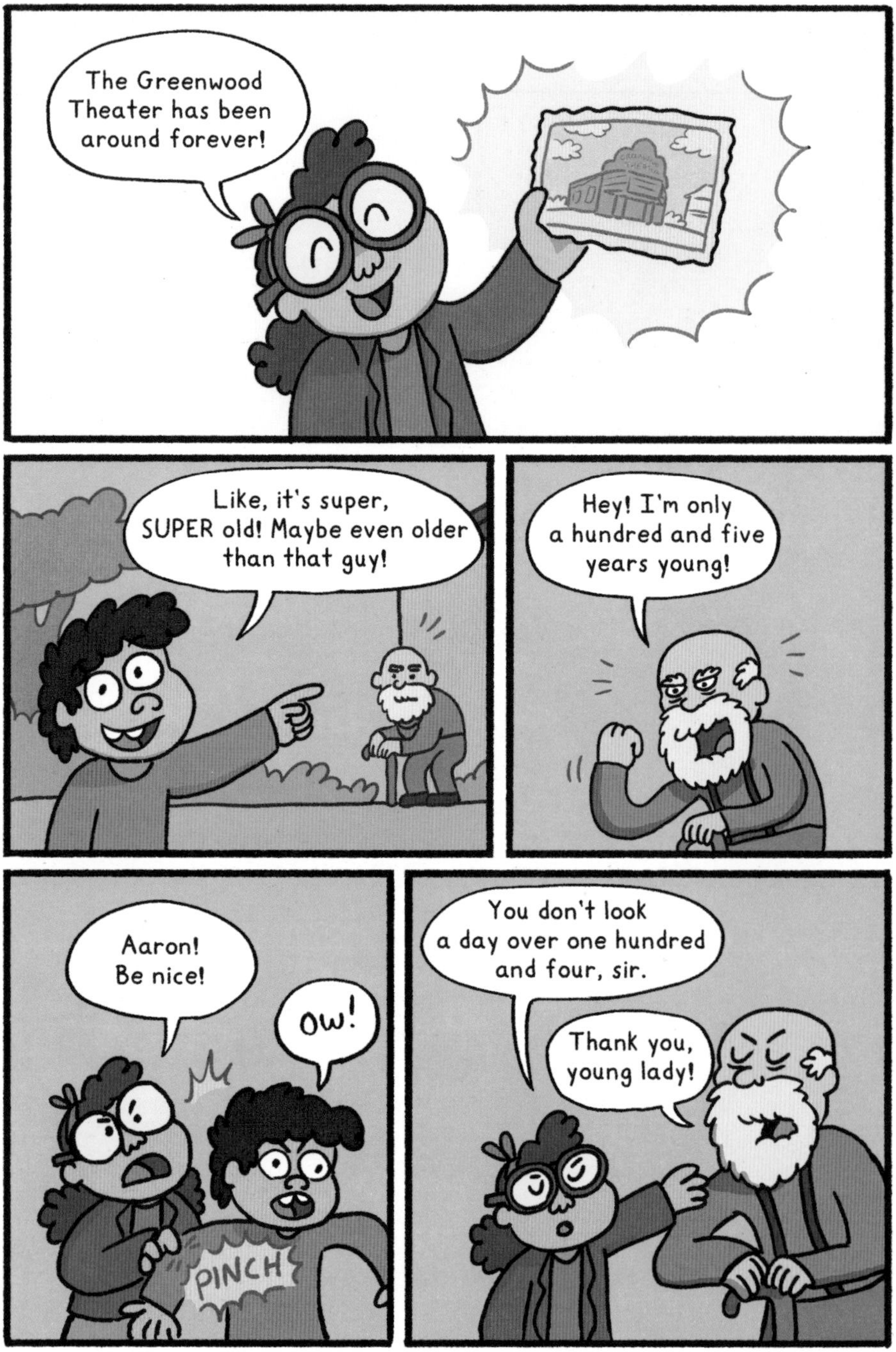
The Greenwood Theater has been around forever!
Like, it's super, SUPER old! Maybe even older than that guy!
Hey! I'm only a hundred and five years young!
Aaron! Be nice!
OW!
PINCH
You don't look a day over one hundred and four, sir.
Thank you, young lady!

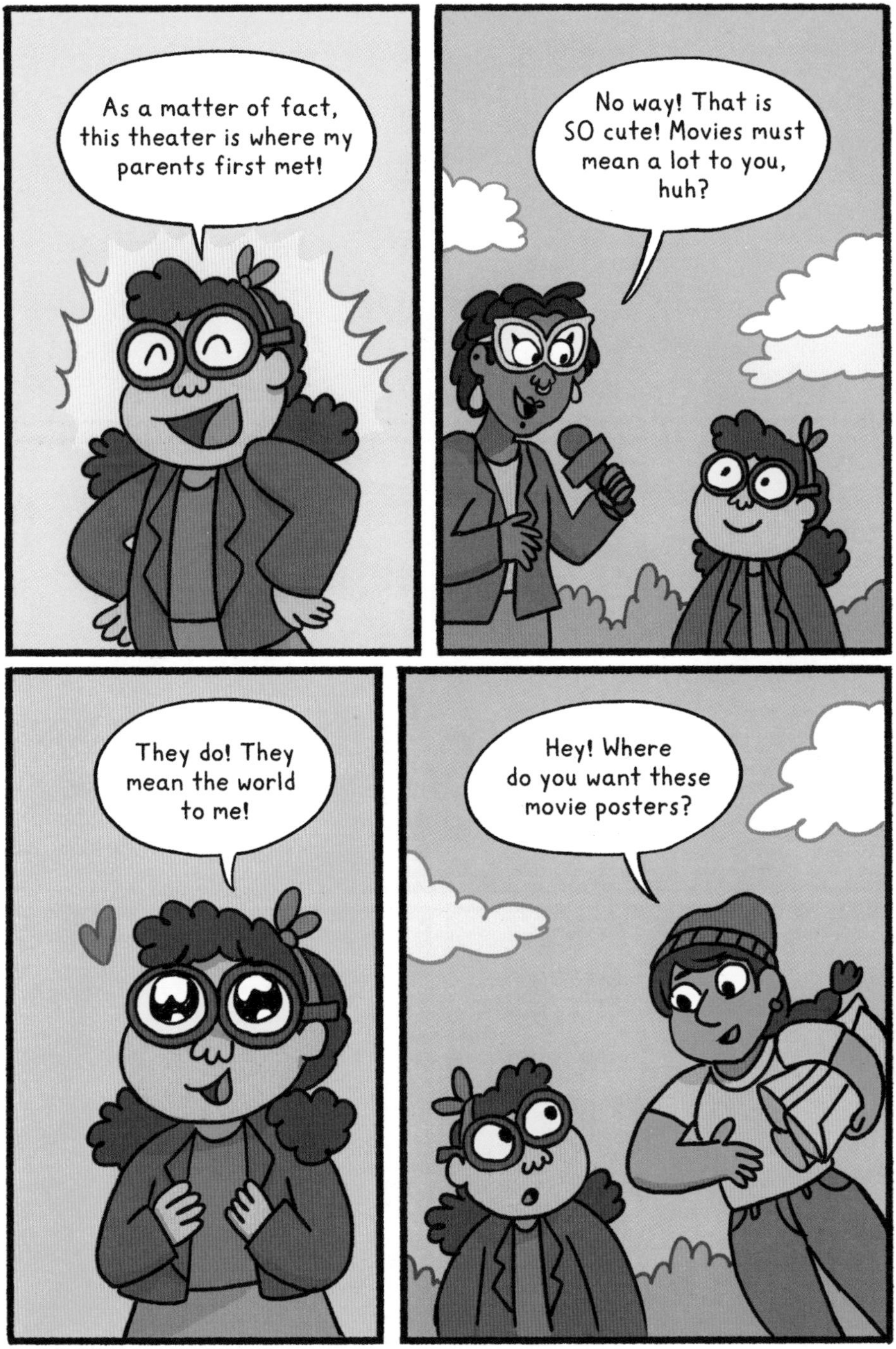
As a matter of fact, this theater is where my parents first met!
No way! That is SO cute! Movies must mean a lot to you, huh?
They do! They mean the world to me!
Hey! Where do you want these movie posters?

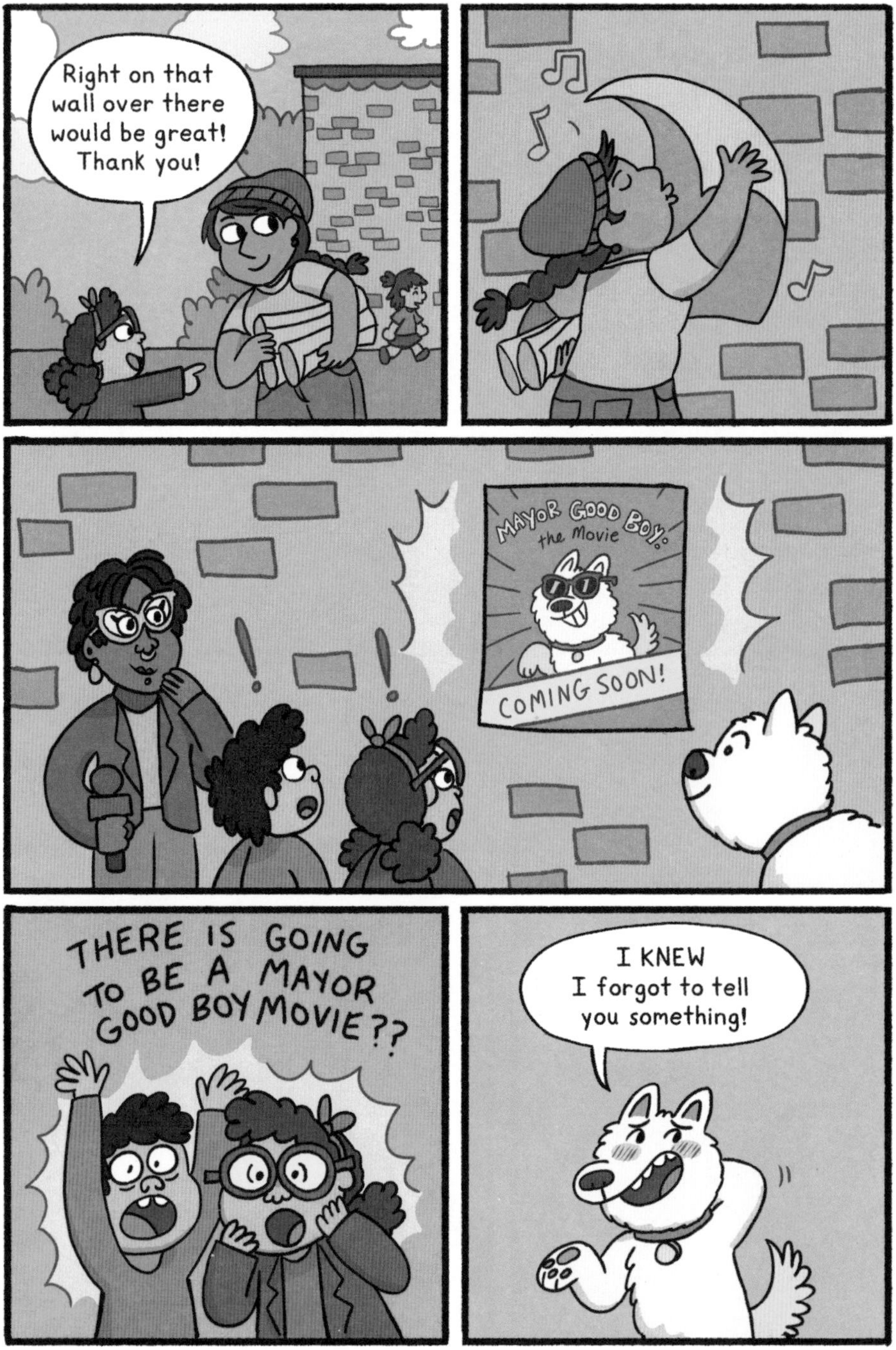
Right on that wall over there would be great! Thank you!
MAYOR GOOD BOY: the Movie
COMING SOON!
THERE IS GOING TO BE A MAYOR GOOD BOY MOVIE??
I KNEW I forgot to tell you something!

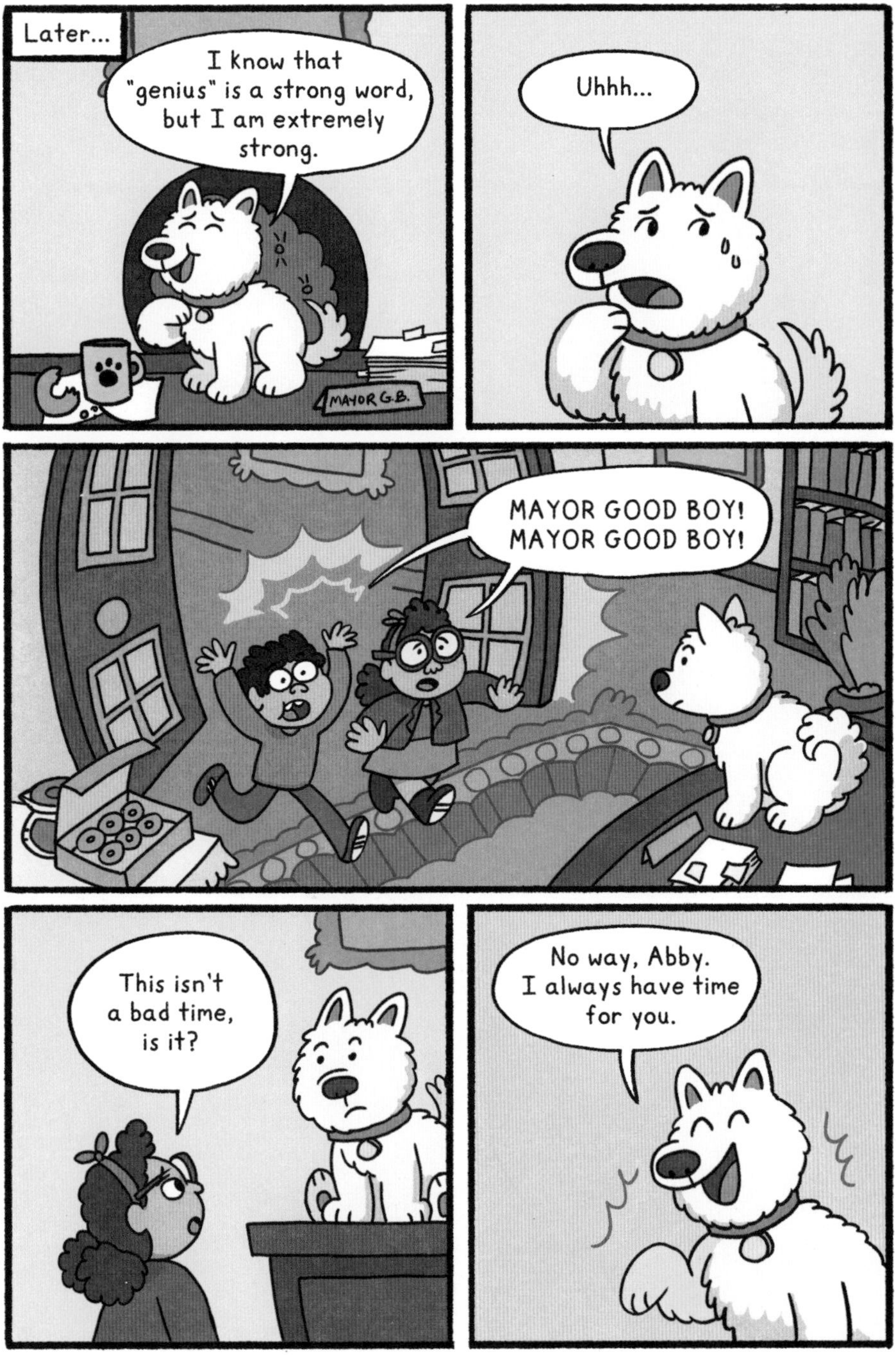
Later...
I know that "genius" is a strong word, but I am extremely strong.
MAYOR G.B.
Uhhh...
MAYOR GOOD BOY! MAYOR GOOD BOY!
This isn't a bad time, is it?
No way, Abby. I always have time for you.

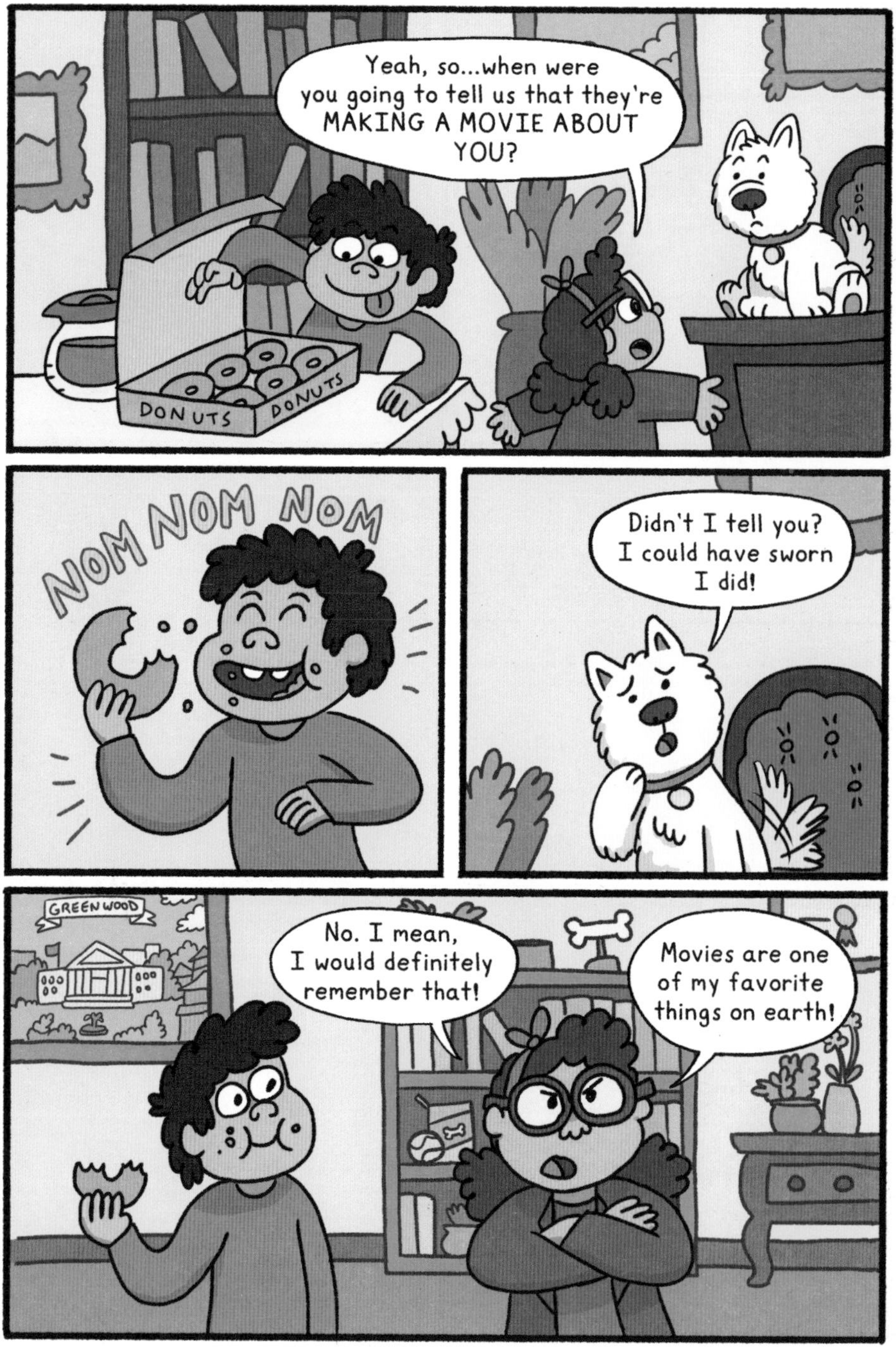
Yeah, so...when were you going to tell us that they're MAKING A MOVIE ABOUT YOU?
DONUTS
DONUTS
NOM NOM NOM
Didn't I tell you? I could have sworn I did!
GREENWOOD
No. I mean, I would definitely remember that!
Movies are one of my favorite things on earth!

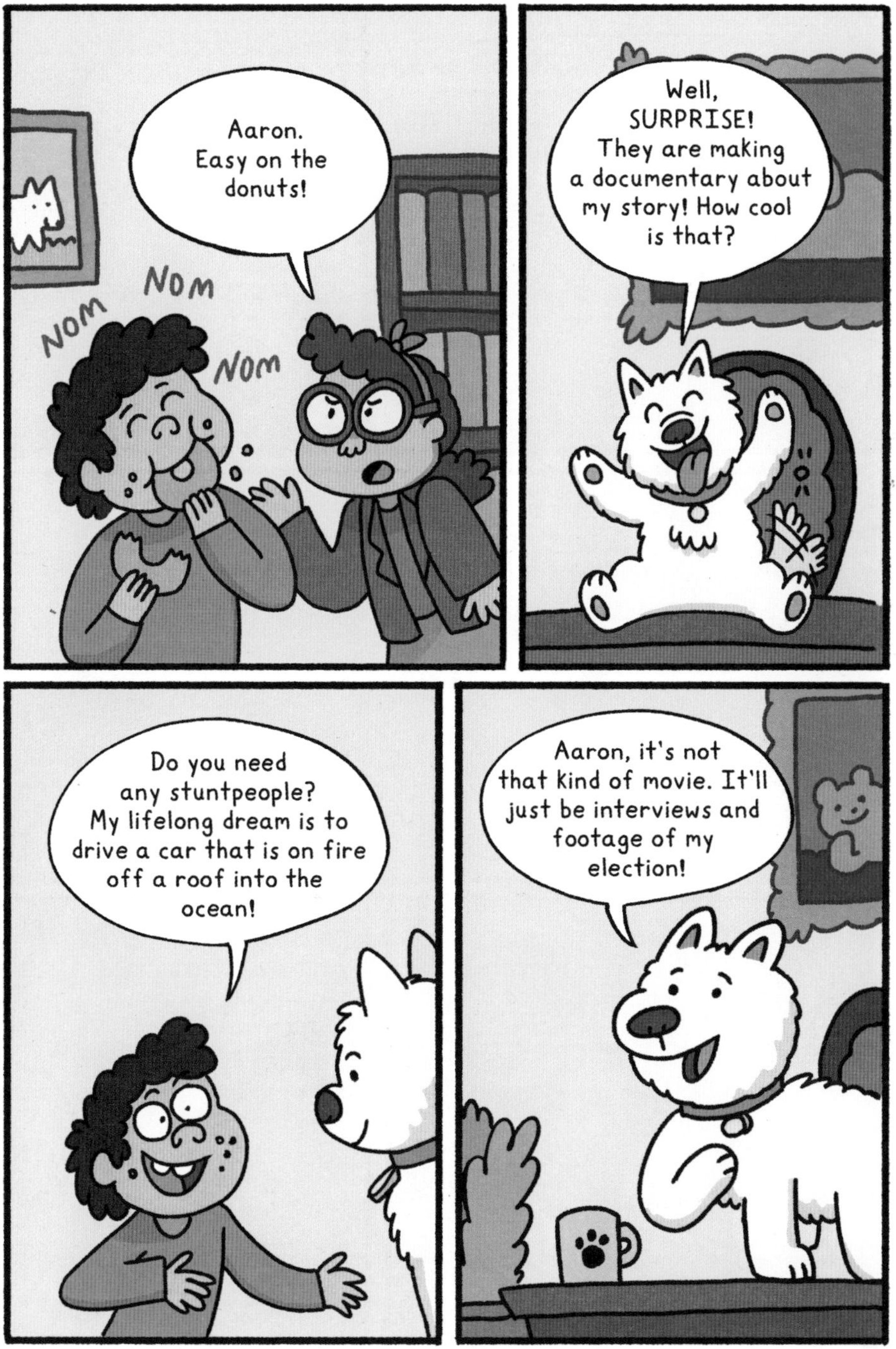
Aaron. Easy on the donuts!
NOM
NOM
NOM
Well, SURPRISE! They are making a documentary about my story! How cool is that?
Do you need any stuntpeople? My lifelong dream is to drive a car that is on fire off a roof into the ocean!
Aaron, it's not that kind of movie. It'll just be interviews and footage of my election!

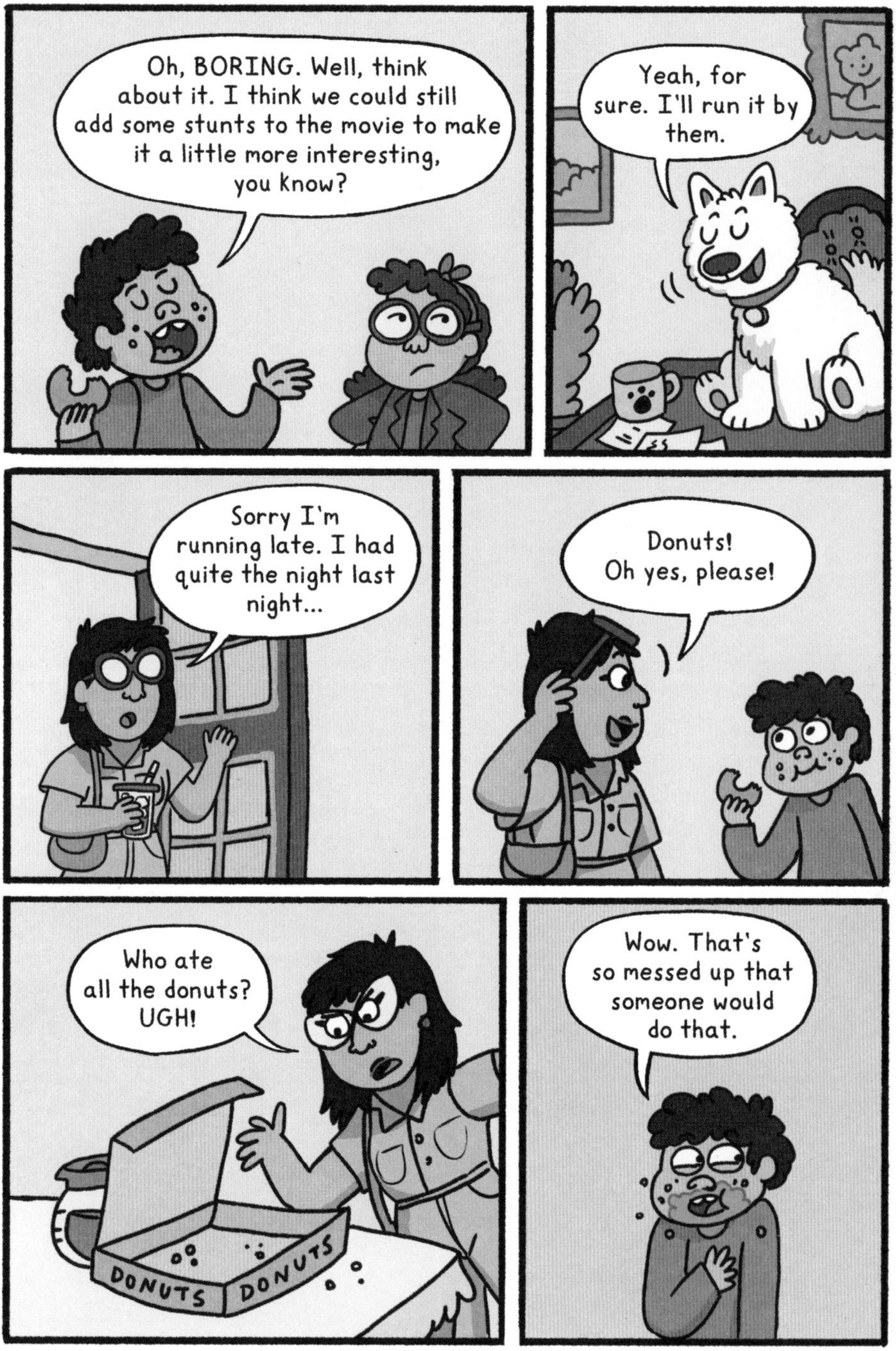
Oh, BORING. Well, think about it. I think we could still add some stunts to the movie to make it a little more interesting, you know?
Yeah, for sure. I'll run it by them.
Sorry I'm running late. I had quite the night last night...
Donuts! Oh yes, please!
Who ate all the donuts? UGH!
DONUTS
DONUTS
Wow. That's so messed up that someone would do that.

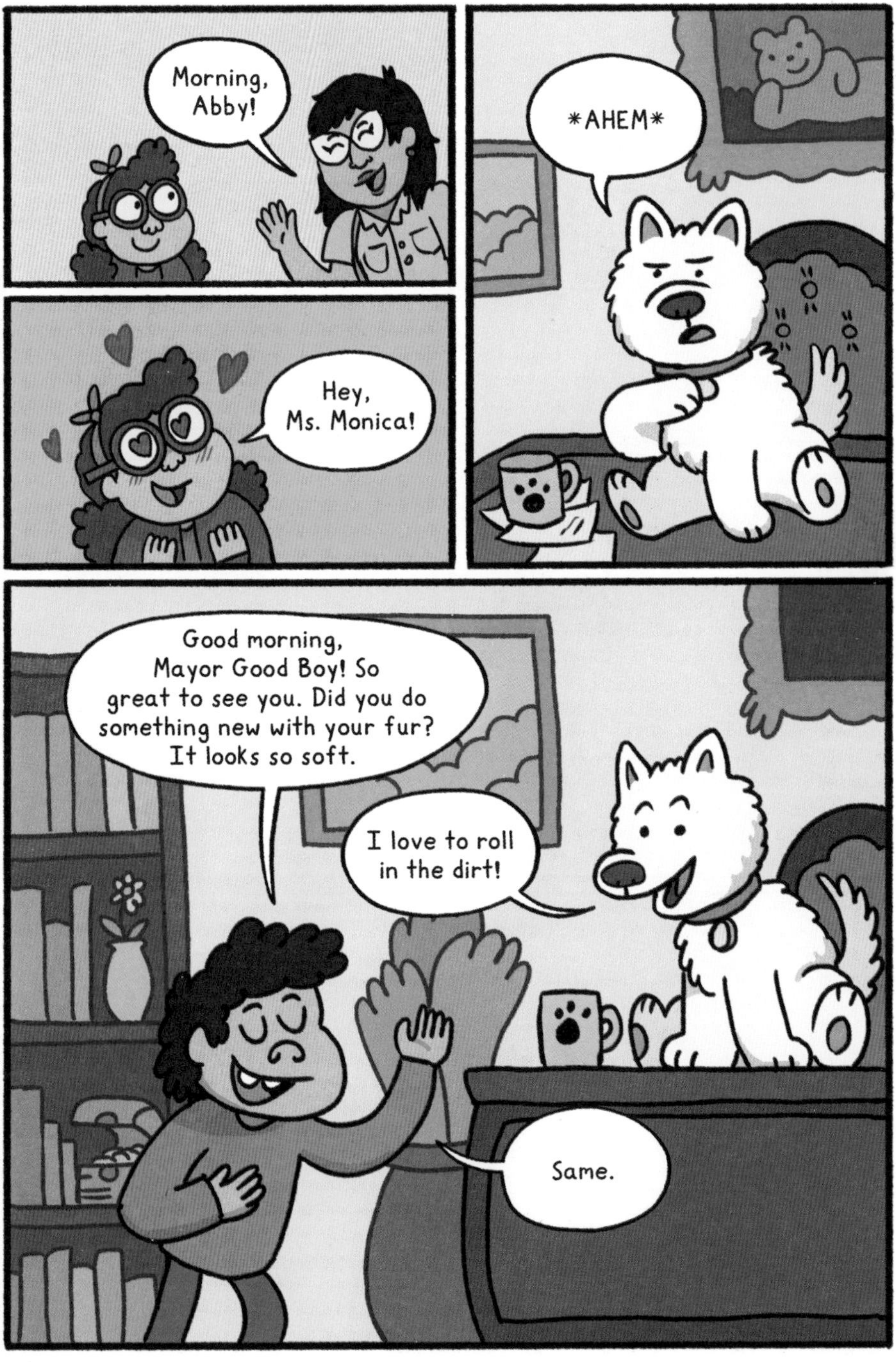
Morning, Abby!
Hey, Ms. Monica!
AHEM
Good morning, Mayor Good Boy! So great to see you. Did you do something new with your fur? It looks so soft.
I love to roll in the dirt!
Same.

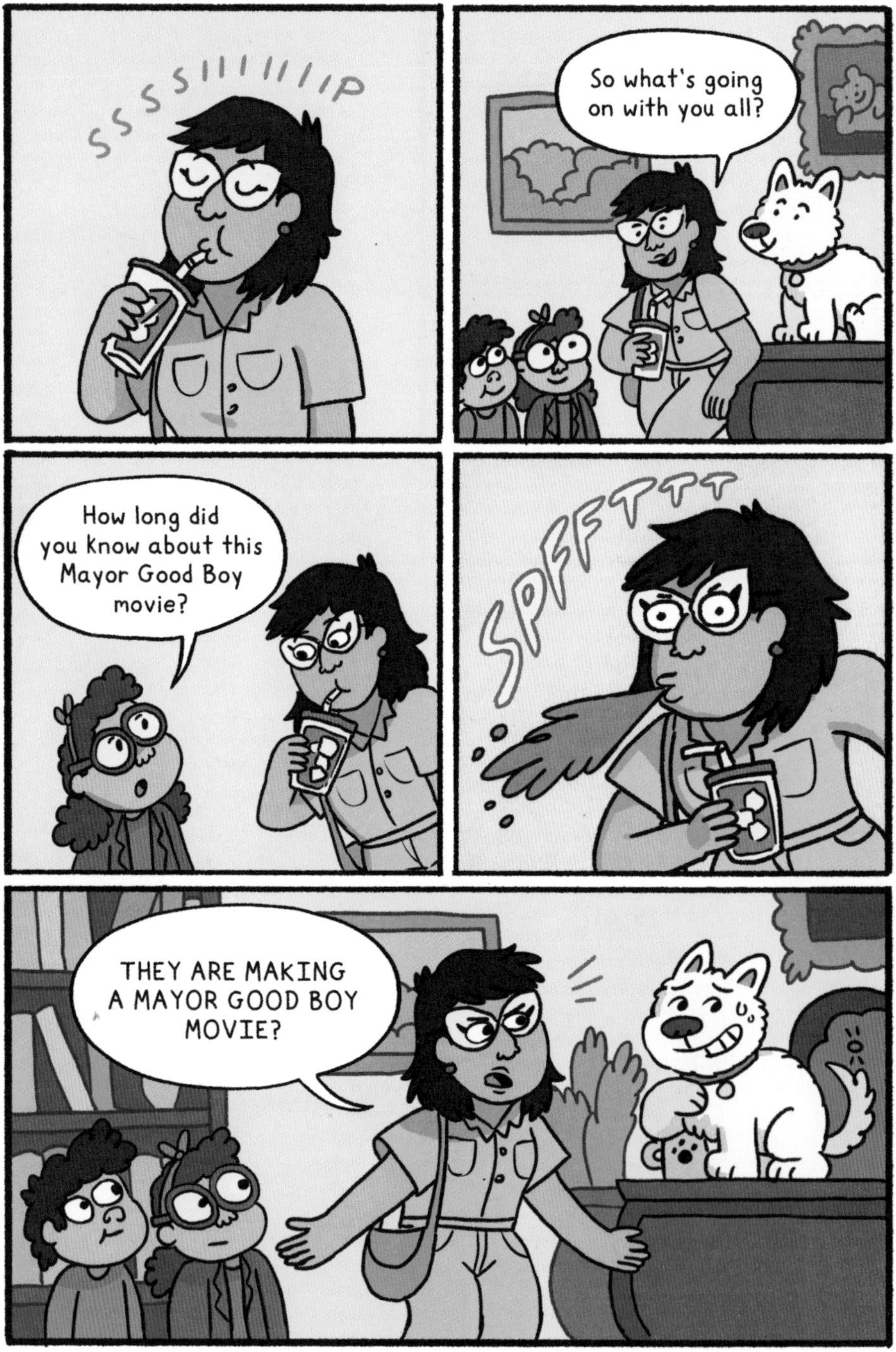
SSSSIIIIIIIIP
So what's going on with you all?
How long did you know about this Mayor Good Boy movie?
SPFFTTT
THEY ARE MAKING A MAYOR GOOD BOY MOVIE?

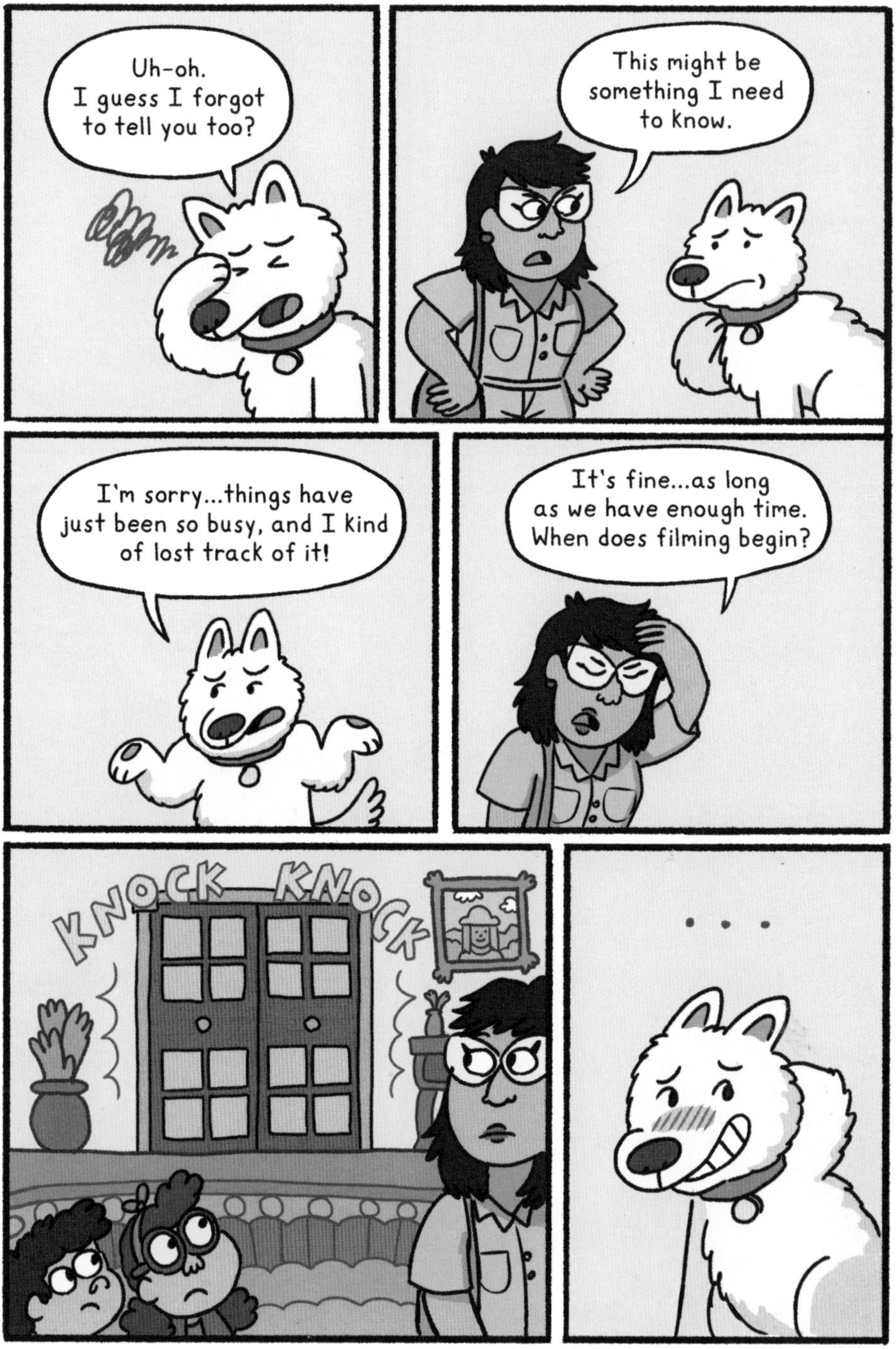
Uh-oh.
I guess I forgot to tell you too?
This might be something I need to know.
I'm sorry...things have just been so busy, and I kind of lost track of it!
It's fine...as long as we have enough time. When does filming begin?
KNOCK KNOCK
...

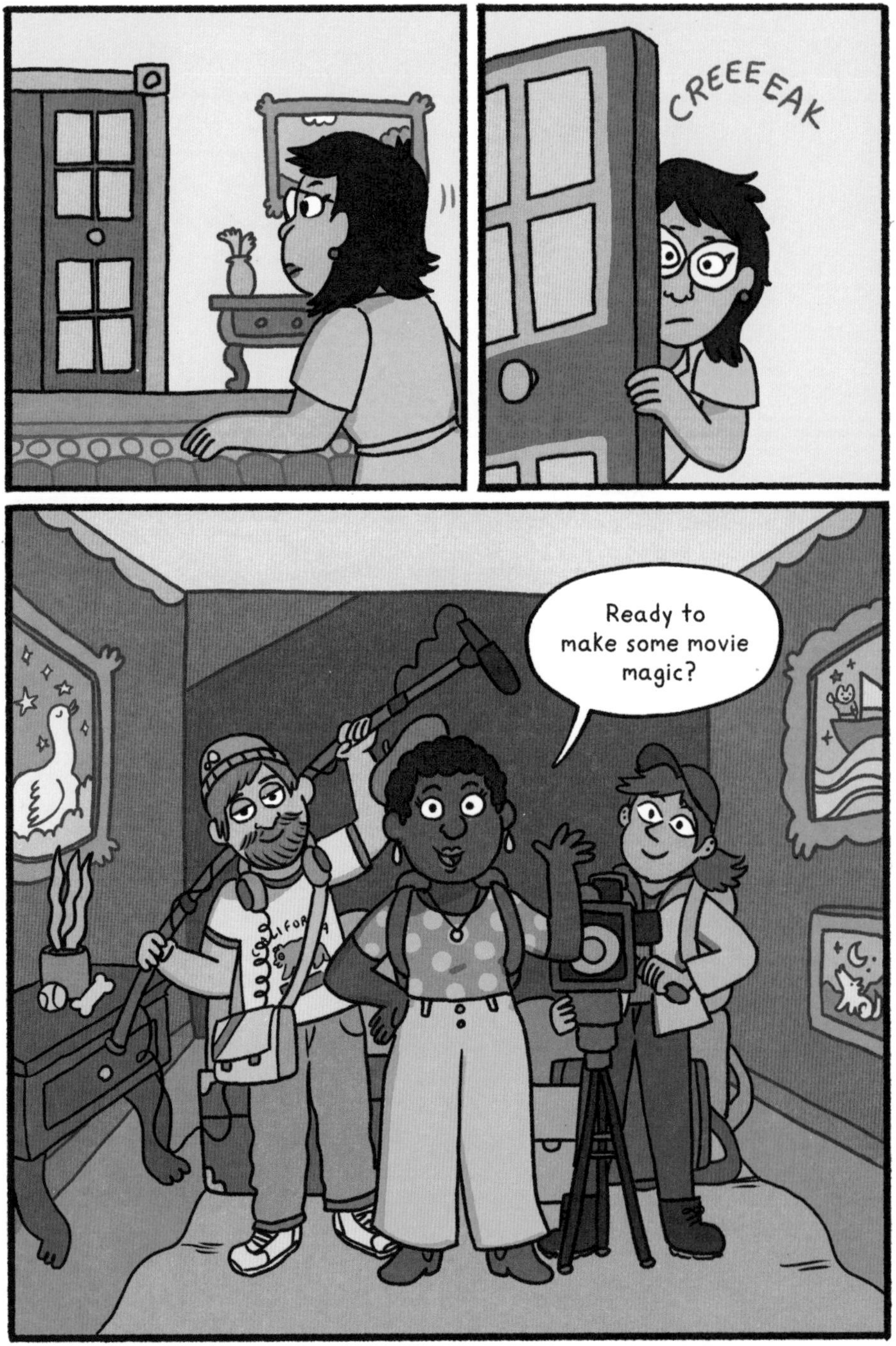
CREEEEEAK
Ready to make some movie magic?

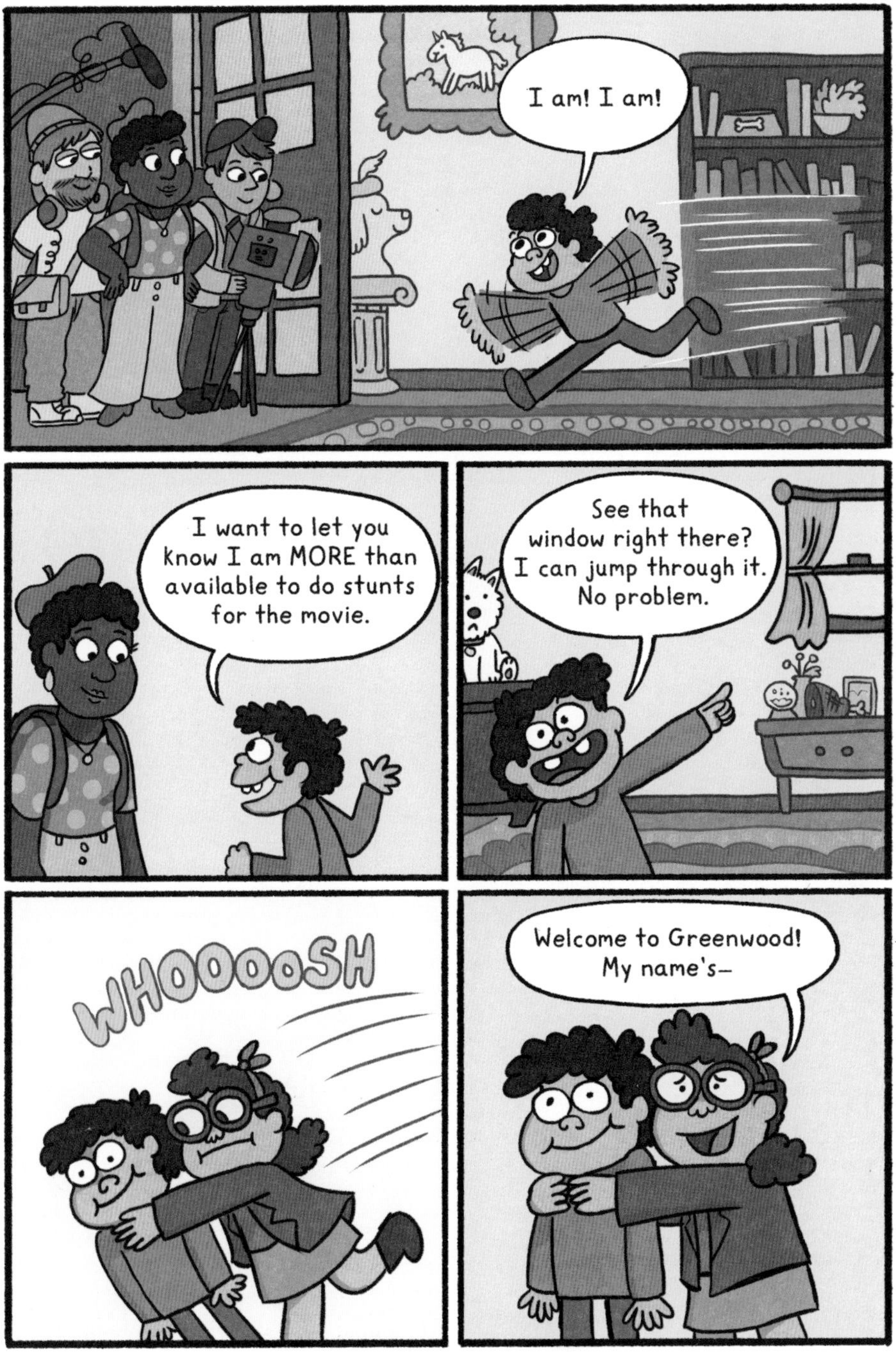
I am! I am!
I want to let you know I am MORE than available to do stunts for the movie.
See that window right there? I can jump through it. No problem.
WHOOOOOSH
Welcome to Greenwood! My name's—

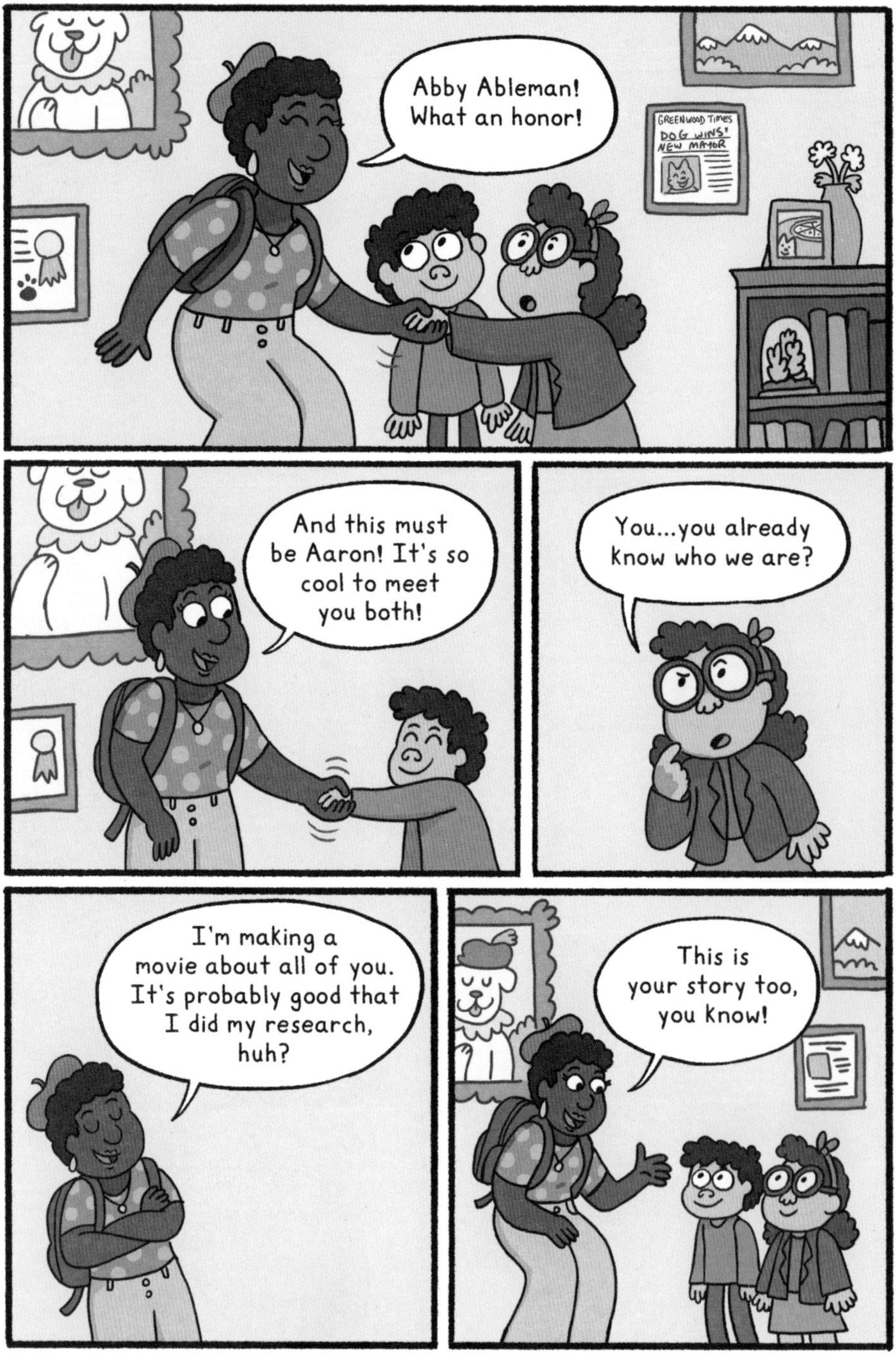
Abby Ableman! What an honor!
GREENWOOD TIMES
DOG WINS! NEW MAYOR
And this must be Aaron! It's so cool to meet you both!
You...you already know who we are?
I'm making a movie about all of you. It's probably good that I did my research, huh?
This is your story too, you know!

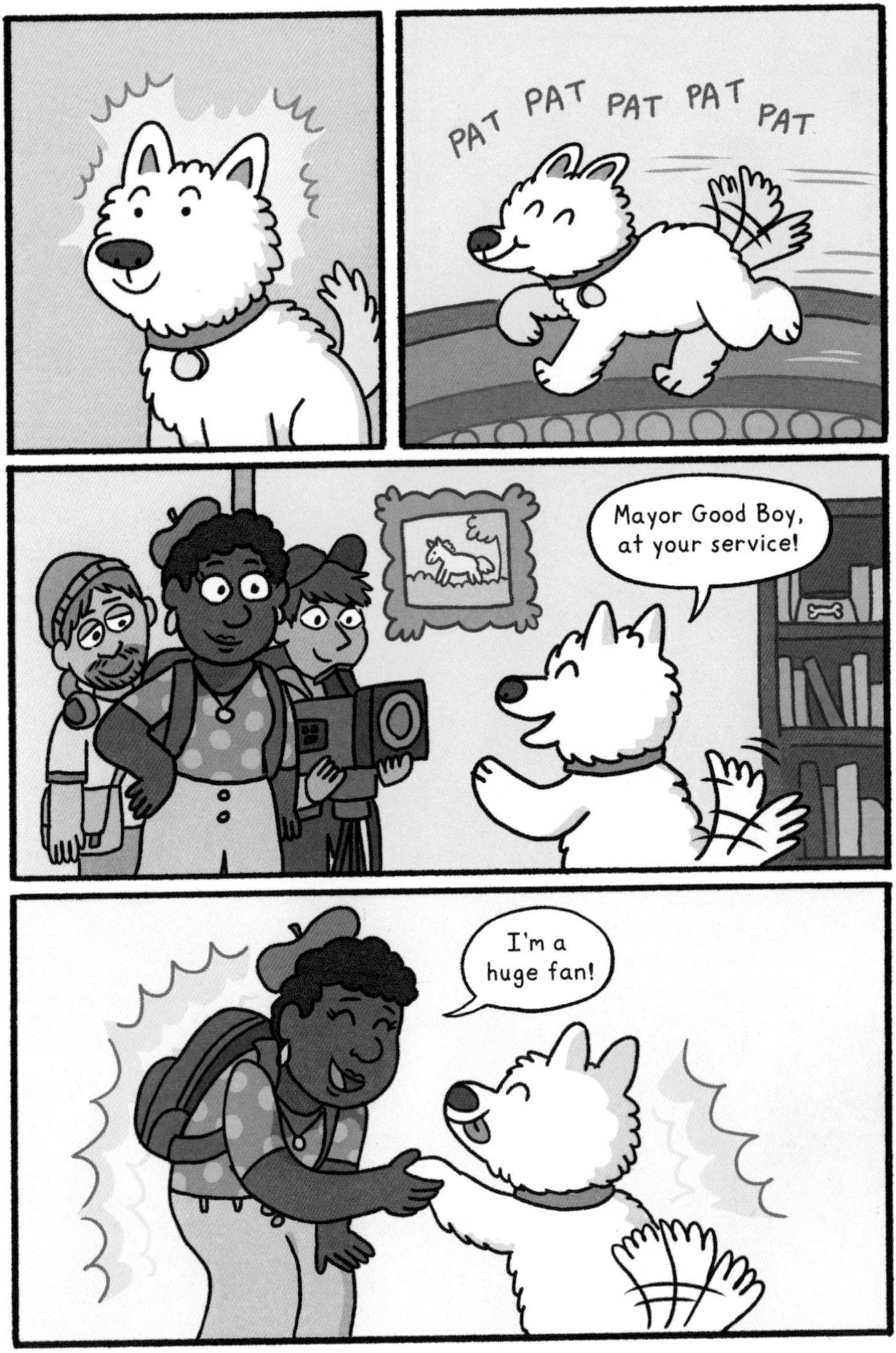
PAT PAT PAT PAT PAT
Mayor Good Boy, at your service!
I'm a huge fan!

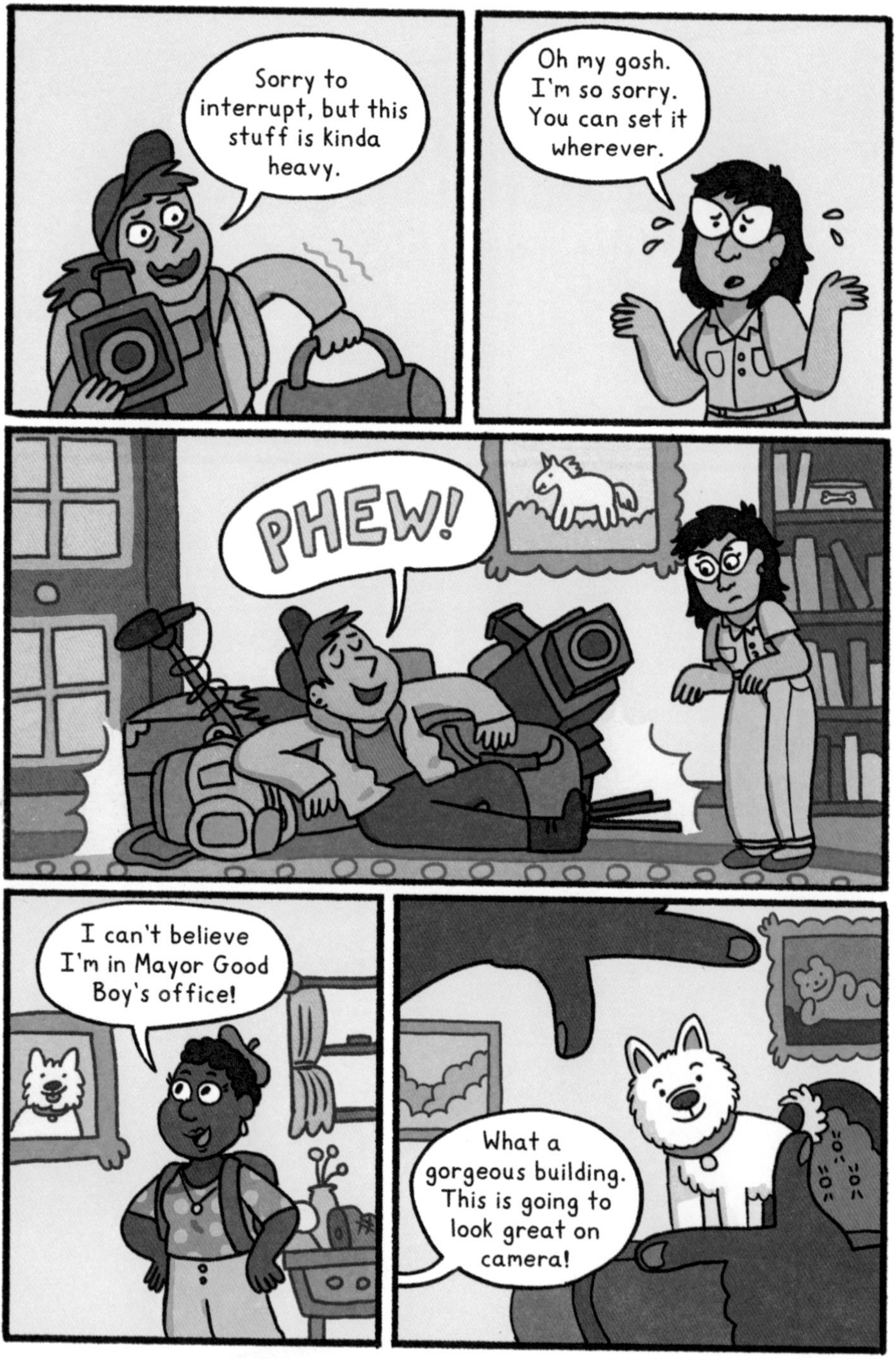
Sorry to interrupt, but this stuff is kinda heavy.
Oh my gosh. I'm so sorry. You can set it wherever.
PHEW!
I can't believe I'm in Mayor Good Boy's office!
What a gorgeous building. This is going to look great on camera!

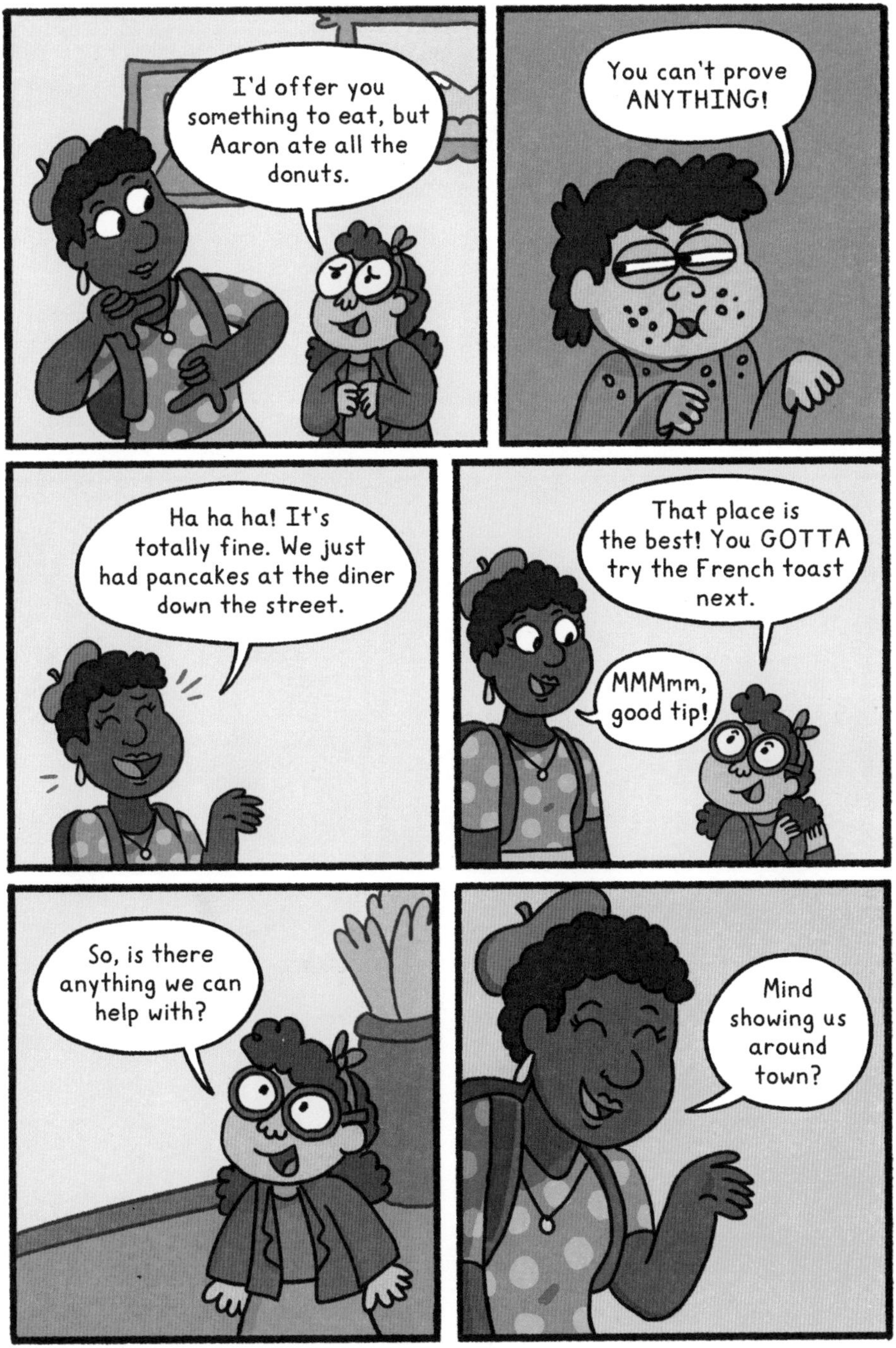
I'd offer you something to eat, but Aaron ate all the donuts.
You can't prove ANYTHING!
Ha ha ha! It's totally fine. We just had pancakes at the diner down the street.
That place is the best! You GOTTA try the French toast next.
MMMmm, good tip!
So, is there anything we can help with?
Mind showing us around town?

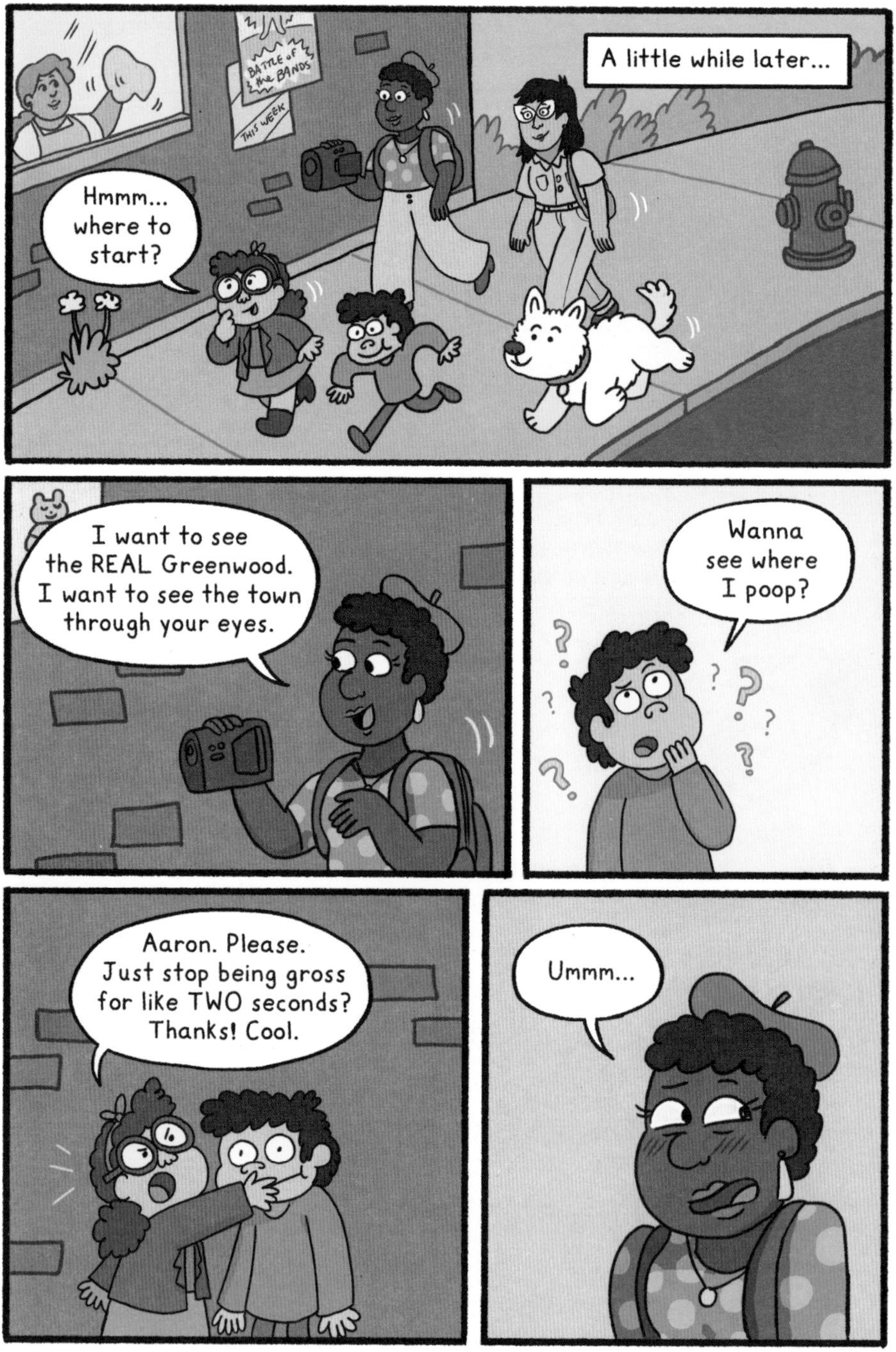
BATTLE of the BANDS
THIS WEEK
A little while later...
Hmmm... where to start?
I want to see the REAL Greenwood. I want to see the town through your eyes.
Wanna see where I poop?
Aaron. Please. Just stop being gross for like TWO seconds? Thanks! Cool.
Ummm...

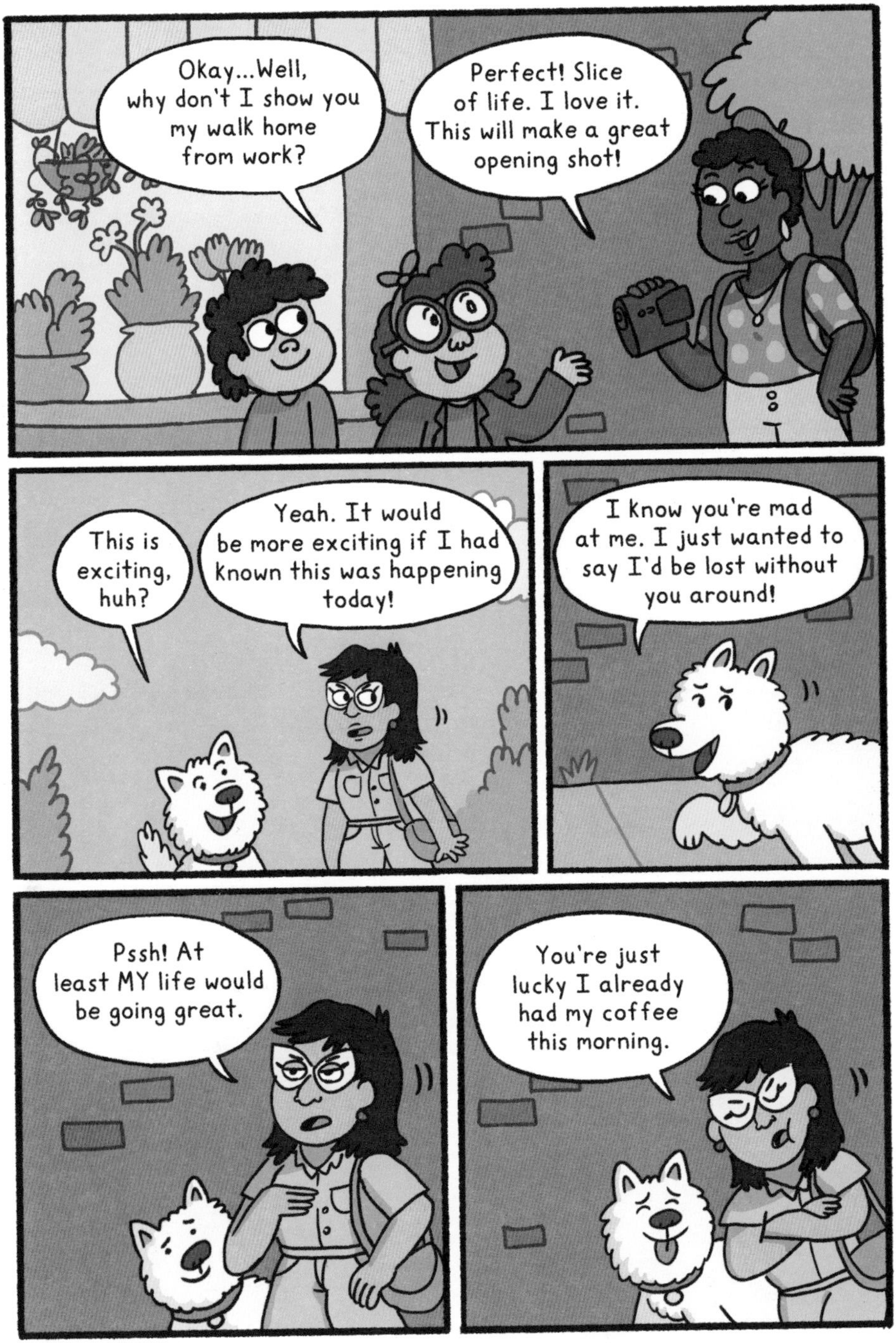
Okay...Well, why don't I show you my walk home from work?
Perfect! Slice of life. I love it. This will make a great opening shot!
This is exciting, huh?
Yeah. It would be more exciting if I had known this was happening today!
I know you're mad at me. I just wanted to say I'd be lost without you around!
Pssh! At least MY life would be going great.
You're just lucky I already had my coffee this morning.

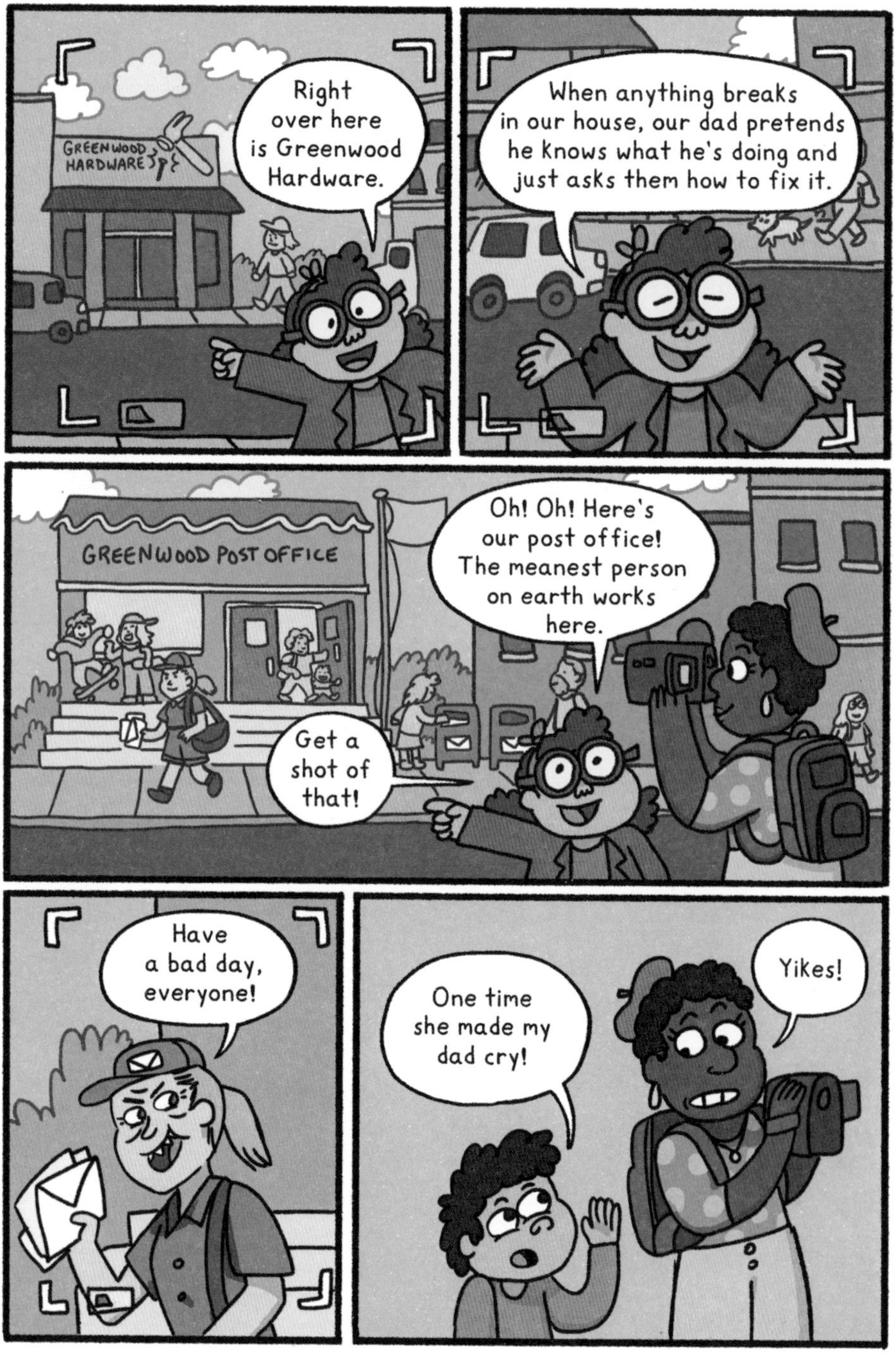
GREENWOOD HARDWARE
Right over here is Greenwood Hardware.
When anything breaks in our house, our dad pretends he knows what he's doing and just asks them how to fix it.
GREENWOOD POST OFFICE
Oh! Oh! Here's our post office! The meanest person on earth works here.
Get a shot of that!
Have a bad day, everyone!
One time she made my dad cry!
Yikes!

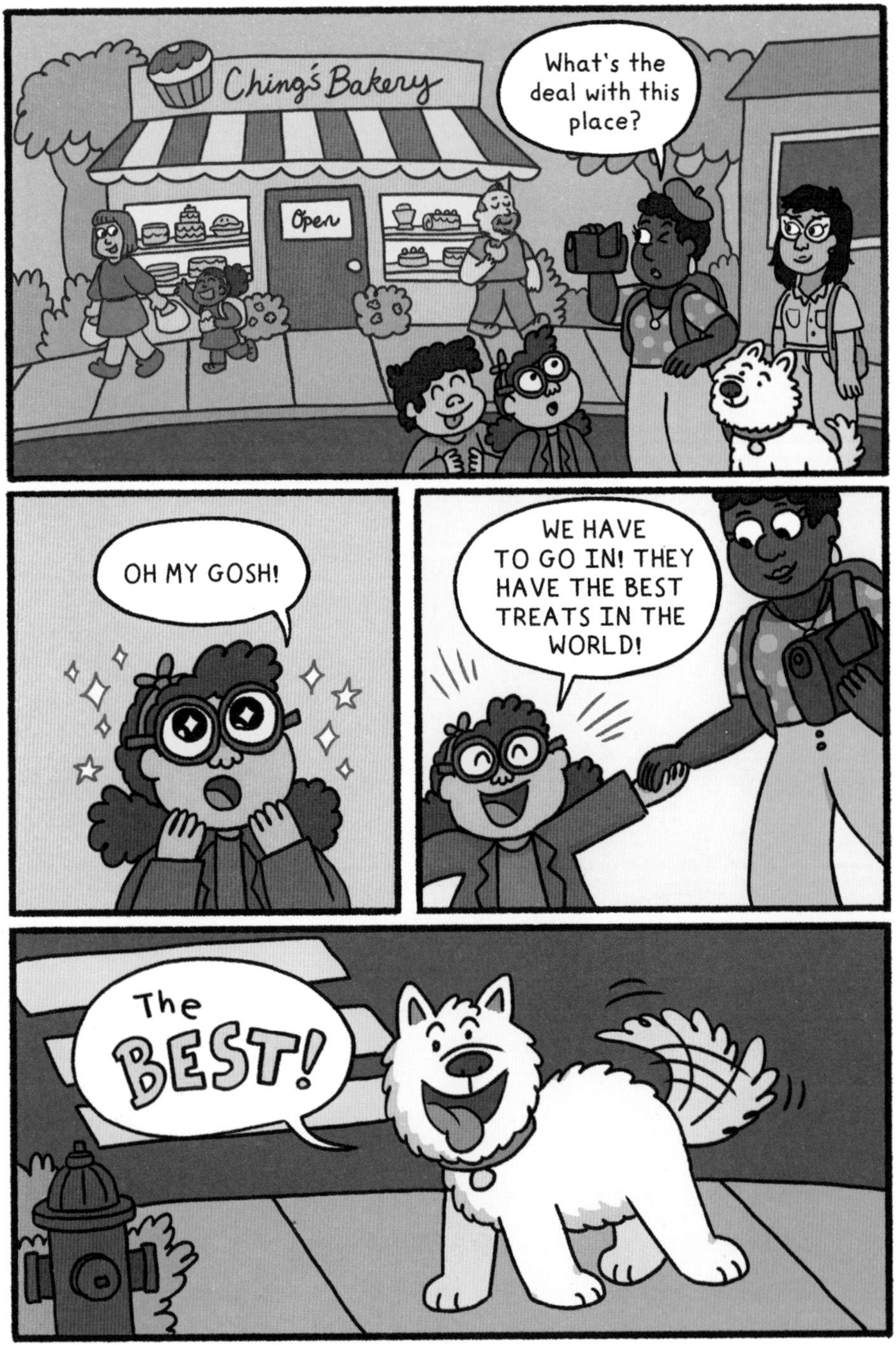
Ching's Bakery
Open
What's the deal with this place?
OH MY GOSH!
WE HAVE TO GO IN! THEY HAVE THE BEST TREATS IN THE WORLD!
The BEST!

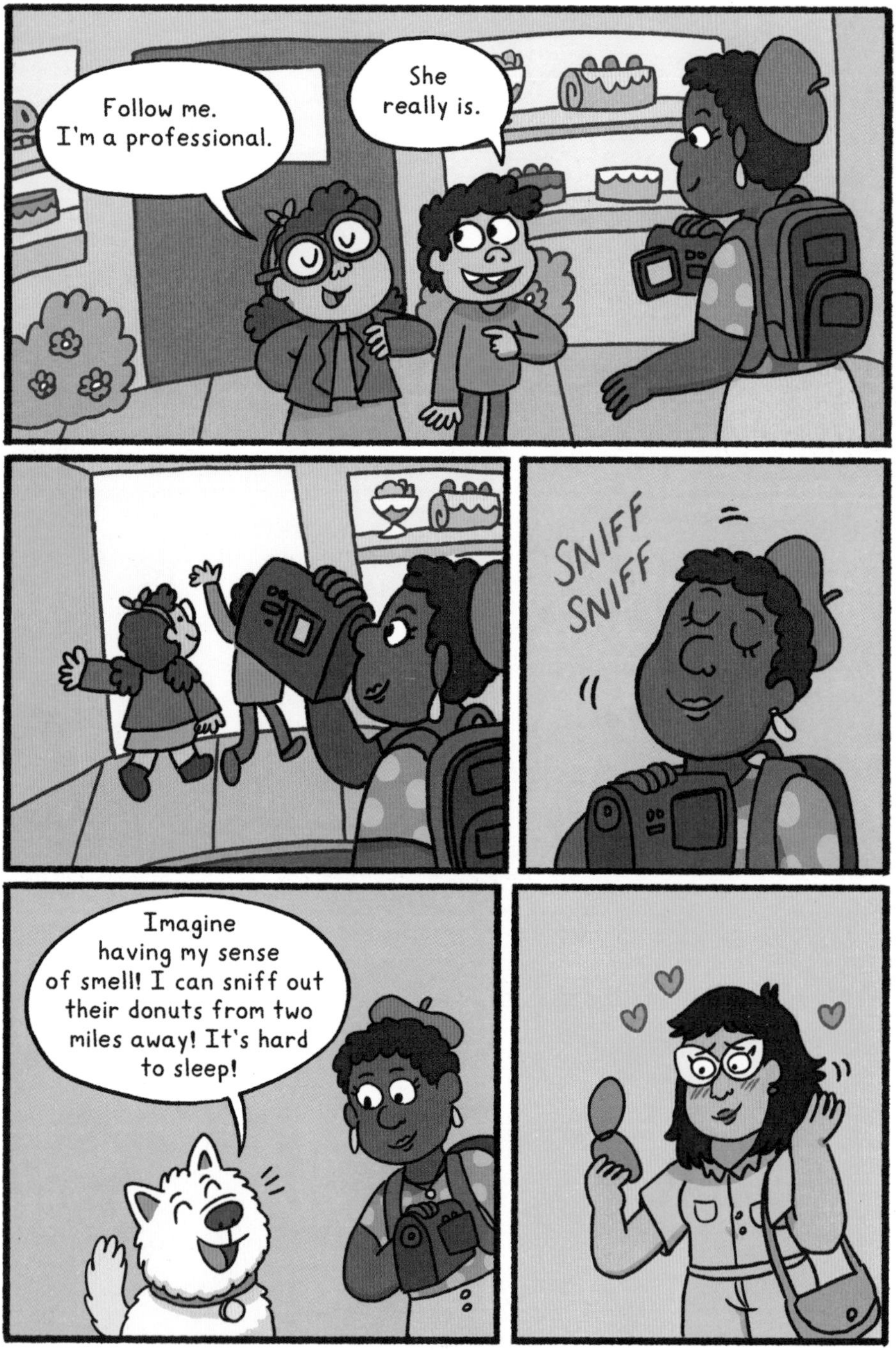
Follow me. I'm a professional.
She really is.
SNIFF SNIFF
Imagine having my sense of smell! I can sniff out their donuts from two miles away! It's hard to sleep!

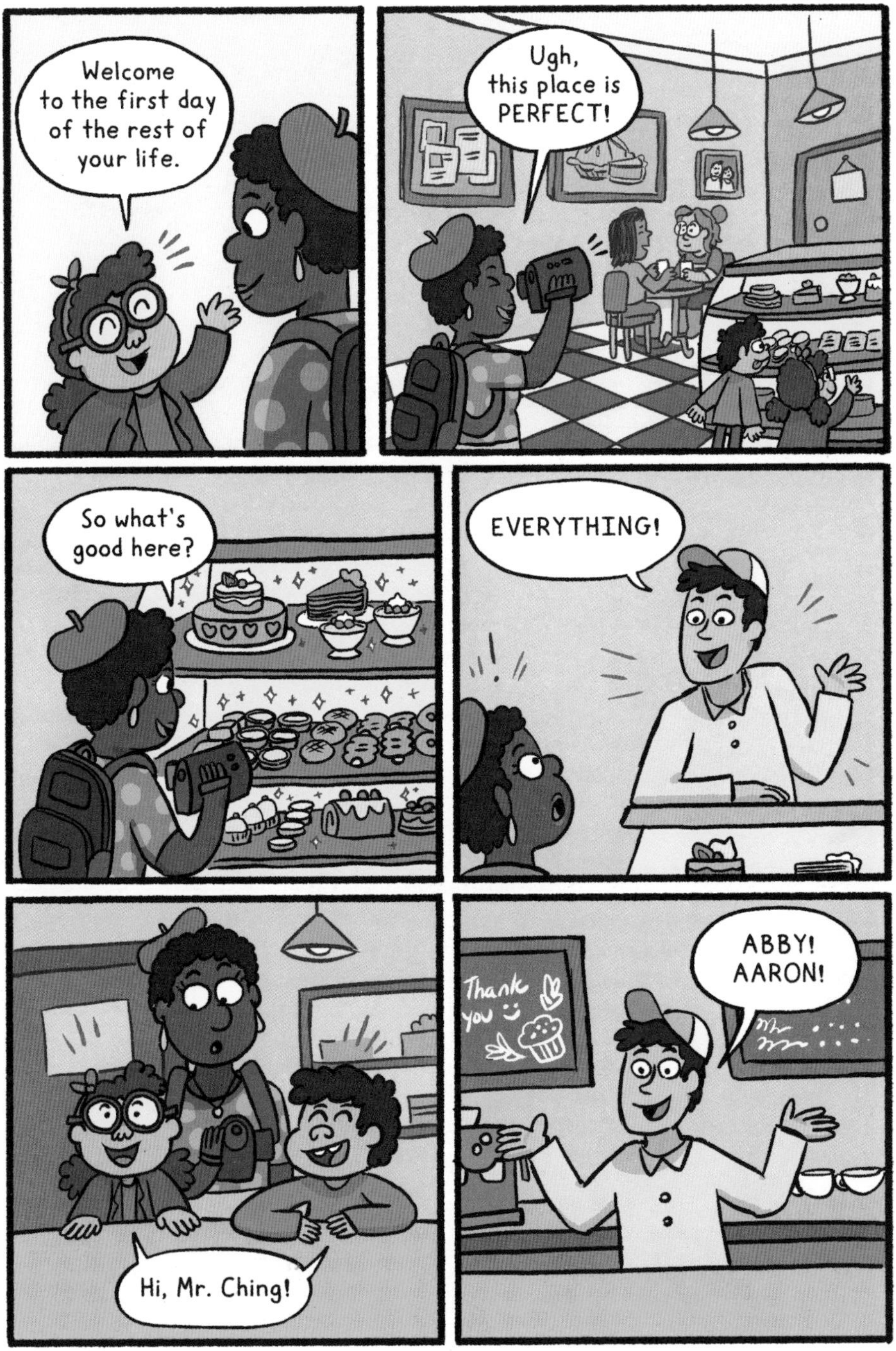
Welcome to the first day of the rest of your life.
Ugh, this place is PERFECT!
So what's good here?
EVERYTHING!
Hi, Mr. Ching!
ABBY! AARON!
Thank you

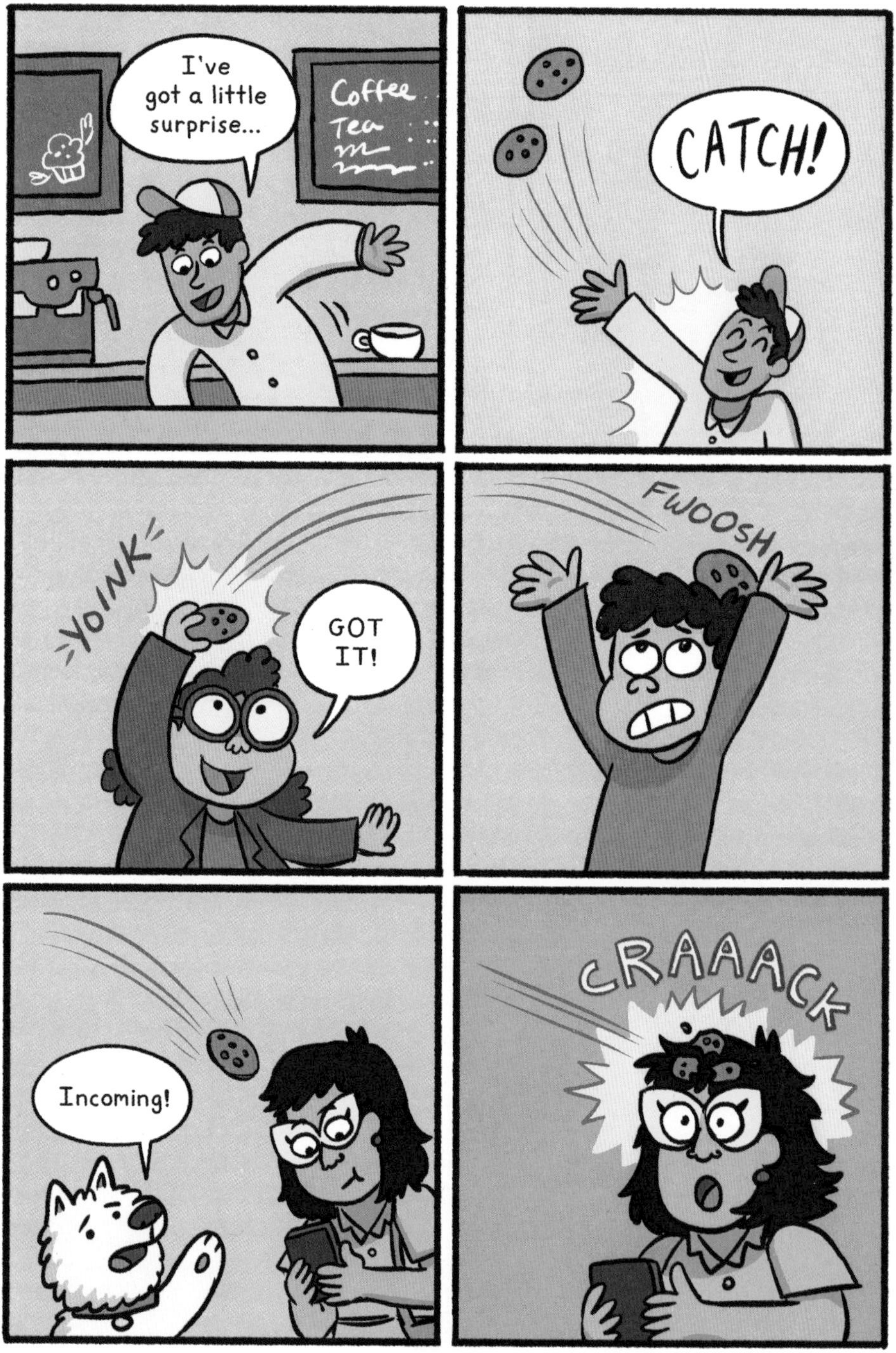
I've got a little surprise...
Coffee
Tea
CATCH!
YOINK
GOT IT!
FWOOSH
Incoming!
CRAAACK

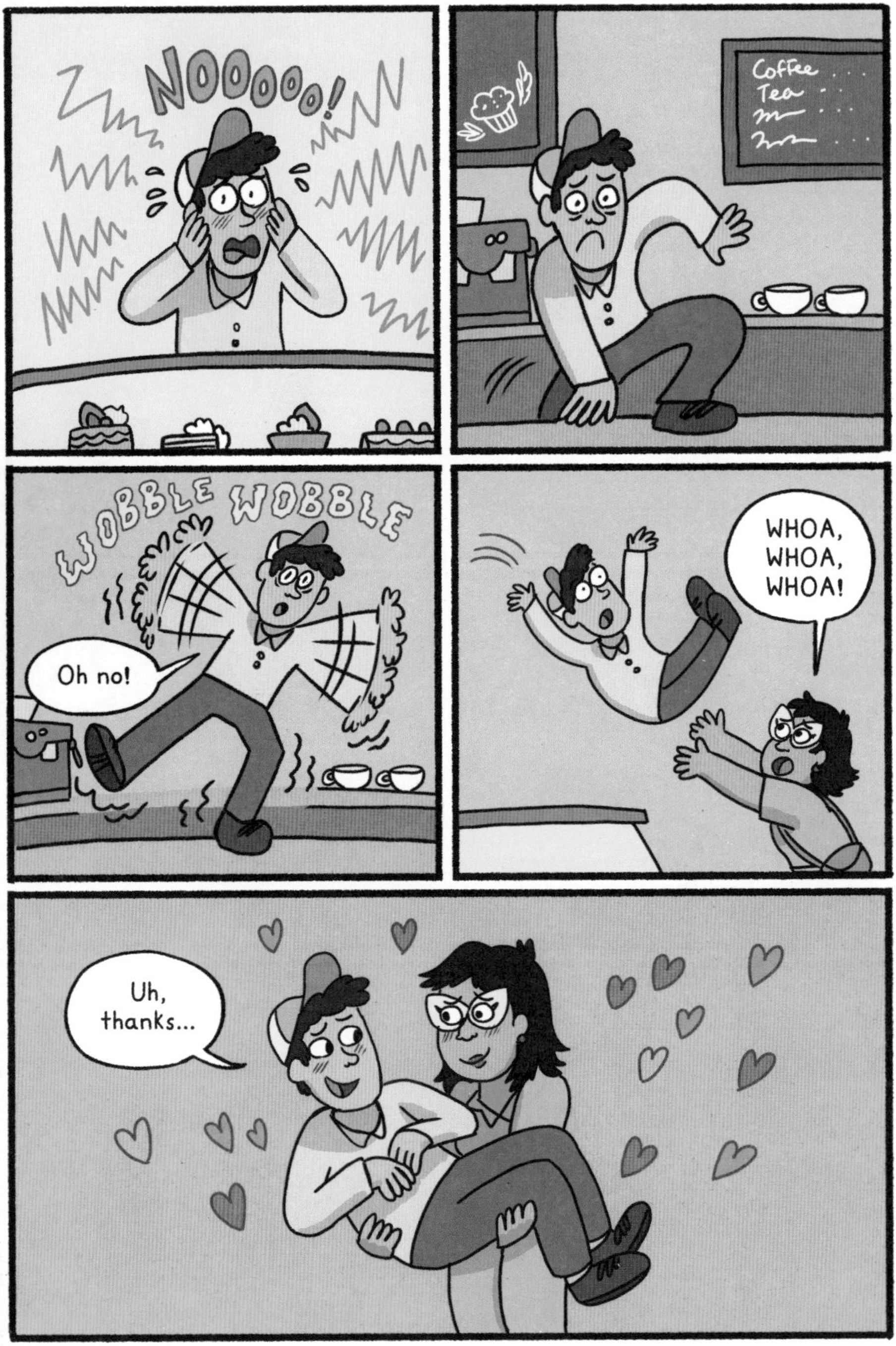
NOOOOOO!
WOBBLE WOBBLE
Oh no!
WHOA, WHOA, WHOA!
Uh, thanks...

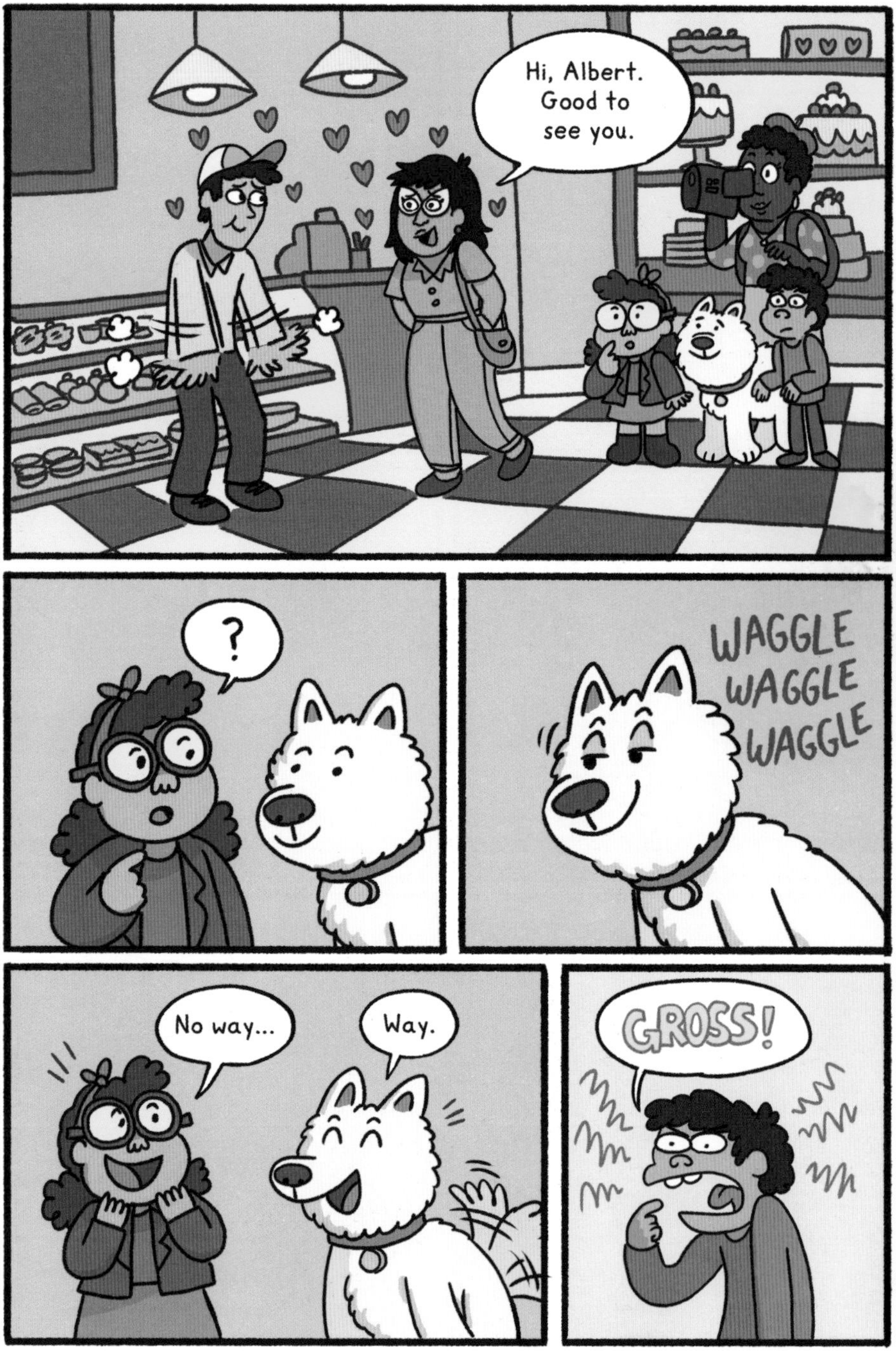
Hi, Albert. Good to see you.
?
WAGGLE
WAGGLE
WAGGLE
No way...
Way.
GROSS!

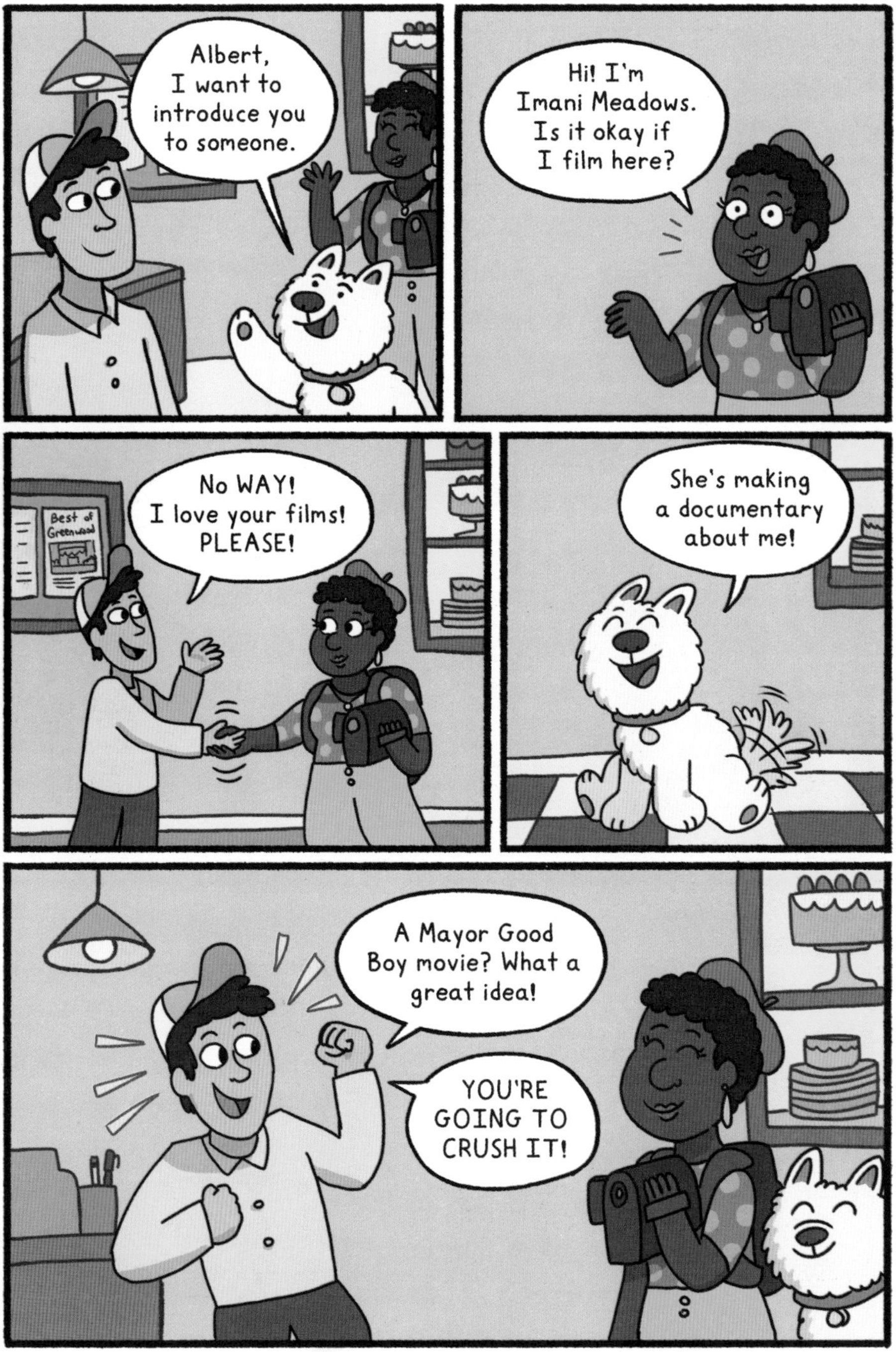
Albert, I want to introduce you to someone.
Hi! I'm Imani Meadows. Is it okay if I film here?
Best of Greenwood
No WAY! I love your films! PLEASE!
She's making a documentary about me!
A Mayor Good Boy movie? What a great idea!
YOU'RE GOING TO CRUSH IT!

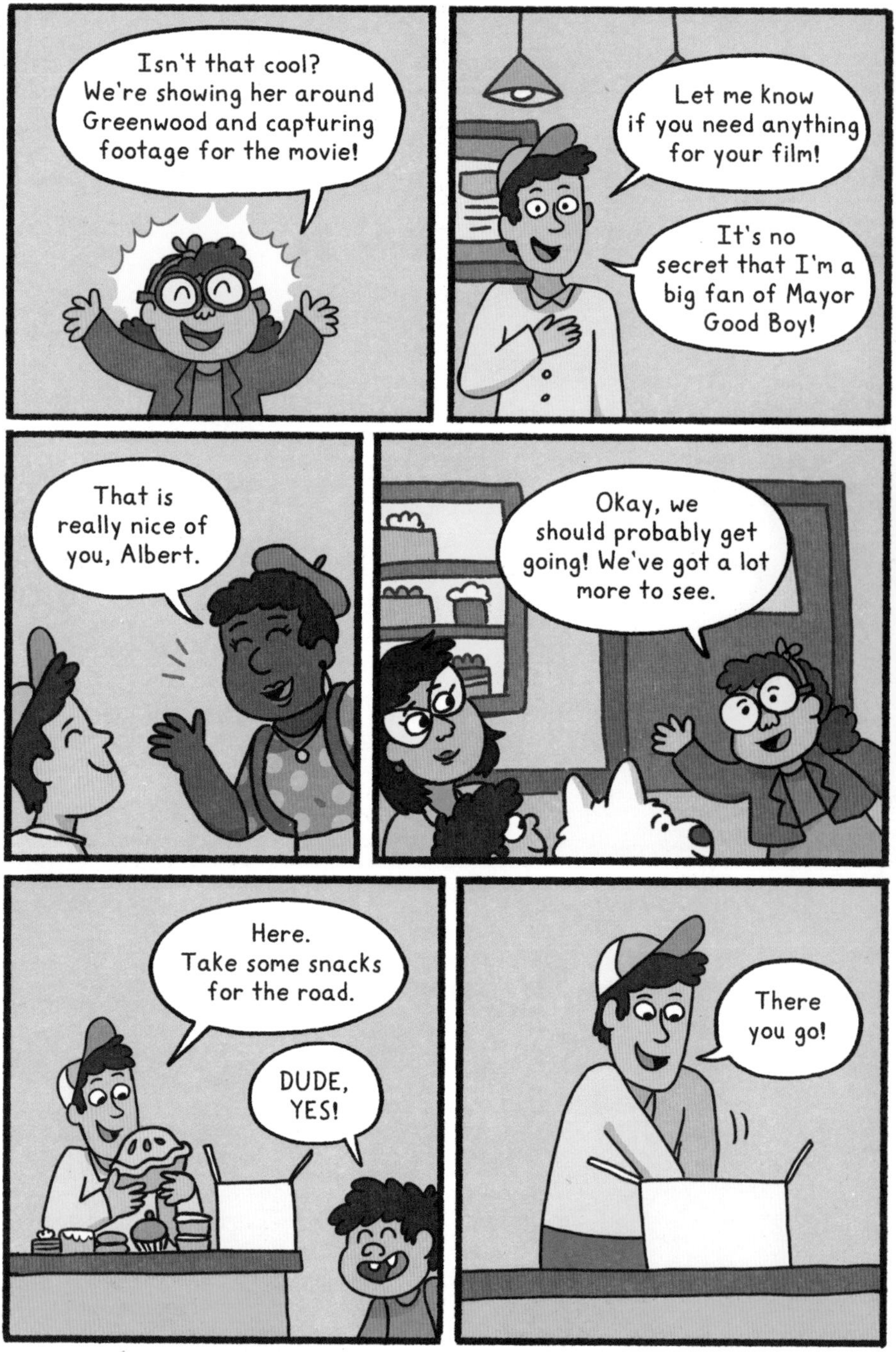

Isn't that cool? We're showing her around Greenwood and capturing footage for the movie!
Let me know if you need anything for your film!
It's no secret that I'm a big fan of Mayor Good Boy!
That is really nice of you, Albert.
Okay, we should probably get going! We've got a lot more to see.
Here. Take some snacks for the road.
DUDE, YES!
There you go!

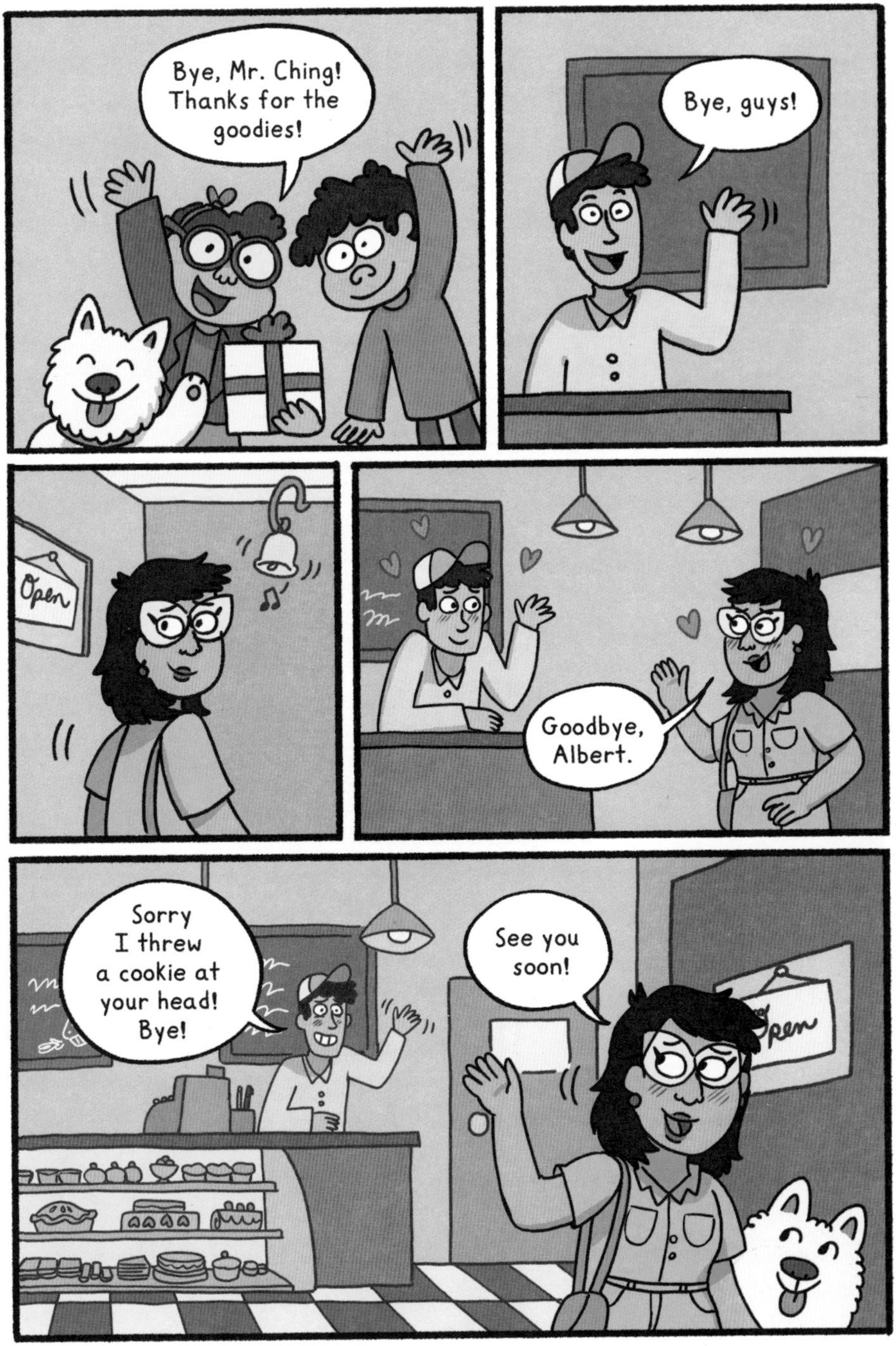
Bye, Mr. Ching! Thanks for the goodies!
Bye, guys!
Open
Goodbye, Albert.
Sorry I threw a cookie at your head! Bye!
See you soon!
Open

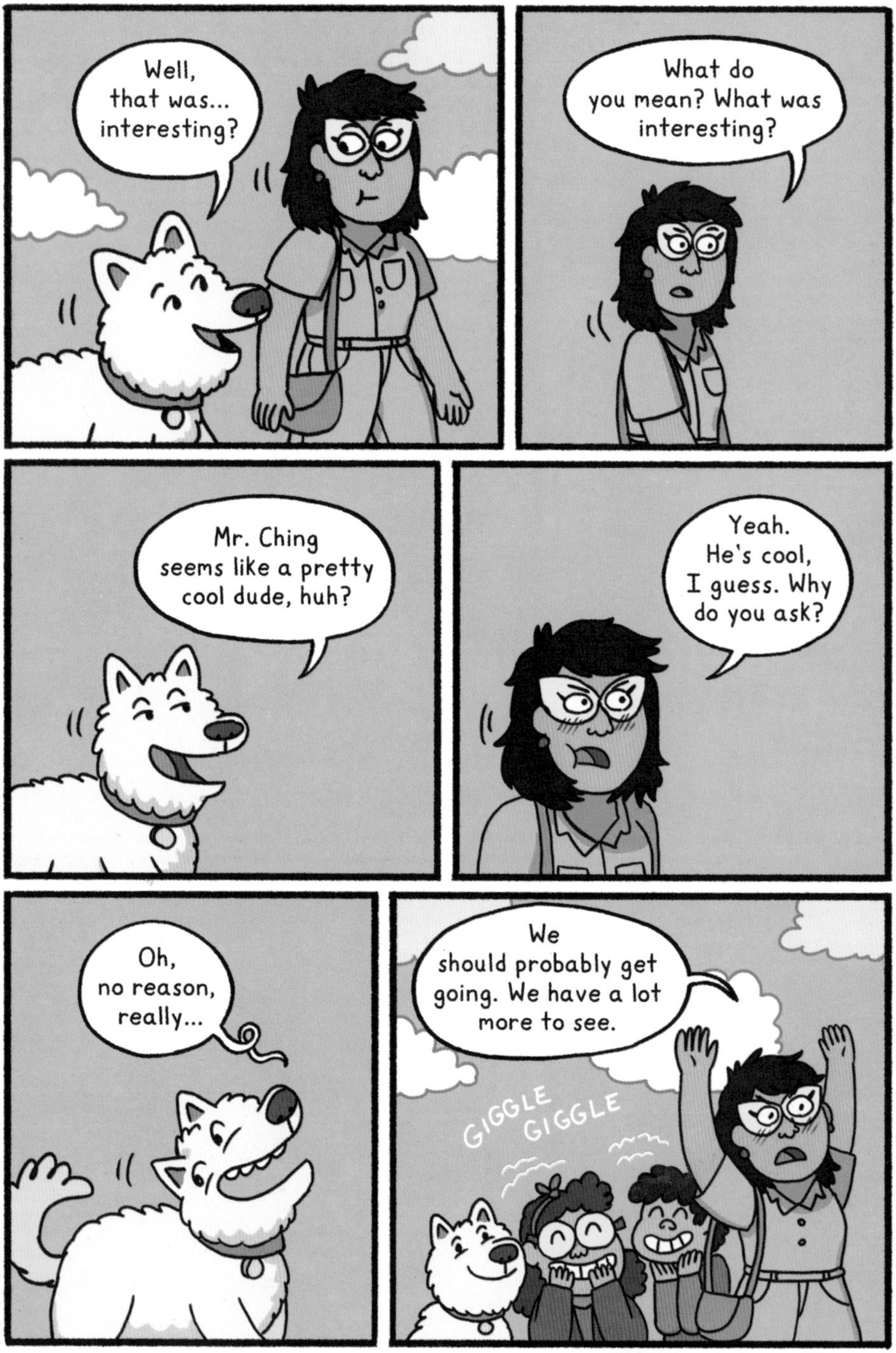
Well, that was... interesting?
What do you mean? What was interesting?
Mr. Ching seems like a pretty cool dude, huh?
Yeah. He's cool, I guess. Why do you ask?
Oh, no reason, really...
We should probably get going. We have a lot more to see.
GIGGLE GIGGLE

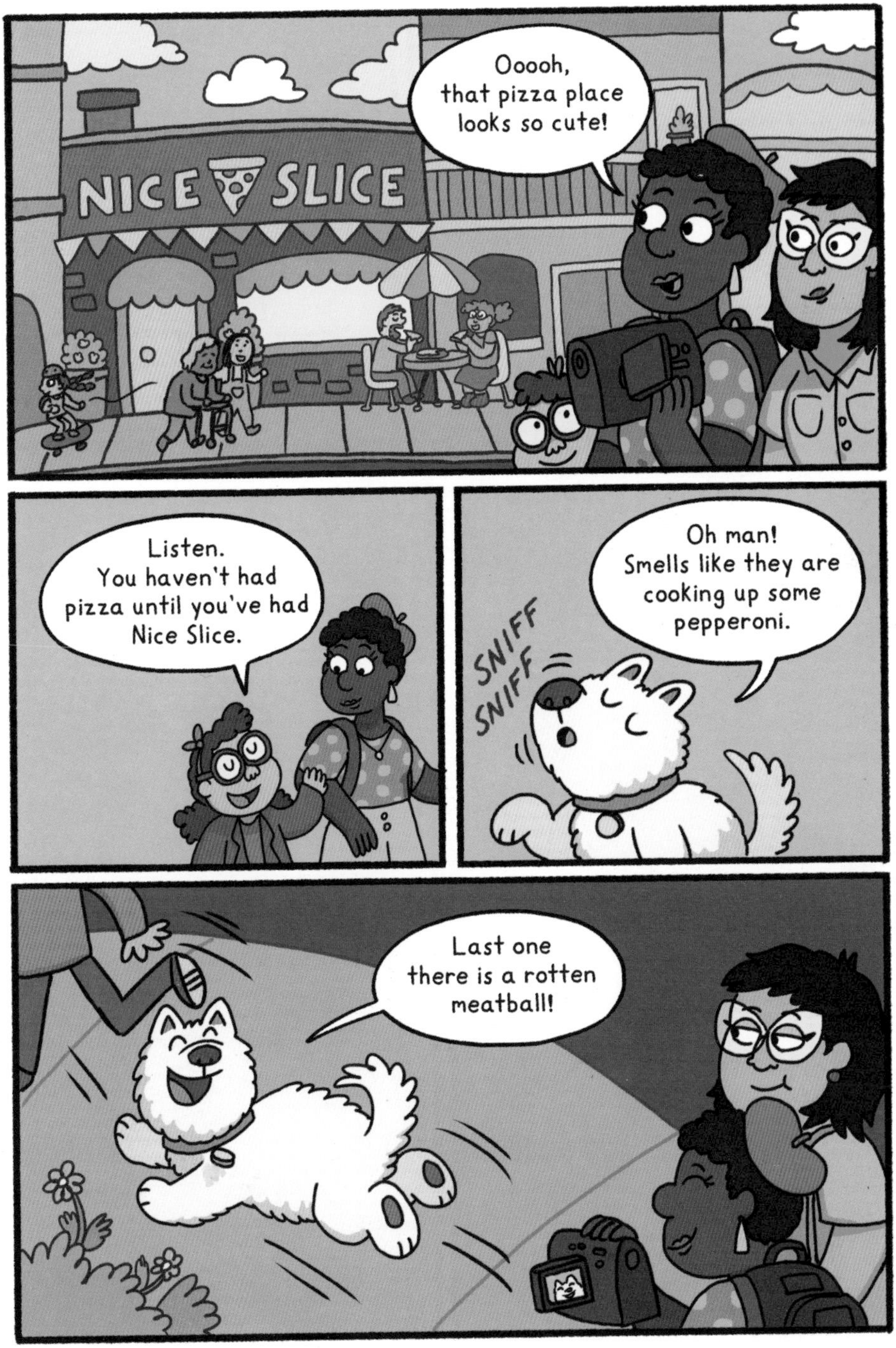
NICE SLICE
Ooooh, that pizza place looks so cute!
Listen. You haven't had pizza until you've had Nice Slice.
SNIFF SNIFF
Oh man! Smells like they are cooking up some pepperoni.
Last one there is a rotten meatball!

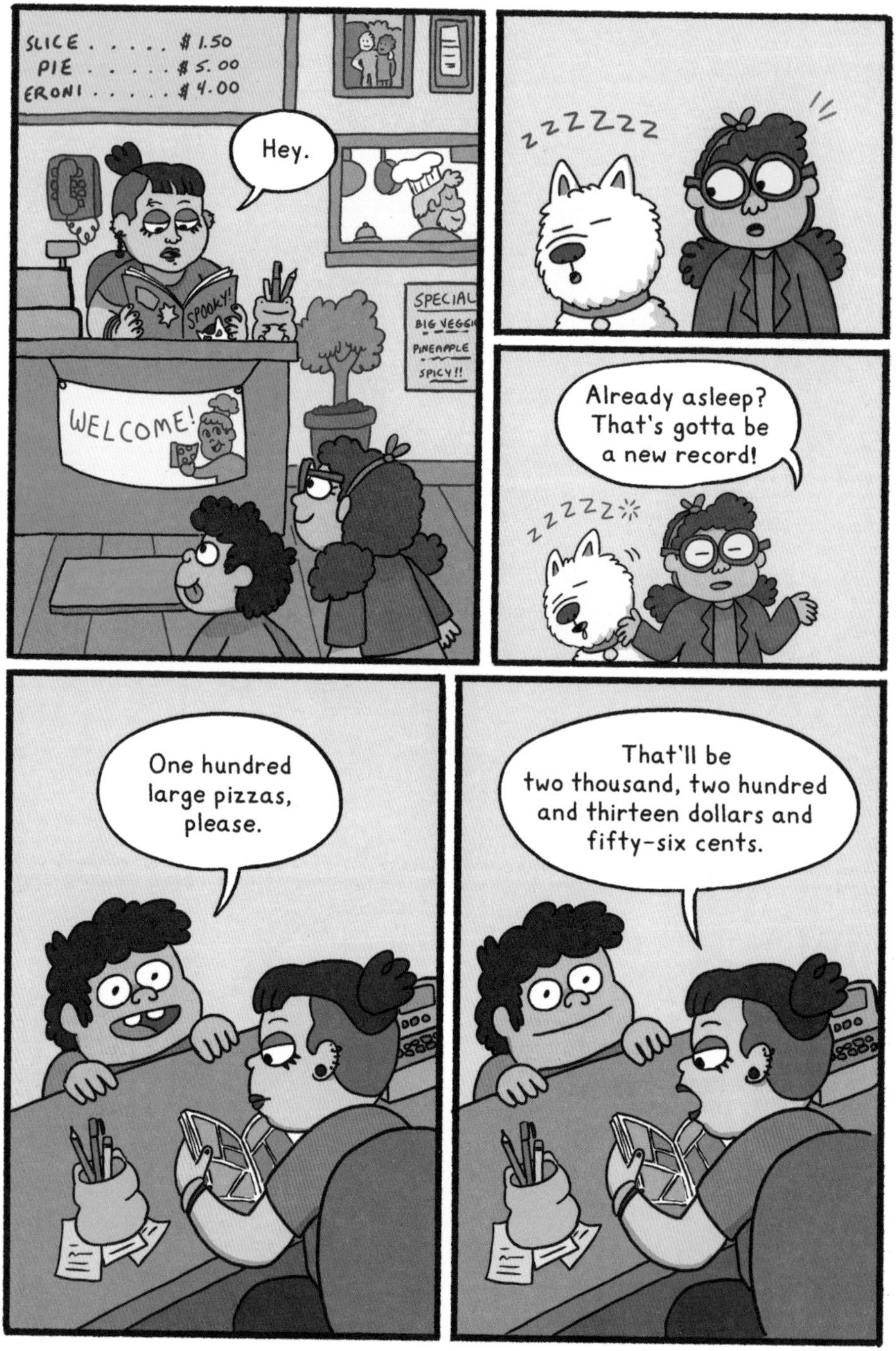
SLICE $1.50
PIE $5.00
ERONI $4.00
Hey.
SPOOKY!
SPECIAL
BIG VEGGI
PINEAPPLE
SPICY!!
WELCOME!
ZZZZZZ
Already asleep? That's gotta be a new record!
ZZZZZ
One hundred large pizzas, please.
That'll be two thousand, two hundred and thirteen dollars and fifty-six cents.

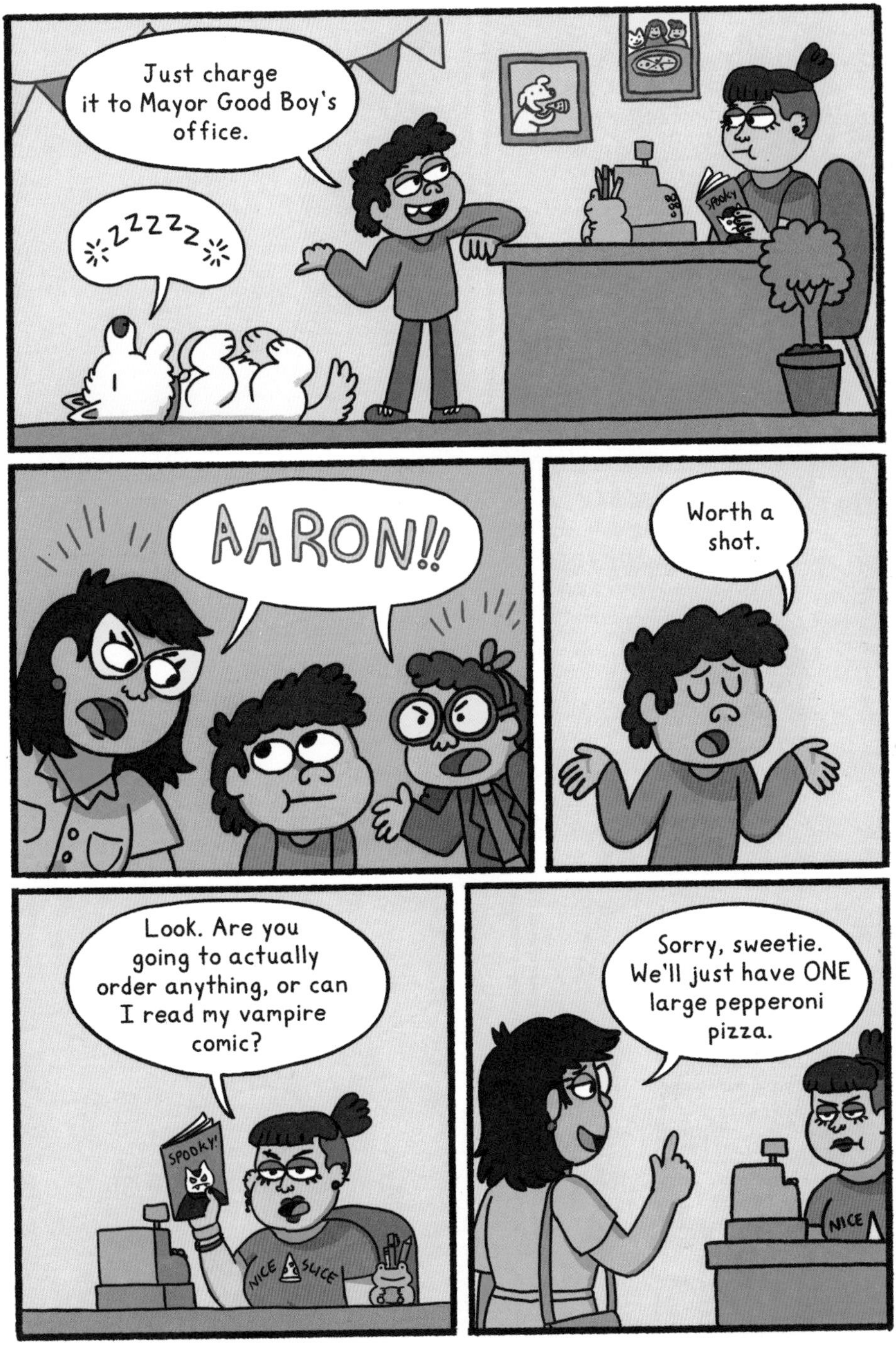
Just charge it to Mayor Good Boy's office.
ZZZZZ
SPOOKY
AARON!!
Worth a shot.
Look. Are you going to actually order anything, or can I read my vampire comic?
SPOOKY!
NICE SLICE
Sorry, sweetie. We'll just have ONE large pepperoni pizza.
NICE

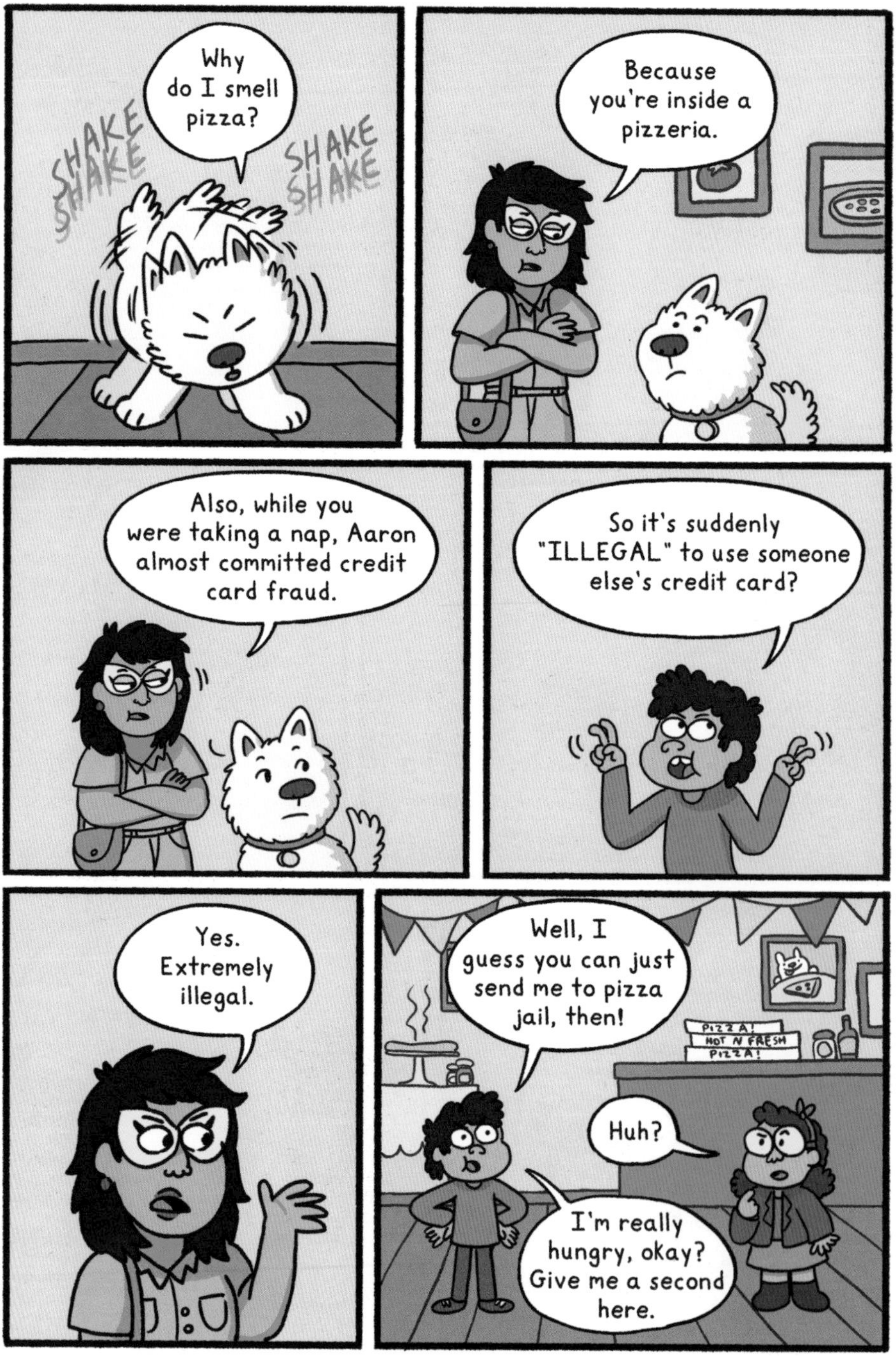
Why do I smell pizza?
SHAKE SHAKE
SHAKE SHAKE
Because you're inside a pizzeria.
Also, while you were taking a nap, Aaron almost committed credit card fraud.
So it's suddenly "ILLEGAL" to use someone else's credit card?
Yes. Extremely illegal.
Well, I guess you can just send me to pizza jail, then!
PIZZA!
HOT N FRESH
PIZZA!
Huh?
I'm really hungry, okay? Give me a second here.

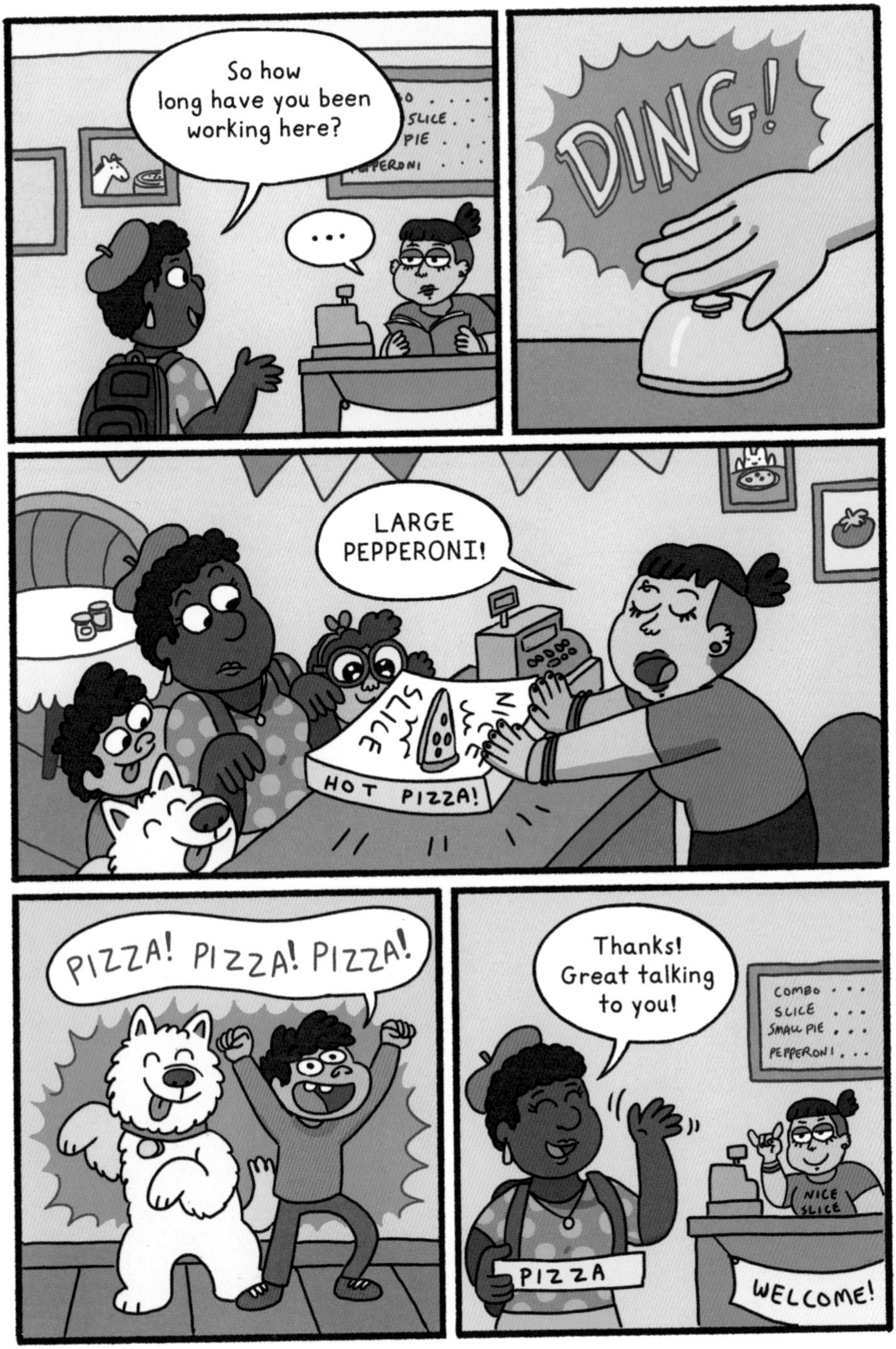
So how long have you been working here?
...
DING!
LARGE PEPPERONI!
NICE SLICE
HOT PIZZA!
PIZZA! PIZZA! PIZZA!
Thanks! Great talking to you!
COMBO
SLICE
SMALL PIE
PEPPERONI
NICE SLICE
PIZZA
WELCOME!

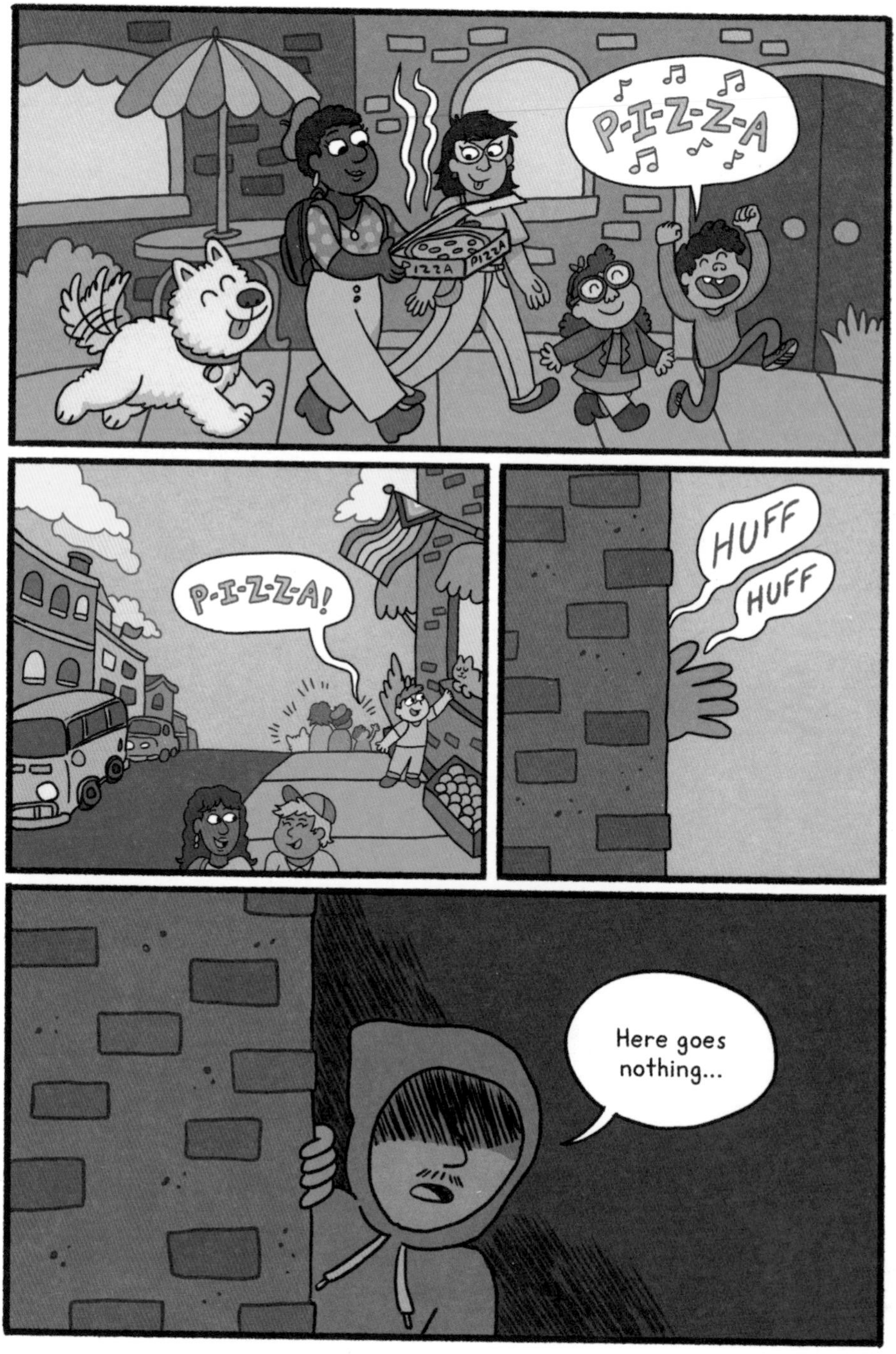
P-I-Z-Z-A
PIZZA
PIZZA
P-I-Z-Z-A!
HUFF
HUFF
Here goes nothing...

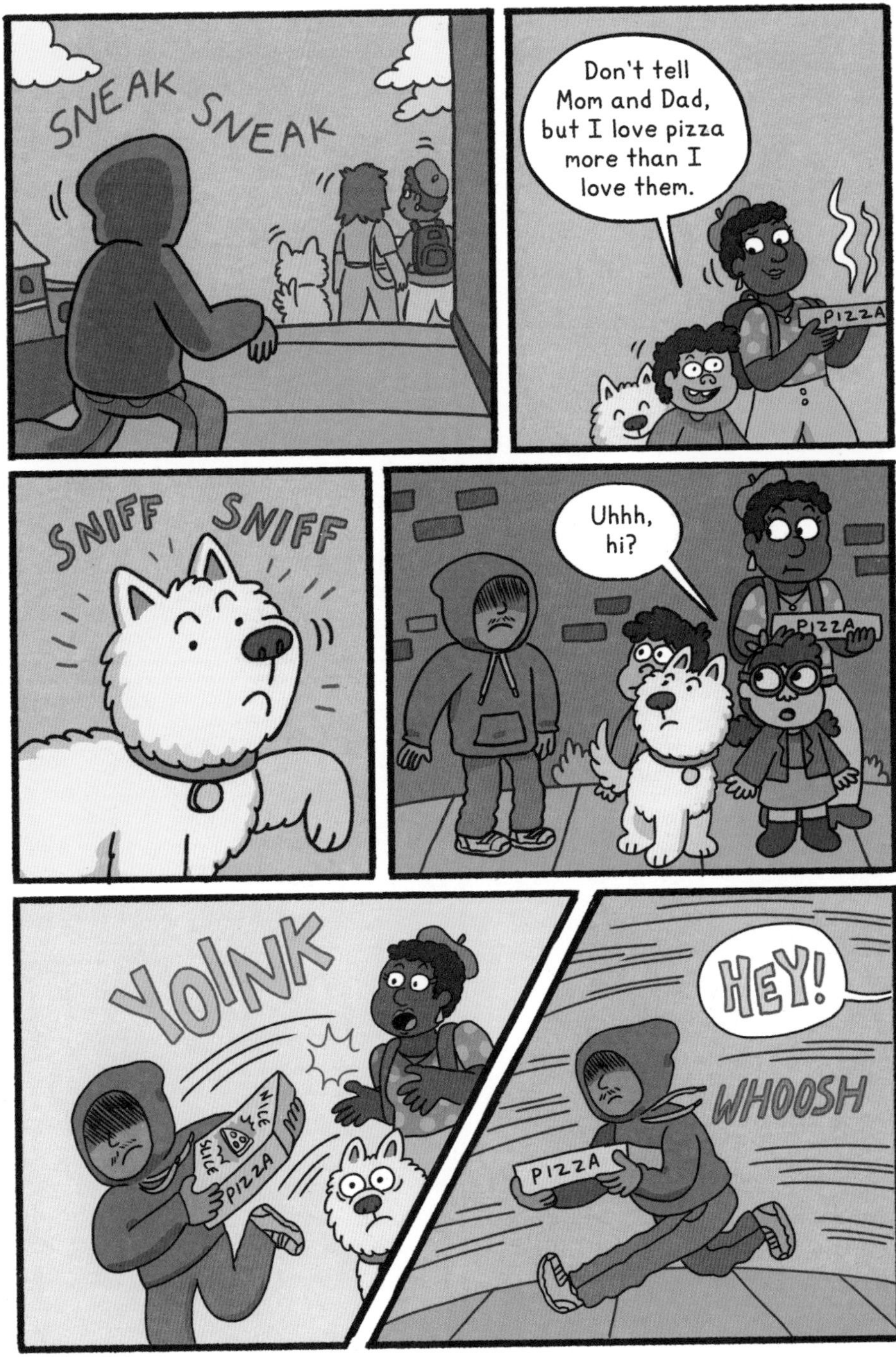
SNEAK SNEAK
Don't tell Mom and Dad, but I love pizza more than I love them.
PIZZA
SNIFF SNIFF
Uhhh, hi?
PIZZA
YOINK
NICE SLICE PIZZA
HEY!
WHOOSH
PIZZA

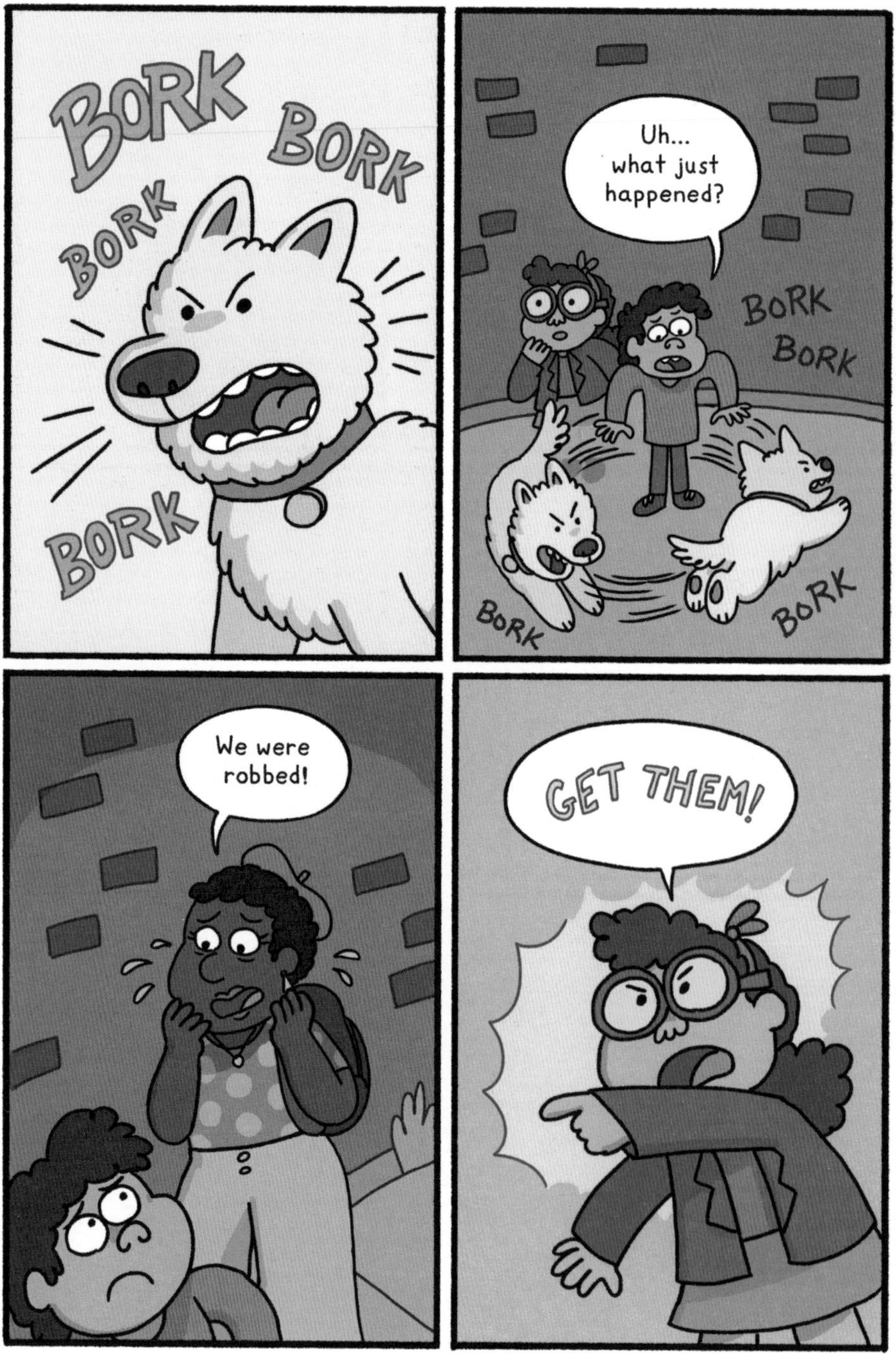
BORK
BORK
BORK
BORK
Uh... what just happened?
BORK
BORK
BORK
BORK
We were robbed!
GET THEM!

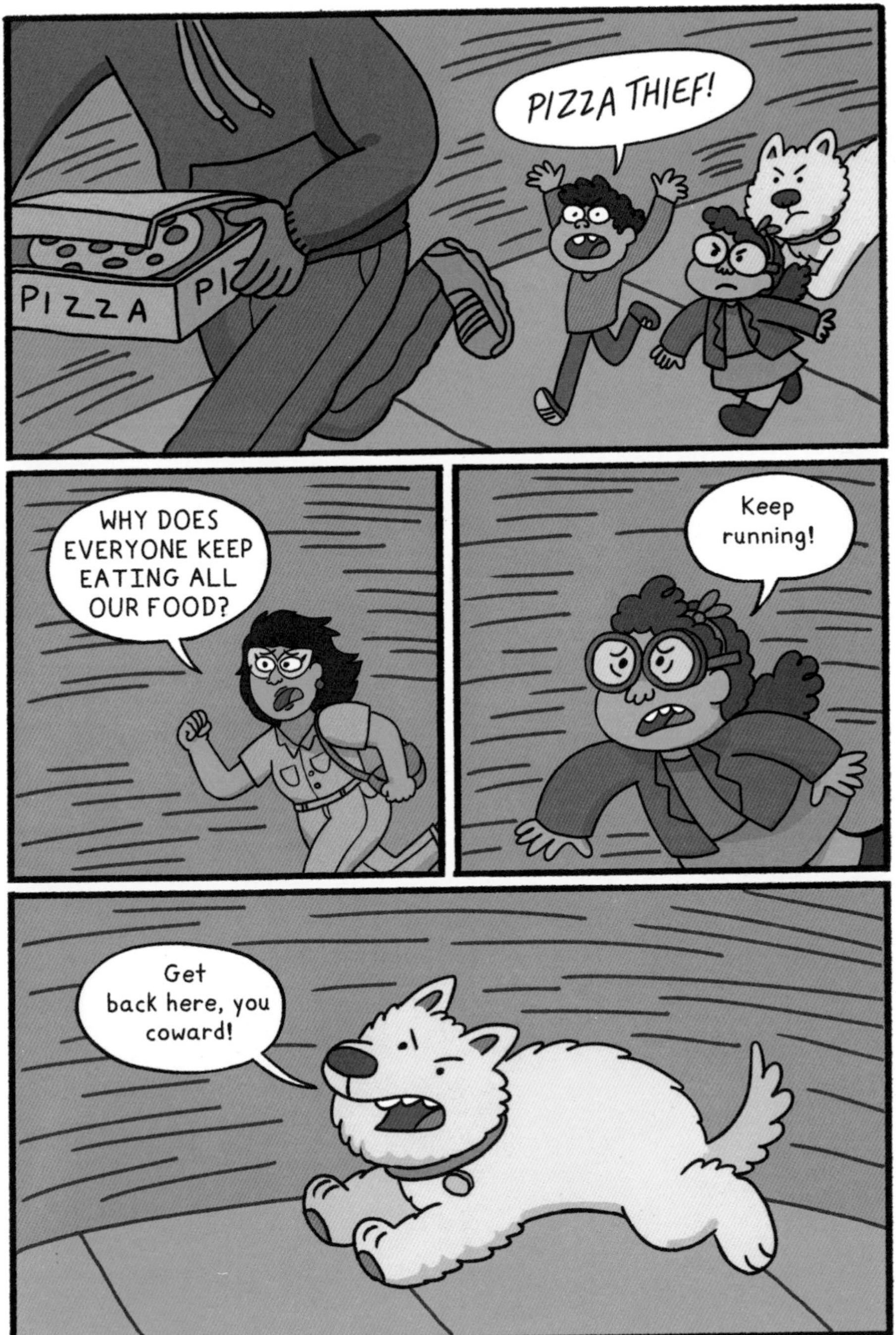
PIZZA
PI
PIZZA THIEF!
WHY DOES EVERYONE KEEP EATING ALL OUR FOOD?
Keep running!
Get back here, you coward!

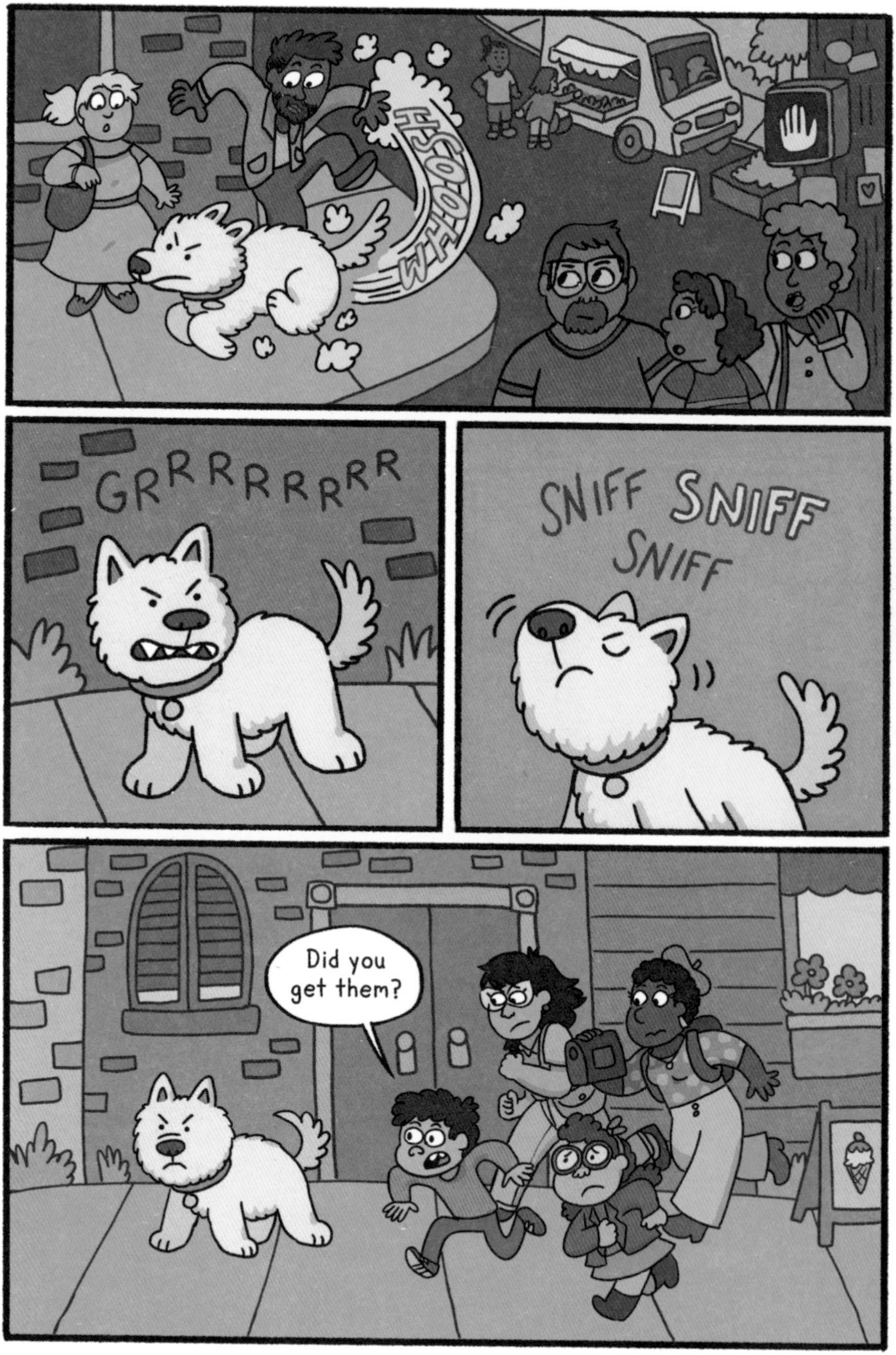
WHOOSH
GRRRRRRRRR
SNIFF SNIFF
SNIFF
Did you get them?

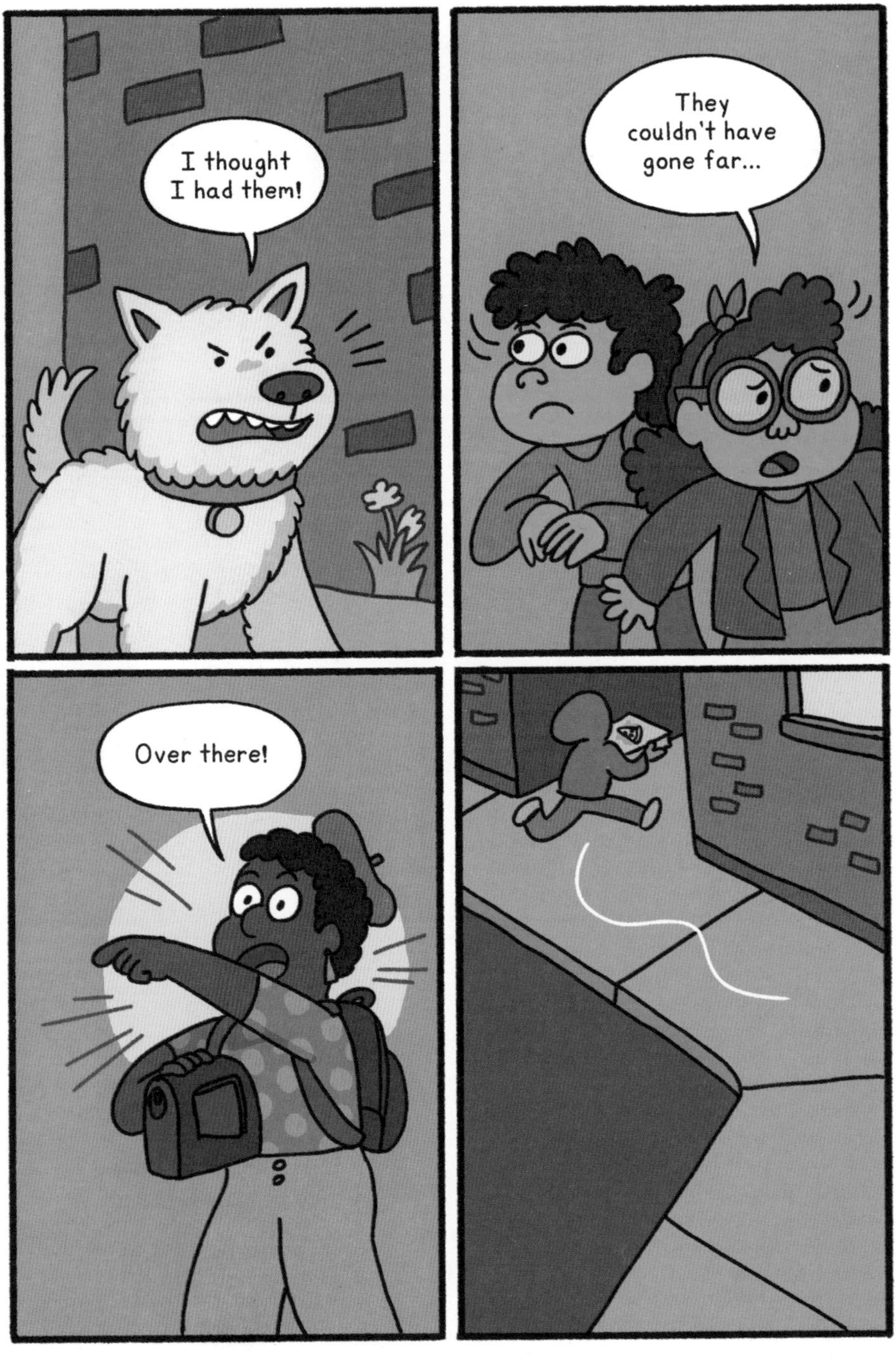
I thought I had them!
They couldn't have gone far...
Over there!

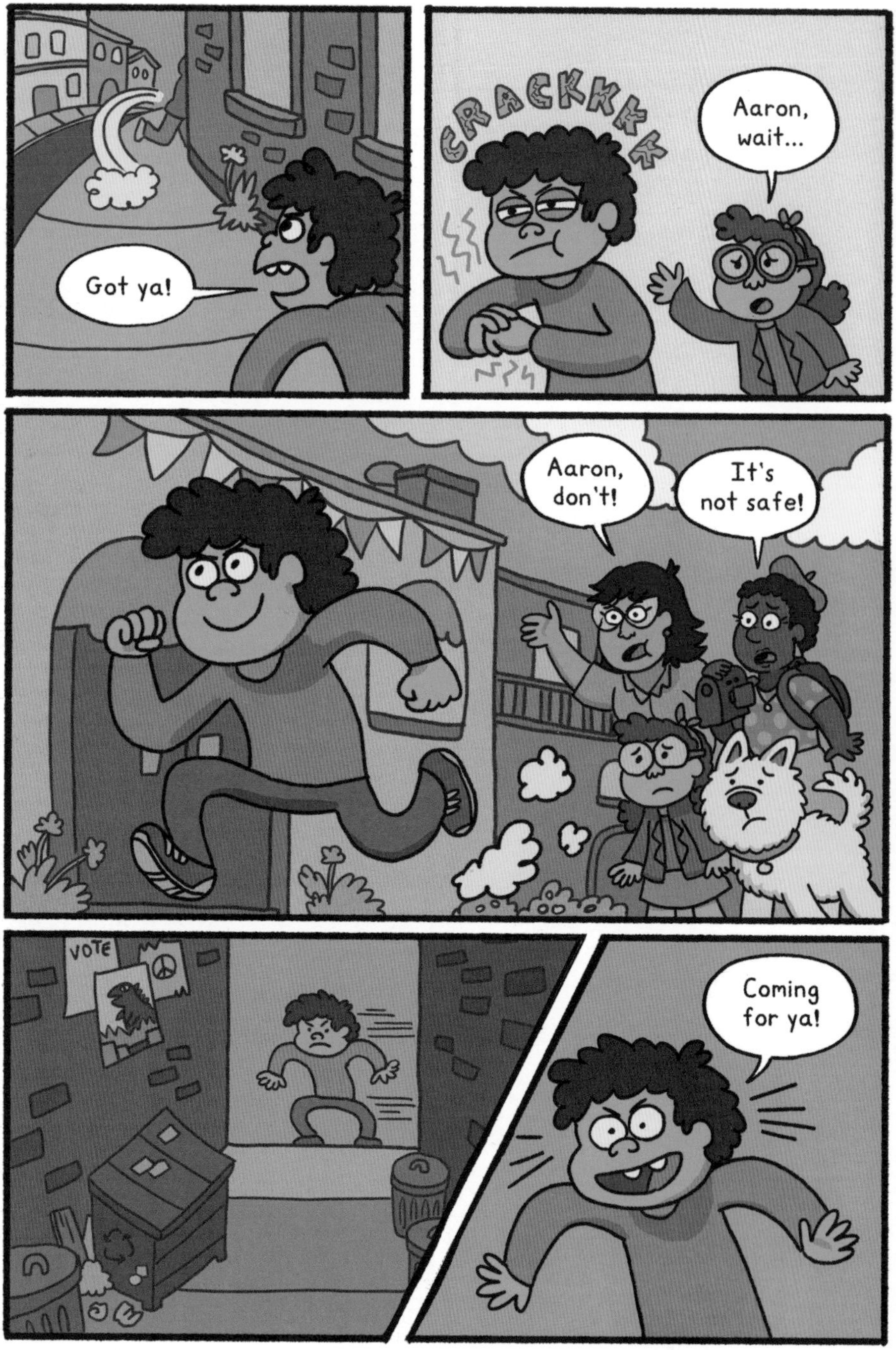
Got ya!
CRACKKKK
Aaron, wait...
Aaron, don't!
It's not safe!
VOTE
Coming for ya!

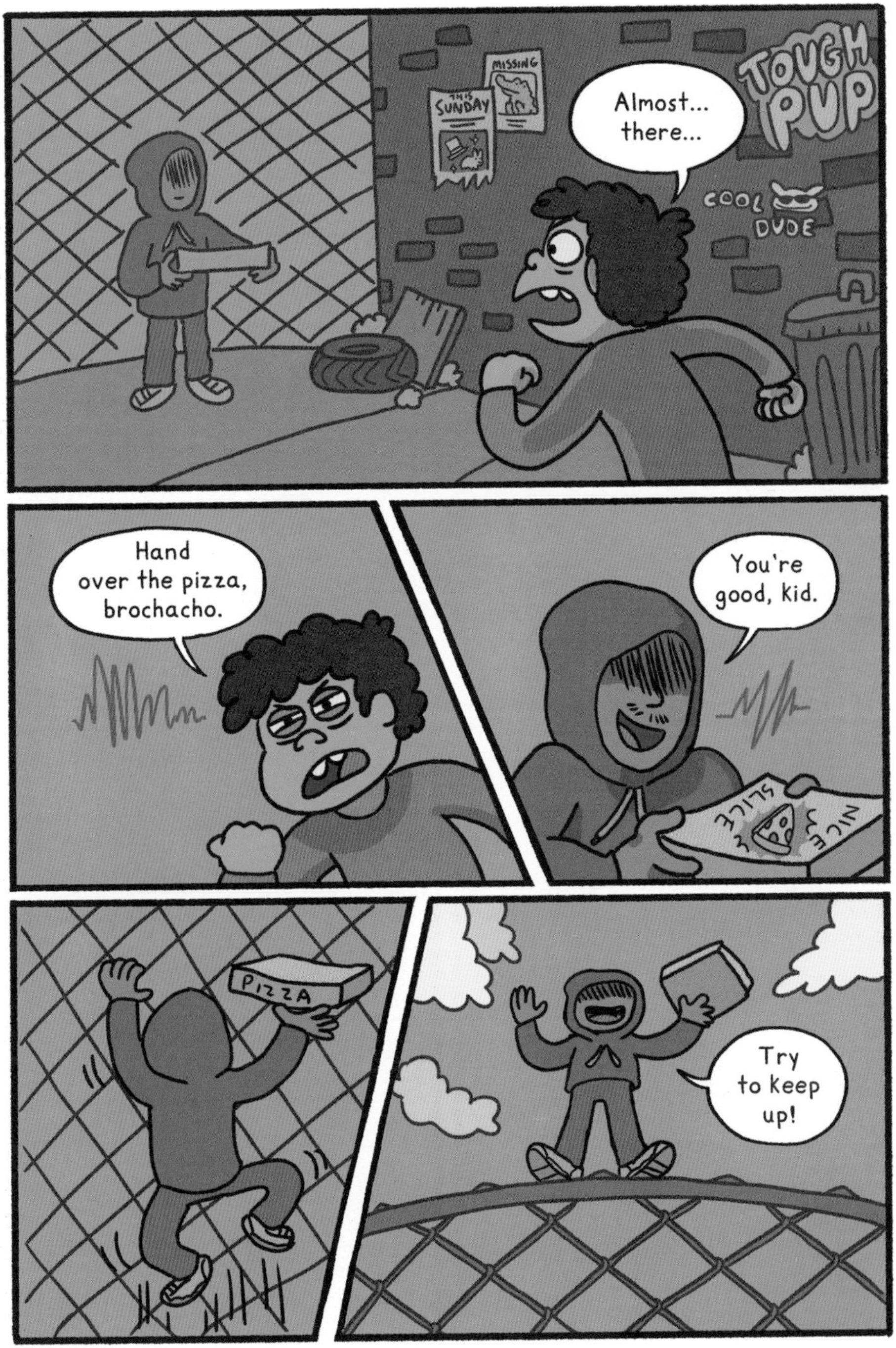
THIS SUNDAY
MISSING
TOUGH PUP
Almost... there...
COOL DUDE
Hand over the pizza, brochacho.
You're good, kid.
NICE SLICE
PIZZA
Try to keep up!

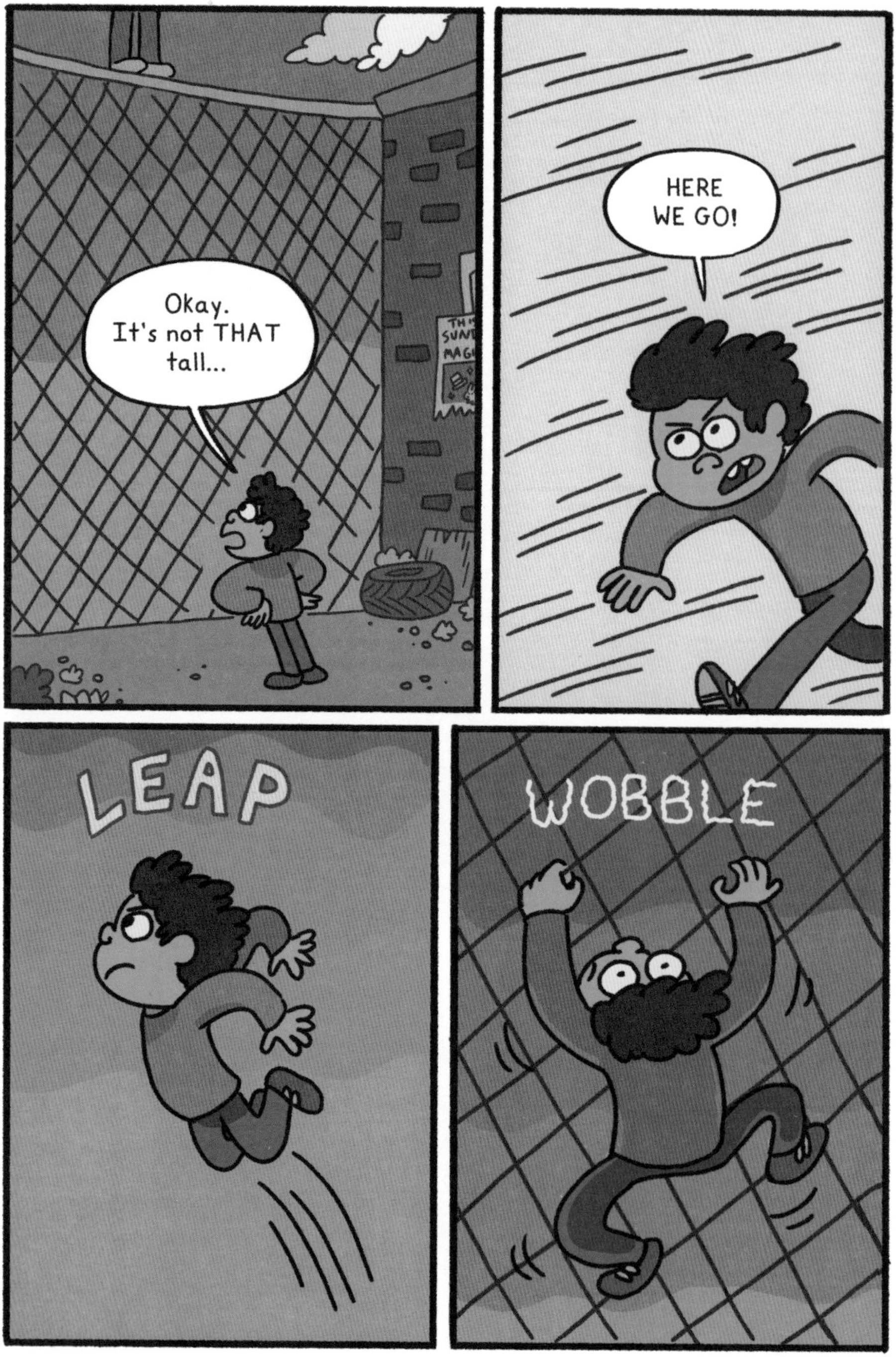
Okay.
It's not THAT
tall...
HERE
WE GO!
LEAP
WOBBLE

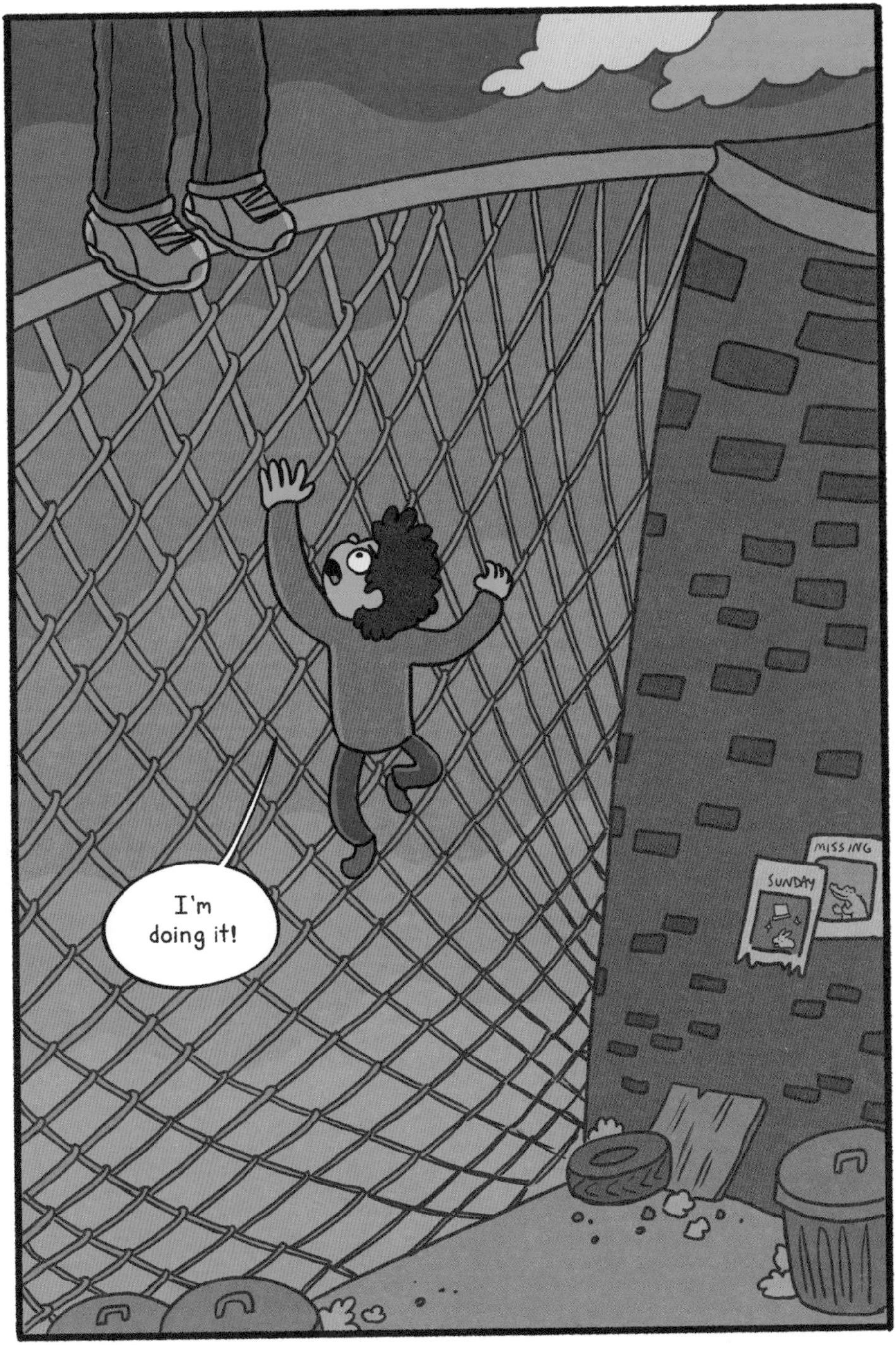
I'm doing it!
SUNDAY
MISSING

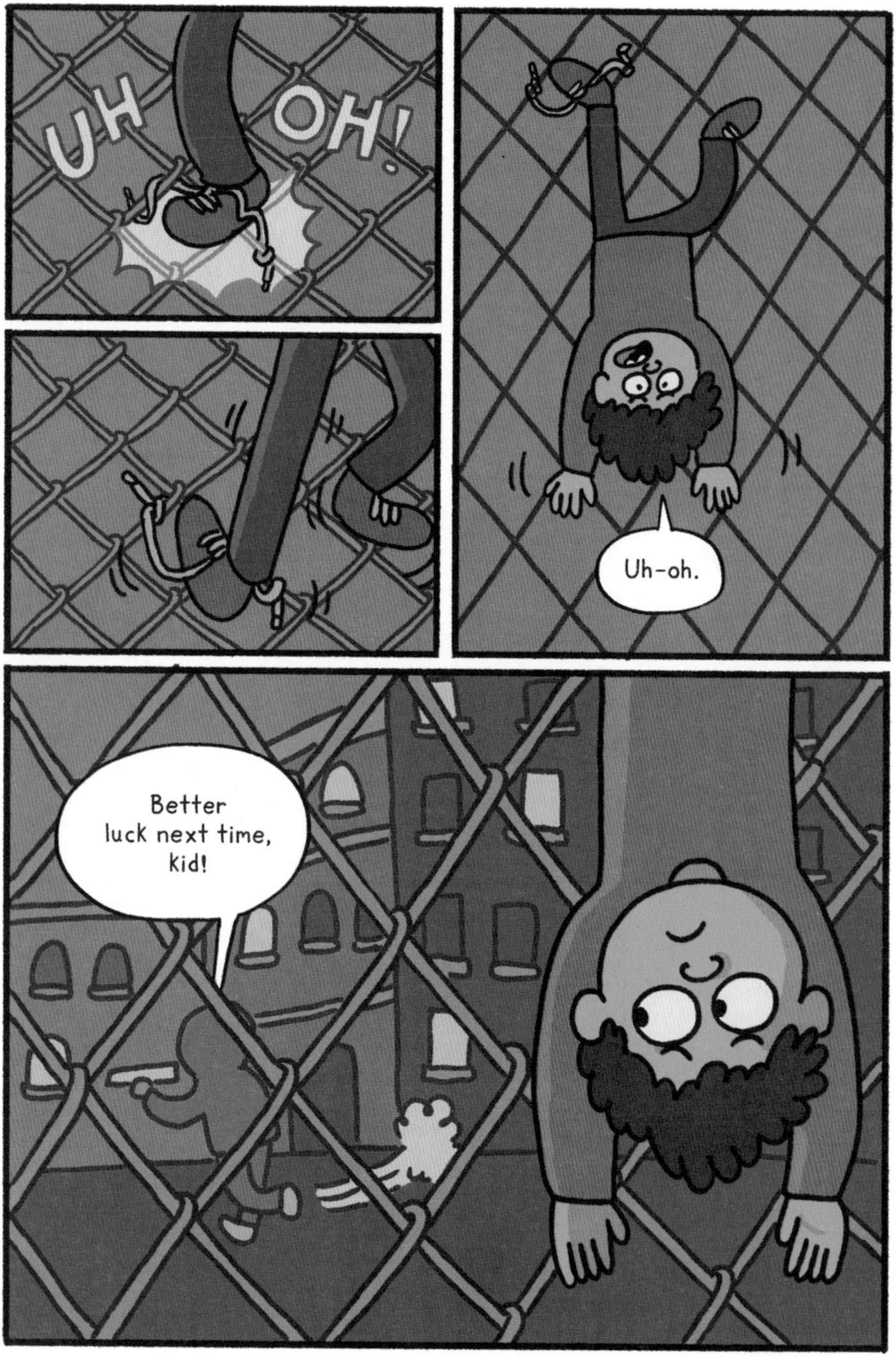
UH OH!
Uh-oh.
Better luck next time, kid!

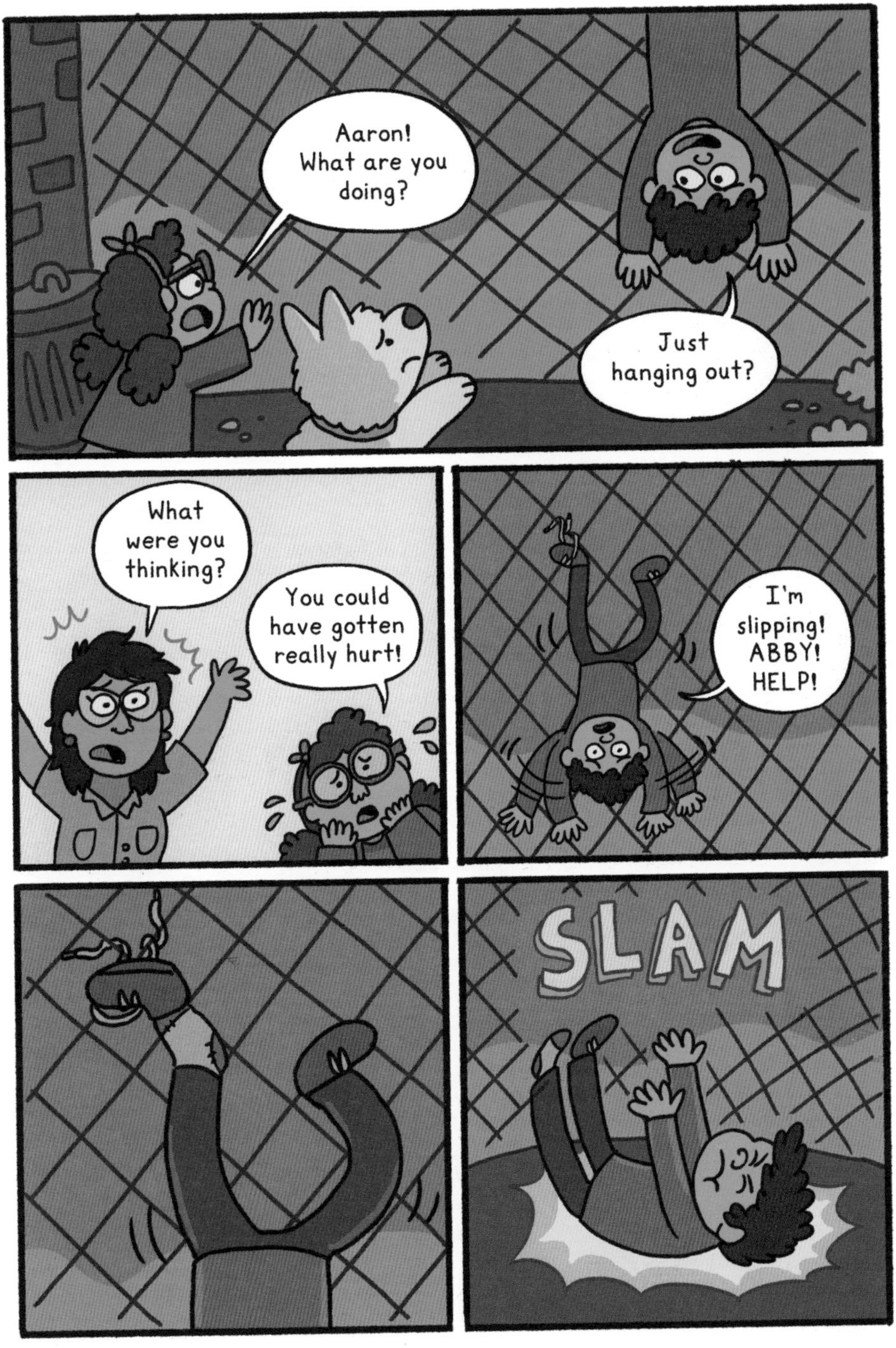
Aaron! What are you doing?
Just hanging out?
What were you thinking?
You could have gotten really hurt!
I'm slipping! ABBY! HELP!
SLAM

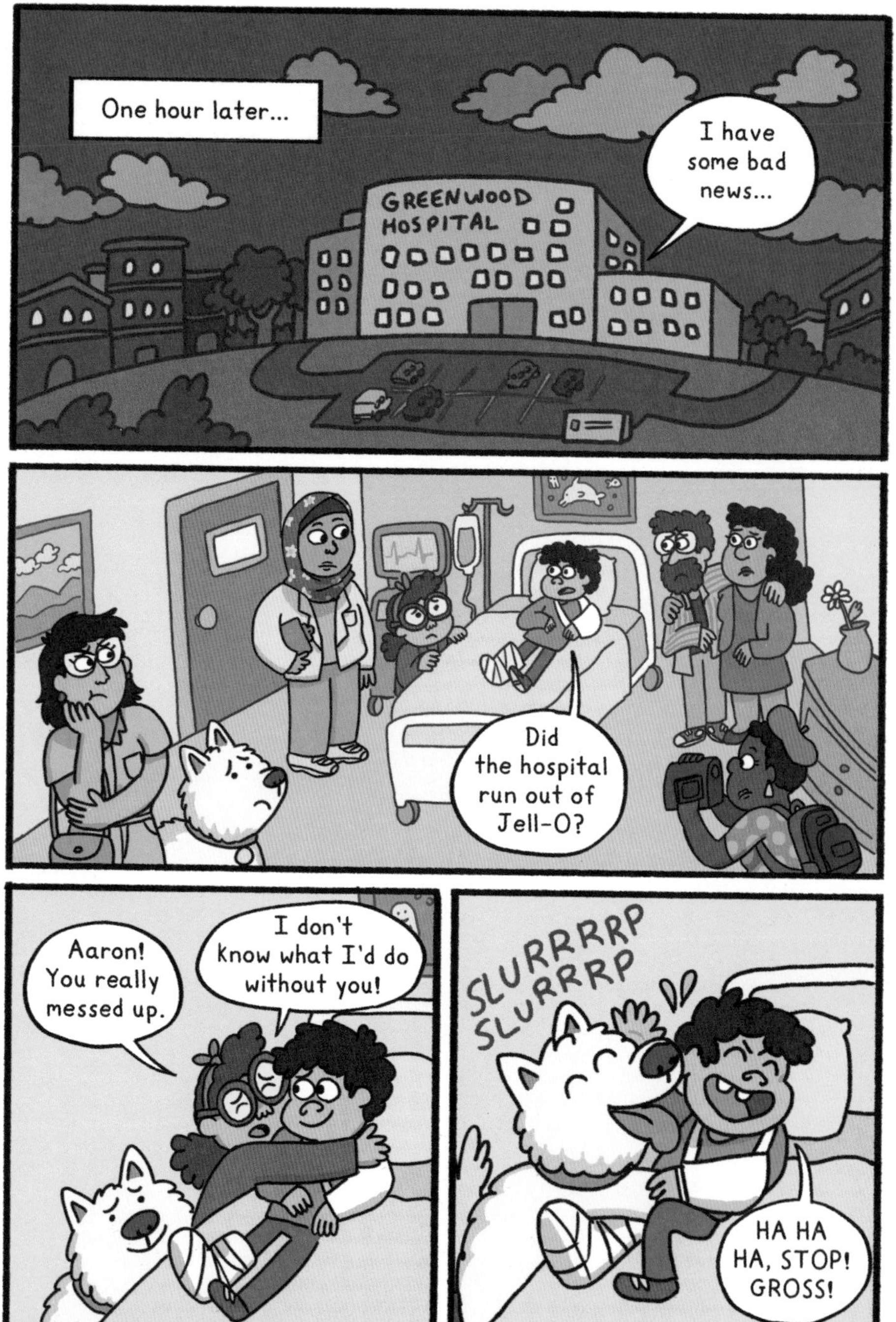
One hour later...
GREENWOOD HOSPITAL
I have some bad news...
Did the hospital run out of Jell-O?
Aaron! You really messed up.
I don't know what I'd do without you!
SLURRRRP SLURRRP
HA HA HA, STOP! GROSS!

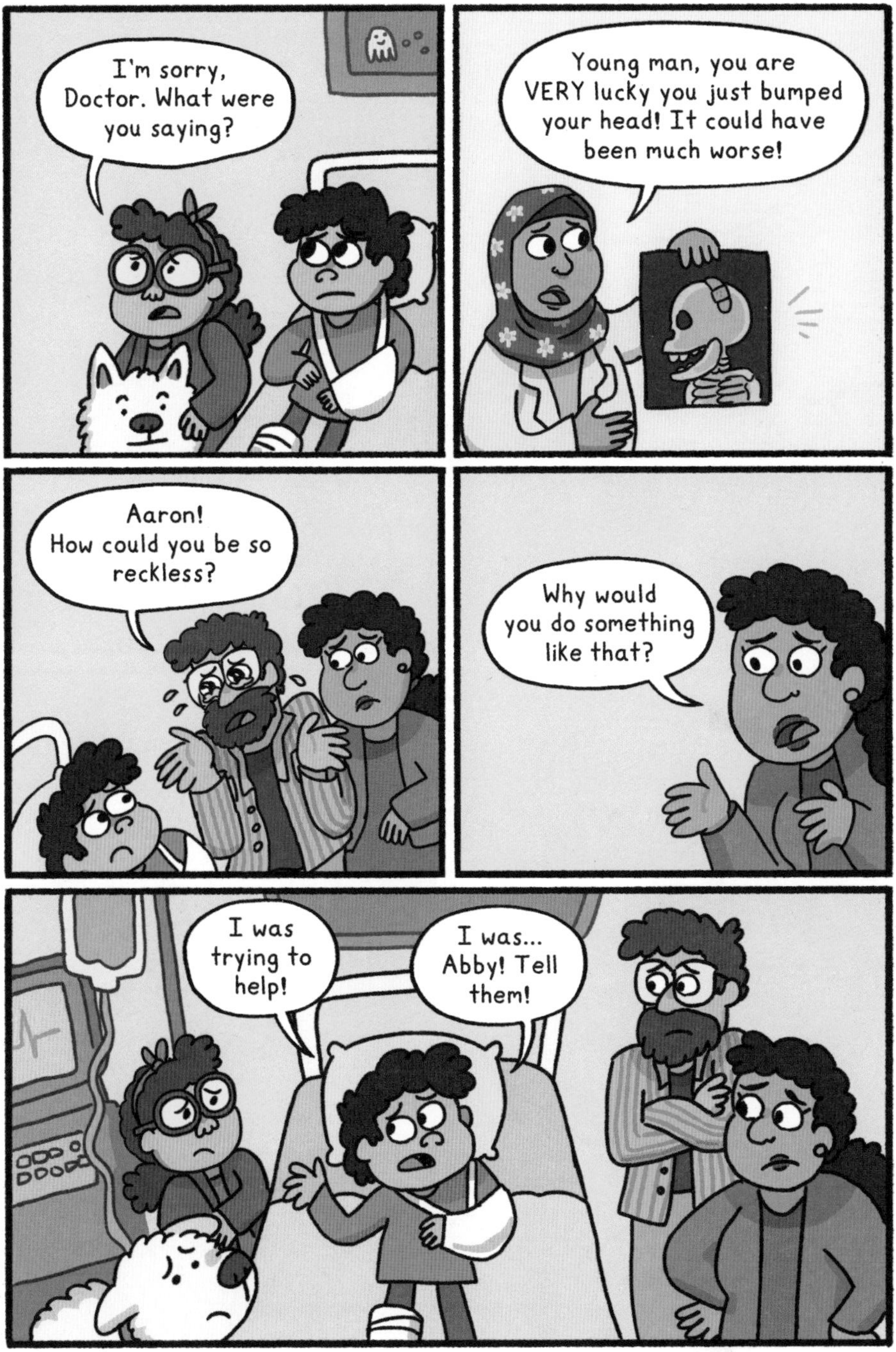
I'm sorry, Doctor. What were you saying?
Young man, you are VERY lucky you just bumped your head! It could have been much worse!
Aaron! How could you be so reckless?
Why would you do something like that?
I was trying to help!
I was... Abby! Tell them!

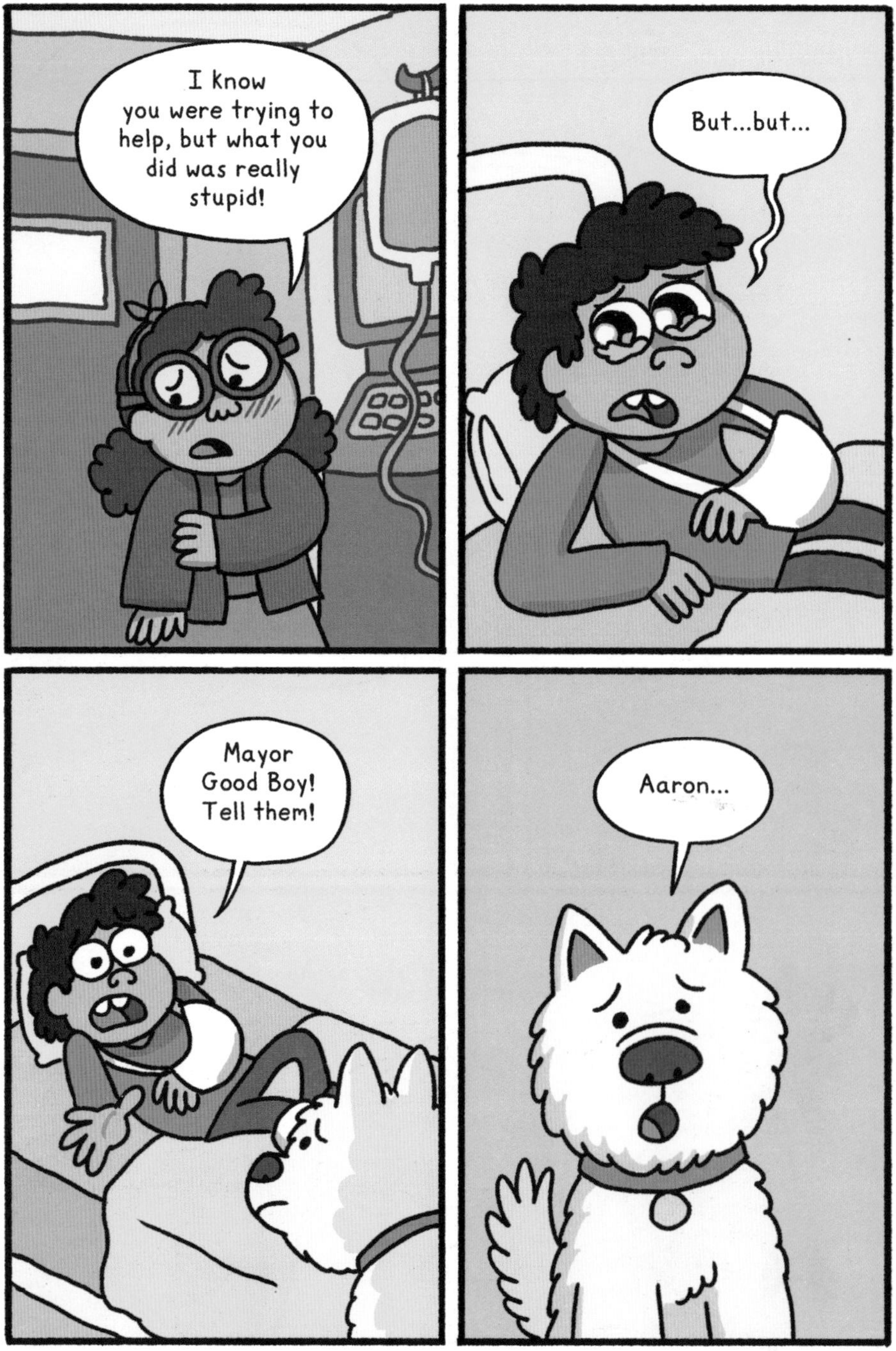
I know you were trying to help, but what you did was really stupid!
But...but...
Mayor Good Boy! Tell them!
Aaron...

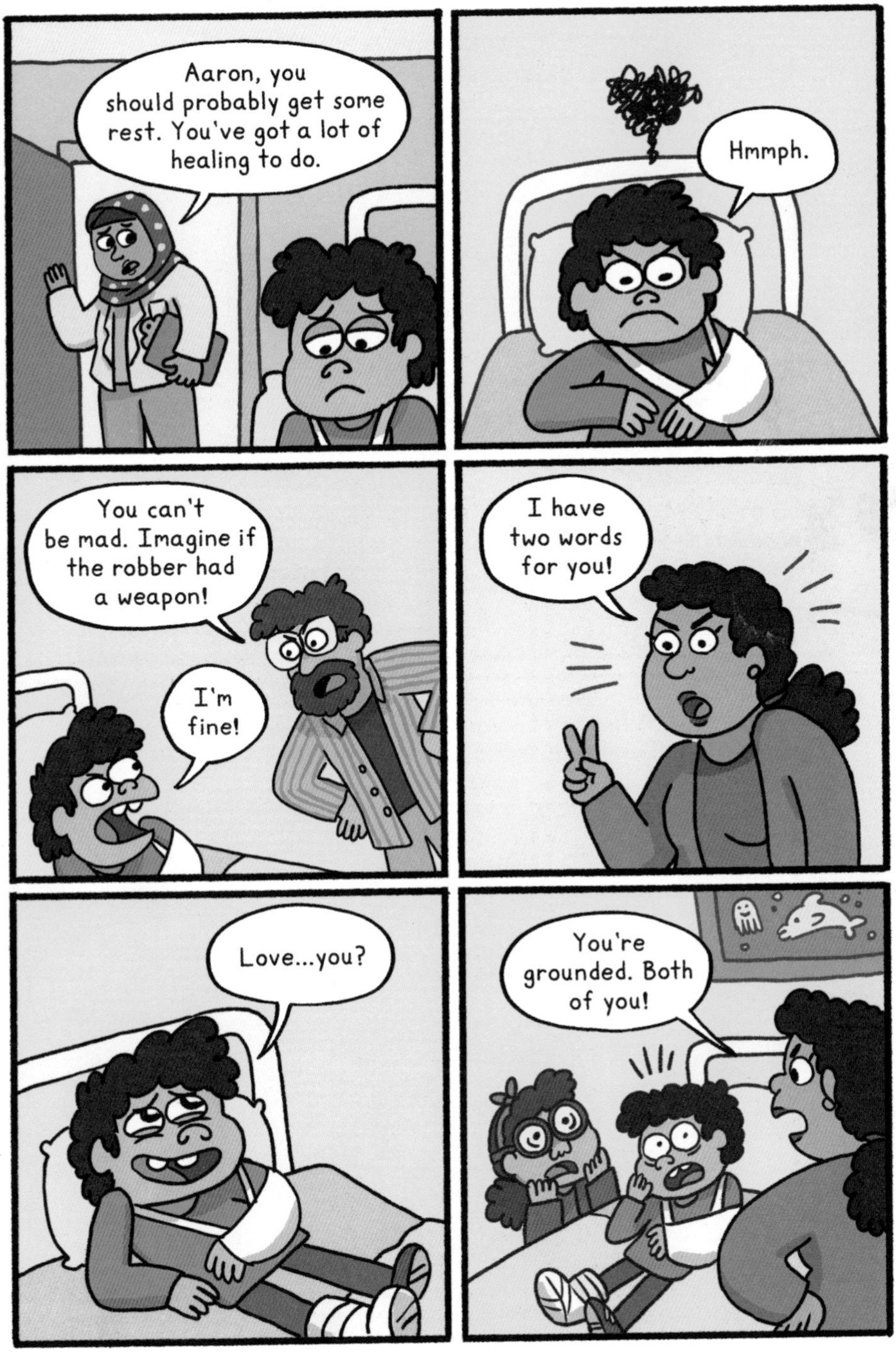
Aaron, you should probably get some rest. You've got a lot of healing to do.
Hmmph.
You can't be mad. Imagine if the robber had a weapon!
I'm fine!
I have two words for you!
Love...you?
You're grounded. Both of you!

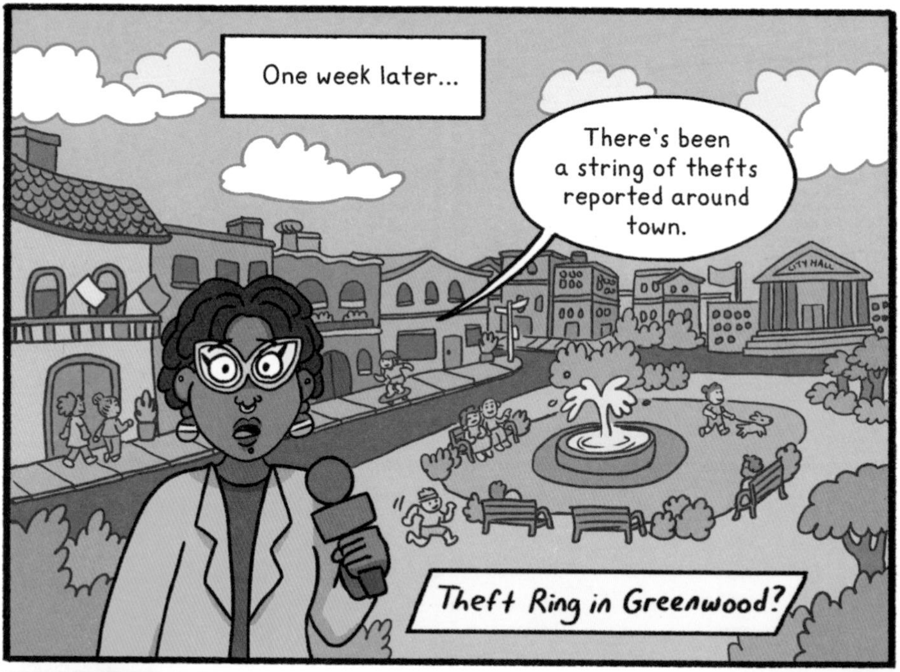
One week later...
There's been a string of thefts reported around town.
CITY HALL
Theft Ring in Greenwood?

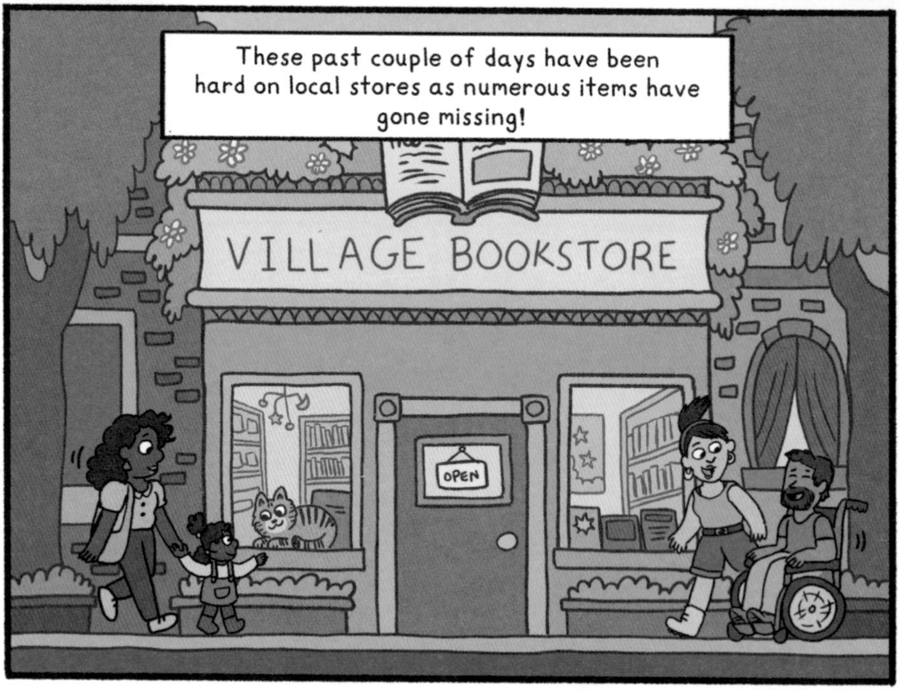
These past couple of days have been hard on local stores as numerous items have gone missing!
VILLAGE BOOKSTORE
OPEN

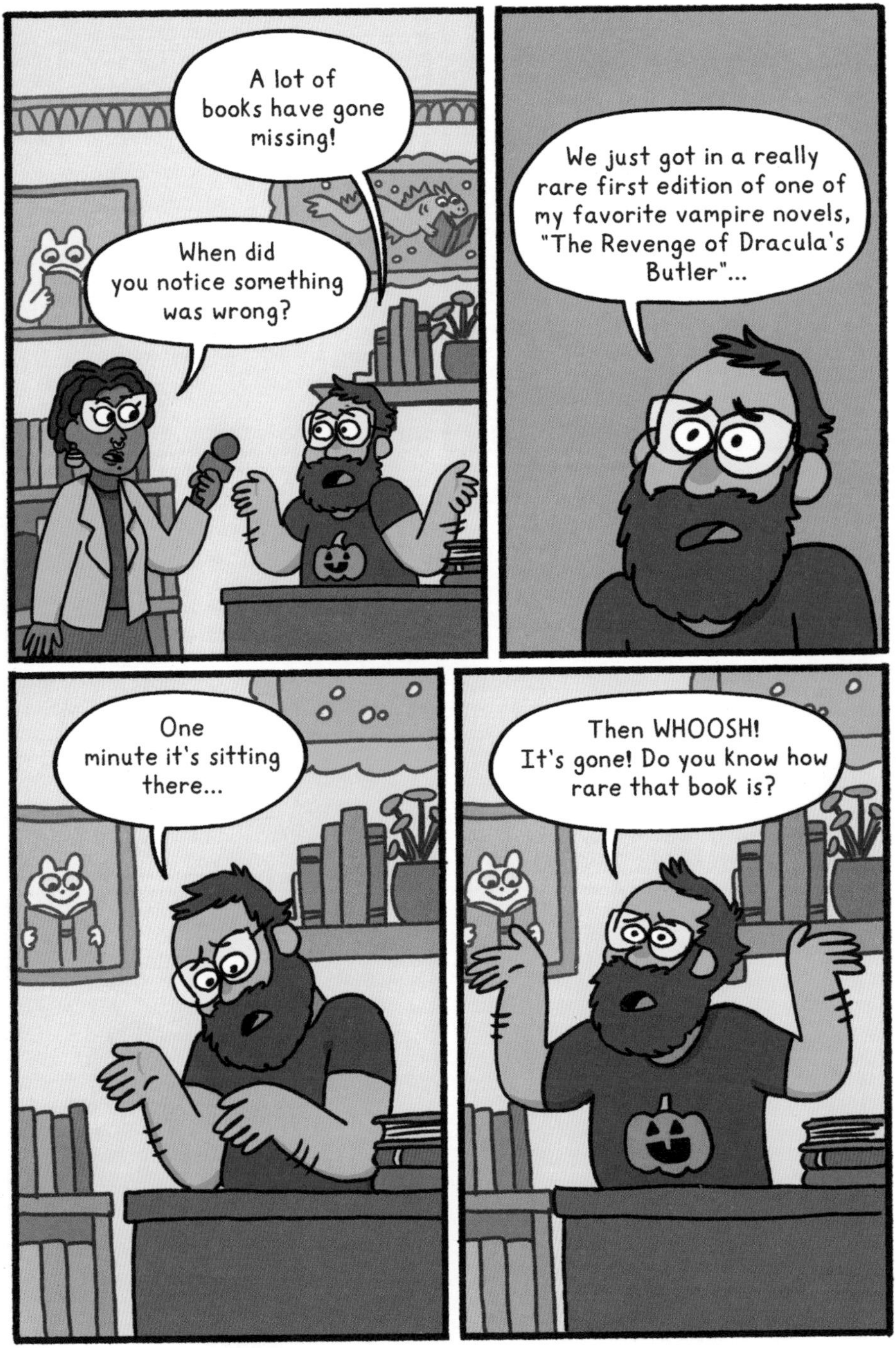
A lot of books have gone missing!
When did you notice something was wrong?
We just got in a really rare first edition of one of my favorite vampire novels, "The Revenge of Dracula's Butler"...
One minute it's sitting there...
Then WHOOSH! It's gone! Do you know how rare that book is?

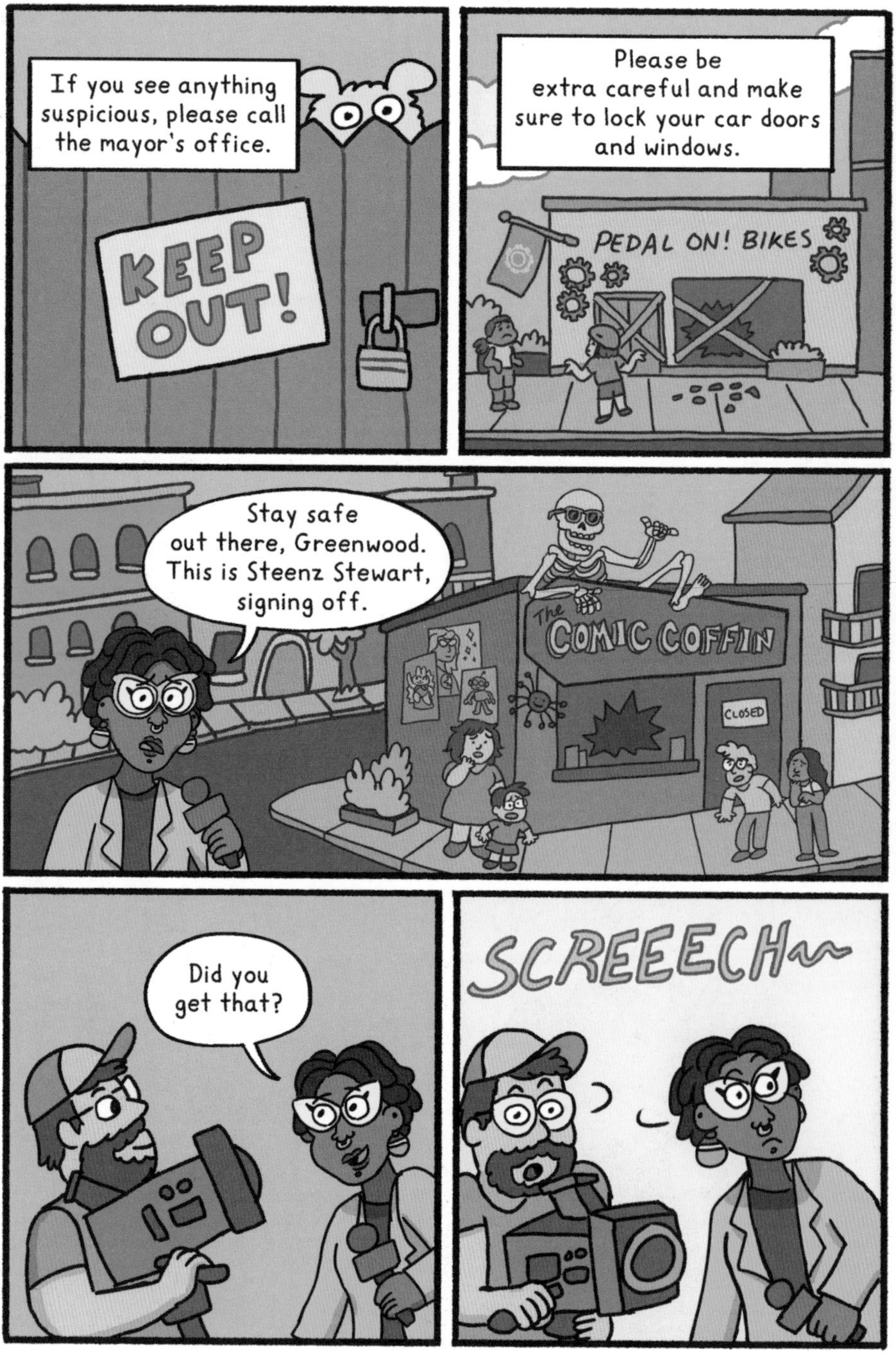

If you see anything suspicious, please call the mayor's office.
KEEP OUT!
Please be extra careful and make sure to lock your car doors and windows.
PEDAL ON! BIKES
Stay safe out there, Greenwood. This is Steenz Stewart, signing off.
The COMIC COFFIN
CLOSED
Did you get that?
SCREEECH

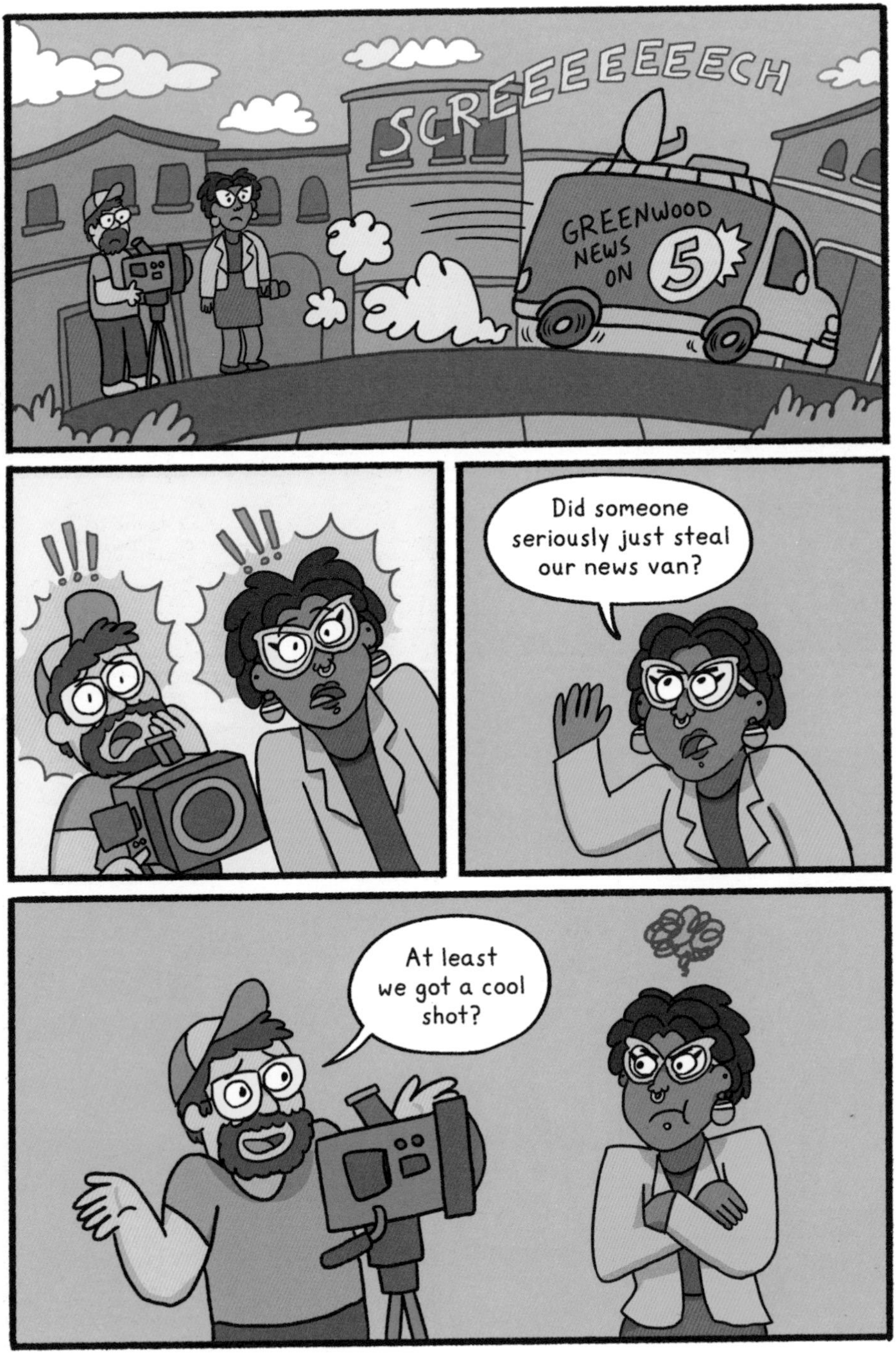
SCREEEEEEEECH
GREENWOOD NEWS ON 5
!!!
!!!
Did someone seriously just steal our news van?
At least we got a cool shot?

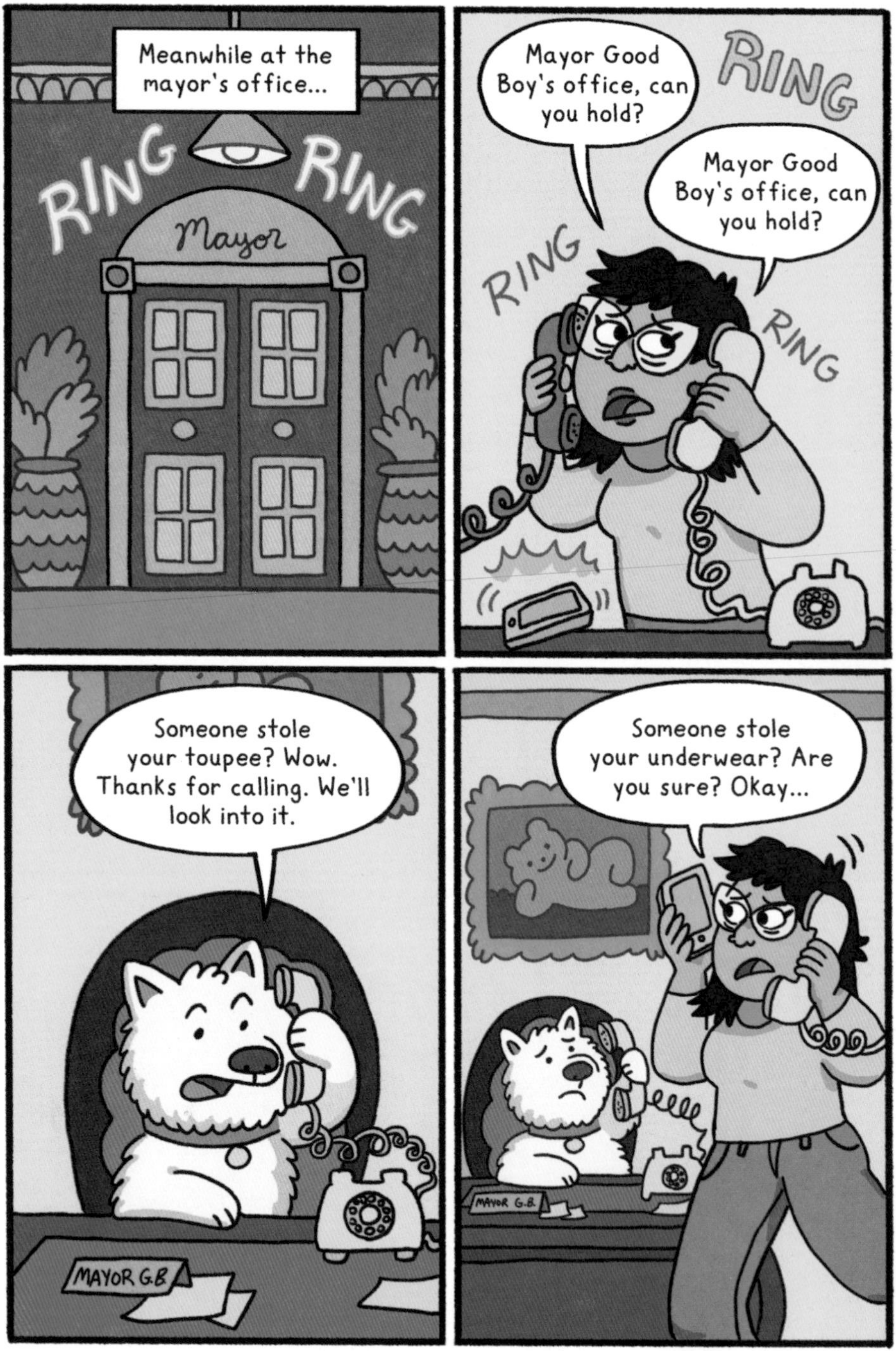
Meanwhile at the mayor's office...
RING RING
Mayor
Mayor Good Boy's office, can you hold?
RING
Mayor Good Boy's office, can you hold?
RING
RING
Someone stole your toupee? Wow. Thanks for calling. We'll look into it.
MAYOR G.B.
Someone stole your underwear? Are you sure? Okay...
MAYOR G.B.

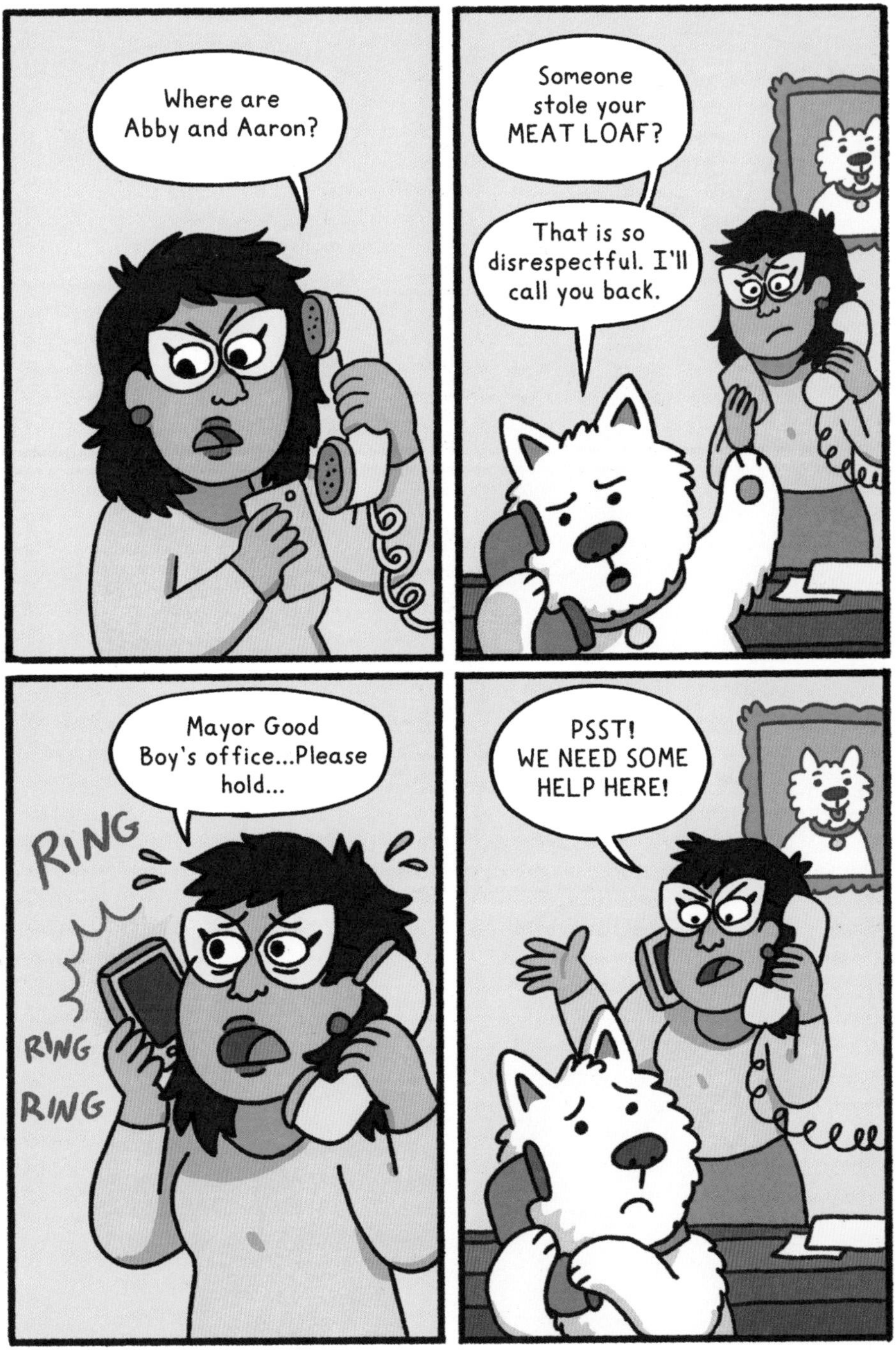
Where are Abby and Aaron?
Someone stole your MEAT LOAF?
That is so disrespectful. I'll call you back.
Mayor Good Boy's office...Please hold...
RING
RING
RING
PSST! WE NEED SOME HELP HERE!

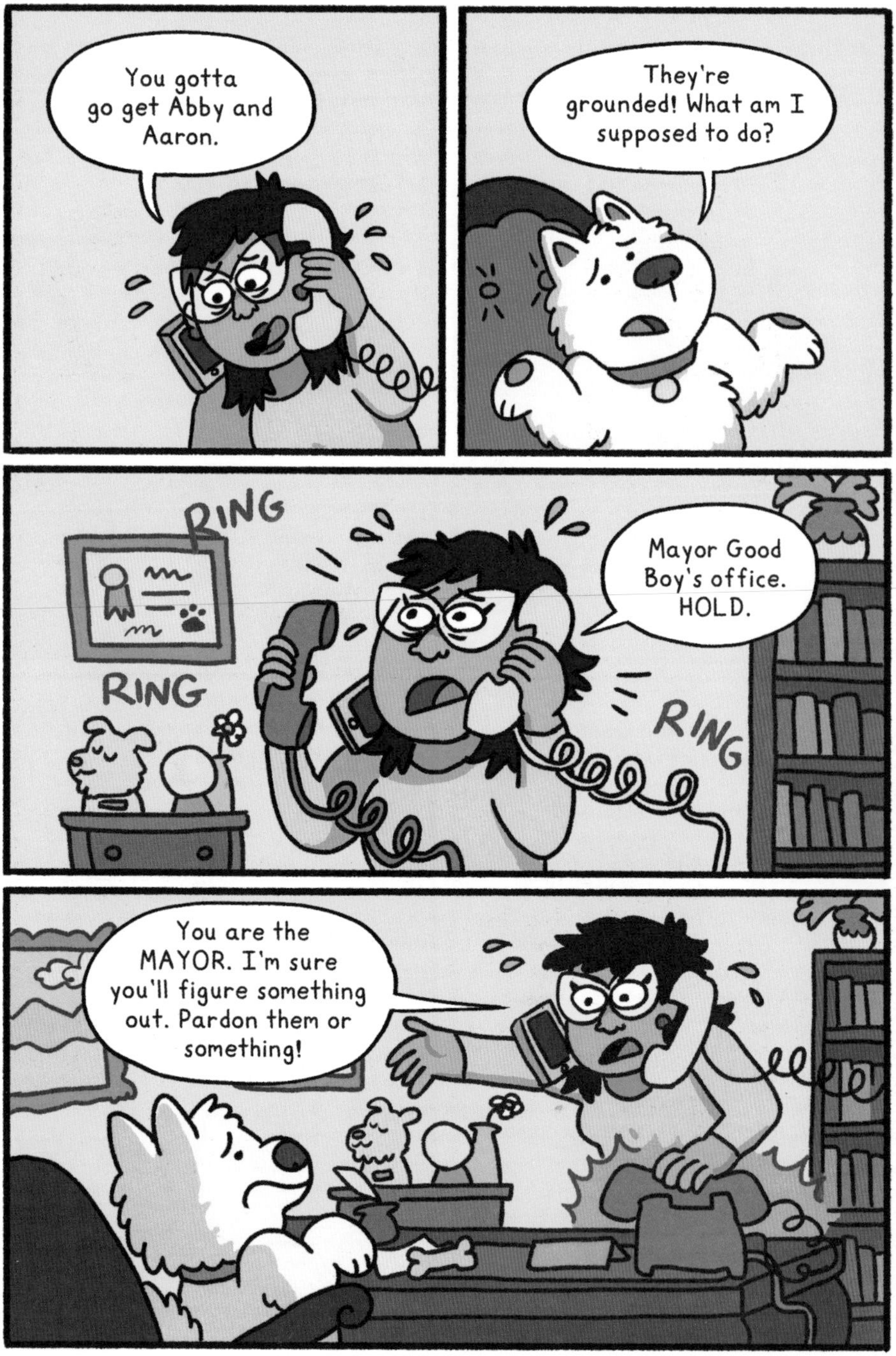
You gotta go get Abby and Aaron.
They're grounded! What am I supposed to do?
RING
RING
Mayor Good Boy's office. HOLD.
RING
You are the MAYOR. I'm sure you'll figure something out. Pardon them or something!

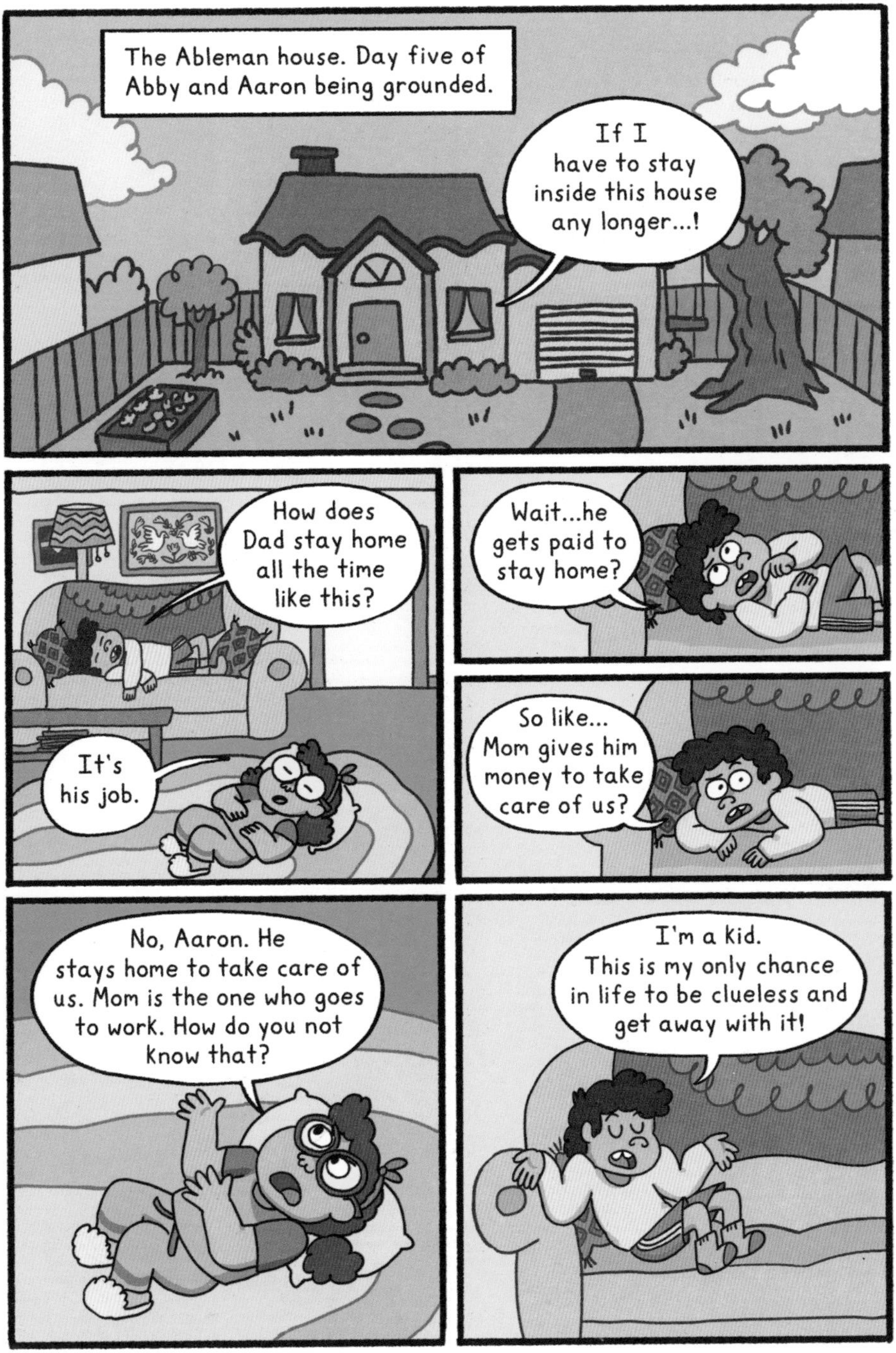

The Ableman house. Day five of Abby and Aaron being grounded.
If I have to stay inside this house any longer...!
How does Dad stay home all the time like this?
It's his job.
Wait...he gets paid to stay home?
So like... Mom gives him money to take care of us?
No, Aaron. He stays home to take care of us. Mom is the one who goes to work. How do you not know that?
I'm a kid. This is my only chance in life to be clueless and get away with it!

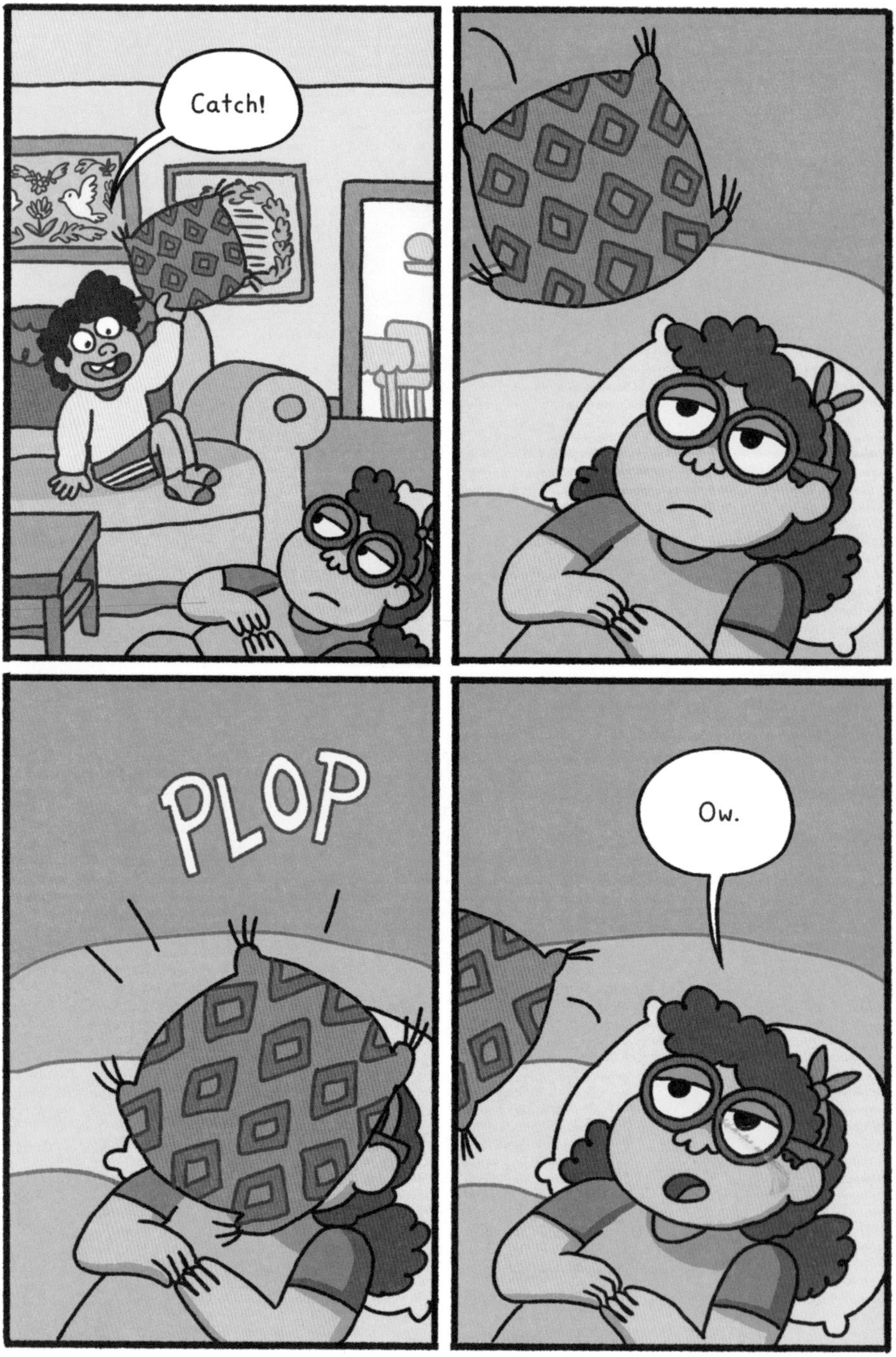
Catch!
PLOP
Ow.

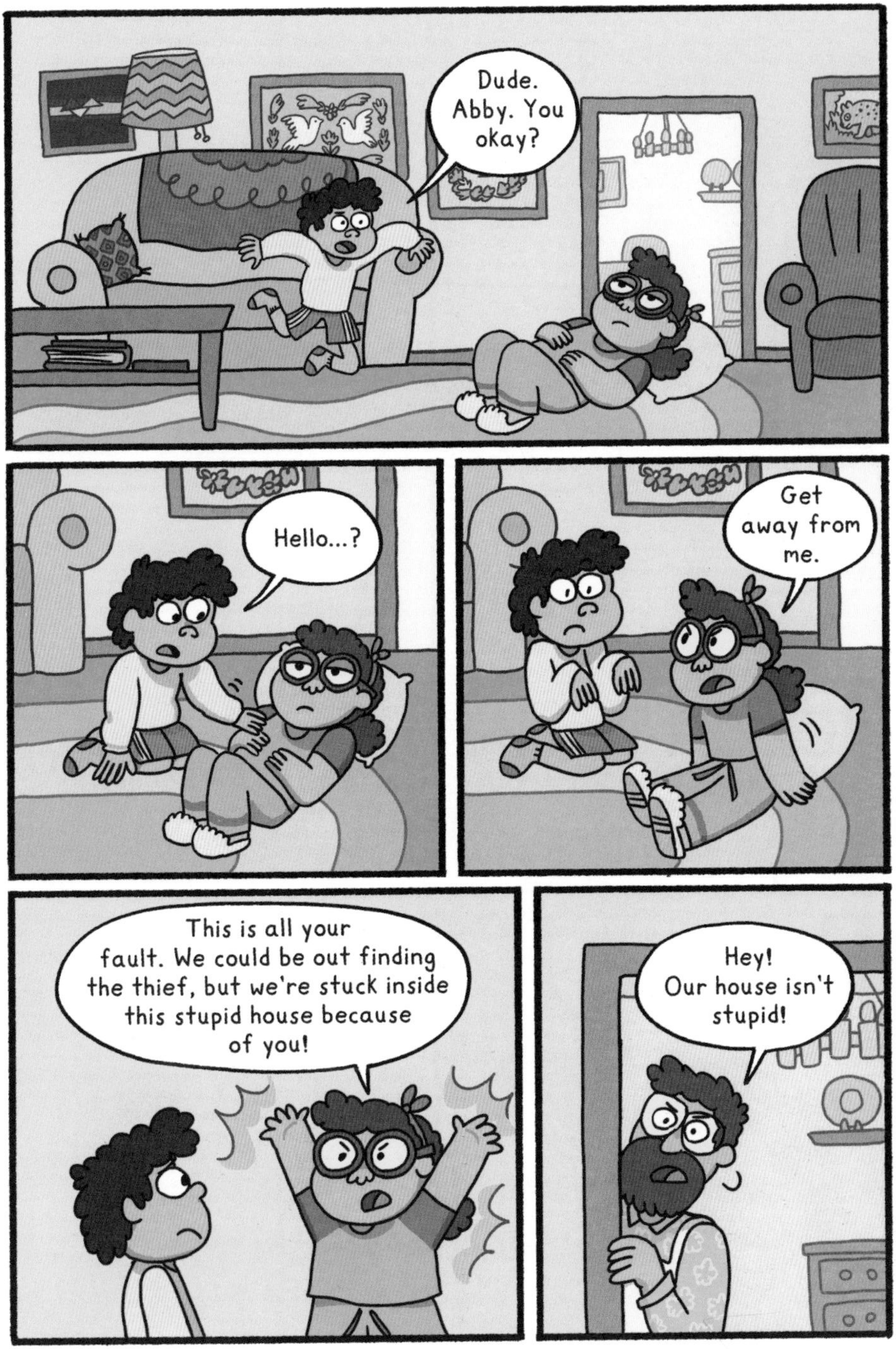
Dude. Abby. You okay?
Hello...?
Get away from me.
This is all your fault. We could be out finding the thief, but we're stuck inside this stupid house because of you!
Hey! Our house isn't stupid!

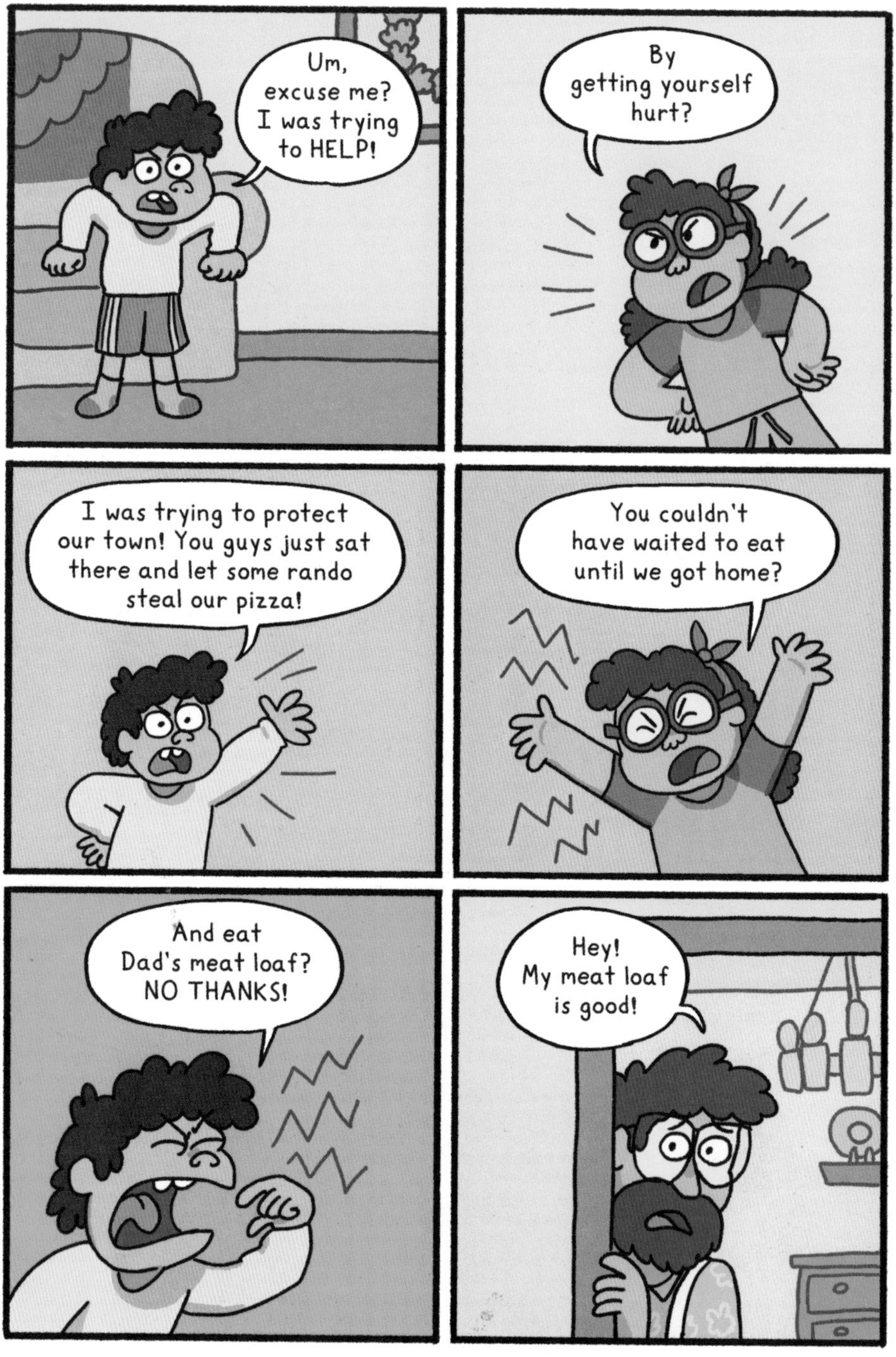
Um, excuse me? I was trying to HELP!
By getting yourself hurt?
I was trying to protect our town! You guys just sat there and let some rando steal our pizza!
You couldn't have waited to eat until we got home?
And eat Dad's meat loaf? NO THANKS!
Hey! My meat loaf is good!

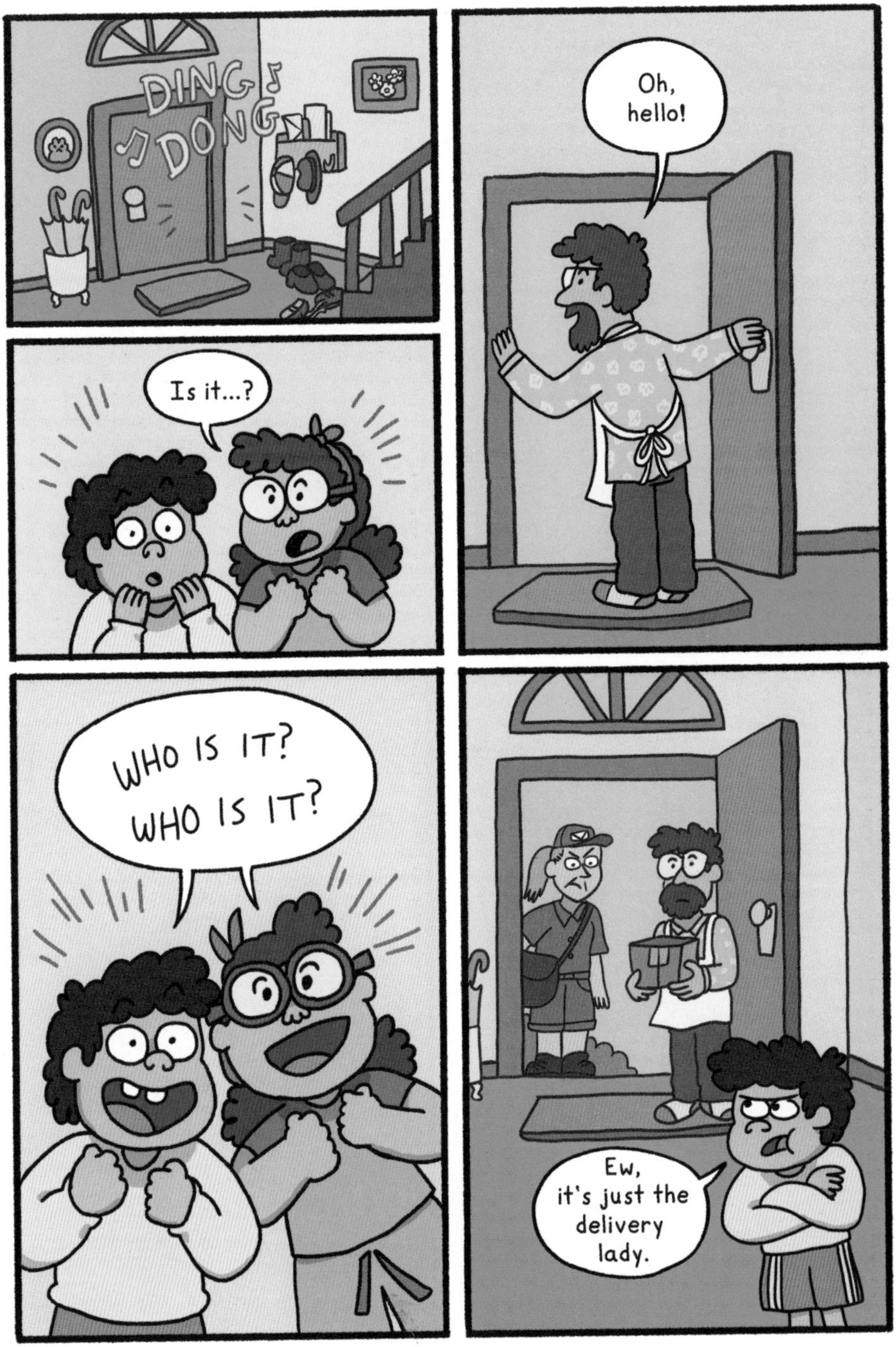
DING DONG
Oh, hello!
Is it...?
WHO IS IT? WHO IS IT?
Ew, it's just the delivery lady.

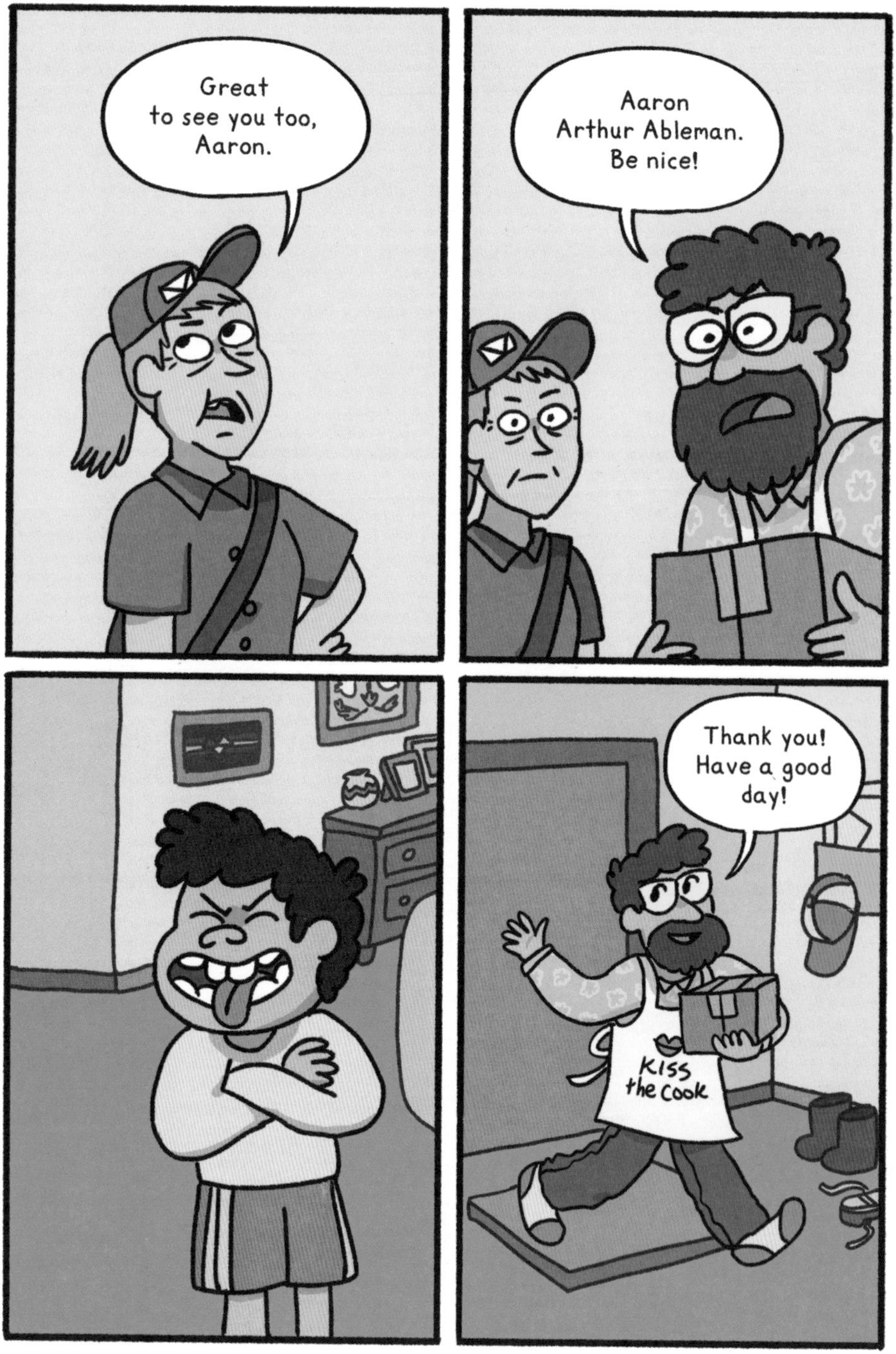
Great to see you too, Aaron.
Aaron Arthur Ableman. Be nice!
Thank you! Have a good day!
Kiss the cook

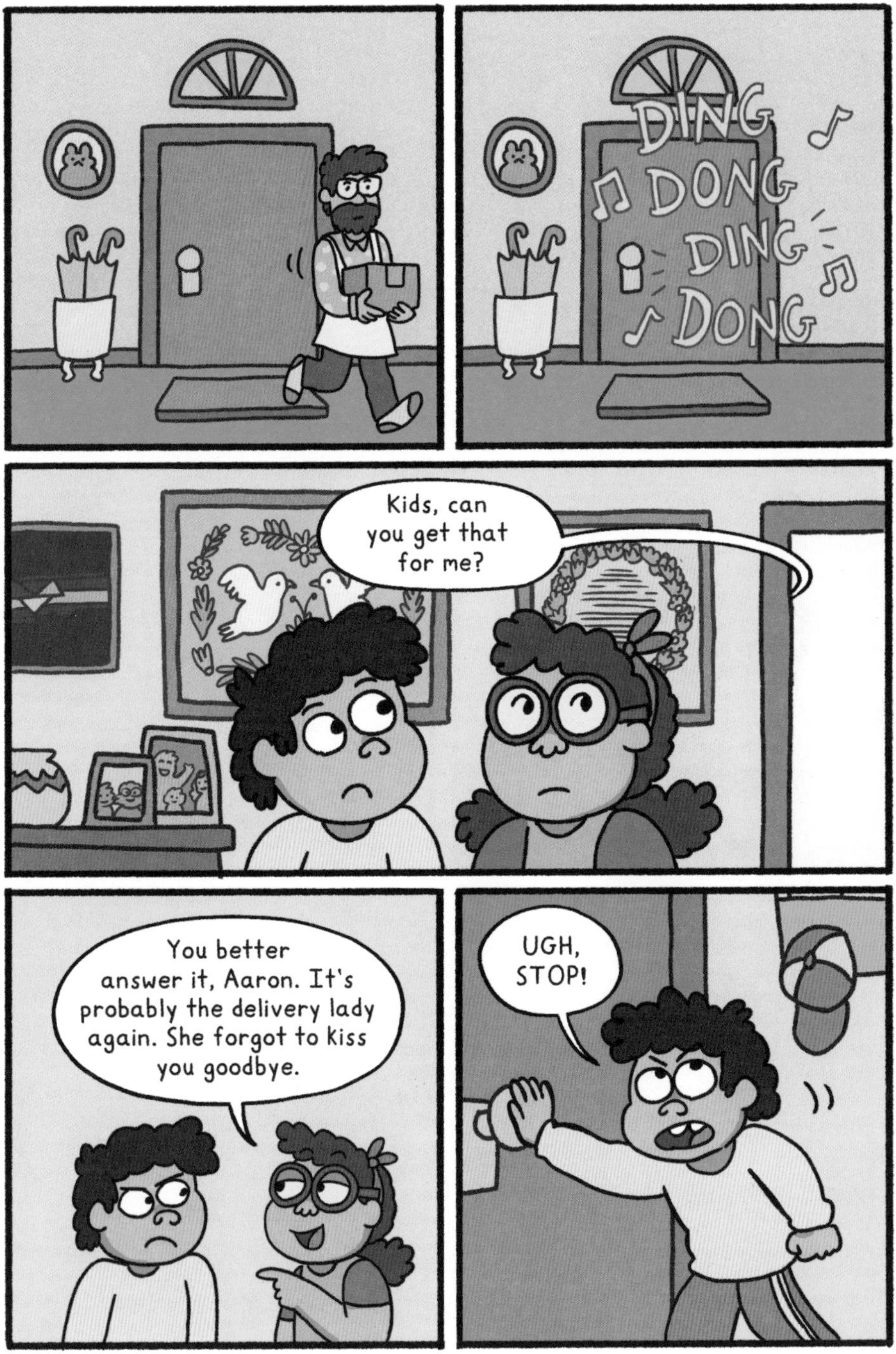
DING
DONG
DING
DONG
Kids, can you get that for me?
You better answer it, Aaron. It's probably the delivery lady again. She forgot to kiss you goodbye.
UGH, STOP!

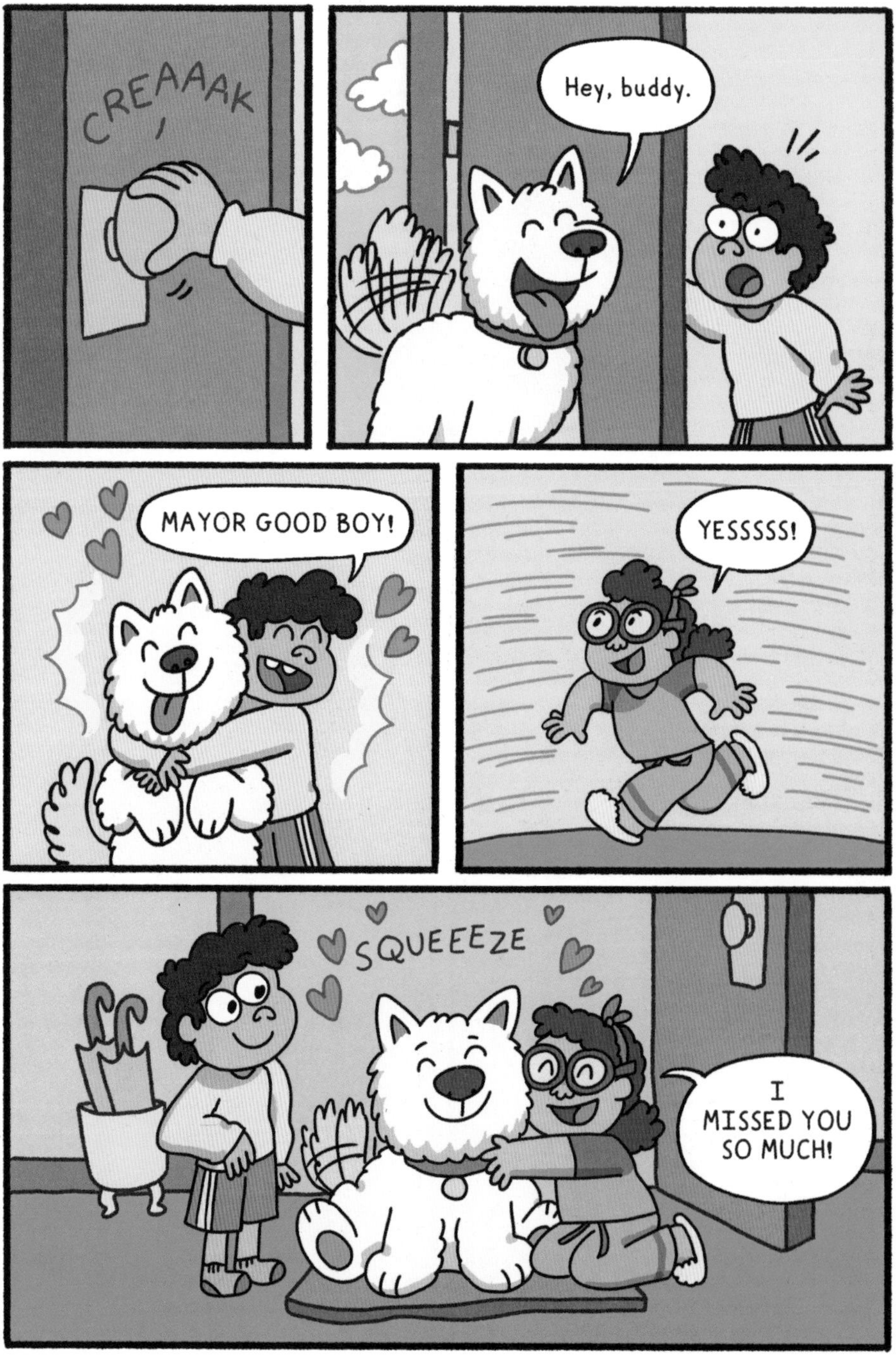
CREAAAK
Hey, buddy.
MAYOR GOOD BOY!
YESSSSS!
SQUEEEZE
I MISSED YOU SO MUCH!

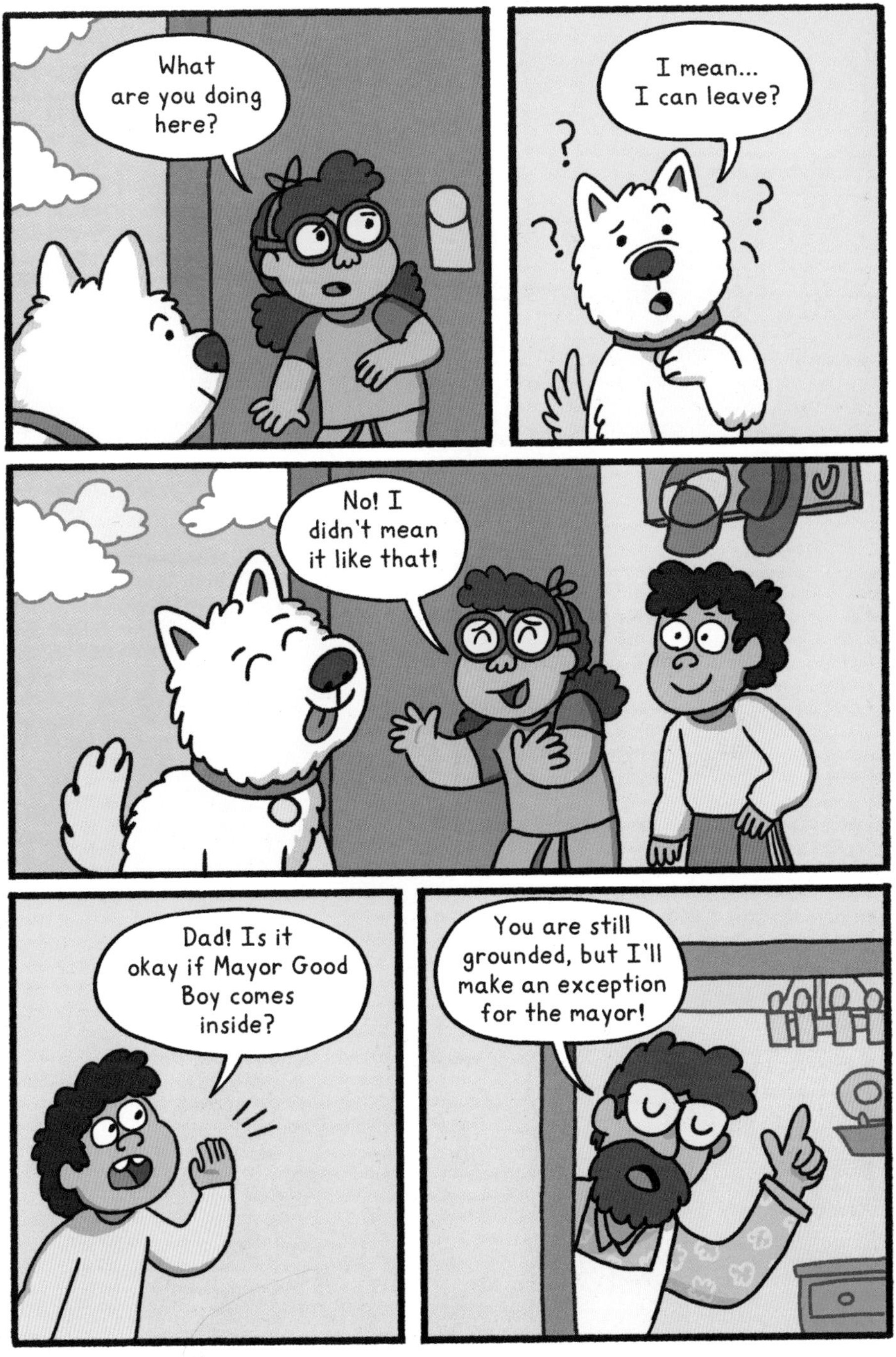

What are you doing here?
I mean... I can leave?
?
?
?
No! I didn't mean it like that!
Dad! Is it okay if Mayor Good Boy comes inside?
You are still grounded, but I'll make an exception for the mayor!

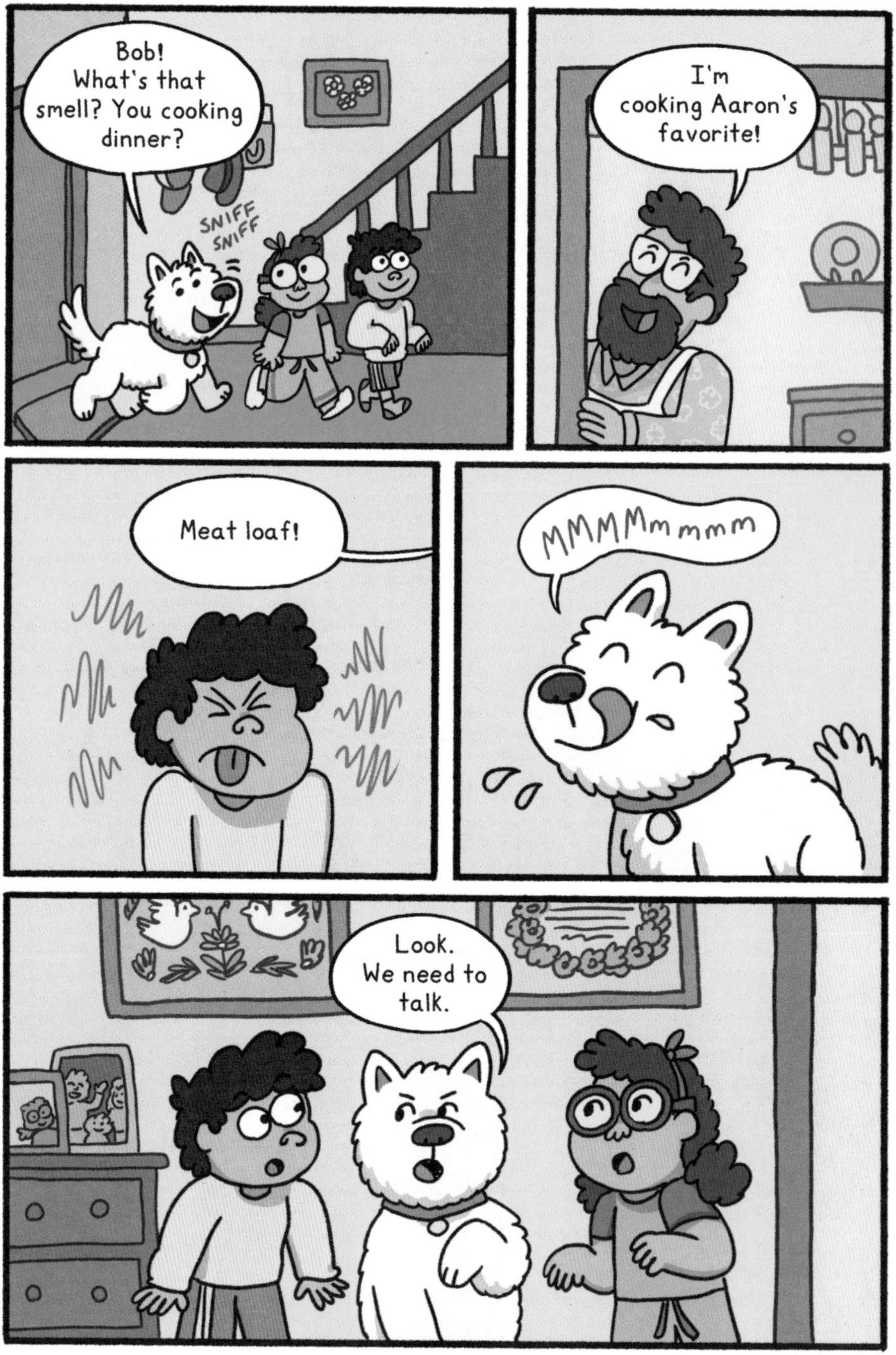
Bob! What's that smell? You cooking dinner?
SNIFF SNIFF
I'm cooking Aaron's favorite!
Meat loaf!
MMMMmmmm
Look. We need to talk.

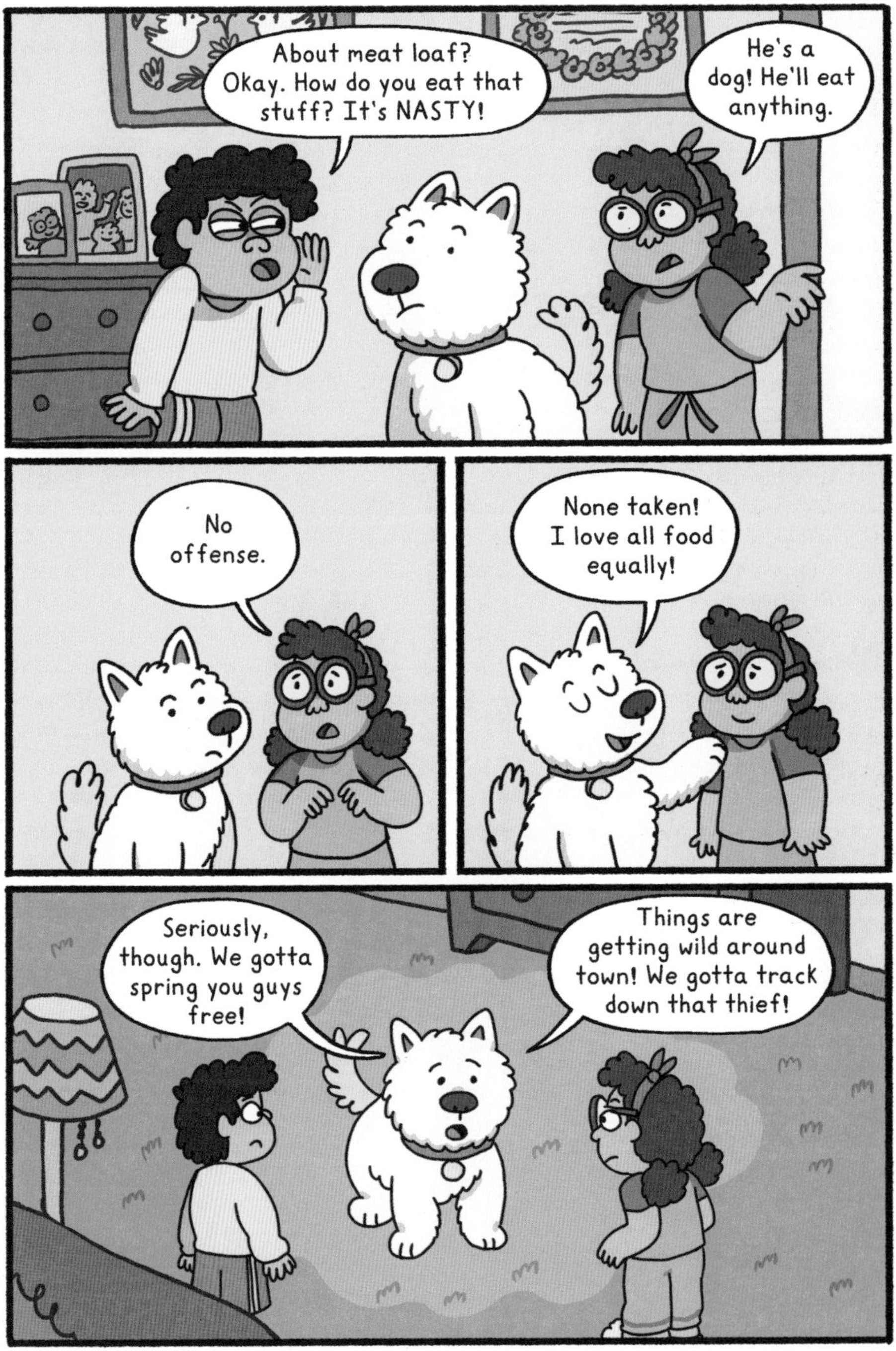
About meat loaf? Okay. How do you eat that stuff? It's NASTY!
He's a dog! He'll eat anything.
No offense.
None taken! I love all food equally!
Seriously, though. We gotta spring you guys free!
Things are getting wild around town! We gotta track down that thief!

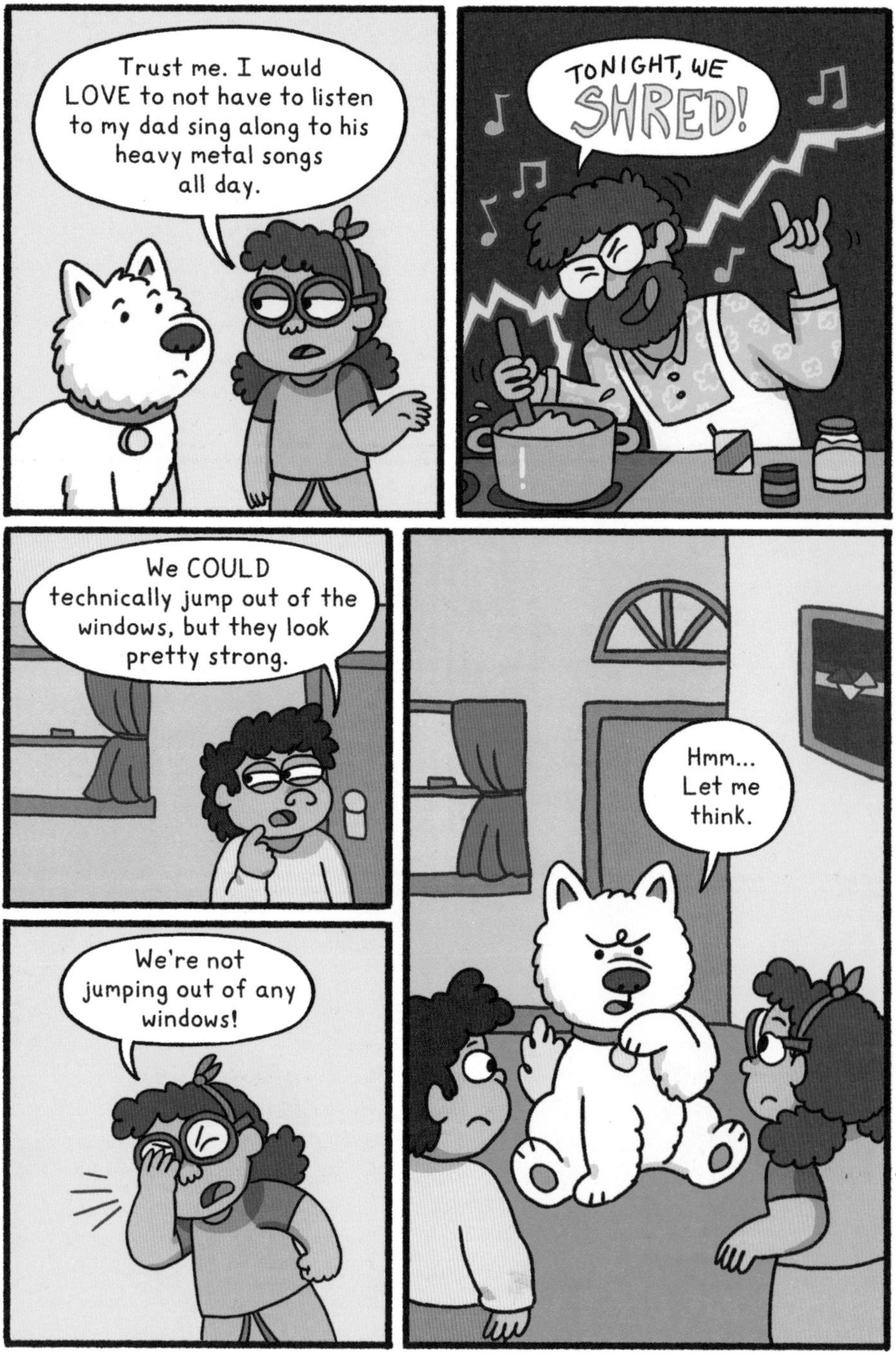
Trust me. I would LOVE to not have to listen to my dad sing along to his heavy metal songs all day.
TONIGHT, WE SHRED!
We COULD technically jump out of the windows, but they look pretty strong.
We're not jumping out of any windows!
Hmm... Let me think.

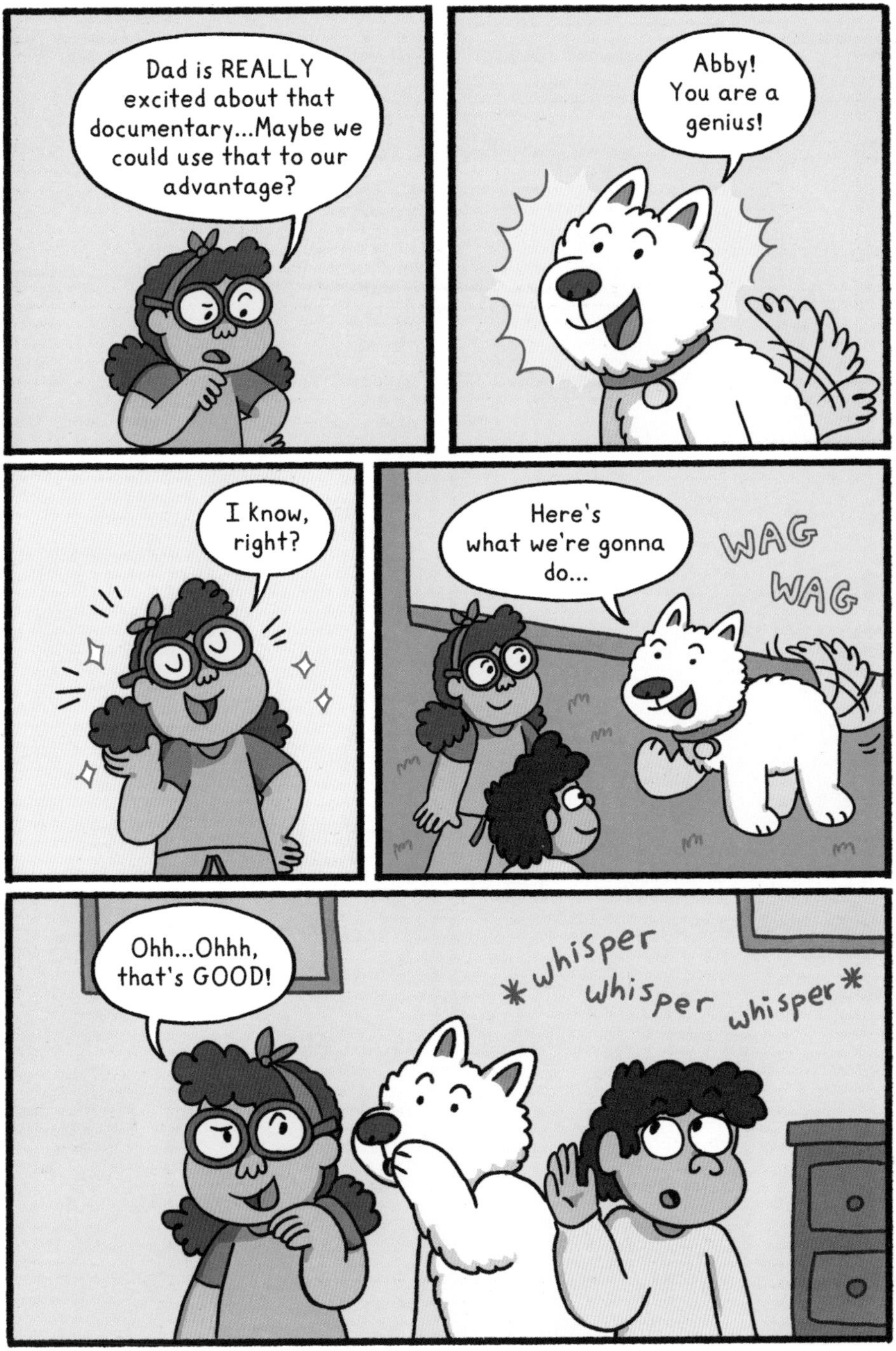
Dad is REALLY excited about that documentary...Maybe we could use that to our advantage?
Abby! You are a genius!
I know, right?
Here's what we're gonna do...
WAG WAG
Ohh...Ohhh, that's GOOD!
whisper whisper whisper

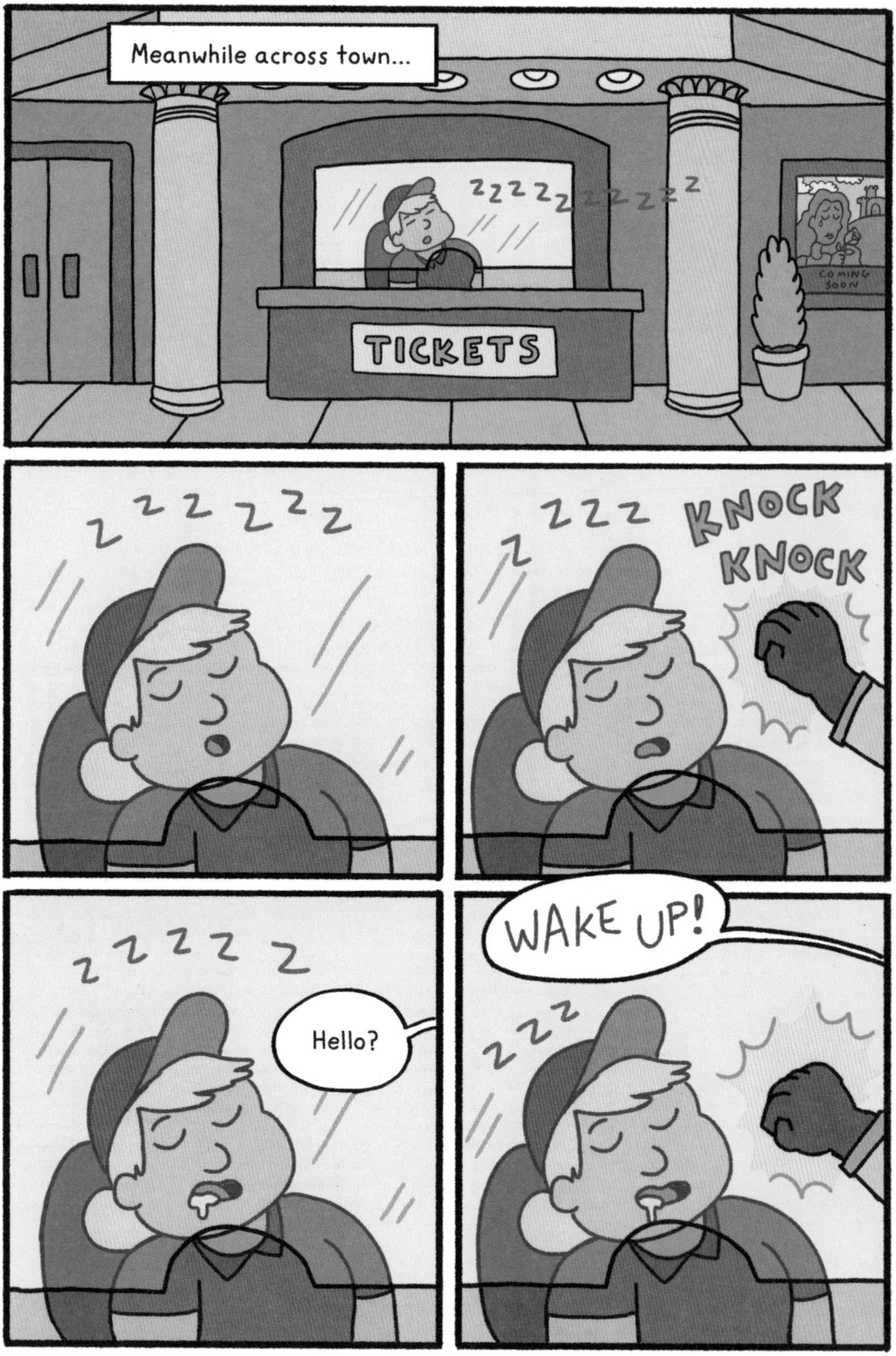
Meanwhile across town...
TICKETS
COMING SOON
KNOCK KNOCK
Hello?
WAKE UP!

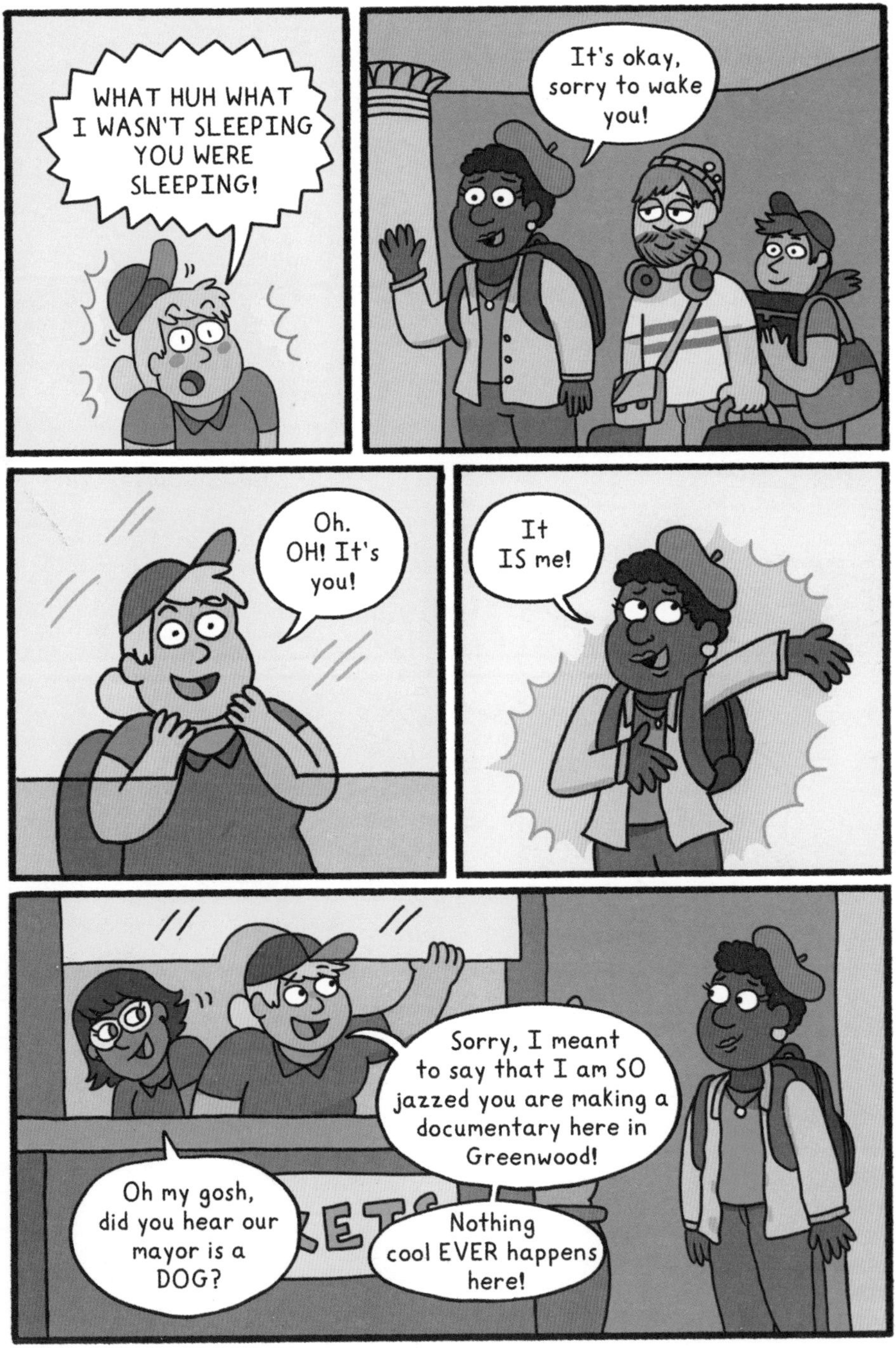
WHAT HUH WHAT I WASN'T SLEEPING YOU WERE SLEEPING!
It's okay, sorry to wake you!
Oh. OH! It's you!
It IS me!
Sorry, I meant to say that I am SO jazzed you are making a documentary here in Greenwood!
Oh my gosh, did you hear our mayor is a DOG?
Nothing cool EVER happens here!

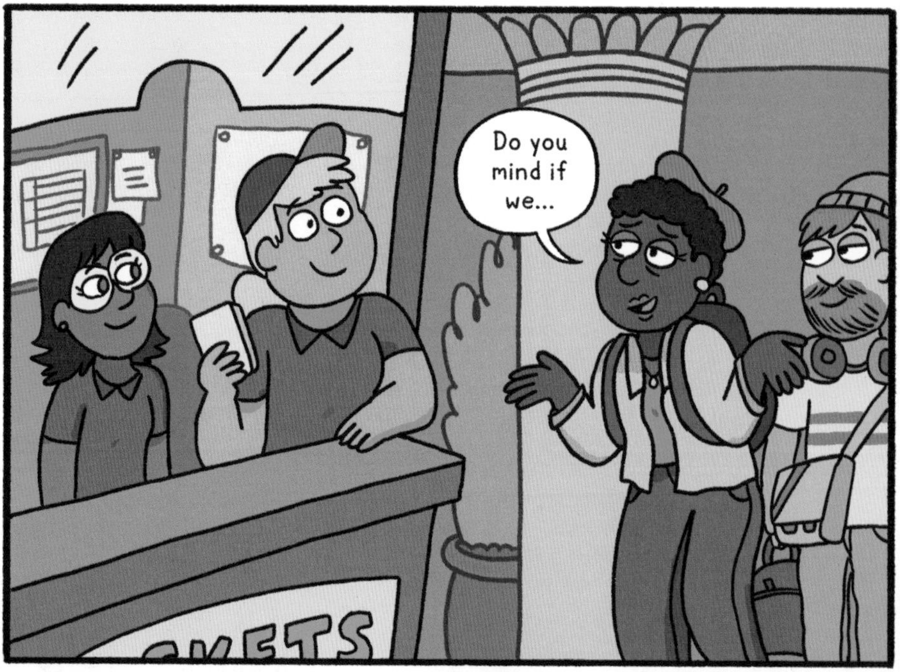
Do you mind if we...
TICKETS

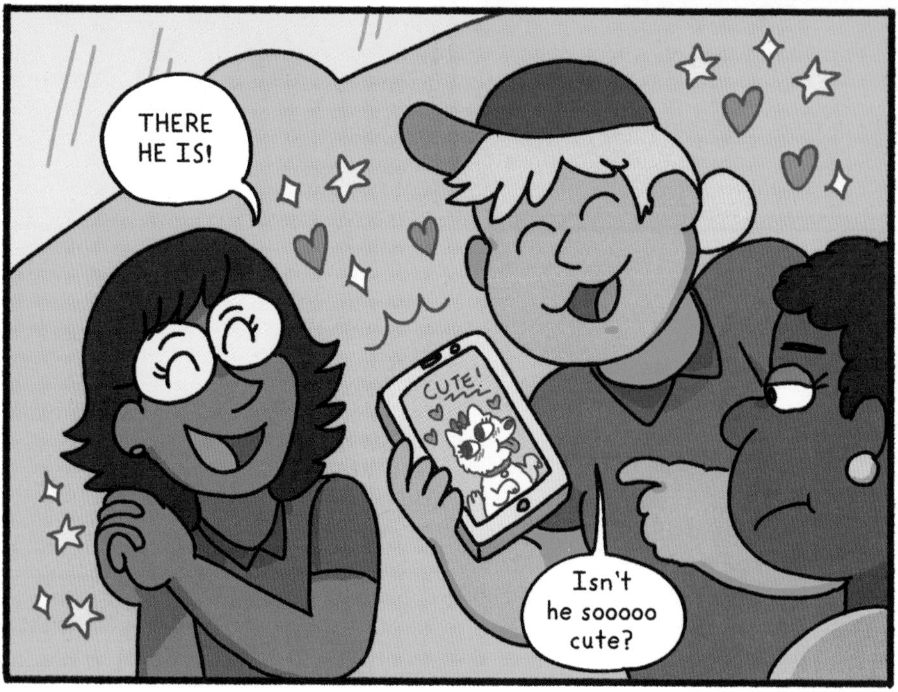
THERE HE IS!
CUTE!
Isn't he sooooo cute?

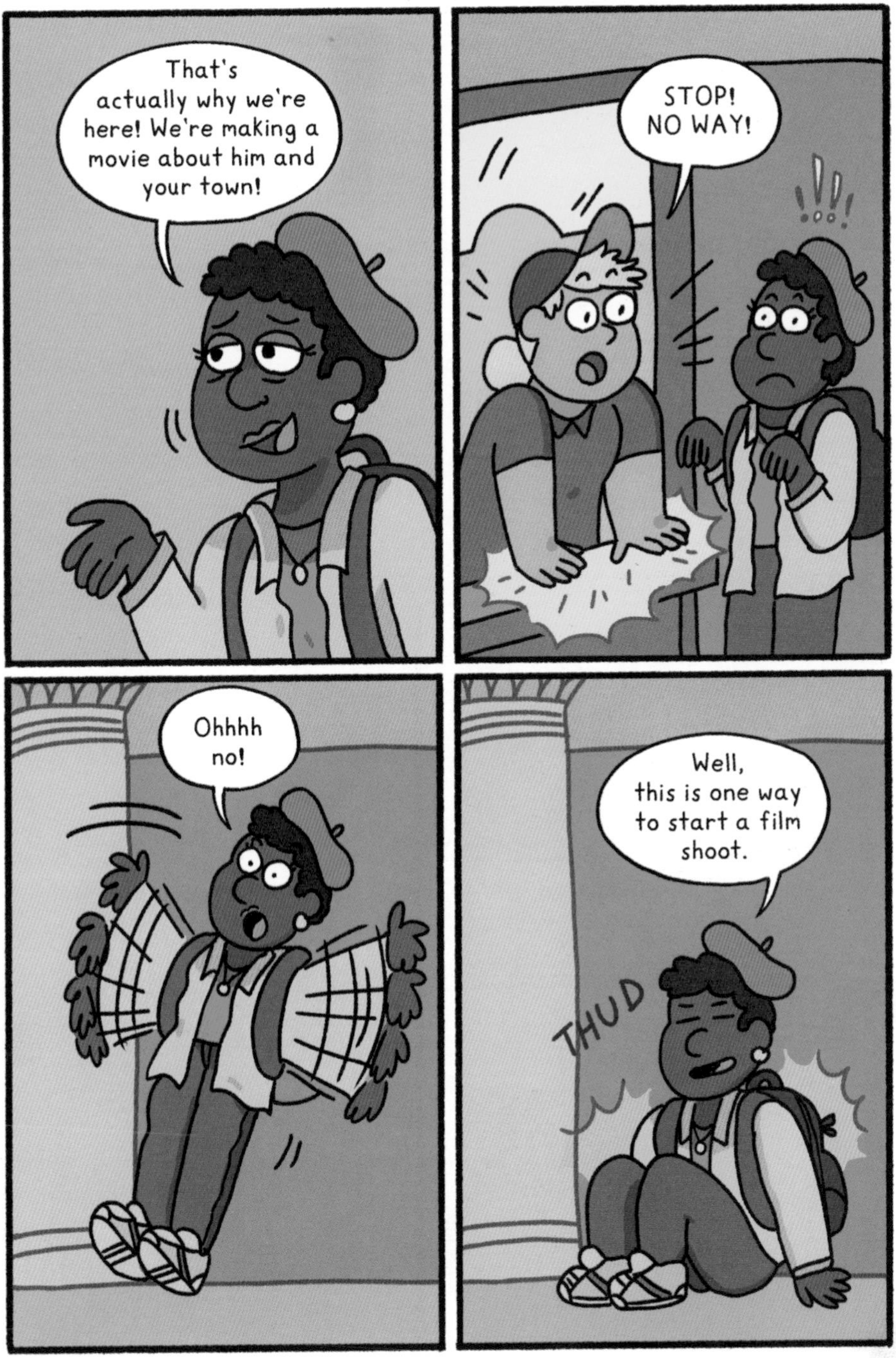
That's actually why we're here! We're making a movie about him and your town!
STOP! NO WAY!
!!!
Ohhhh no!
THUD
Well, this is one way to start a film shoot.

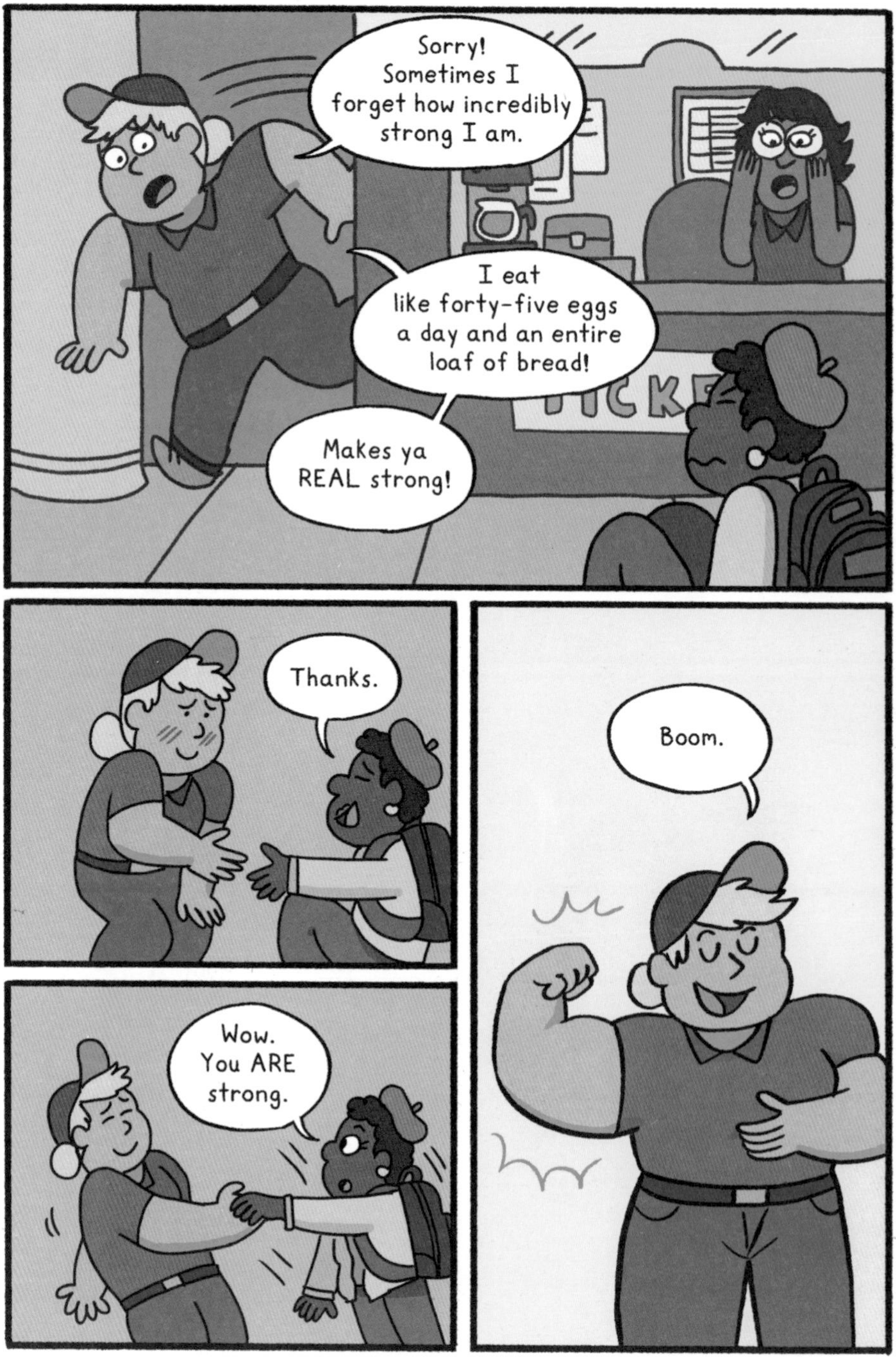
Sorry! Sometimes I forget how incredibly strong I am.
I eat like forty-five eggs a day and an entire loaf of bread!
Makes ya REAL strong!
Thanks.
Wow. You ARE strong.
Boom.

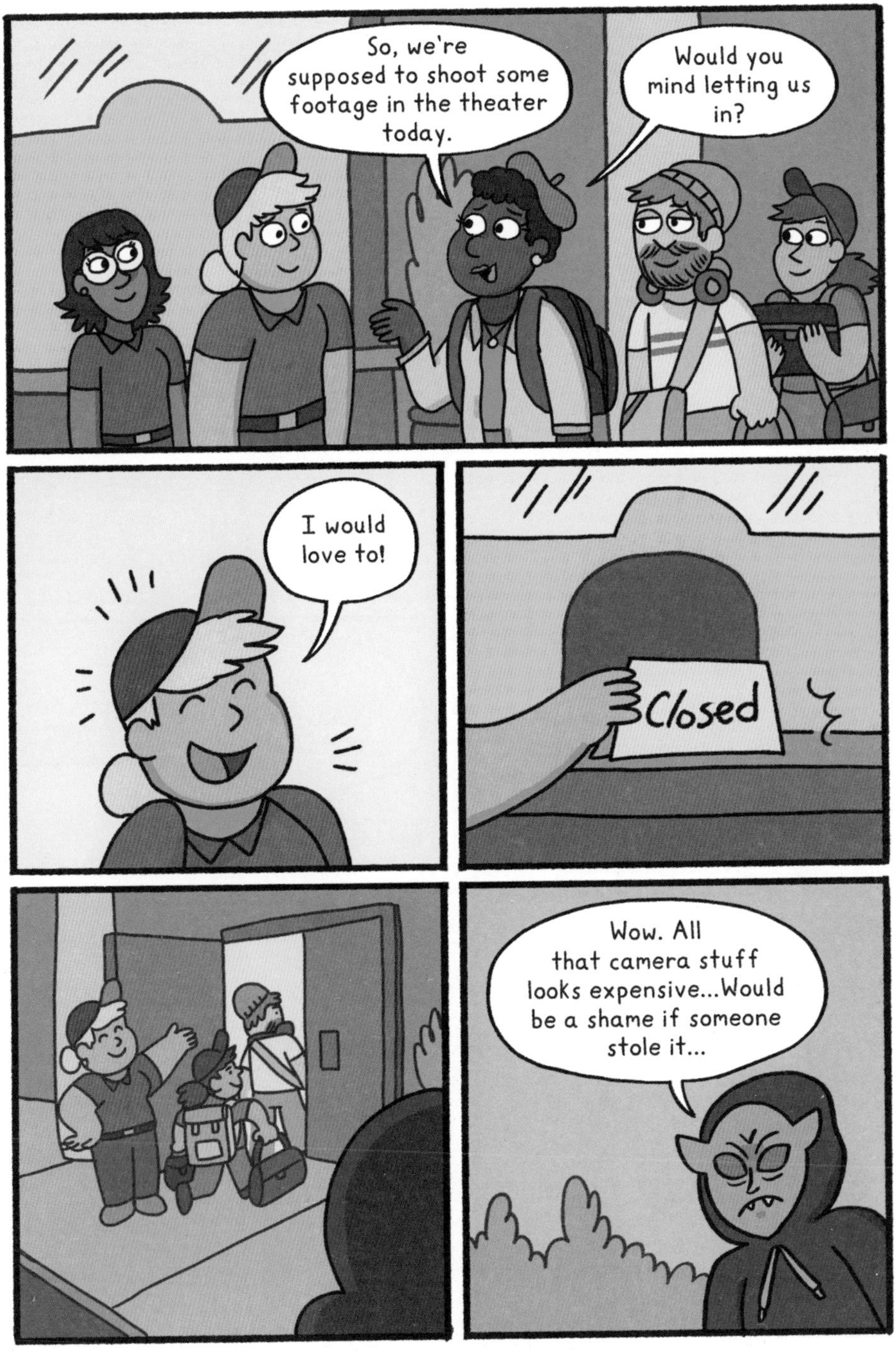
So, we're supposed to shoot some footage in the theater today.
Would you mind letting us in?
I would love to!
Closed
Wow. All that camera stuff looks expensive...Would be a shame if someone stole it...

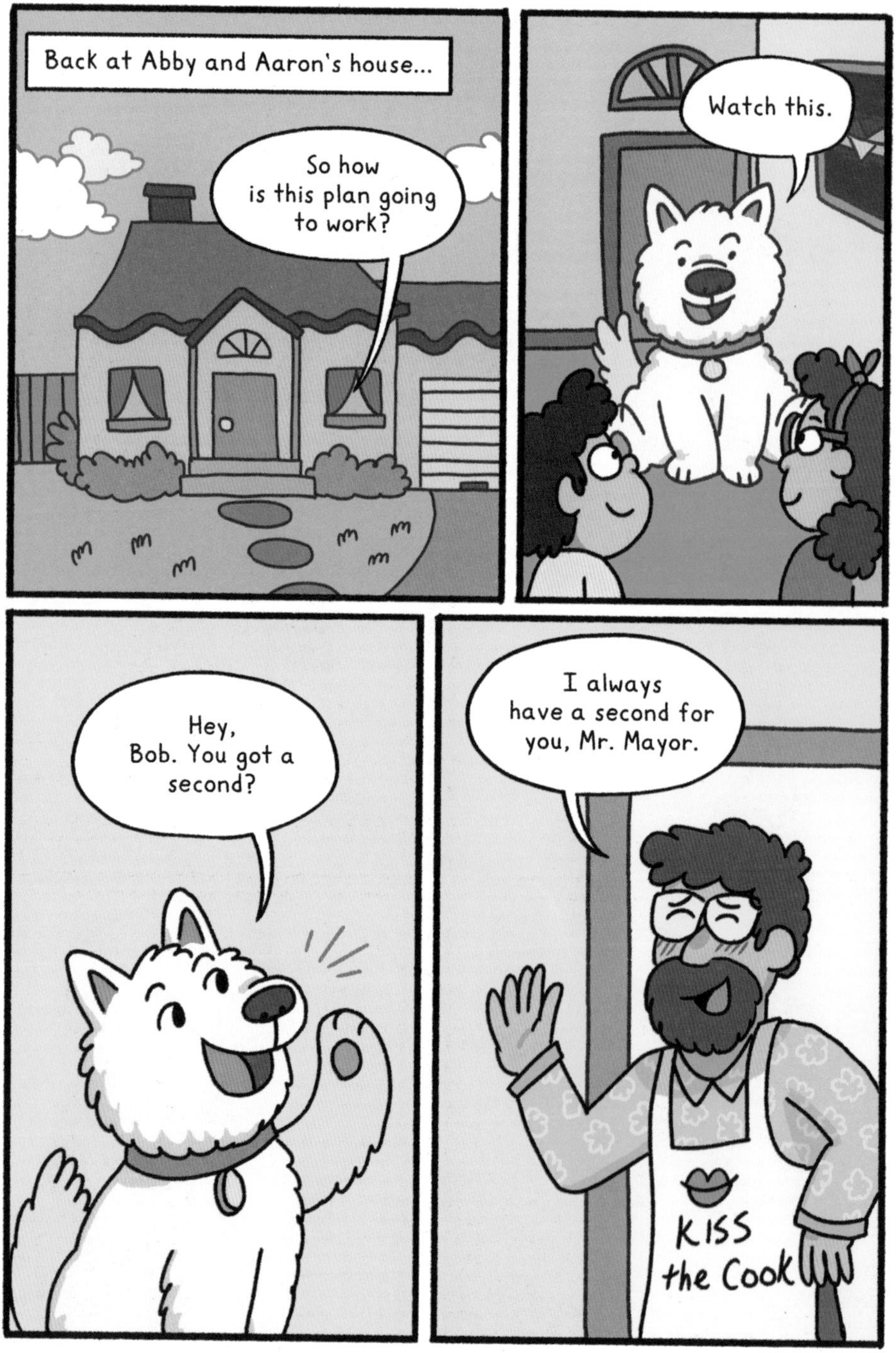
Back at Abby and Aaron's house...
So how is this plan going to work?
Watch this.
Hey, Bob. You got a second?
I always have a second for you, Mr. Mayor.
KISS the Cook

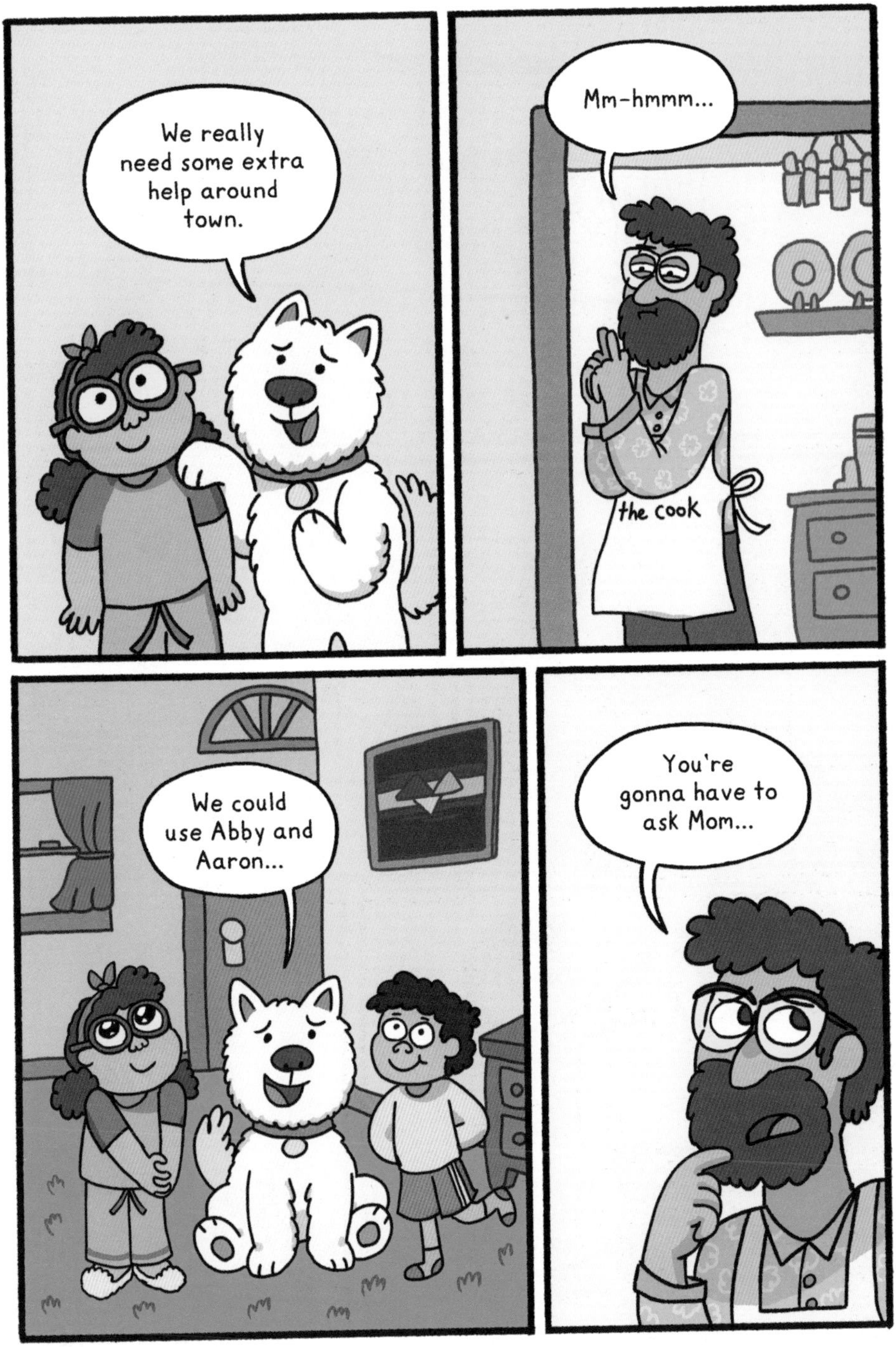
We really need some extra help around town.
Mm-hmmm...
the cook
We could use Abby and Aaron...
You're gonna have to ask Mom...

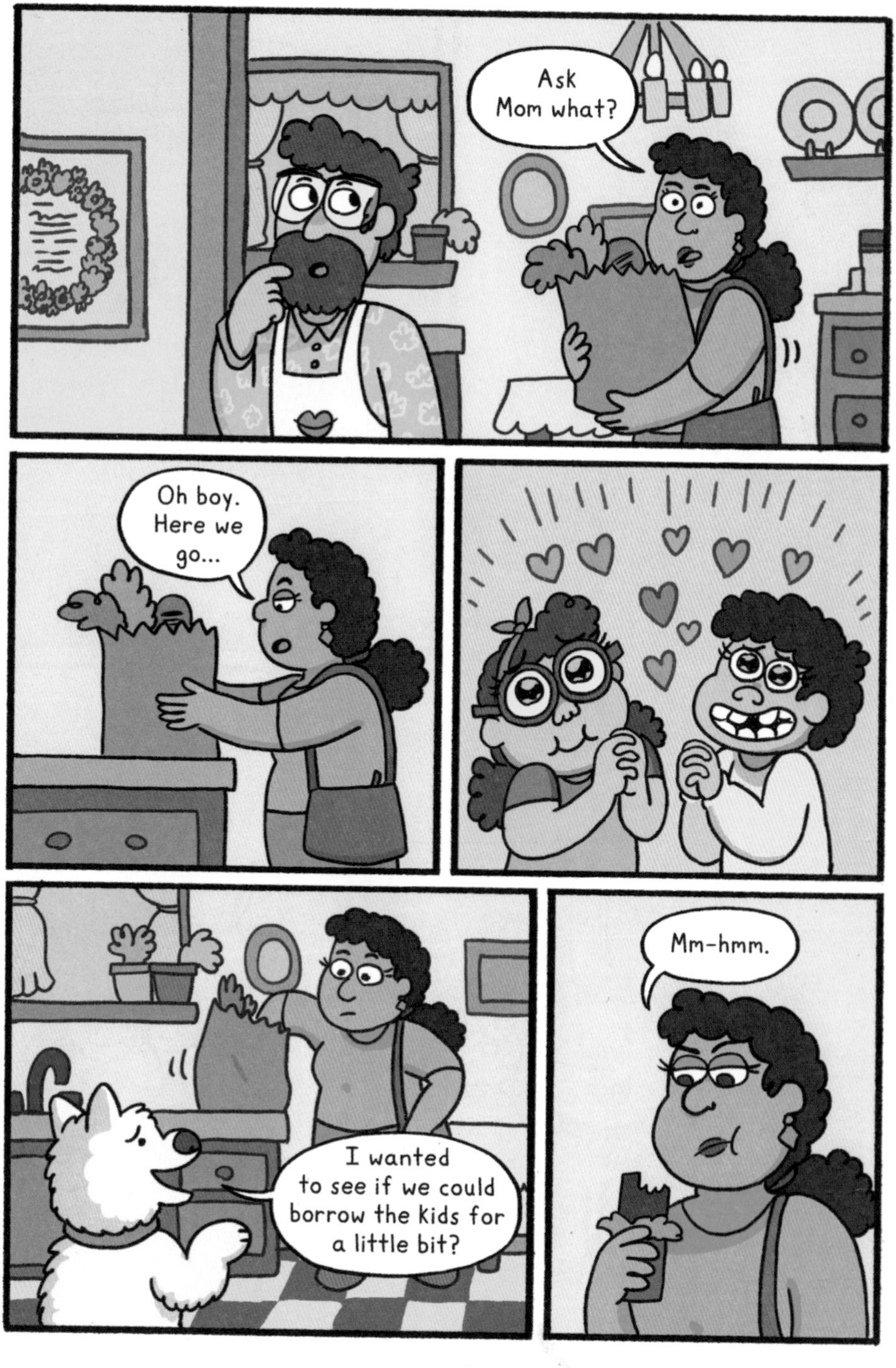
Ask Mom what?
Oh boy. Here we go...
I wanted to see if we could borrow the kids for a little bit?
Mm-hmm.

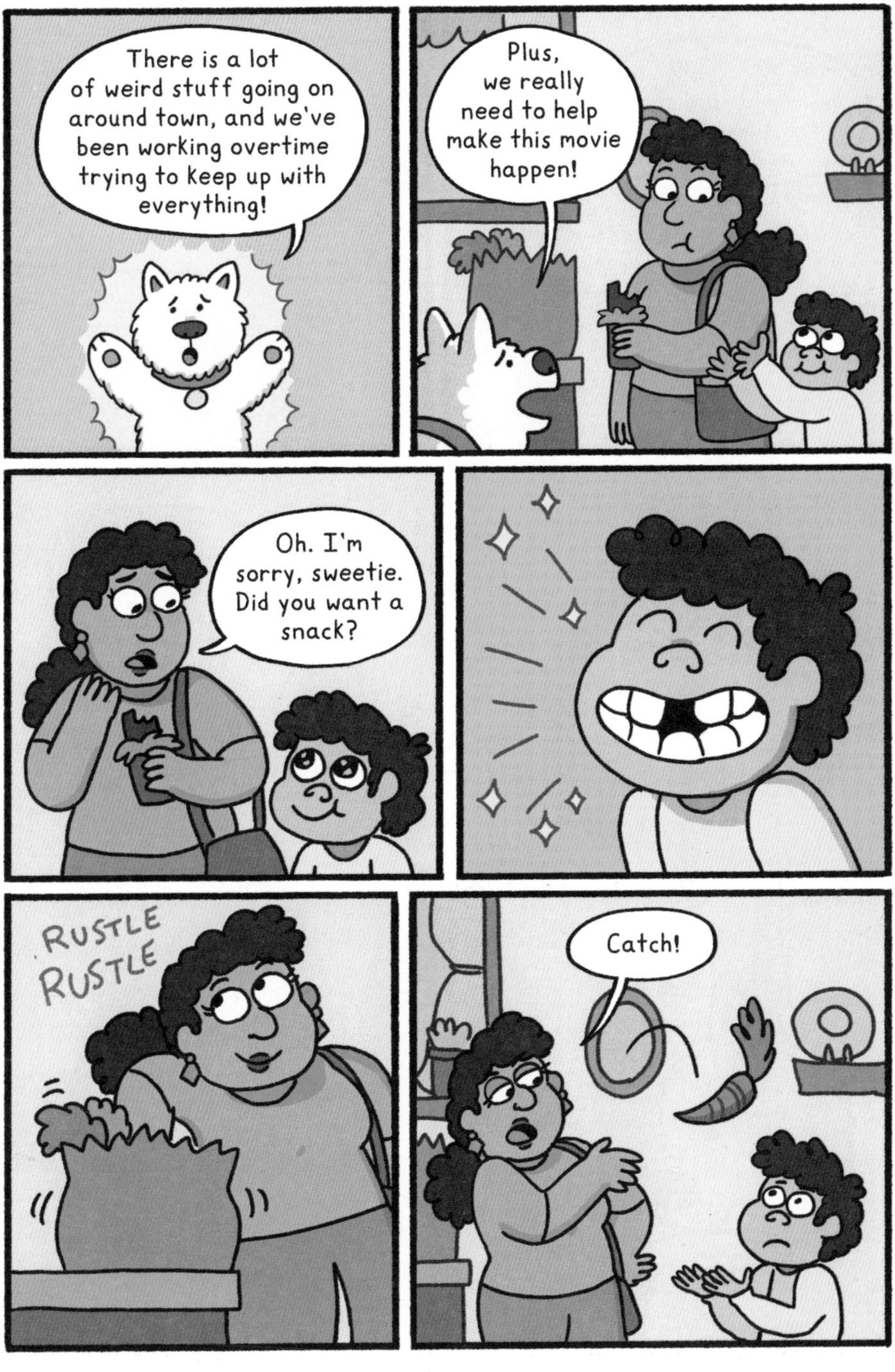

There is a lot of weird stuff going on around town, and we've been working overtime trying to keep up with everything!
Plus, we really need to help make this movie happen!
Oh. I'm sorry, sweetie. Did you want a snack?
RUSTLE RUSTLE
Catch!

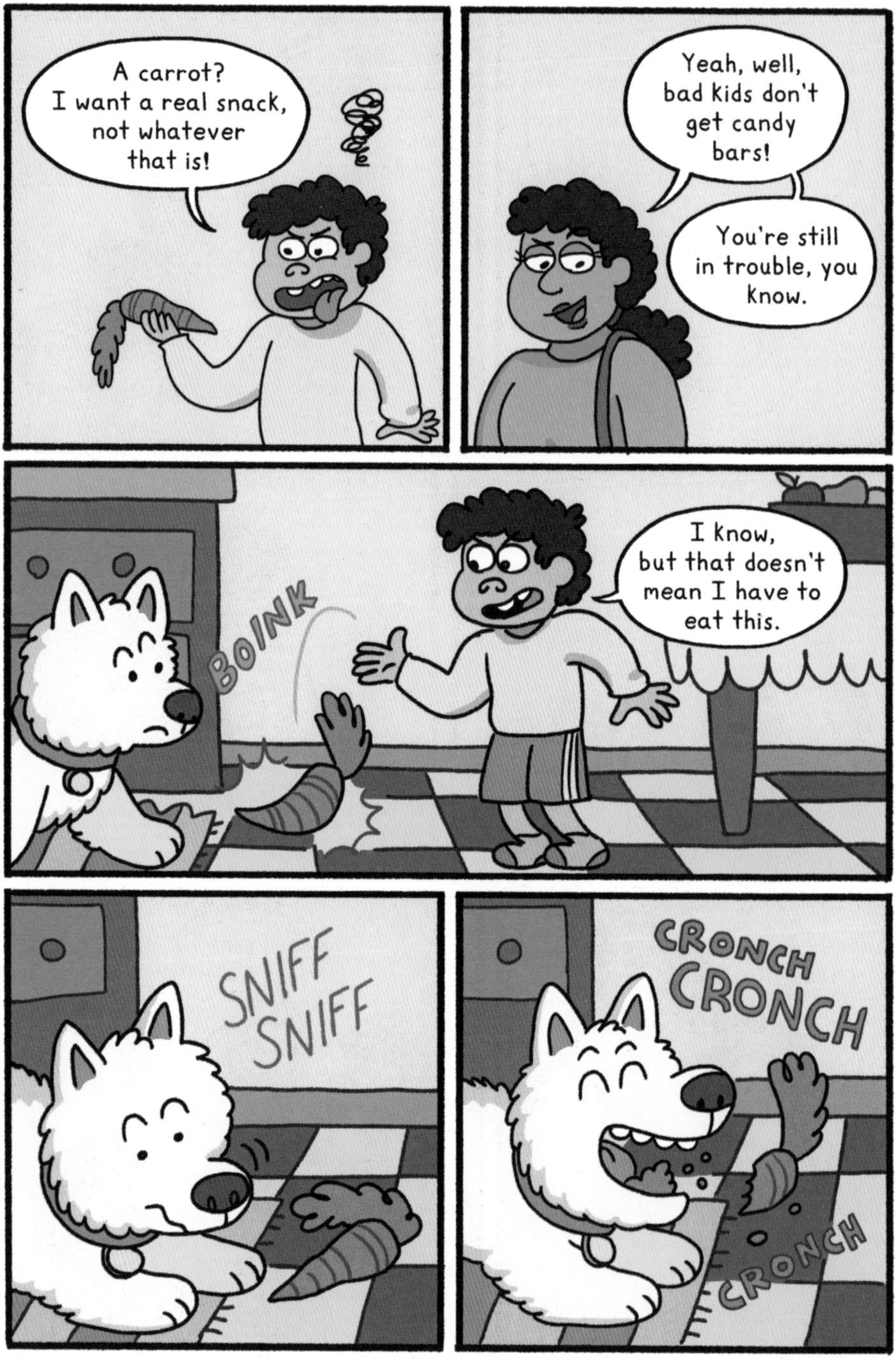

A carrot? I want a real snack, not whatever that is!
Yeah, well, bad kids don't get candy bars!
You're still in trouble, you know.
BOINK
I know, but that doesn't mean I have to eat this.
SNIFF SNIFF
CRONCH CRONCH
CRONCH

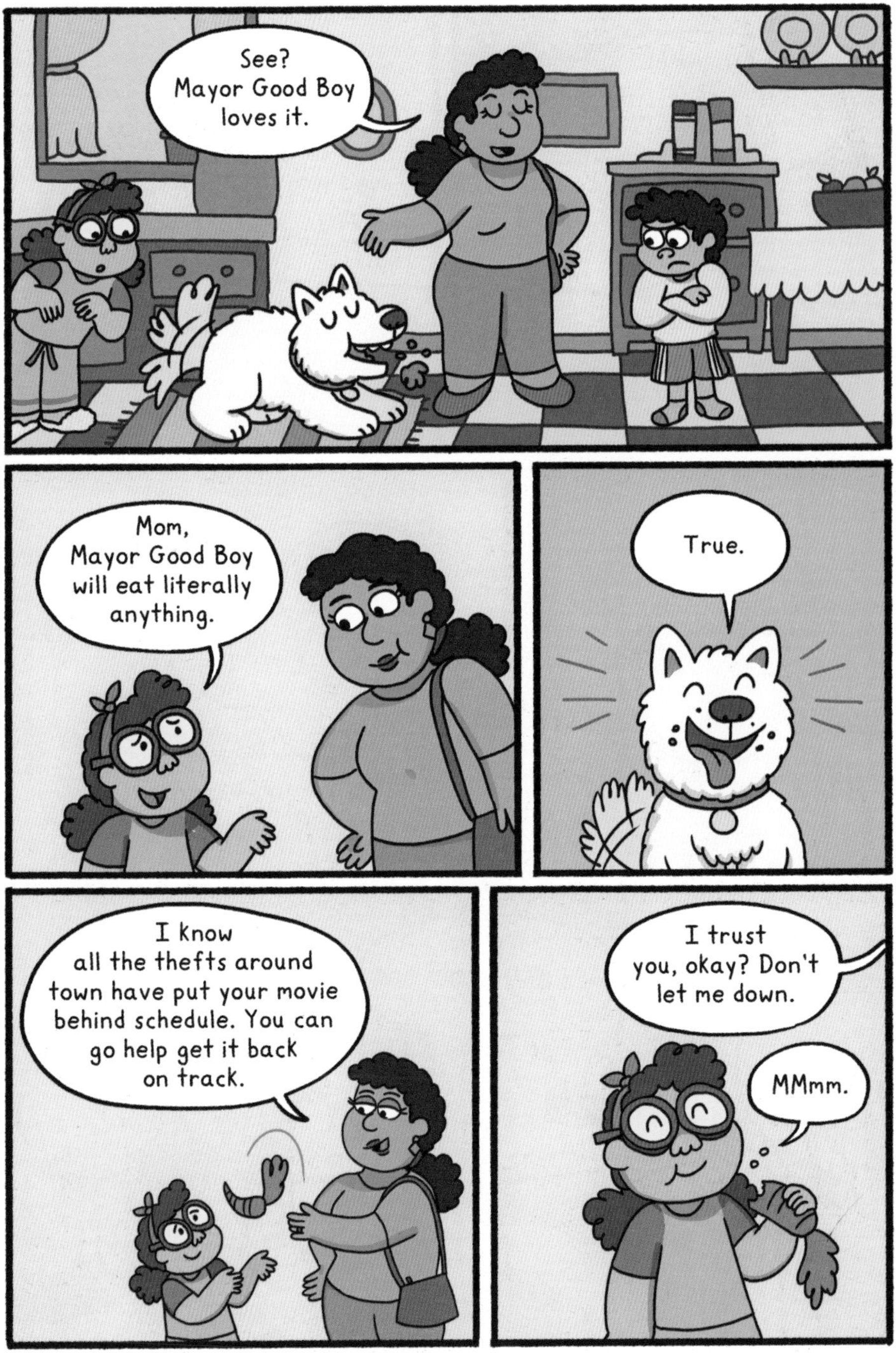
See?
Mayor Good Boy
loves it.
Mom,
Mayor Good Boy
will eat literally
anything.
True.
I know
all the thefts around
town have put your movie
behind schedule. You can
go help get it back
on track.
I trust
you, okay? Don't
let me down.
MMmm.

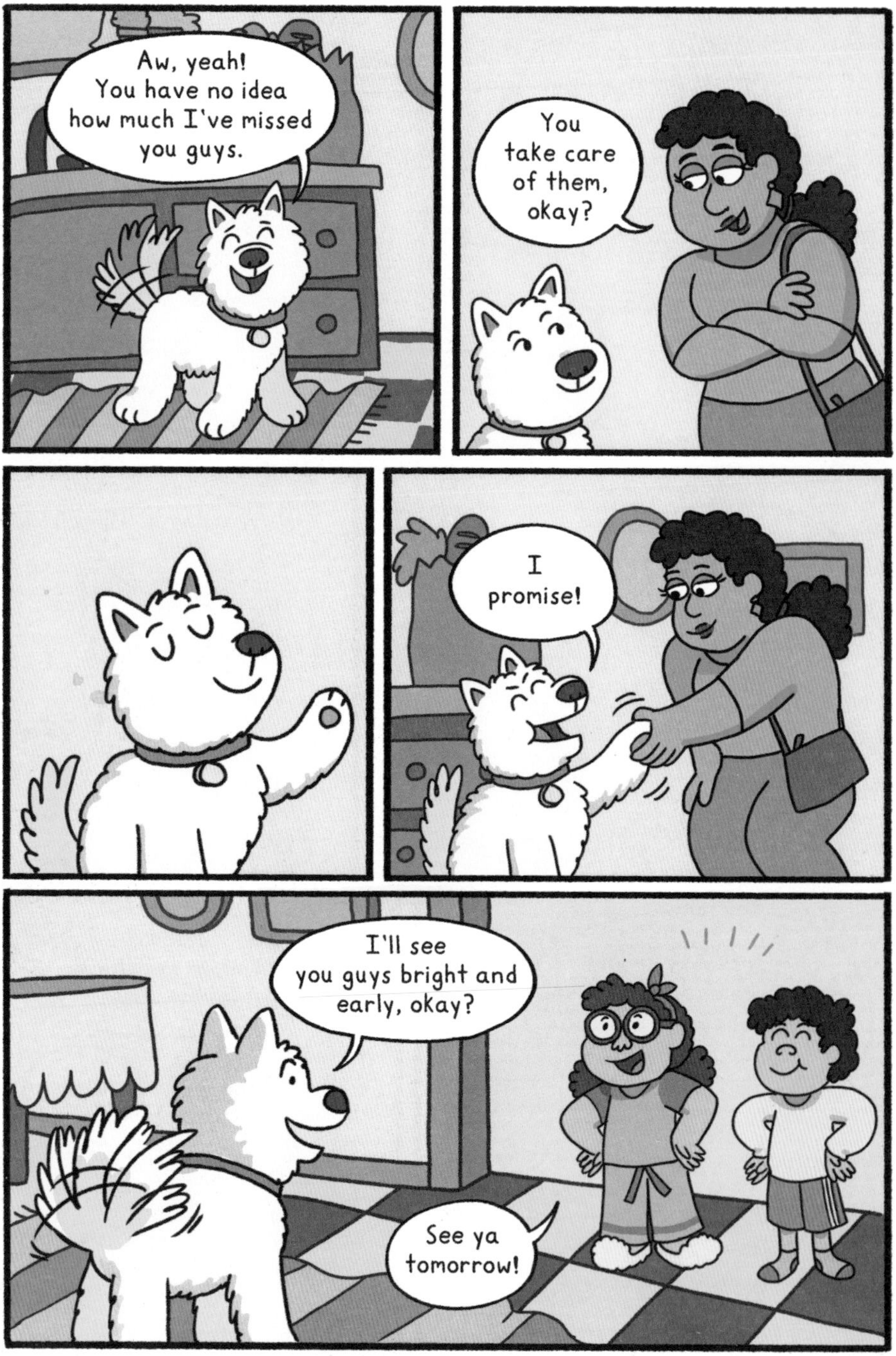
Aw, yeah! You have no idea how much I've missed you guys.
You take care of them, okay?
I promise!
I'll see you guys bright and early, okay?
See ya tomorrow!

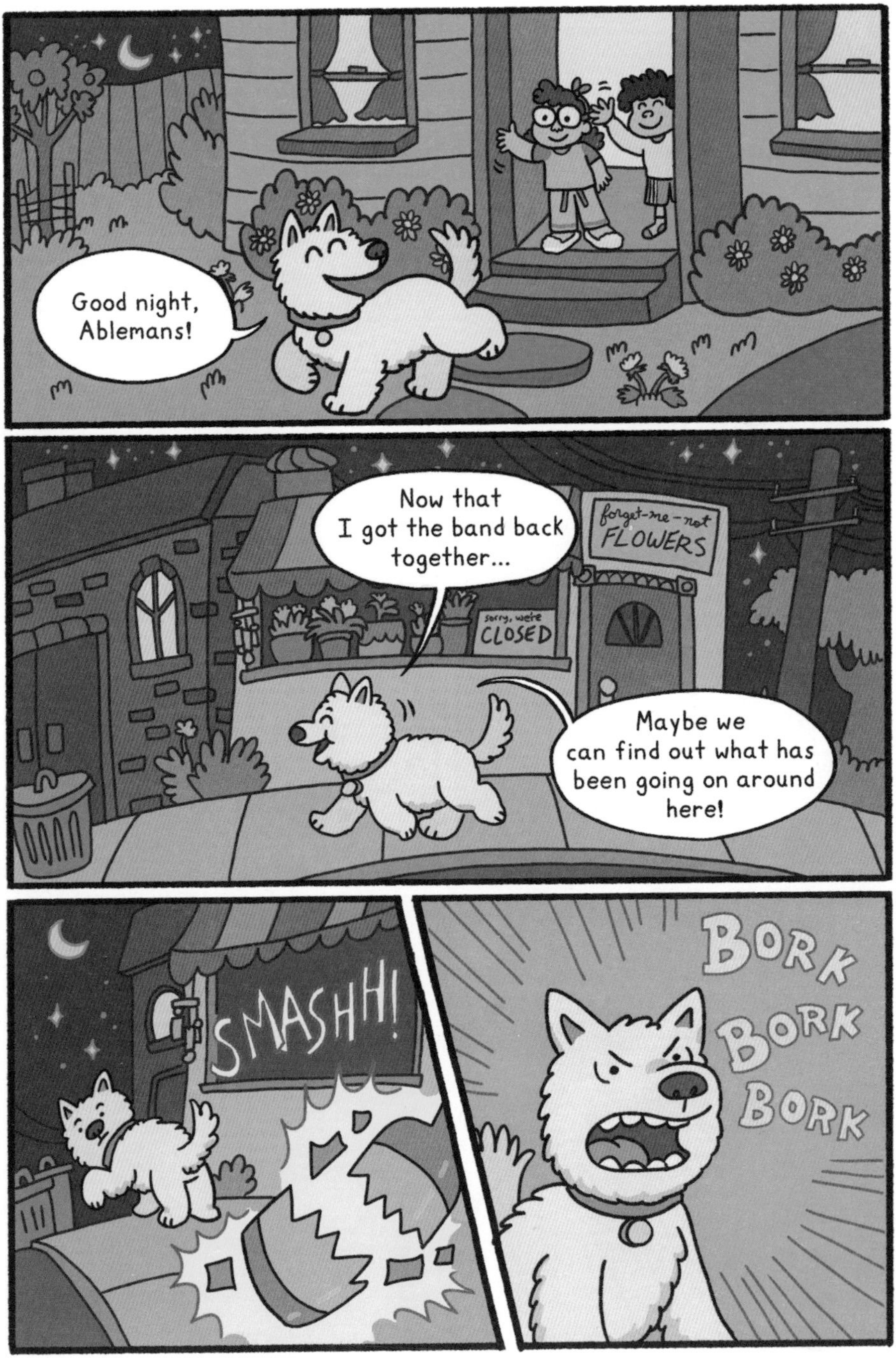
Good night, Ablemans!
Now that I got the band back together...
forget-me-not FLOWERS
sorry, we're CLOSED
Maybe we can find out what has been going on around here!
SMASHH!
BORK
BORK
BORK

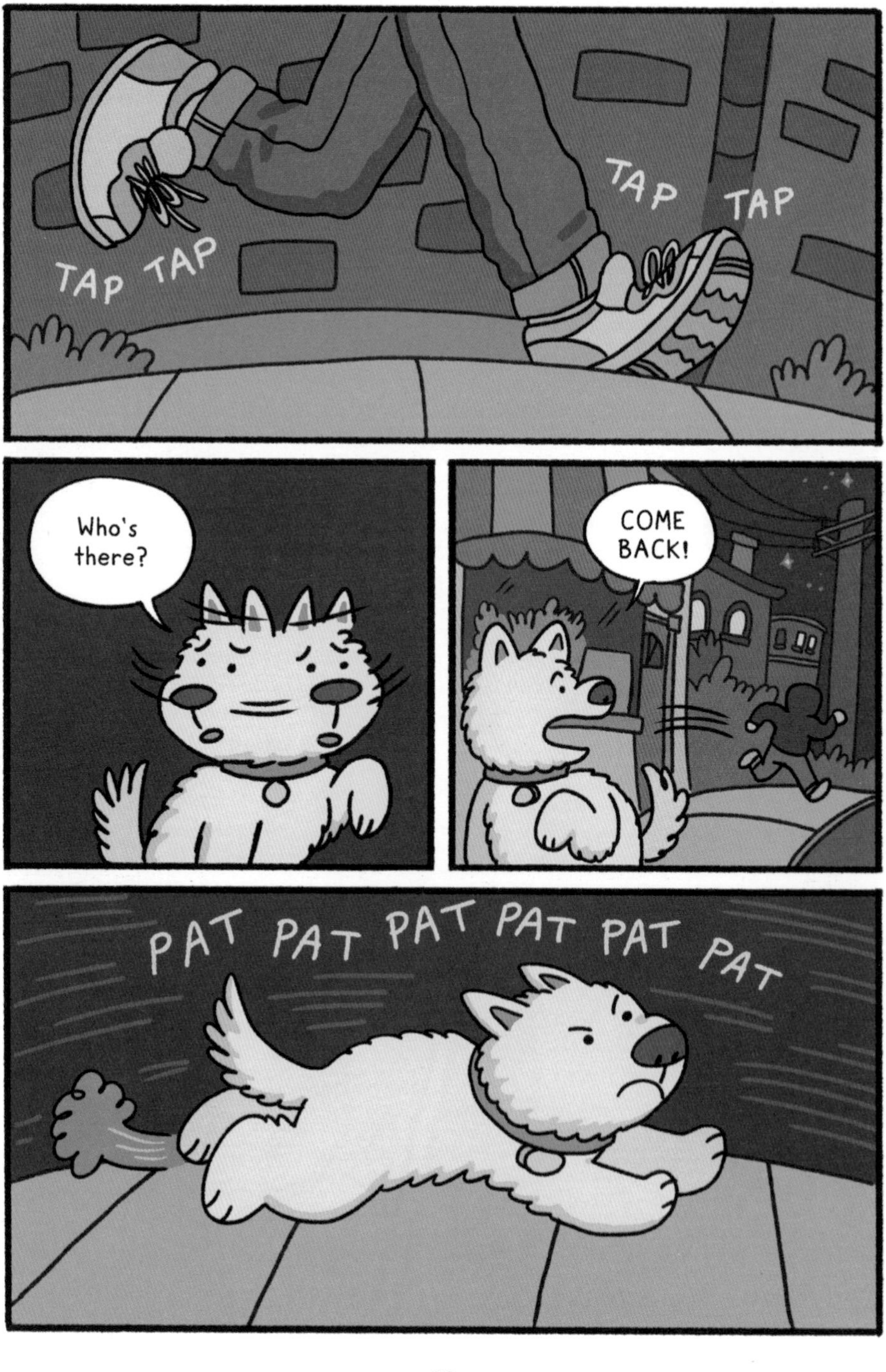
TAP TAP
TAP TAP
Who's there?
COME BACK!
PAT PAT PAT PAT PAT PAT

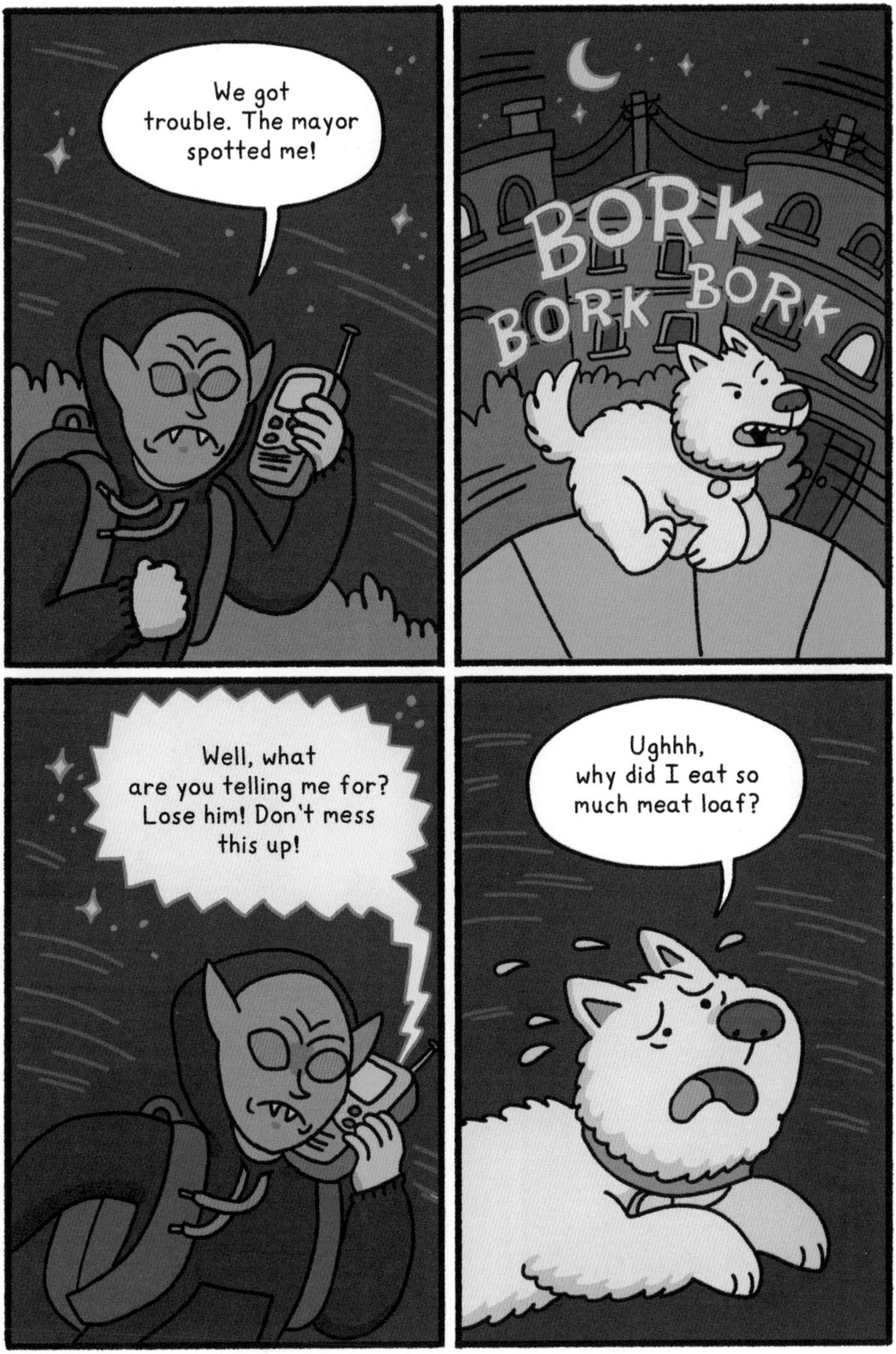
We got trouble. The mayor spotted me!
BORK
BORK BORK BORK
Well, what are you telling me for? Lose him! Don't mess this up!
Ughhh, why did I eat so much meat loaf?

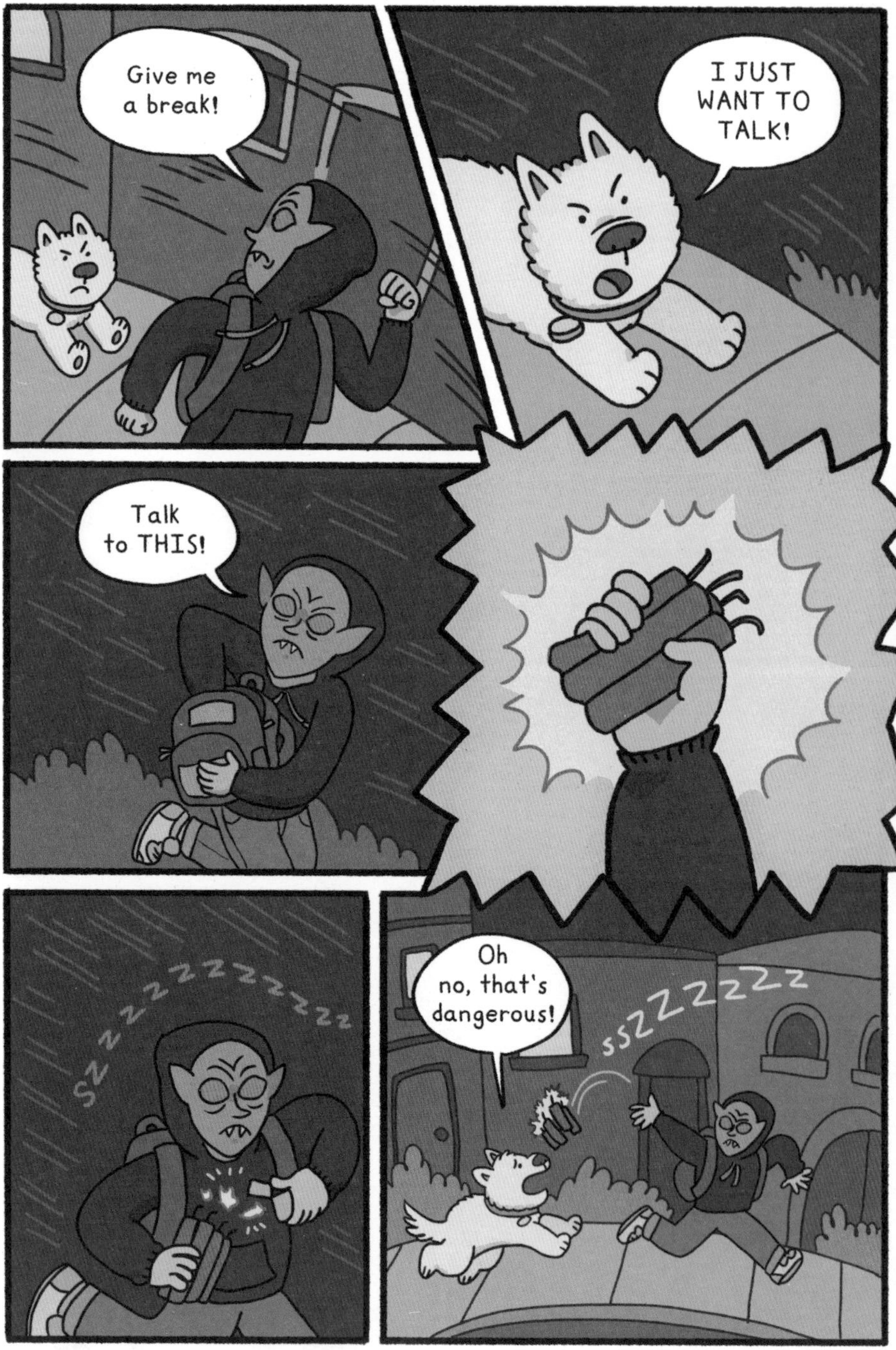

Give me a break!
I JUST WANT TO TALK!
Talk to THIS!
sszzzzzzzzzzz
Oh no, that's dangerous!
sszZZZZzz

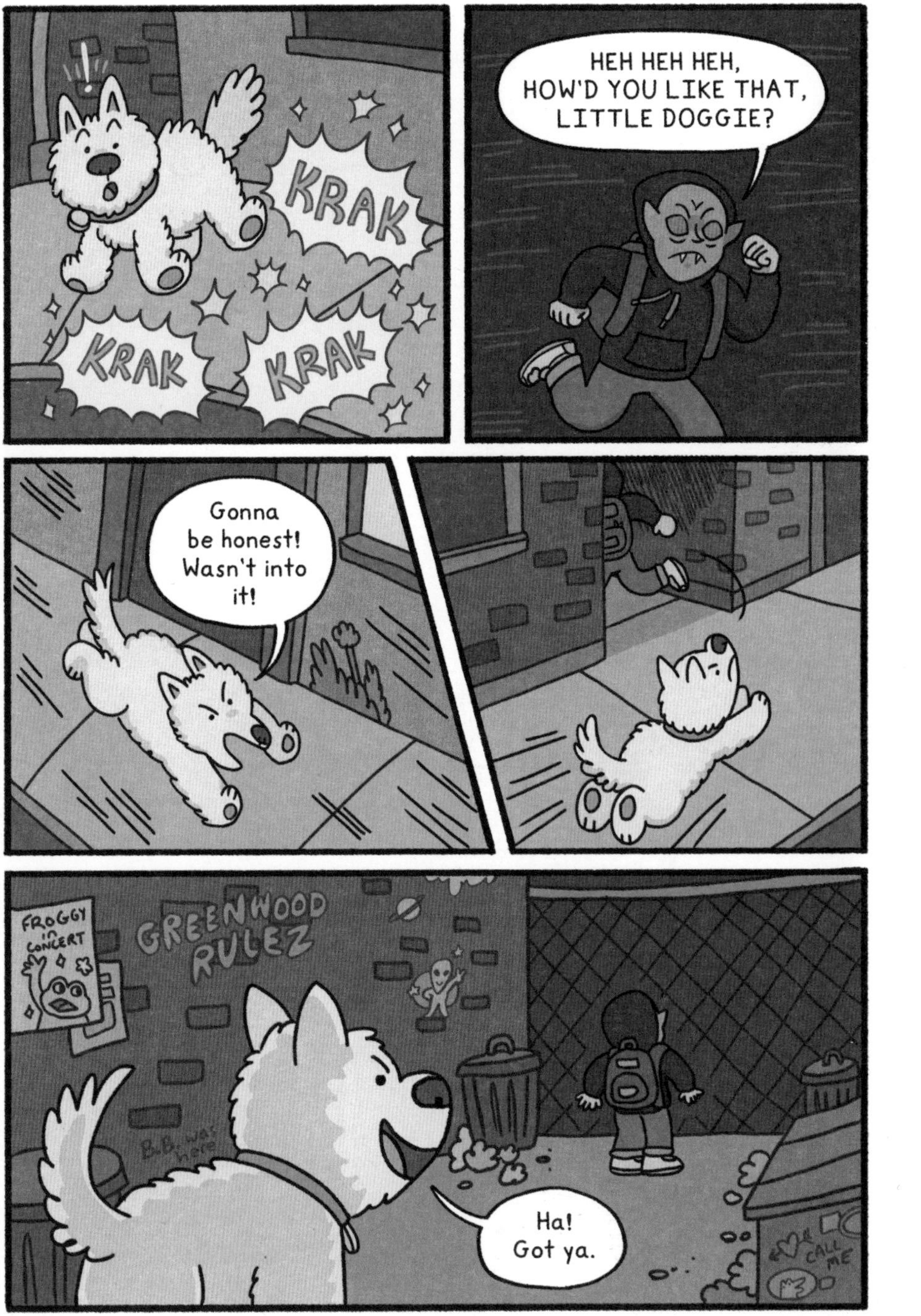
KRAK
KRAK
KRAK
HEH HEH HEH, HOW'D YOU LIKE THAT, LITTLE DOGGIE?
Gonna be honest! Wasn't into it!
FROGGY in CONCERT
GREENWOOD RULEZ
B.B. was here
Ha! Got ya.
CALL ME

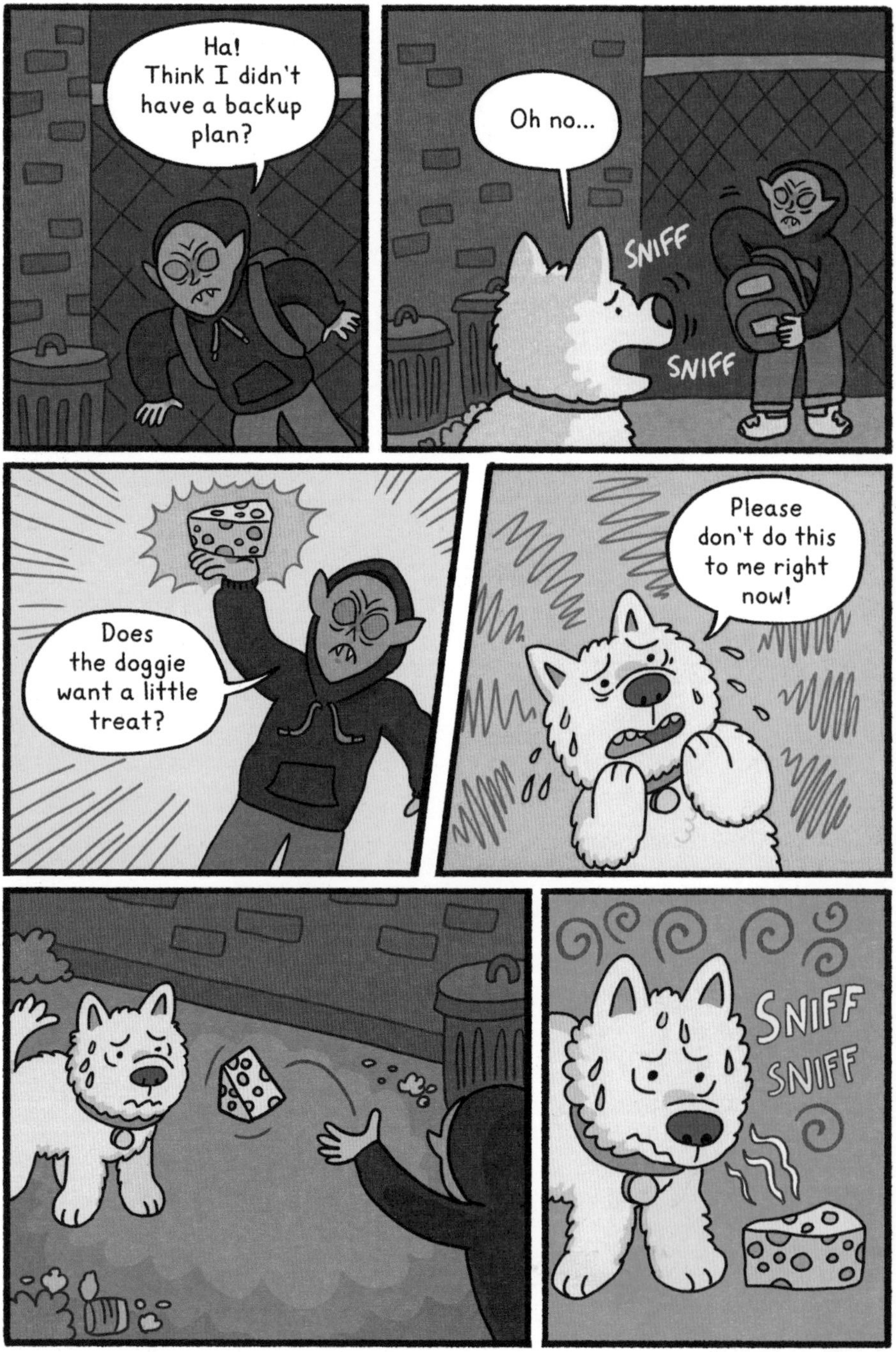
Ha!
Think I didn't have a backup plan?
Oh no...
SNIFF
SNIFF
Does the doggie want a little treat?
Please don't do this to me right now!
SNIFF
SNIFF

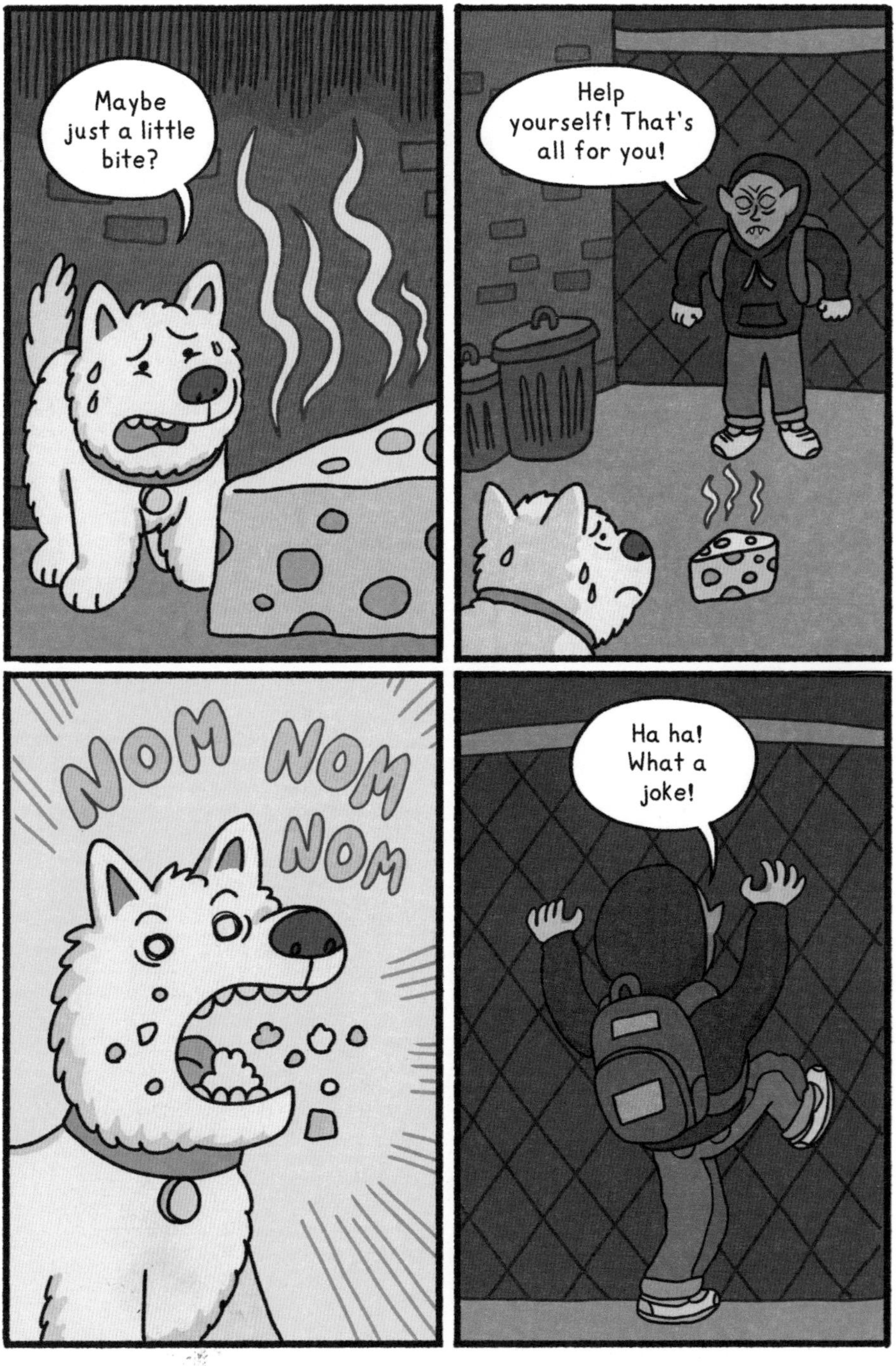
Maybe just a little bite?
Help yourself! That's all for you!
NOM NOM NOM
Ha ha! What a joke!

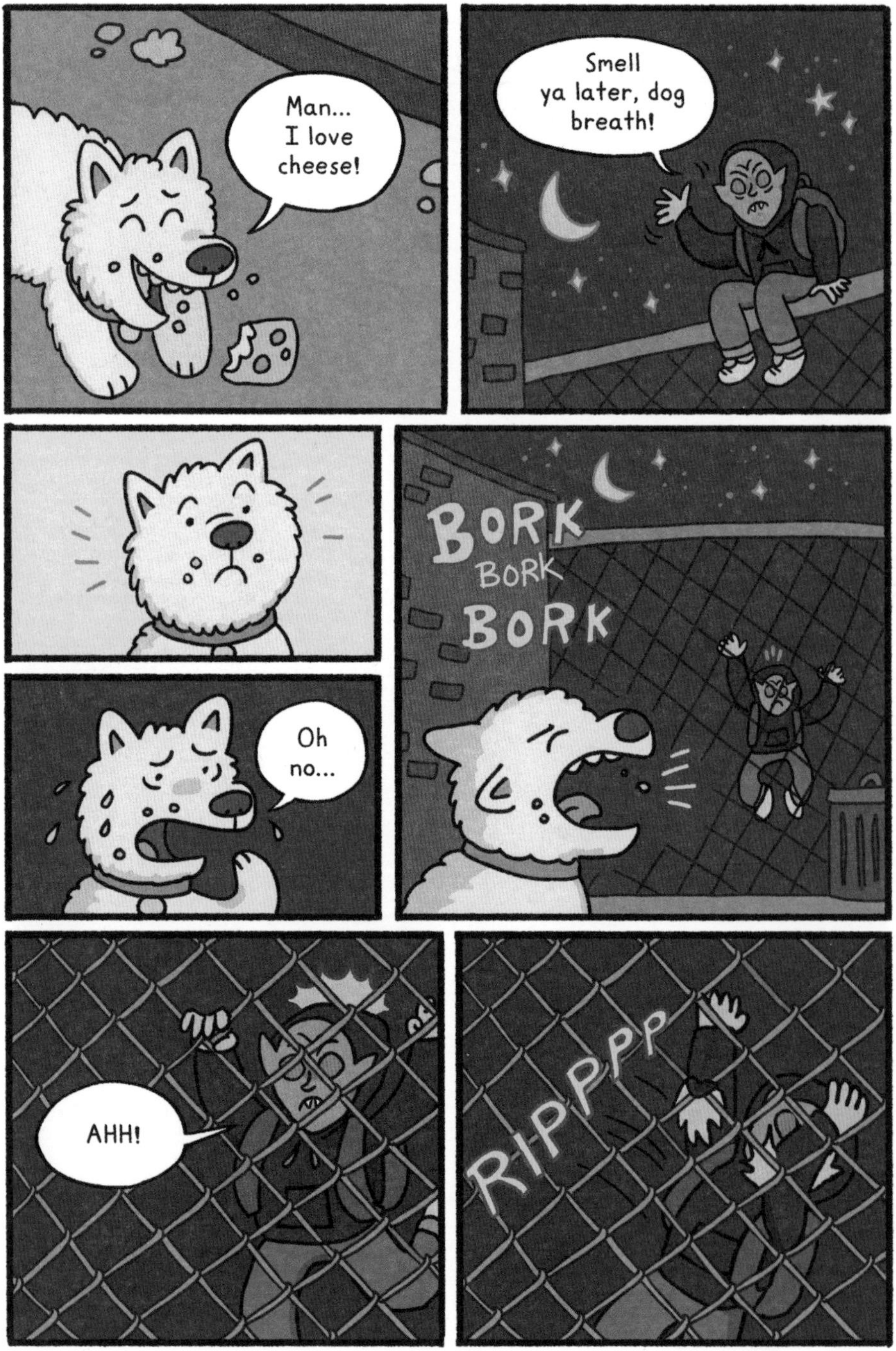
Man... I love cheese!
Smell ya later, dog breath!
Oh no...
BORK
BORK
BORK
AHH!
RIPPPP

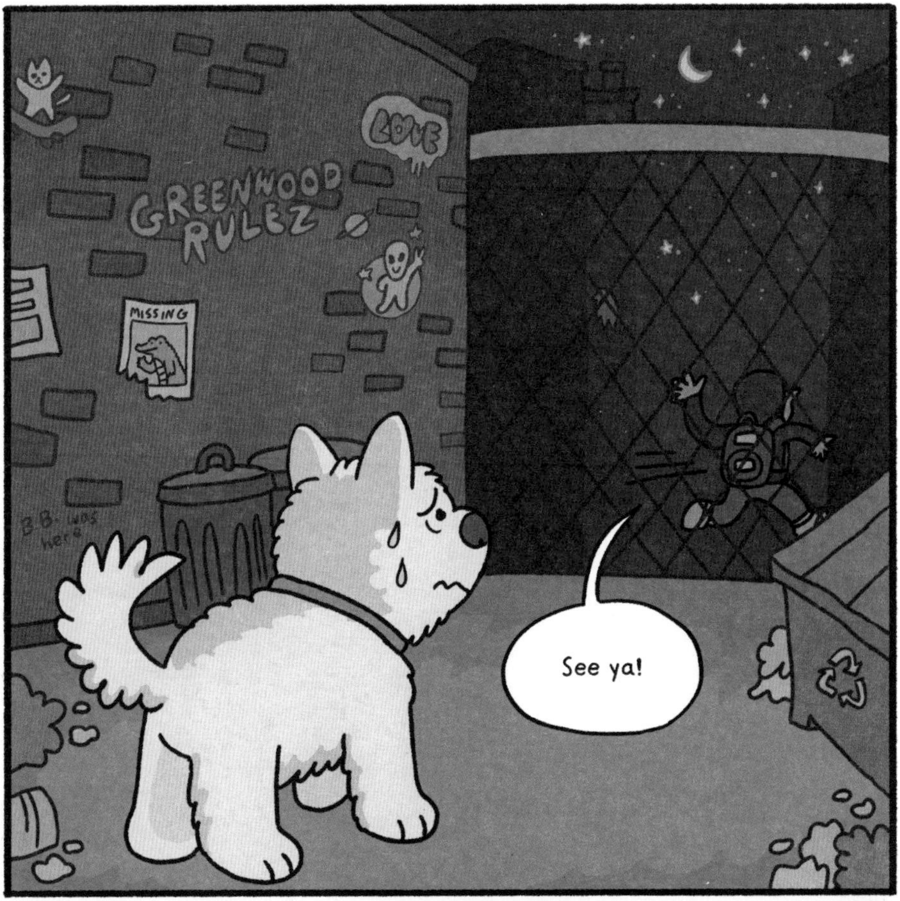
GREENWOOD RULEZ
LOVE
MISSING
B.B. was here
See ya!

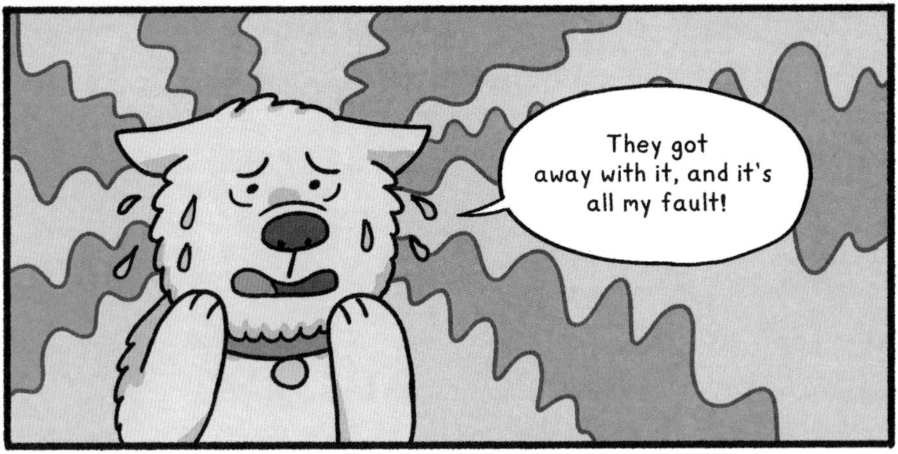
They got away with it, and it's all my fault!

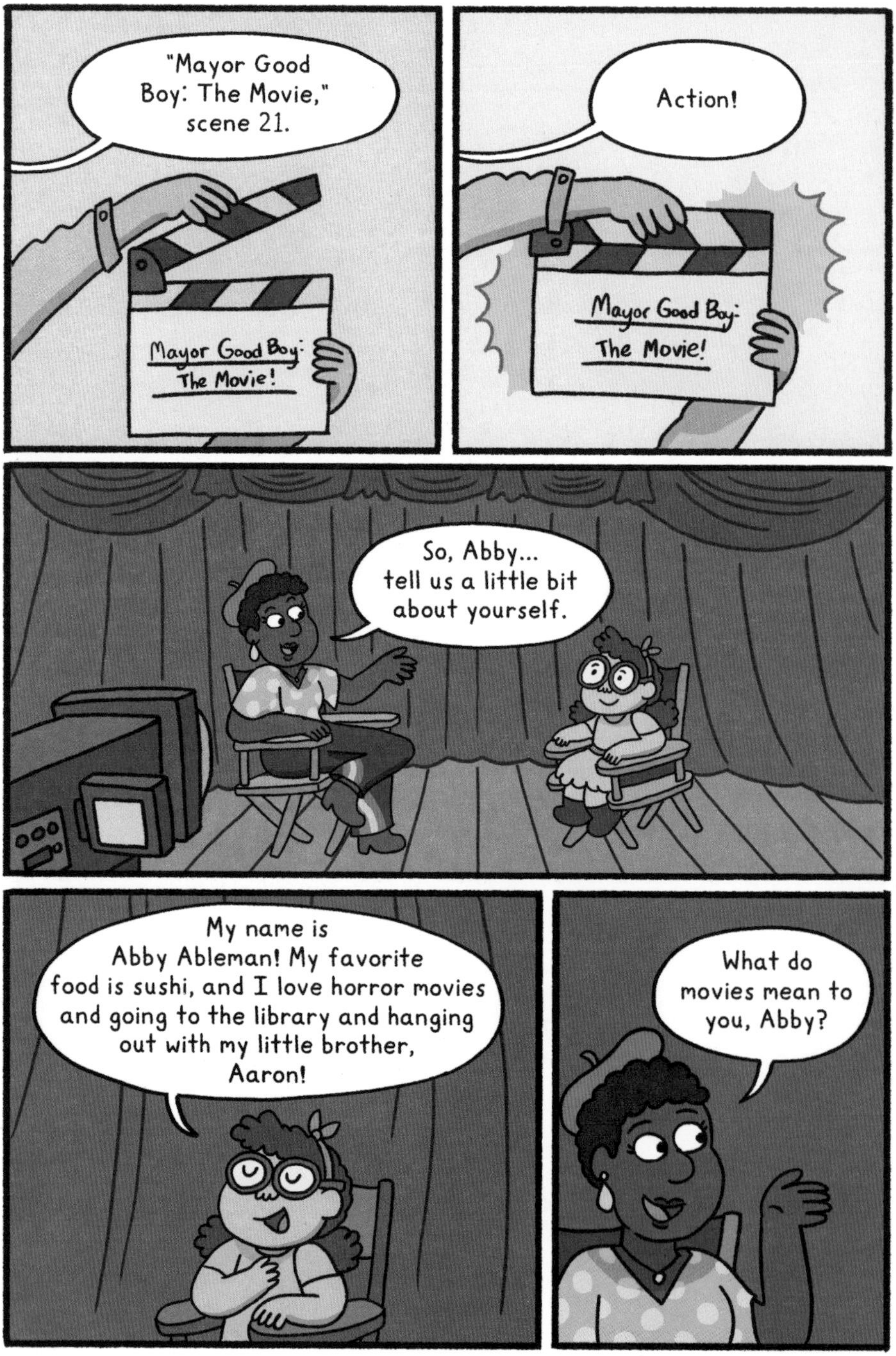
"Mayor Good Boy: The Movie," scene 21.
Mayor Good Boy: The Movie!
Action!
Mayor Good Boy: The Movie!
So, Abby... tell us a little bit about yourself.
My name is Abby Ableman! My favorite food is sushi, and I love horror movies and going to the library and hanging out with my little brother, Aaron!
What do movies mean to you, Abby?

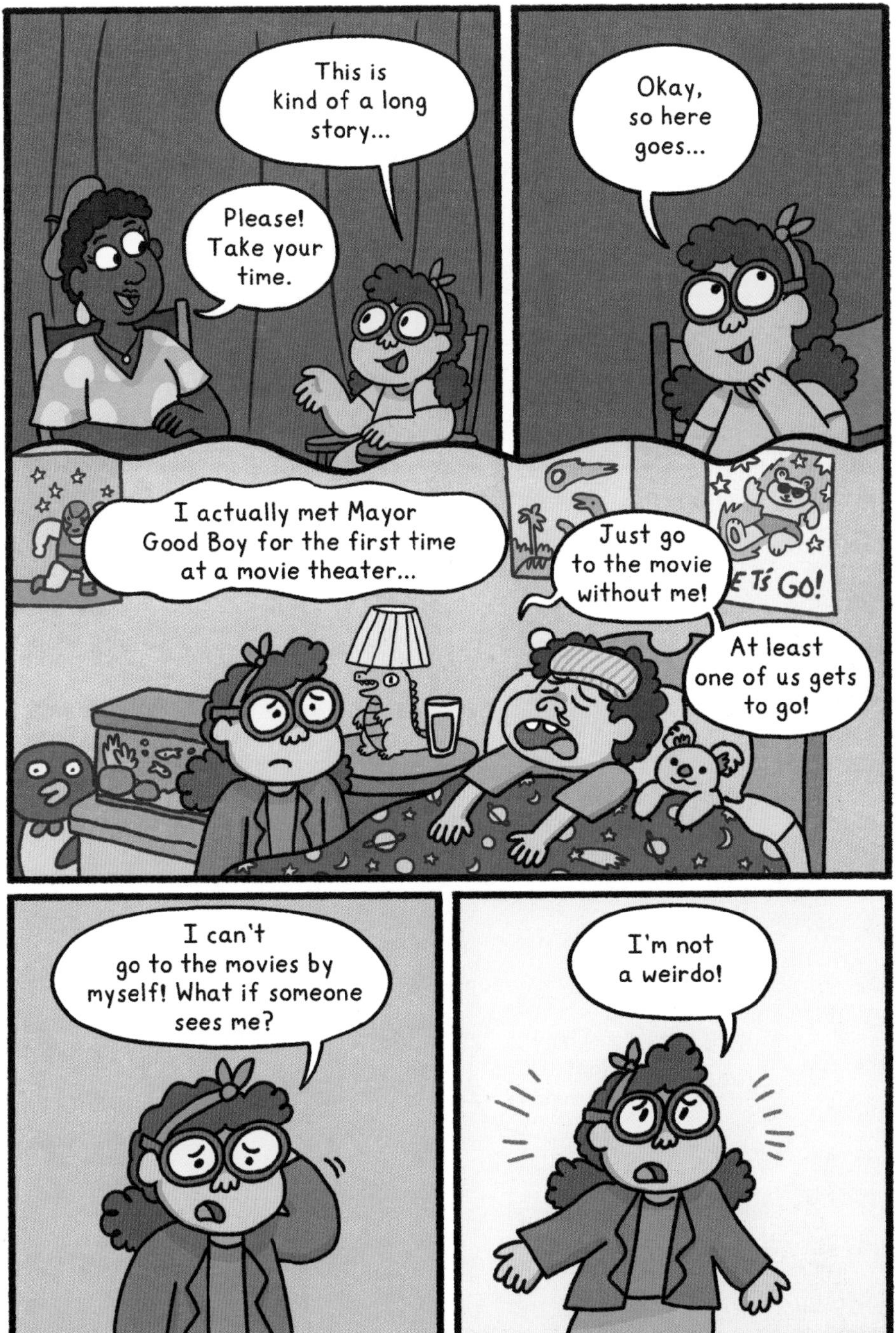
This is kind of a long story...
Please! Take your time.
Okay, so here goes...
I actually met Mayor Good Boy for the first time at a movie theater...
Just go to the movie without me!
At least one of us gets to go!
LETS GO!
I can't go to the movies by myself! What if someone sees me?
I'm not a weirdo!

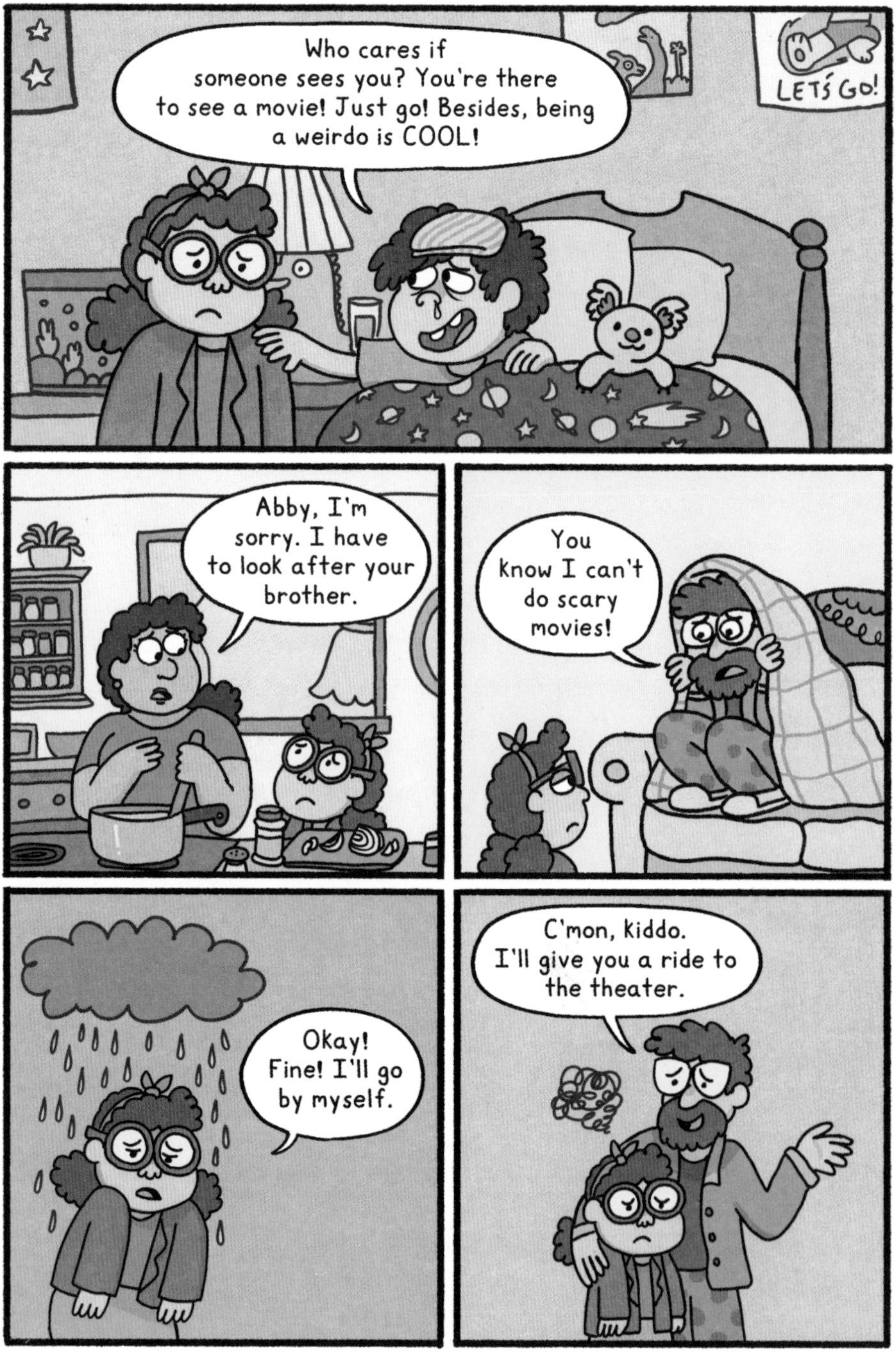
Who cares if someone sees you? You're there to see a movie! Just go! Besides, being a weirdo is COOL!
LET'S GO!
Abby, I'm sorry. I have to look after your brother.
You know I can't do scary movies!
Okay! Fine! I'll go by myself.
C'mon, kiddo. I'll give you a ride to the theater.

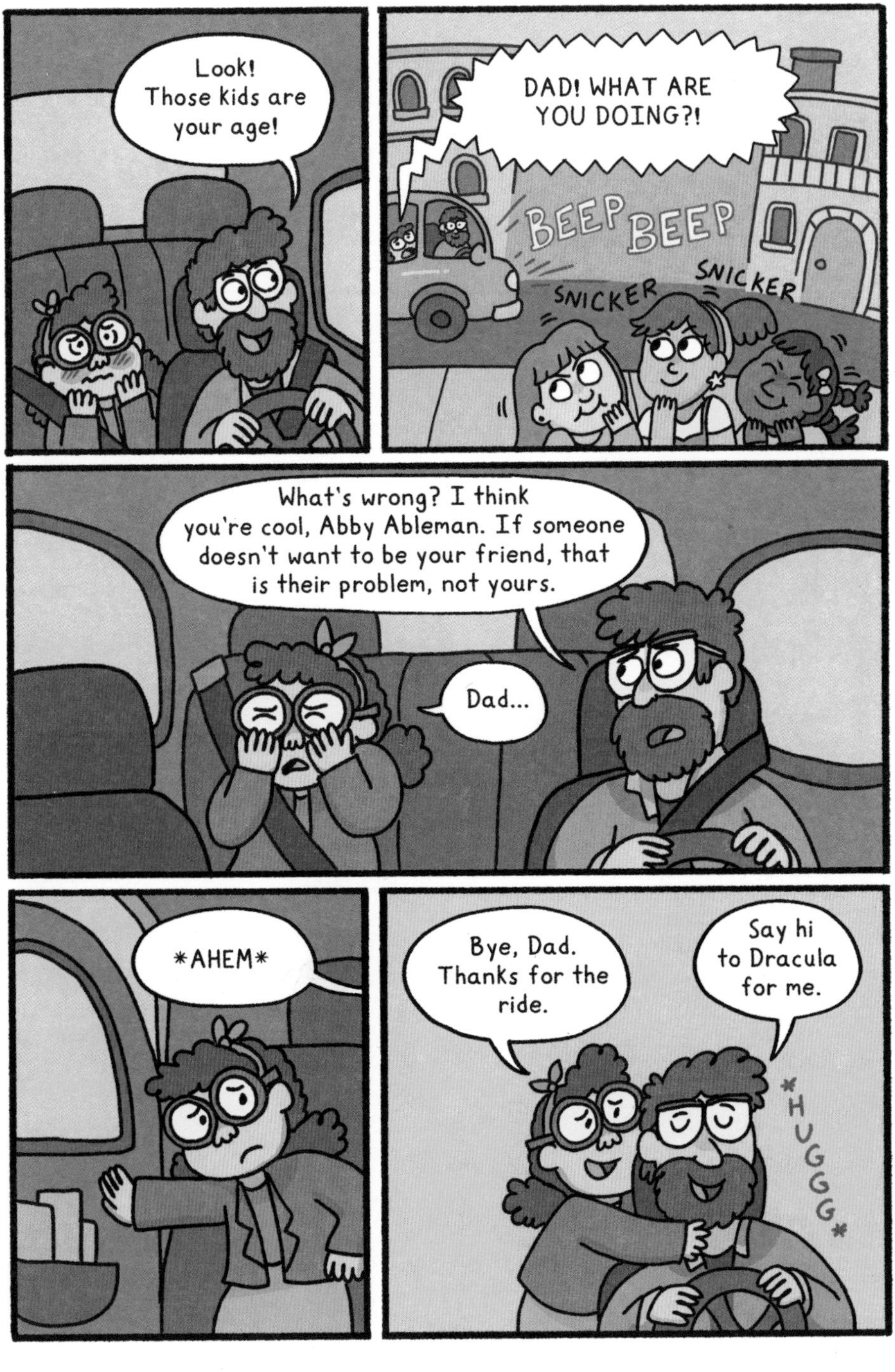
Look! Those kids are your age!
DAD! WHAT ARE YOU DOING?!
BEEP BEEP
SNICKER
SNICKER
What's wrong? I think you're cool, Abby Ableman. If someone doesn't want to be your friend, that is their problem, not yours.
Dad...
AHEM
Bye, Dad. Thanks for the ride.
Say hi to Dracula for me.
HUGGG

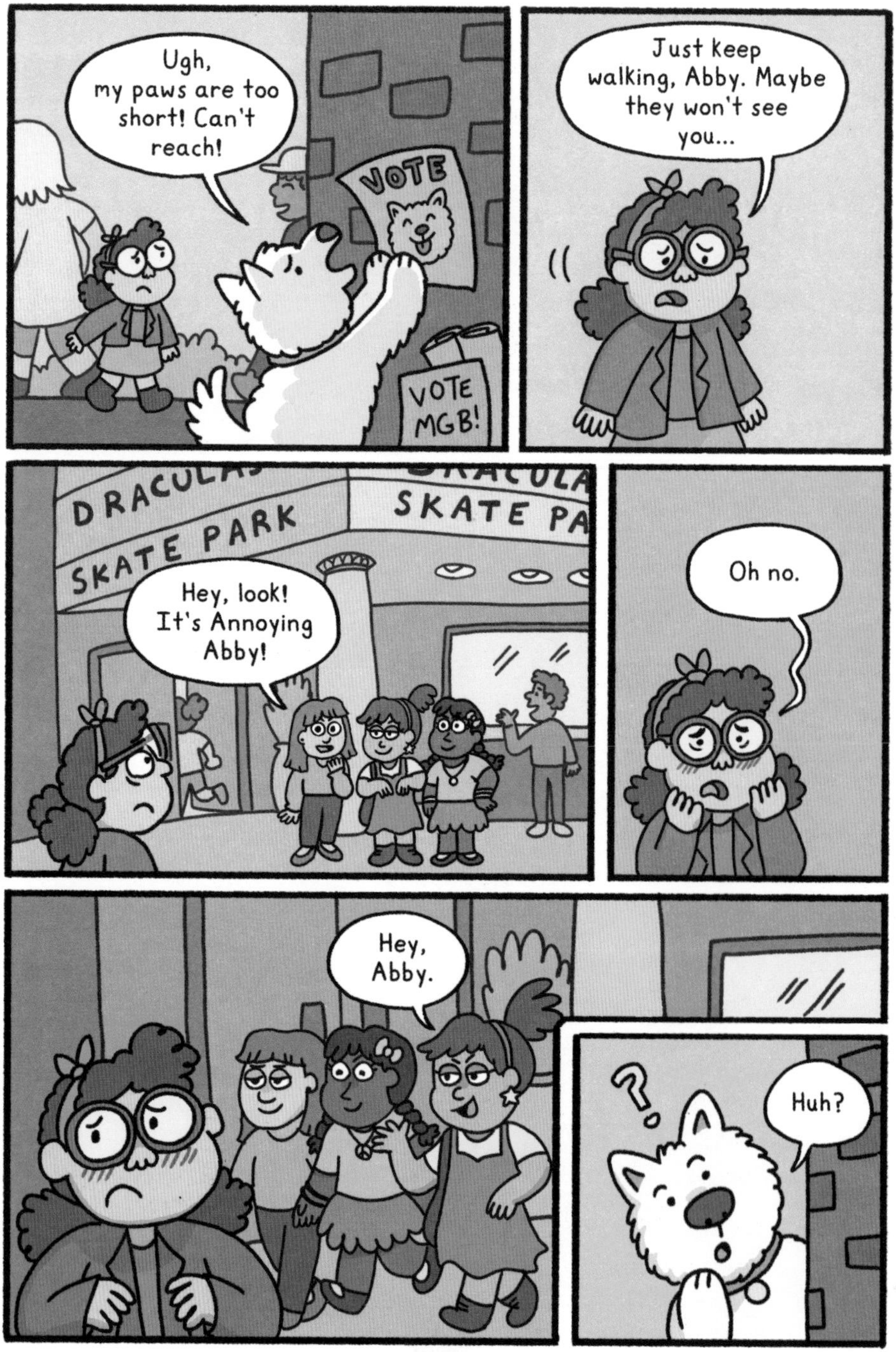

Ugh, my paws are too short! Can't reach!
VOTE
VOTE MGB!
Just keep walking, Abby. Maybe they won't see you...
DRACULAS SKATE PARK
DRACULA SKATE PA
Hey, look! It's Annoying Abby!
Oh no.
Hey, Abby.
Huh?

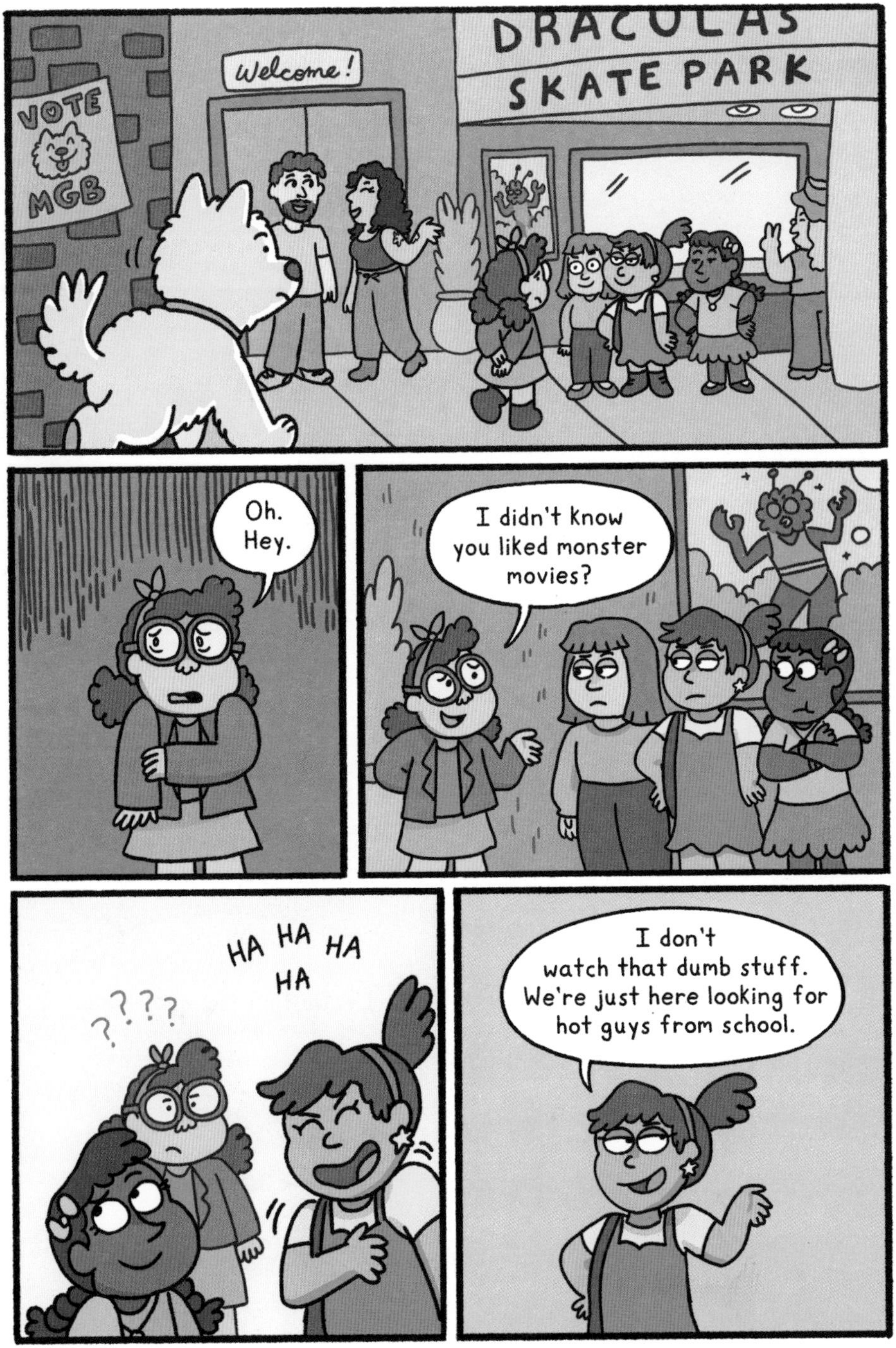
VOTE MGB
Welcome!
DRACULAS
SKATE PARK
Oh.
Hey.
I didn't know you liked monster movies?
???
HA HA HA
HA
I don't watch that dumb stuff. We're just here looking for hot guys from school.

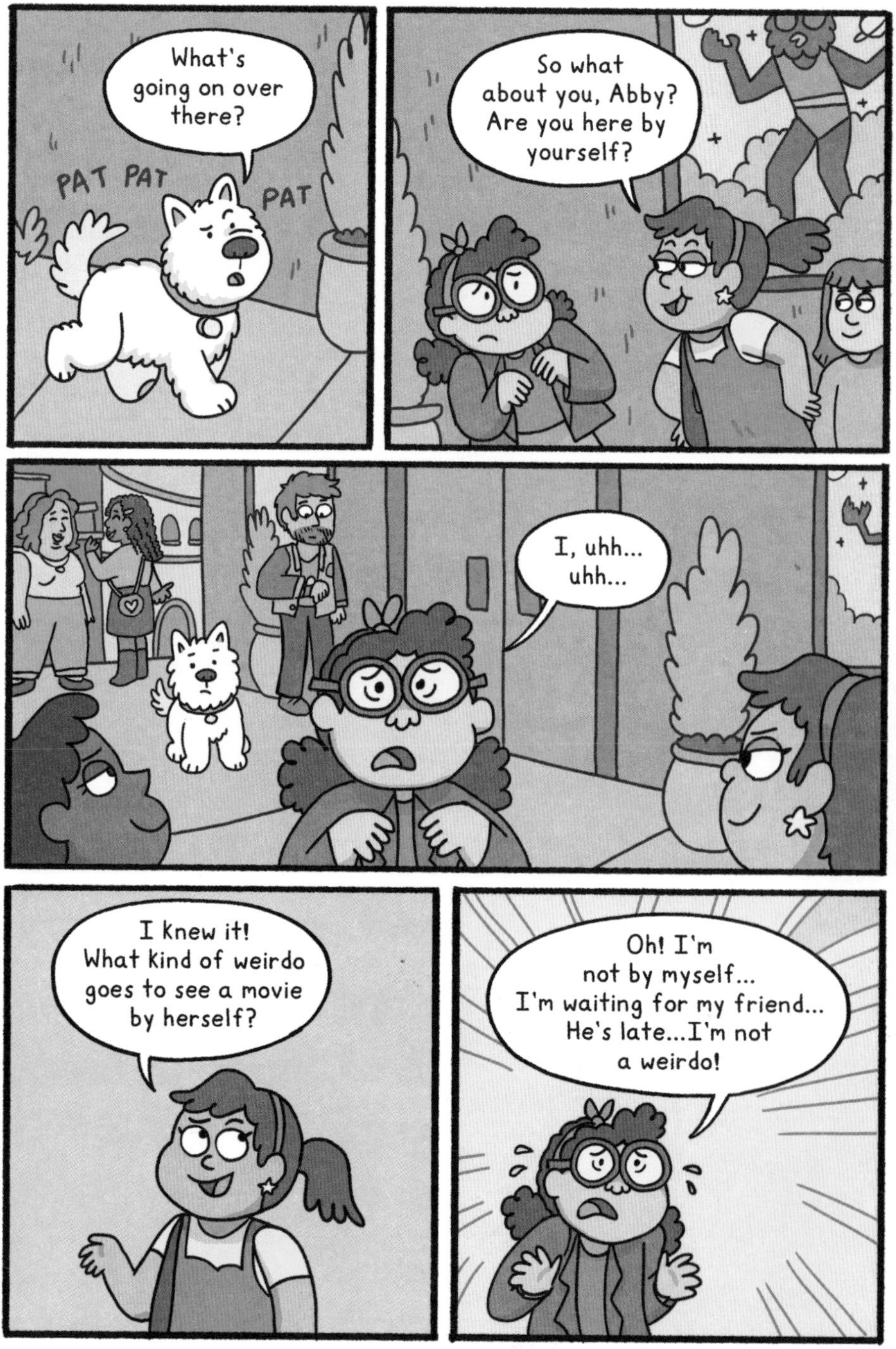
What's going on over there?
PAT PAT
PAT
So what about you, Abby? Are you here by yourself?
I, uhh... uhh...
I knew it! What kind of weirdo goes to see a movie by herself?
Oh! I'm not by myself... I'm waiting for my friend... He's late...I'm not a weirdo!

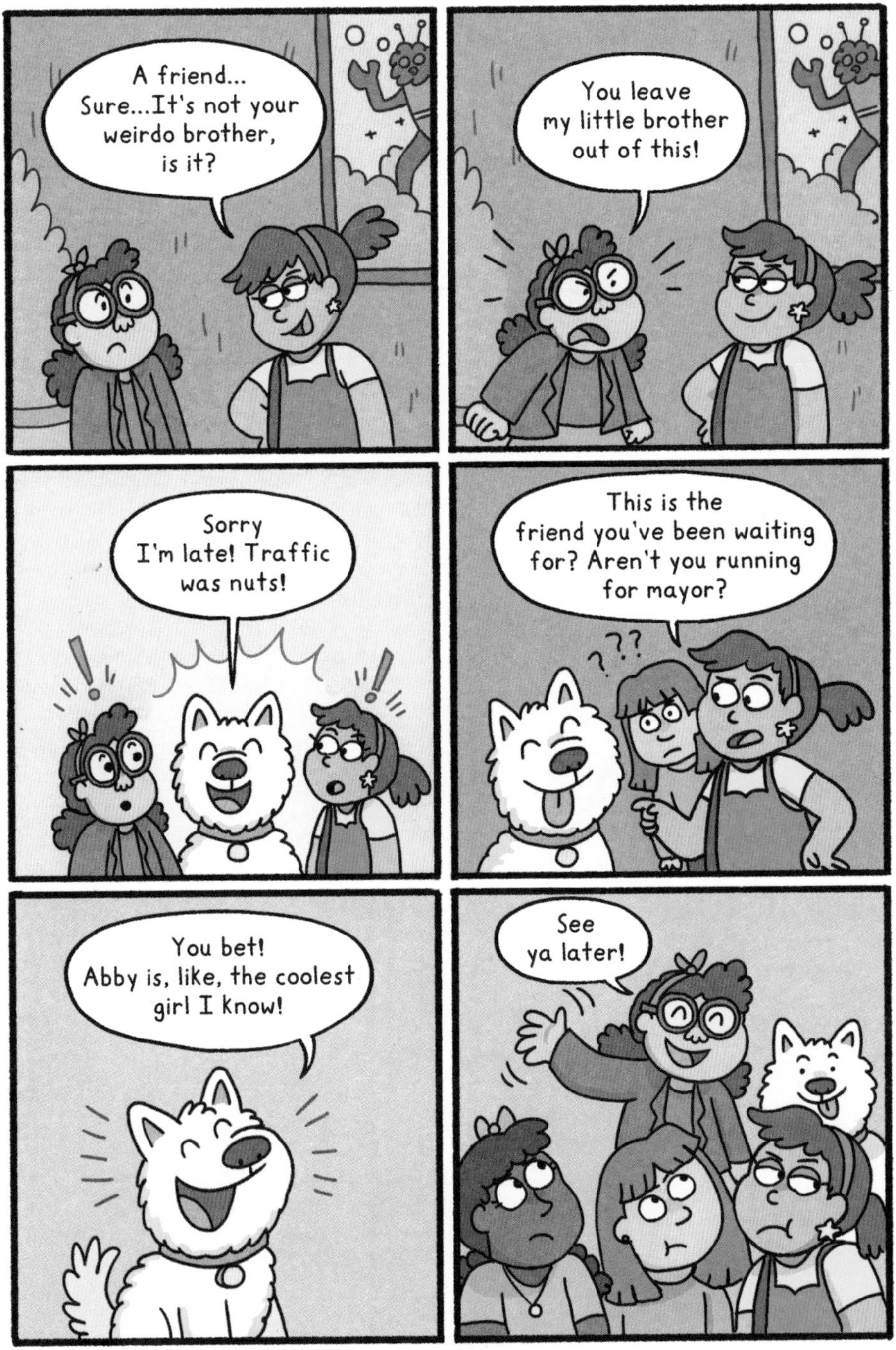
A friend... Sure...It's not your weirdo brother, is it?
You leave my little brother out of this!
Sorry I'm late! Traffic was nuts!
This is the friend you've been waiting for? Aren't you running for mayor?
???
You bet! Abby is, like, the coolest girl I know!
See ya later!

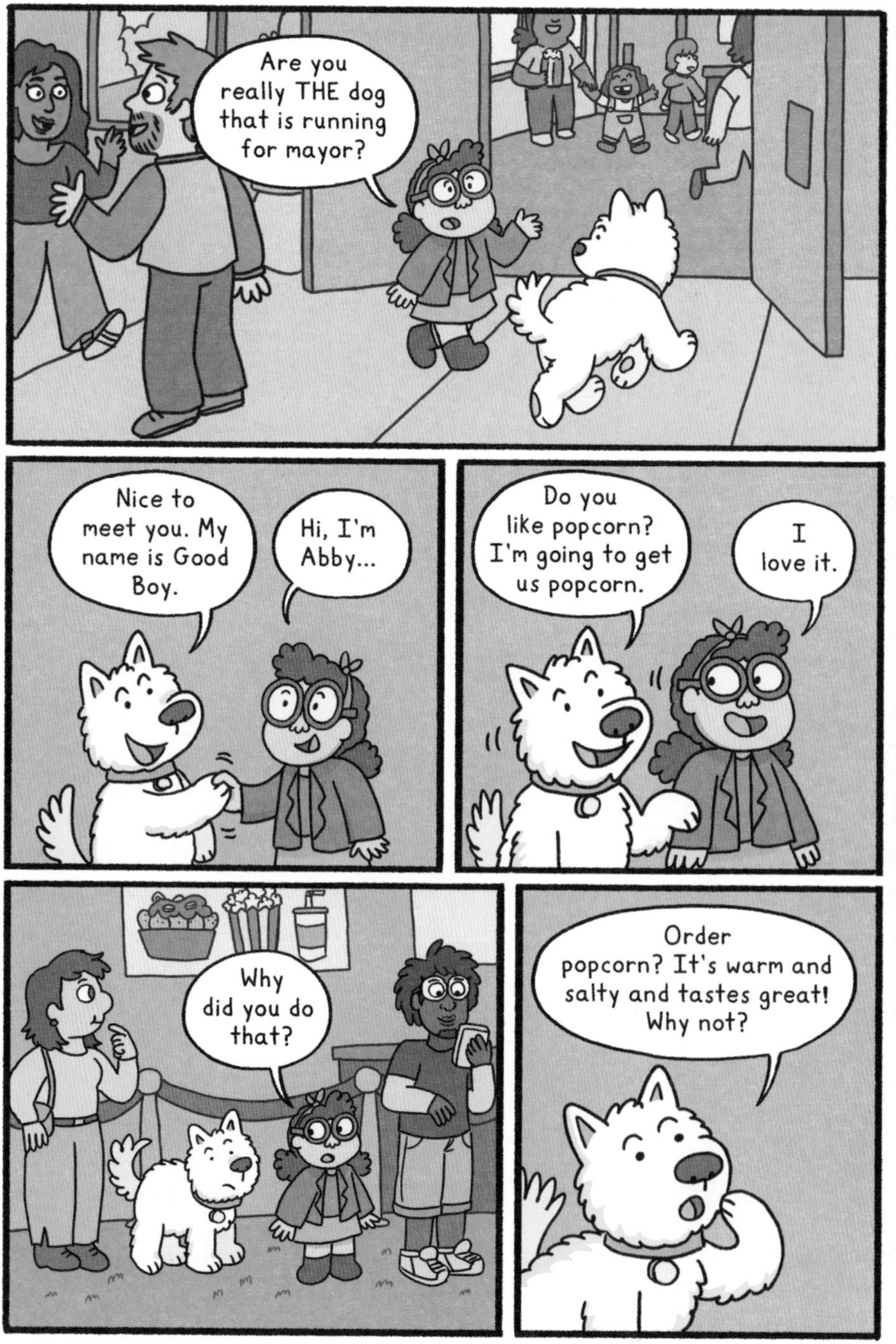
Are you really THE dog that is running for mayor?
Nice to meet you. My name is Good Boy.
Hi, I'm Abby...
Do you like popcorn? I'm going to get us popcorn.
I love it.
Why did you do that?
Order popcorn? It's warm and salty and tastes great! Why not?

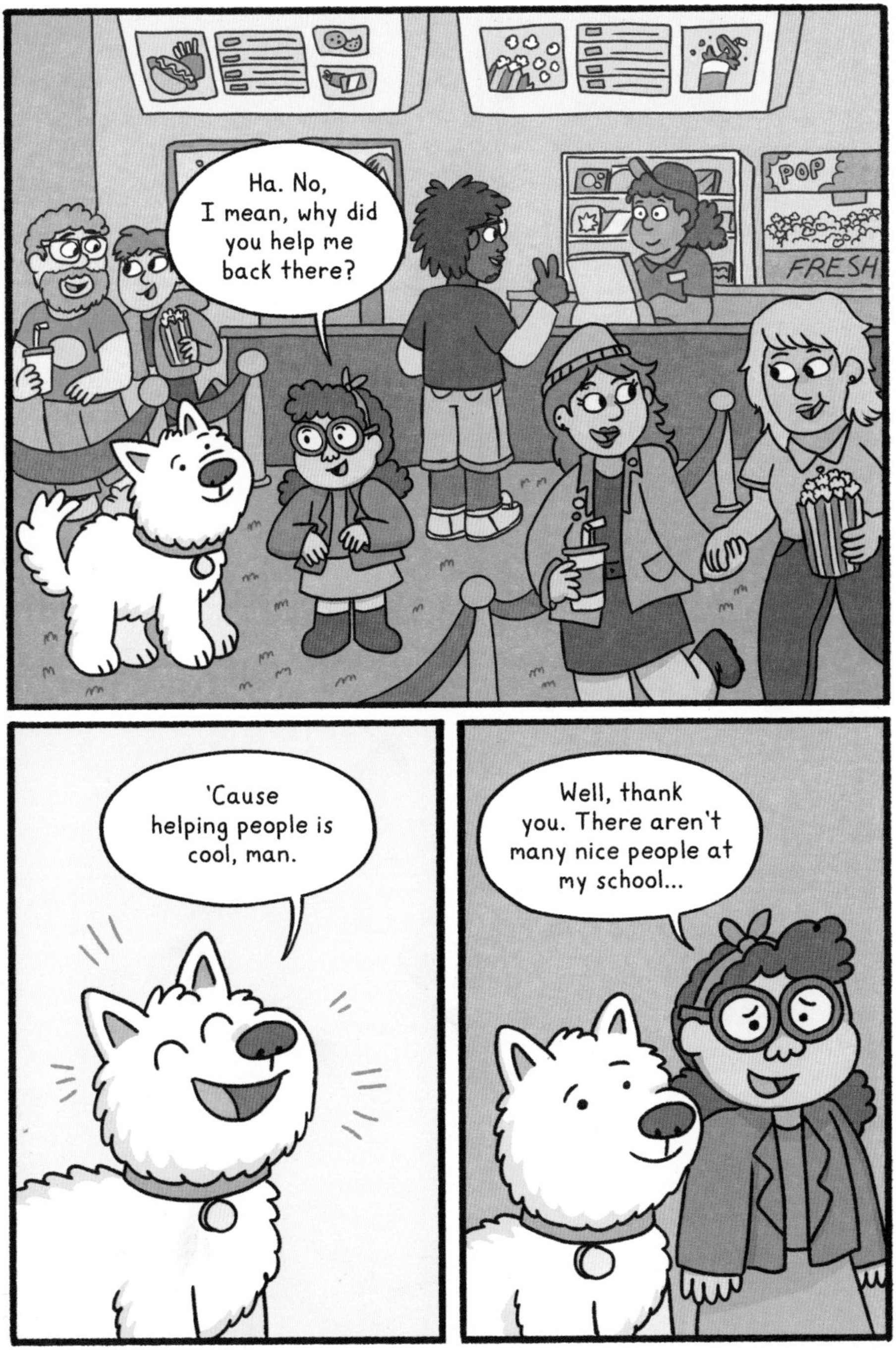
POP
FRESH
Ha. No, I mean, why did you help me back there?
'Cause helping people is cool, man.
Well, thank you. There aren't many nice people at my school...

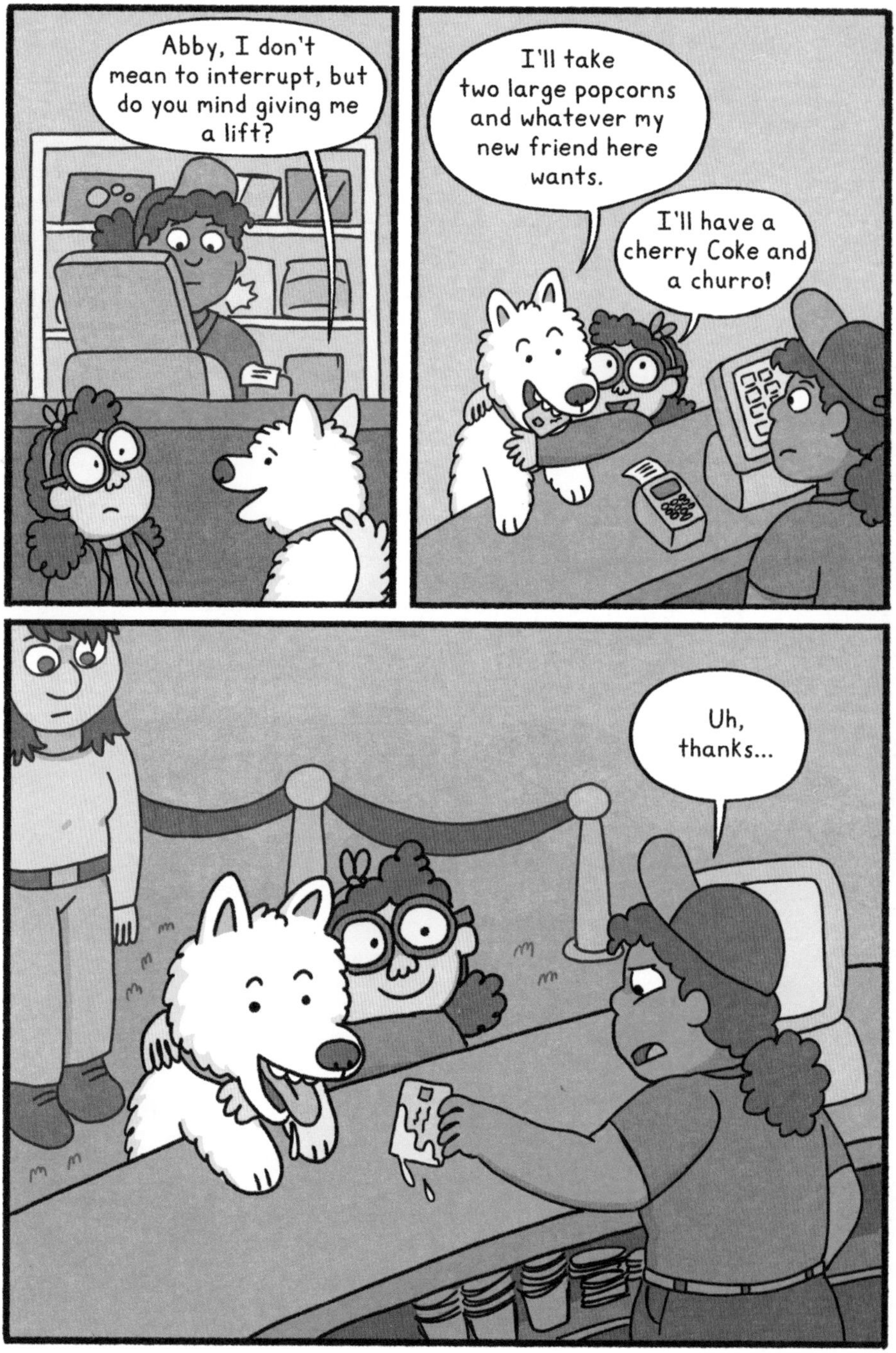
Abby, I don't mean to interrupt, but do you mind giving me a lift?
I'll take two large popcorns and whatever my new friend here wants.
I'll have a cherry Coke and a churro!
Uh, thanks...

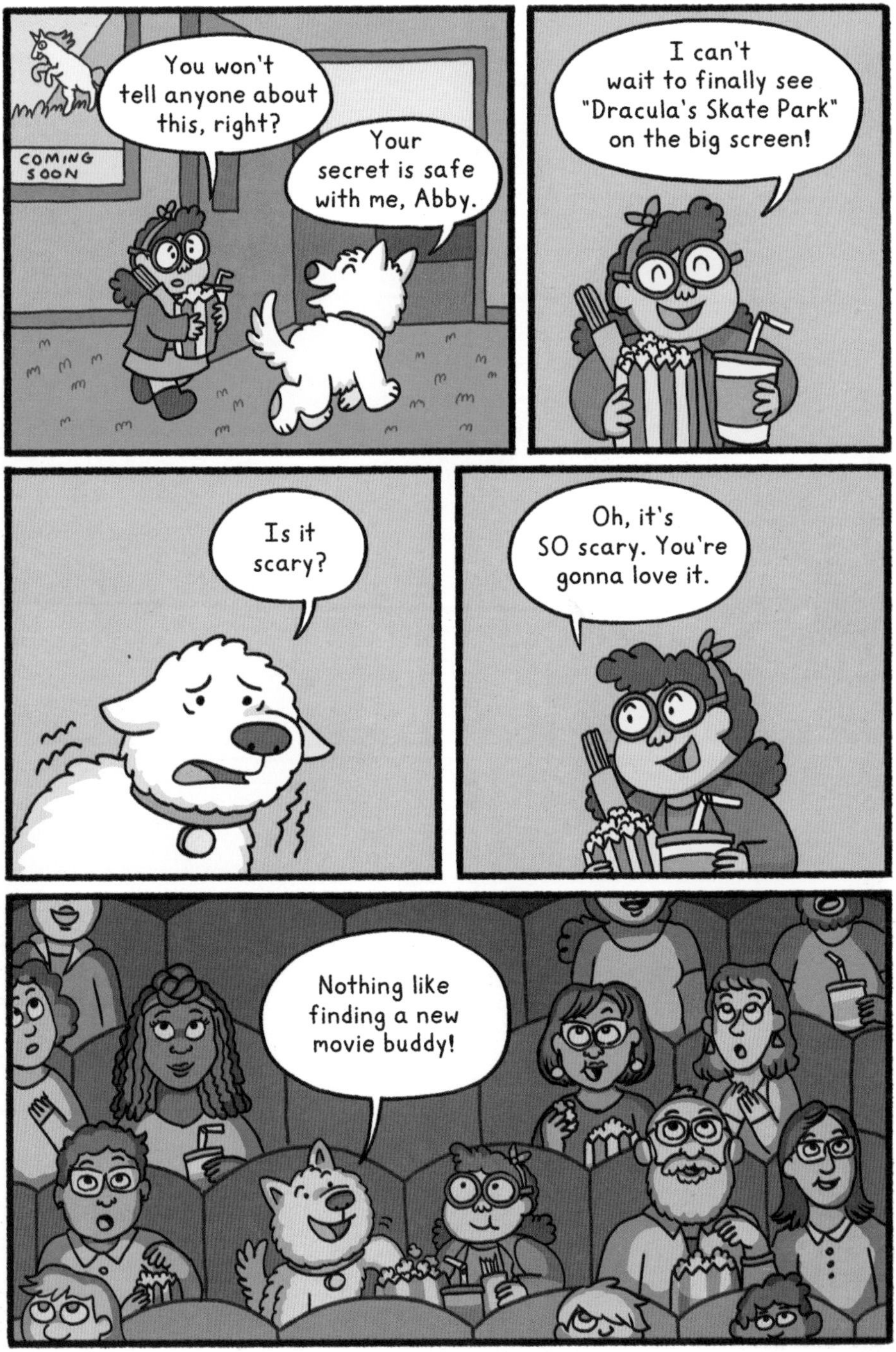
COMING SOON
You won't tell anyone about this, right?
Your secret is safe with me, Abby.
I can't wait to finally see "Dracula's Skate Park" on the big screen!
Is it scary?
Oh, it's SO scary. You're gonna love it.
Nothing like finding a new movie buddy!

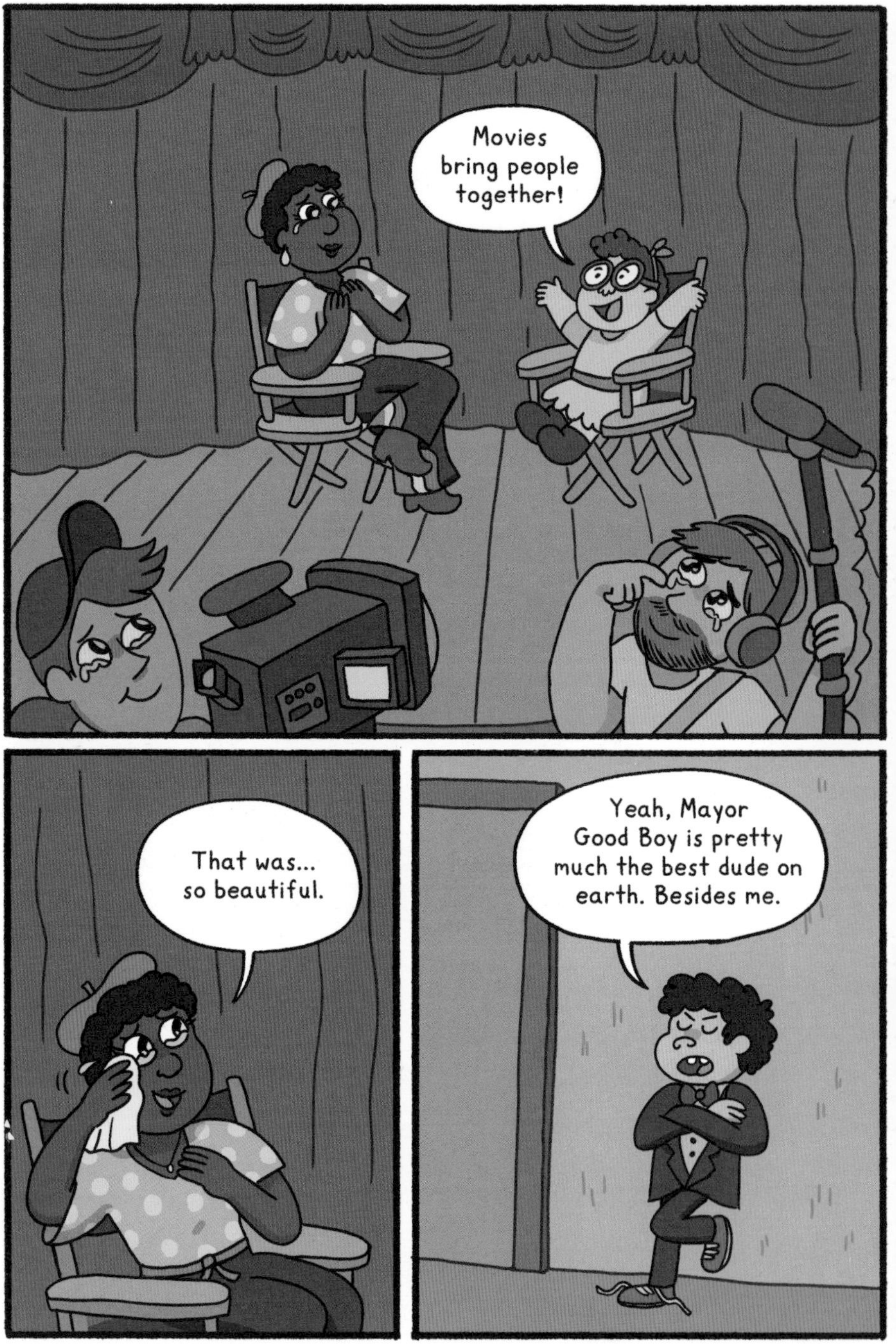
Movies bring people together!
That was... so beautiful.
Yeah, Mayor Good Boy is pretty much the best dude on earth. Besides me.

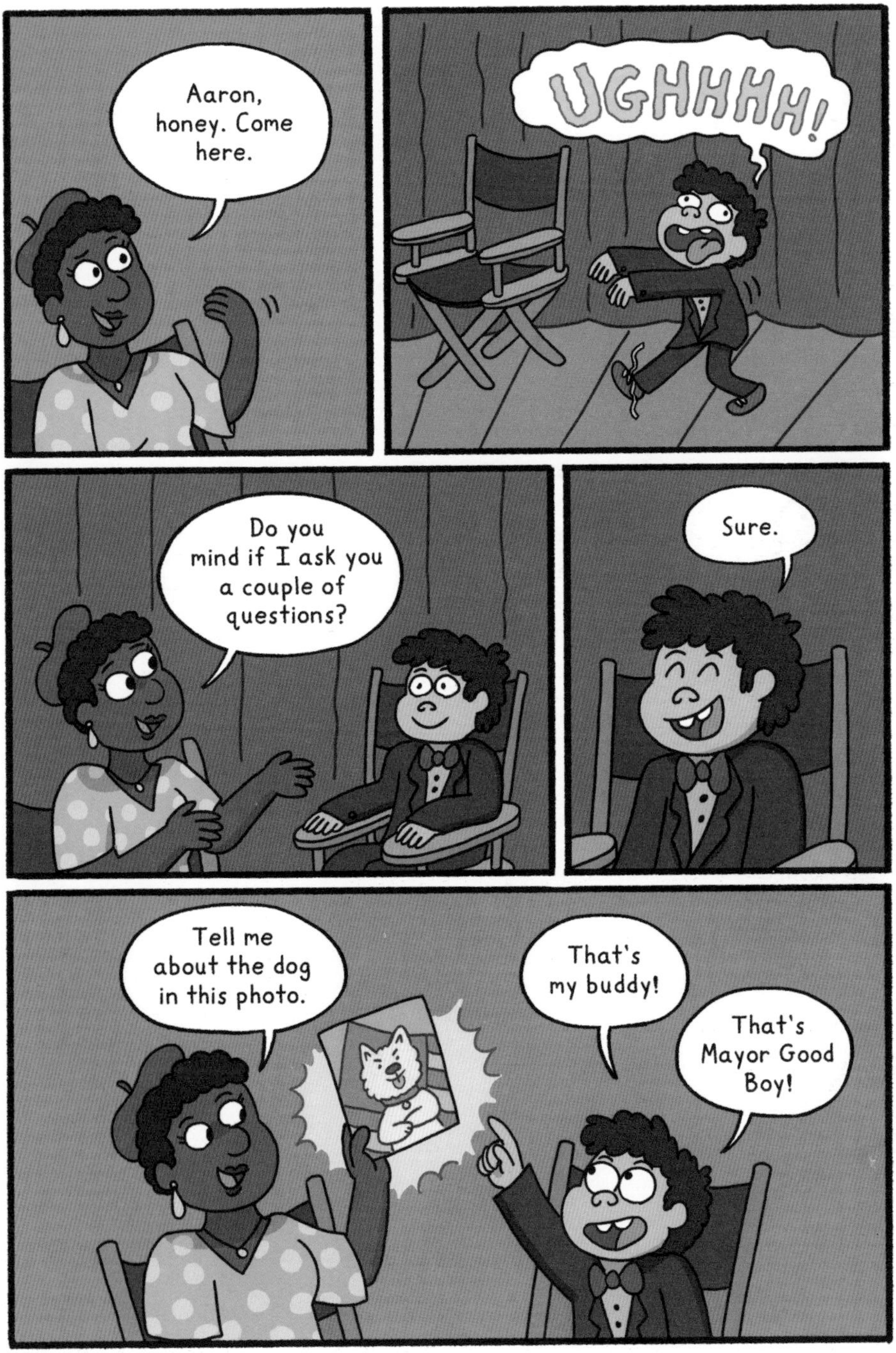
Aaron, honey. Come here.
UGHHHH!
Do you mind if I ask you a couple of questions?
Sure.
Tell me about the dog in this photo.
That's my buddy!
That's Mayor Good Boy!

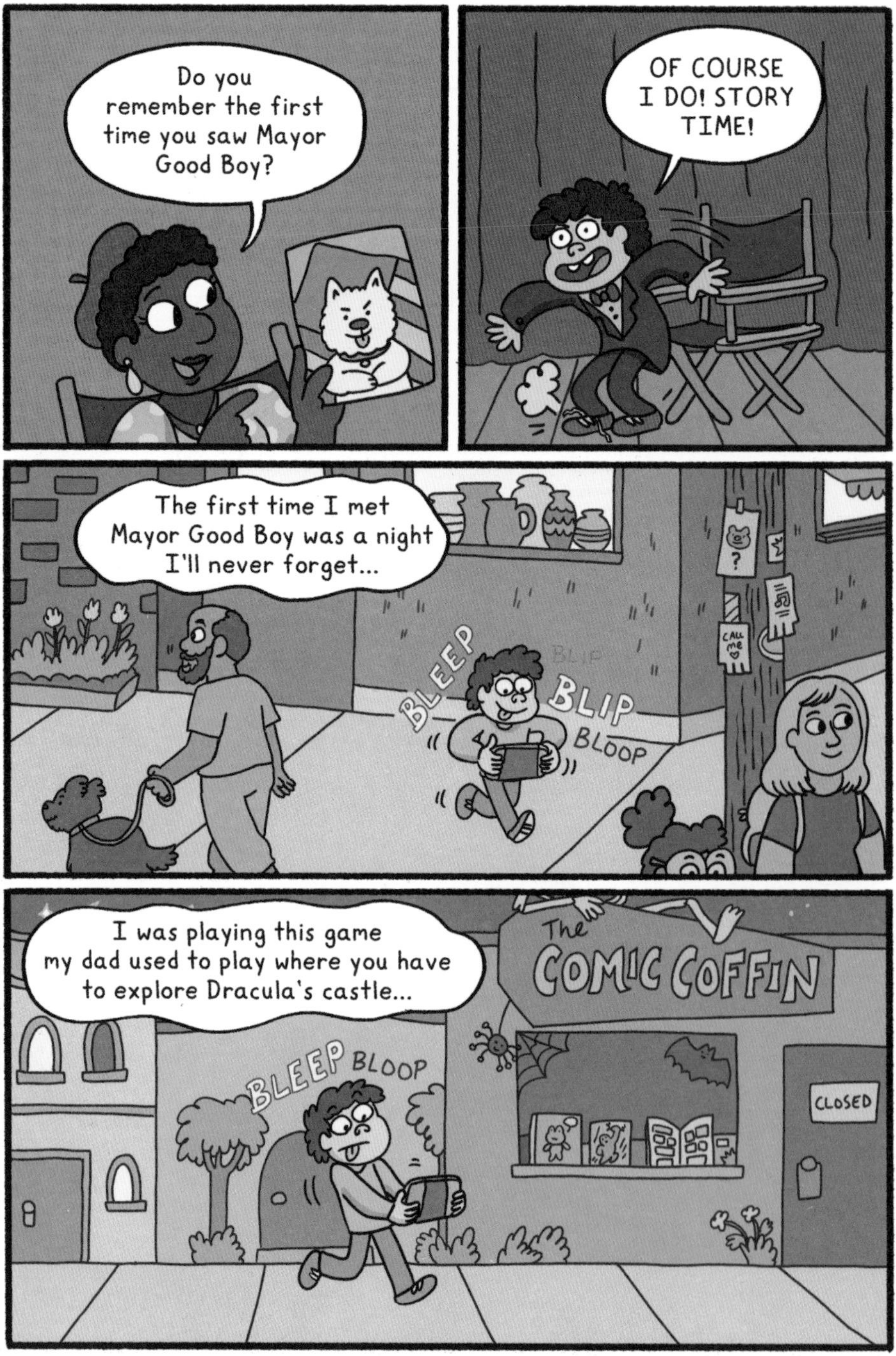
Do you remember the first time you saw Mayor Good Boy?
OF COURSE I DO! STORY TIME!
The first time I met Mayor Good Boy was a night I'll never forget...
BLEEP
BLIP
BLIP
BLOOP
CALL me
I was playing this game my dad used to play where you have to explore Dracula's castle...
The COMIC COFFIN
BLEEP BLOOP
CLOSED

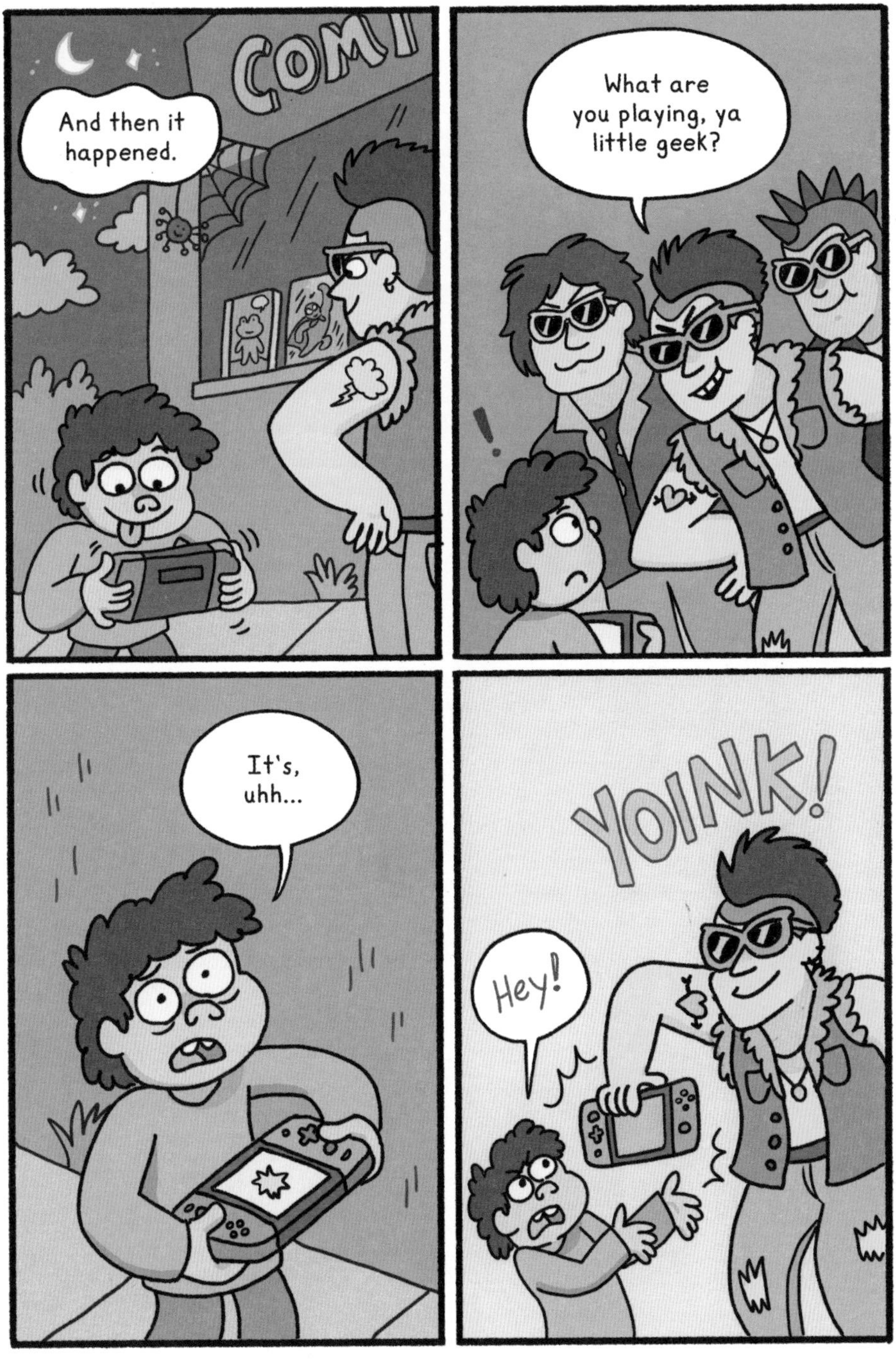
COMI
And then it happened.
What are you playing, ya little geek?
!
It's, uhh...
YOINK!
Hey!

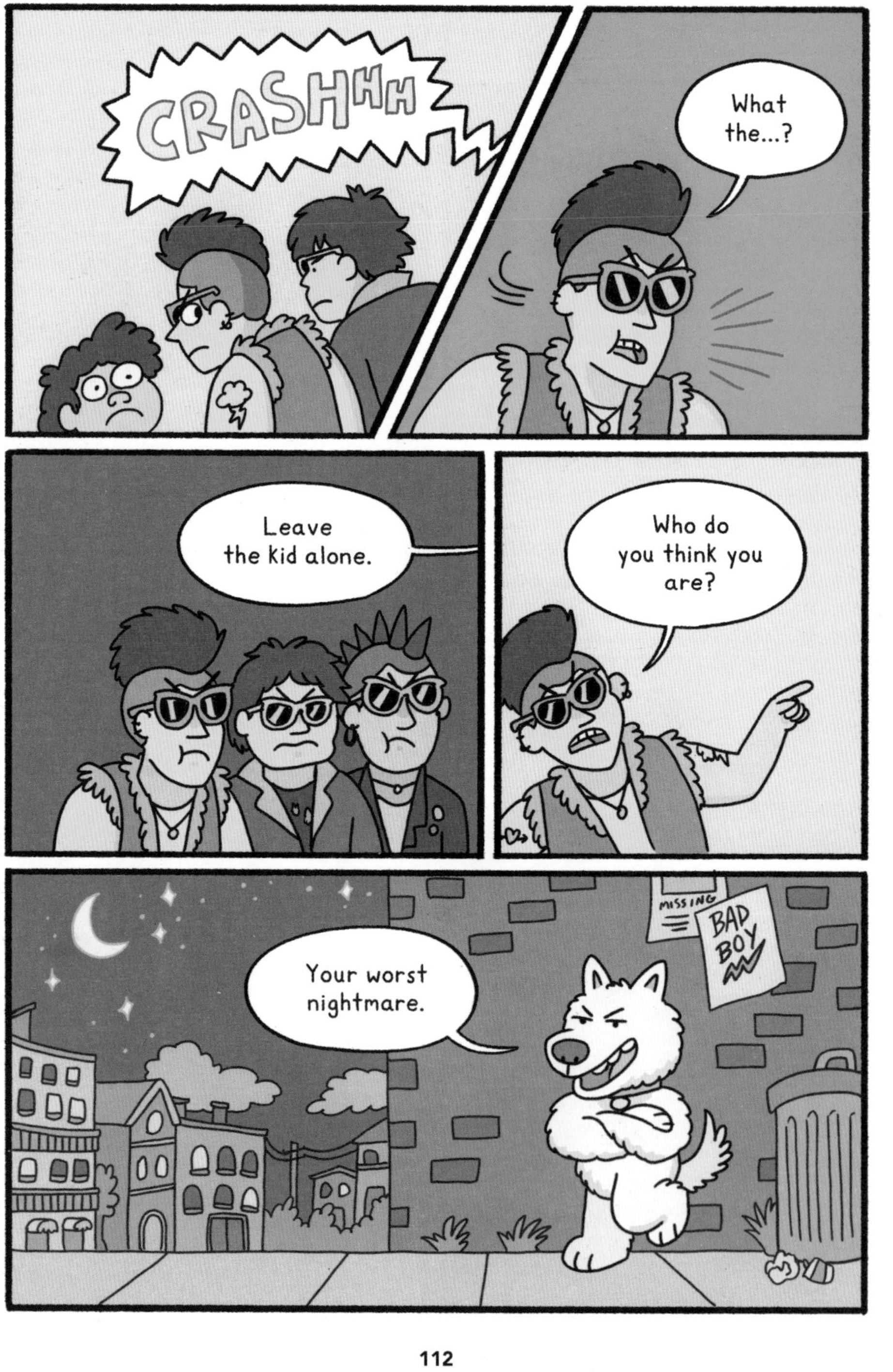
CRASHHH
What the...?
Leave the kid alone.
Who do you think you are?
MISSING
BAD BOY
Your worst nightmare.

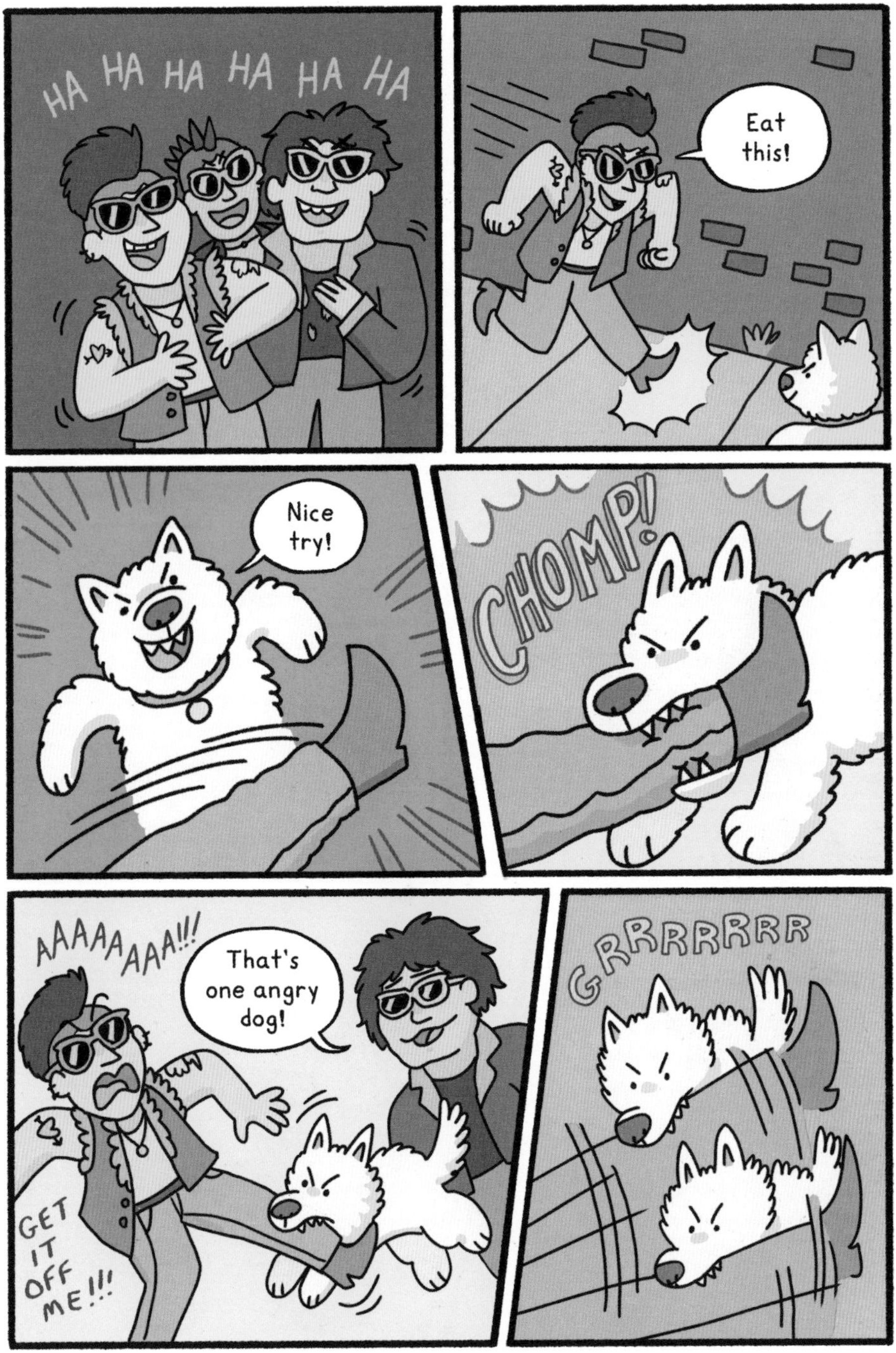
HA HA HA HA HA HA
Eat this!
Nice try!
CHOMP!
AAAAAAAA!!!
That's one angry dog!
GET IT OFF ME!!!
GRRRRRRR

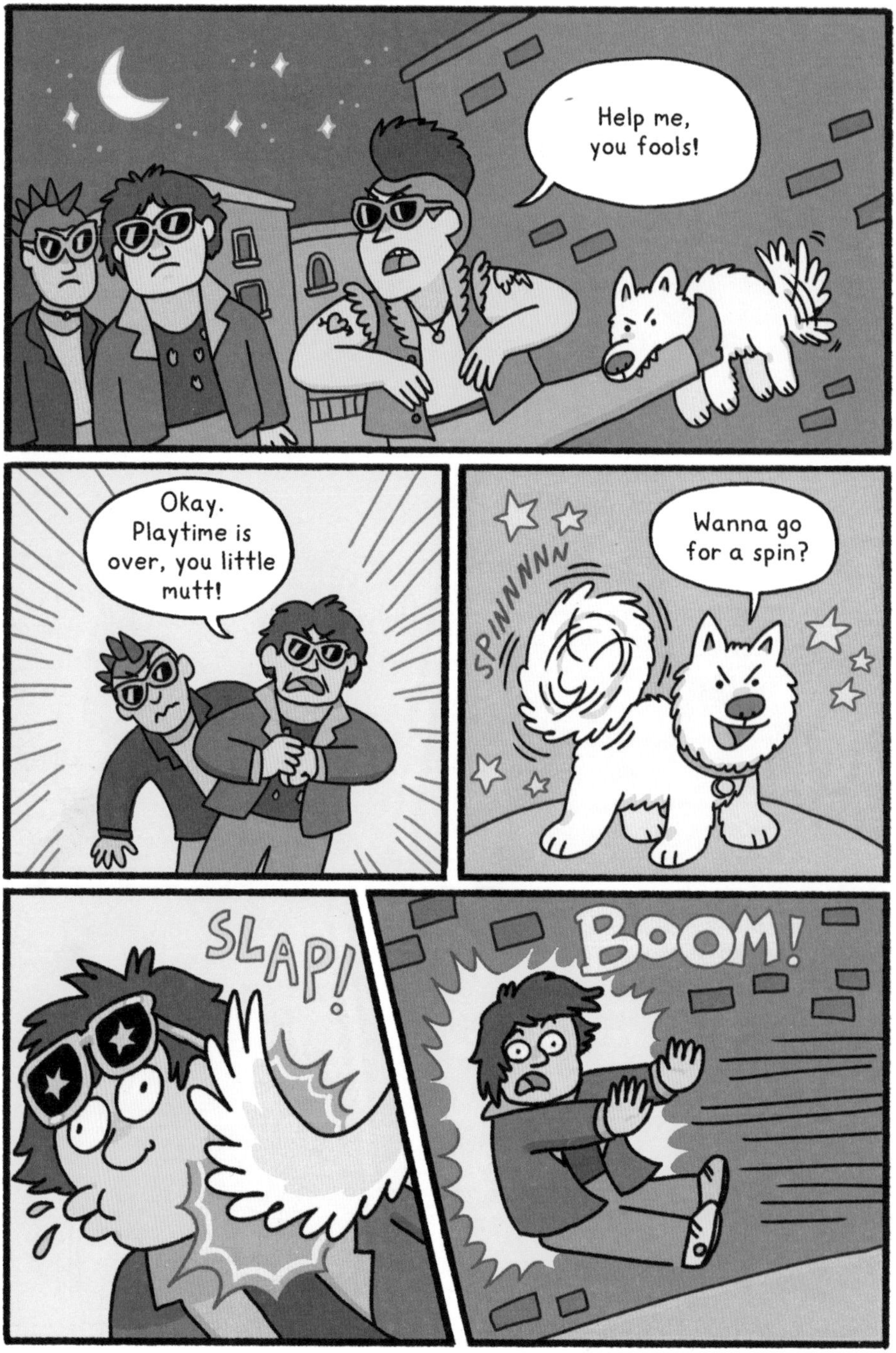
Help me, you fools!
Okay. Playtime is over, you little mutt!
SPINNNNN
Wanna go for a spin?
SLAP!
BOOM!

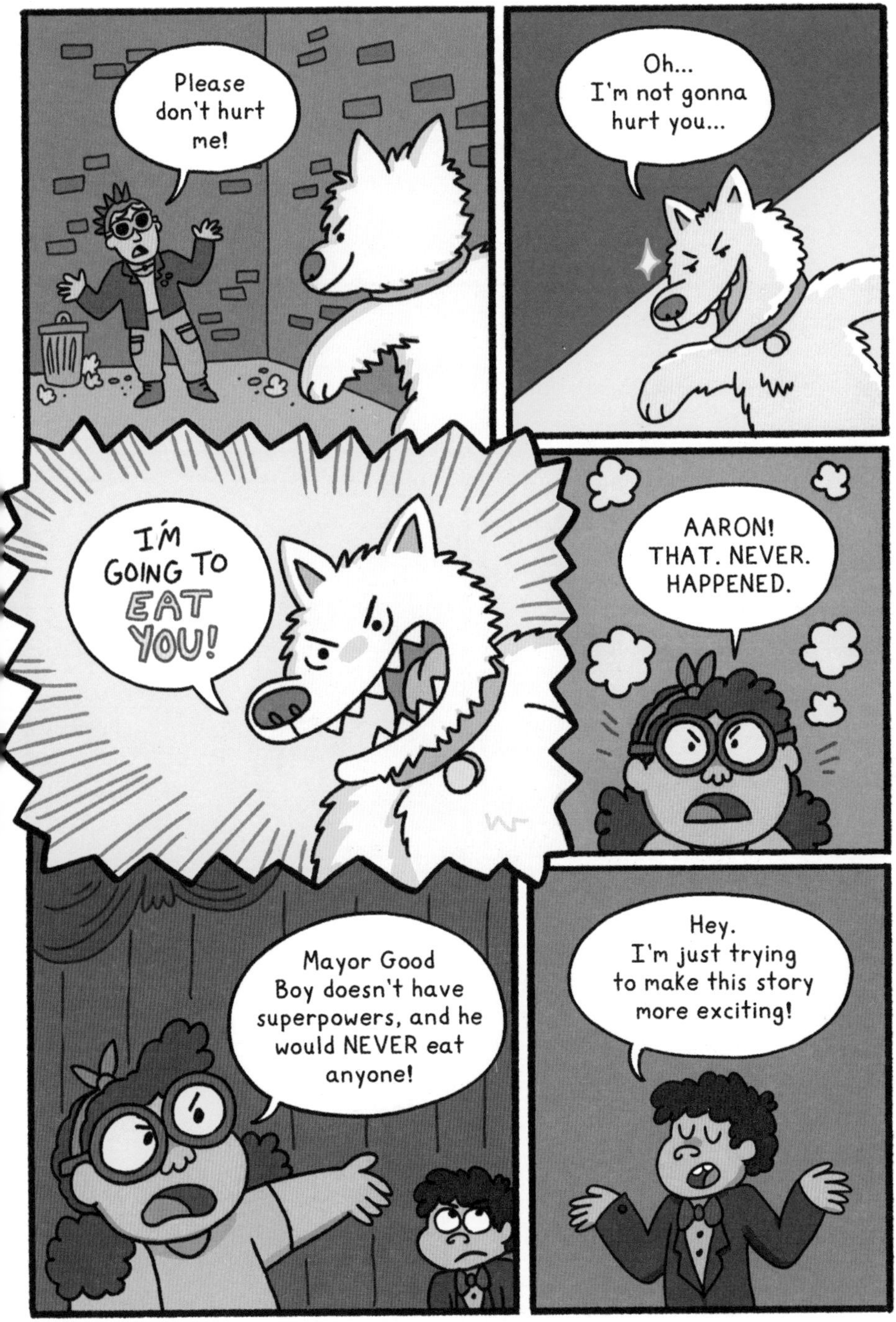
Please don't hurt me!
Oh... I'm not gonna hurt you...
I'M GOING TO EAT YOU!
AARON! THAT. NEVER. HAPPENED.
Mayor Good Boy doesn't have superpowers, and he would NEVER eat anyone!
Hey. I'm just trying to make this story more exciting!

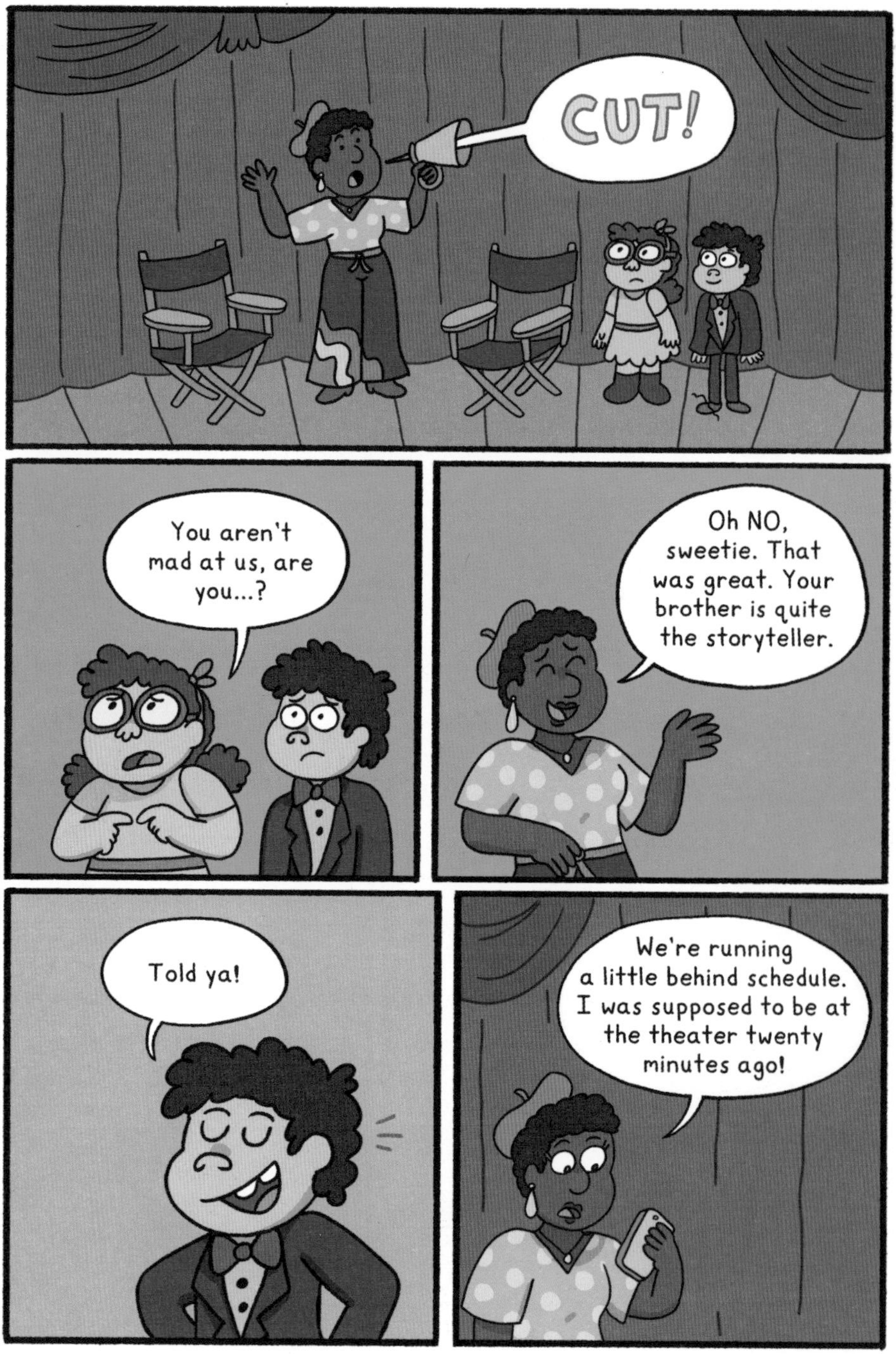
CUT!
You aren't mad at us, are you...?
Oh NO, sweetie. That was great. Your brother is quite the storyteller.
Told ya!
We're running a little behind schedule. I was supposed to be at the theater twenty minutes ago!

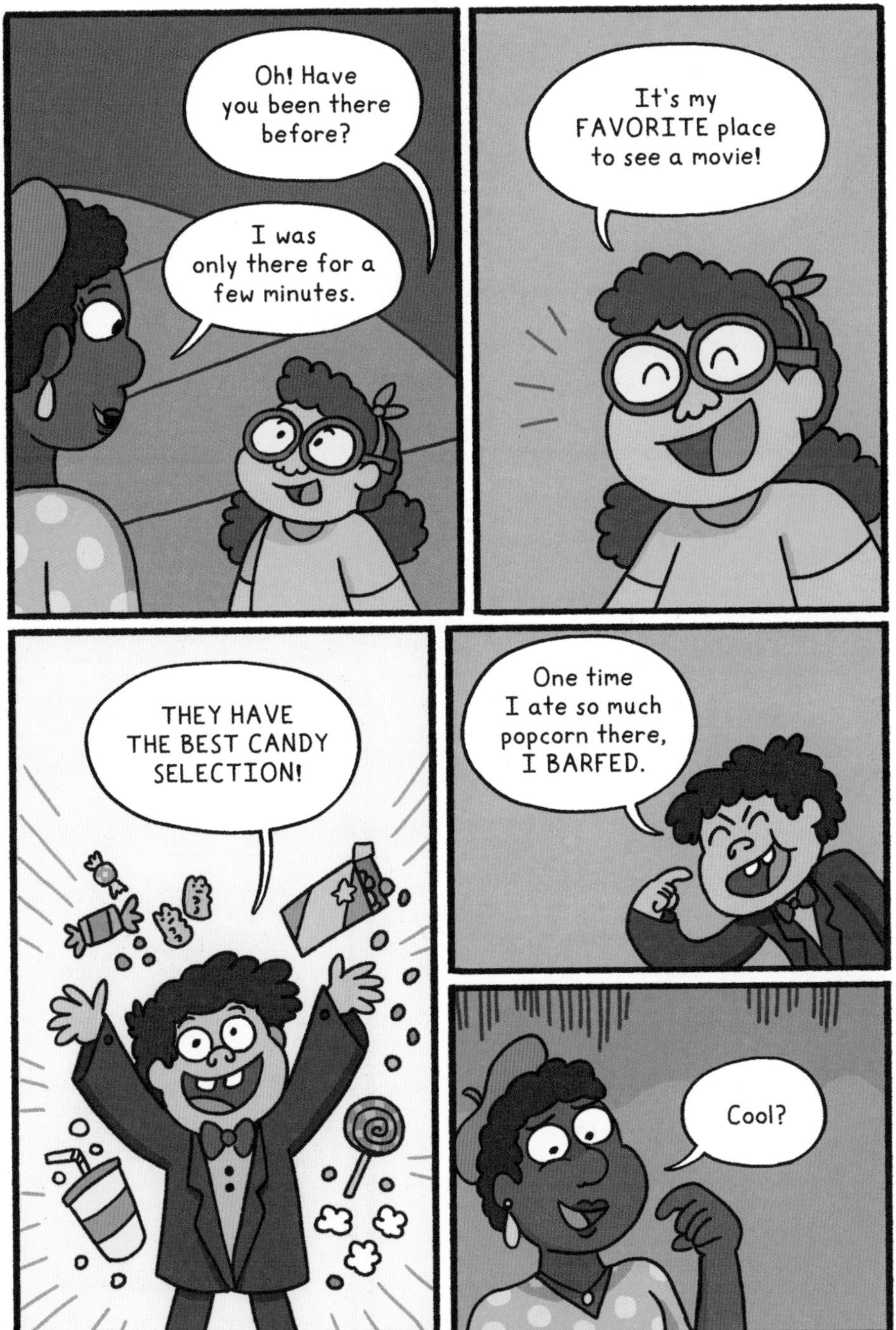
Oh! Have you been there before?
I was only there for a few minutes.
It's my FAVORITE place to see a movie!
THEY HAVE THE BEST CANDY SELECTION!
One time I ate so much popcorn there, I BARFED.
Cool?

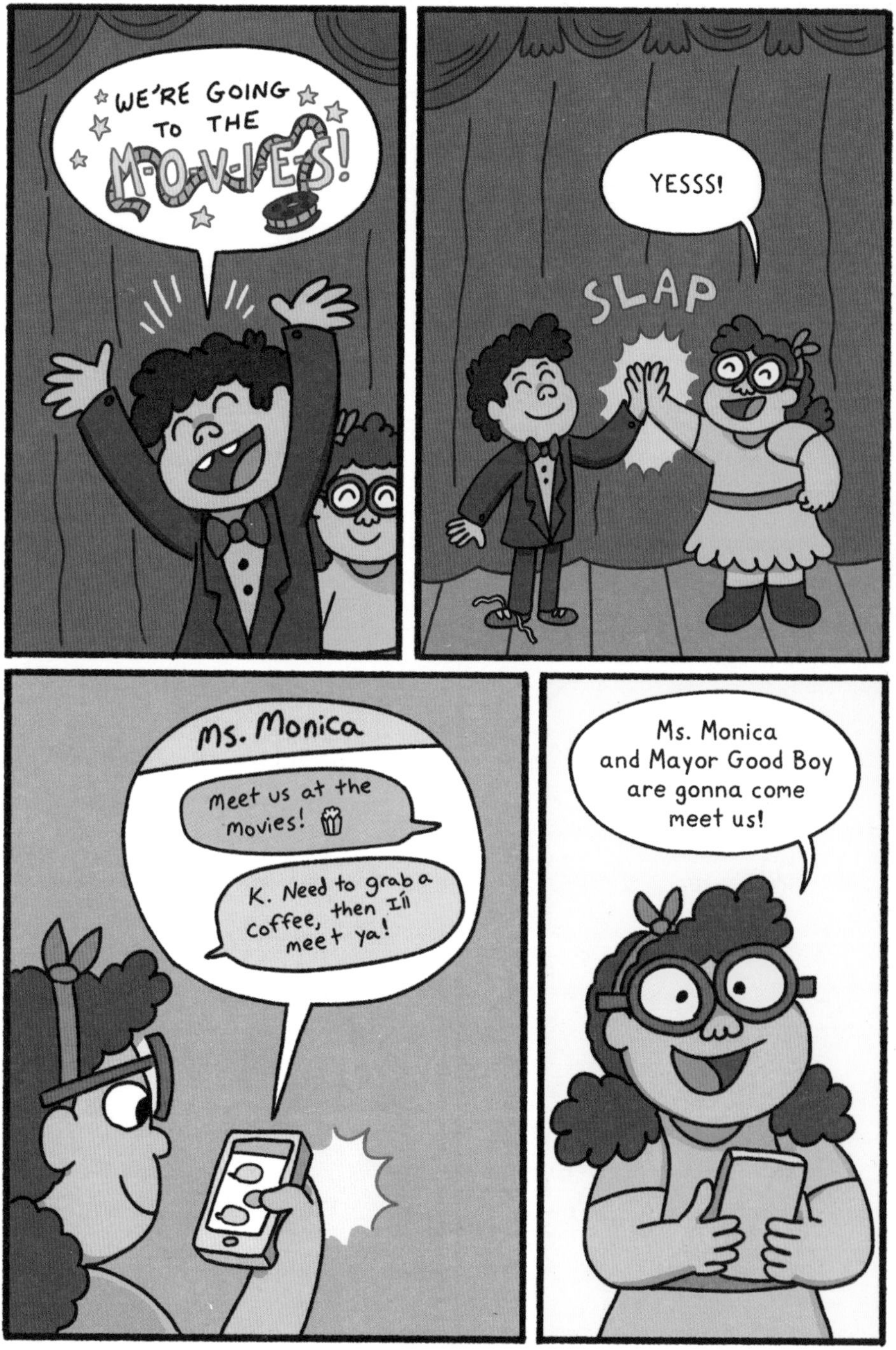
WE'RE GOING TO THE M-O-V-I-E-S!
YESSS!
SLAP
Ms. Monica
meet us at the movies!
K. Need to grab a coffee, then I'll meet ya!
Ms. Monica and Mayor Good Boy are gonna come meet us!

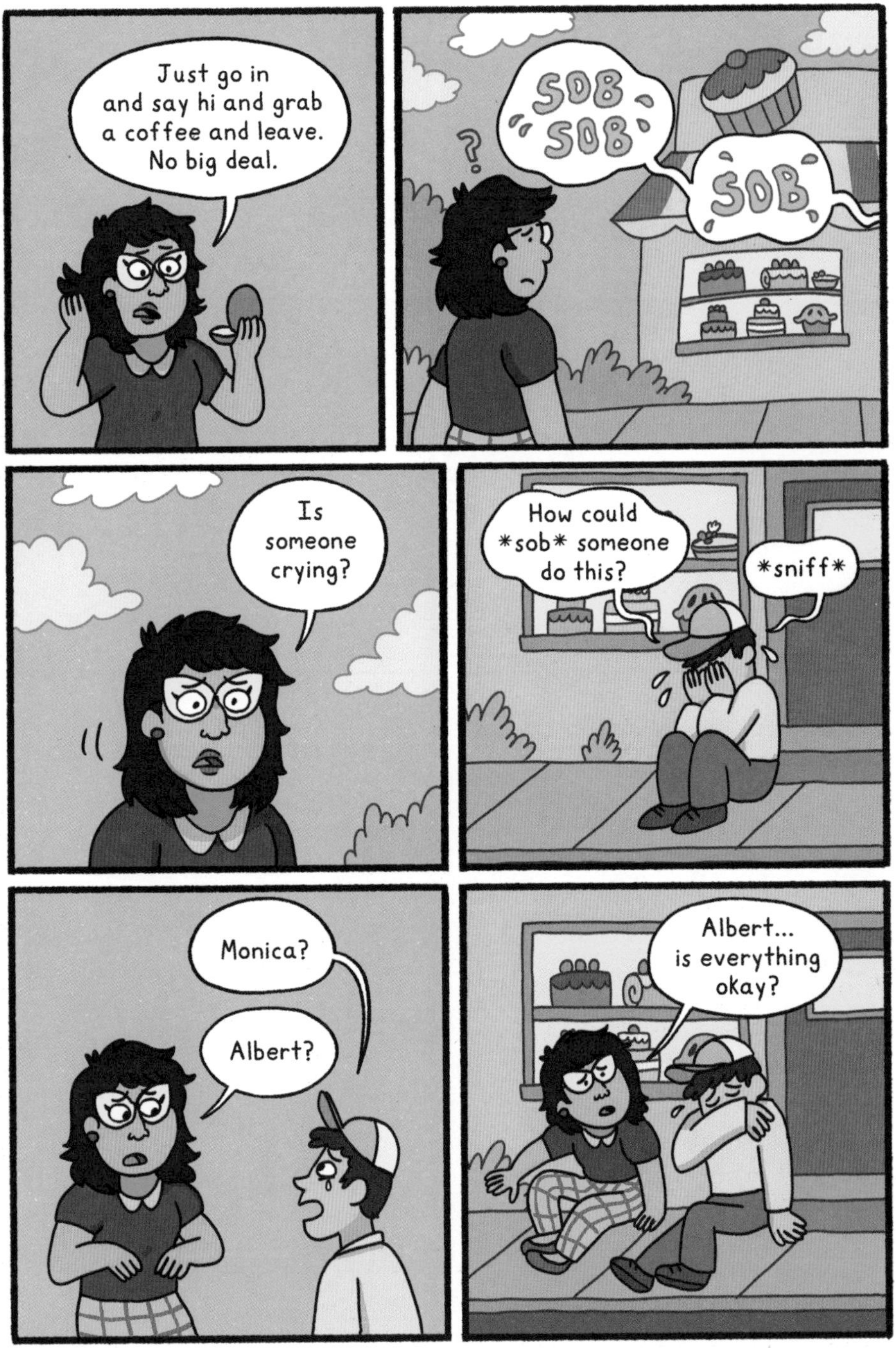
Just go in and say hi and grab a coffee and leave. No big deal.
SOB SOB
SOB
?
Is someone crying?
How could *sob* someone do this?
sniff
Monica?
Albert?
Albert... is everything okay?

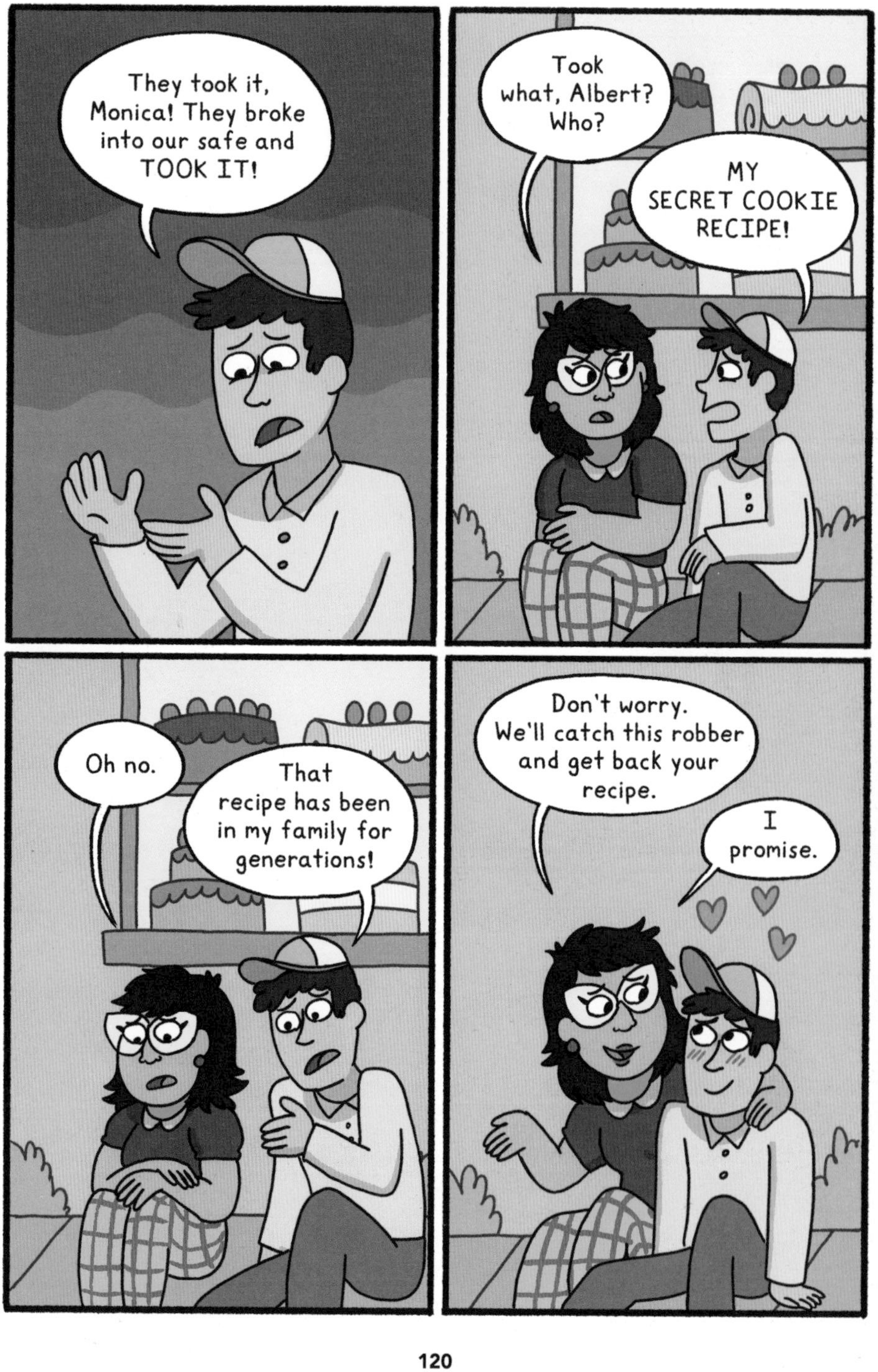
They took it, Monica! They broke into our safe and TOOK IT!
Took what, Albert? Who?
MY SECRET COOKIE RECIPE!
Oh no.
That recipe has been in my family for generations!
Don't worry. We'll catch this robber and get back your recipe.
I promise.

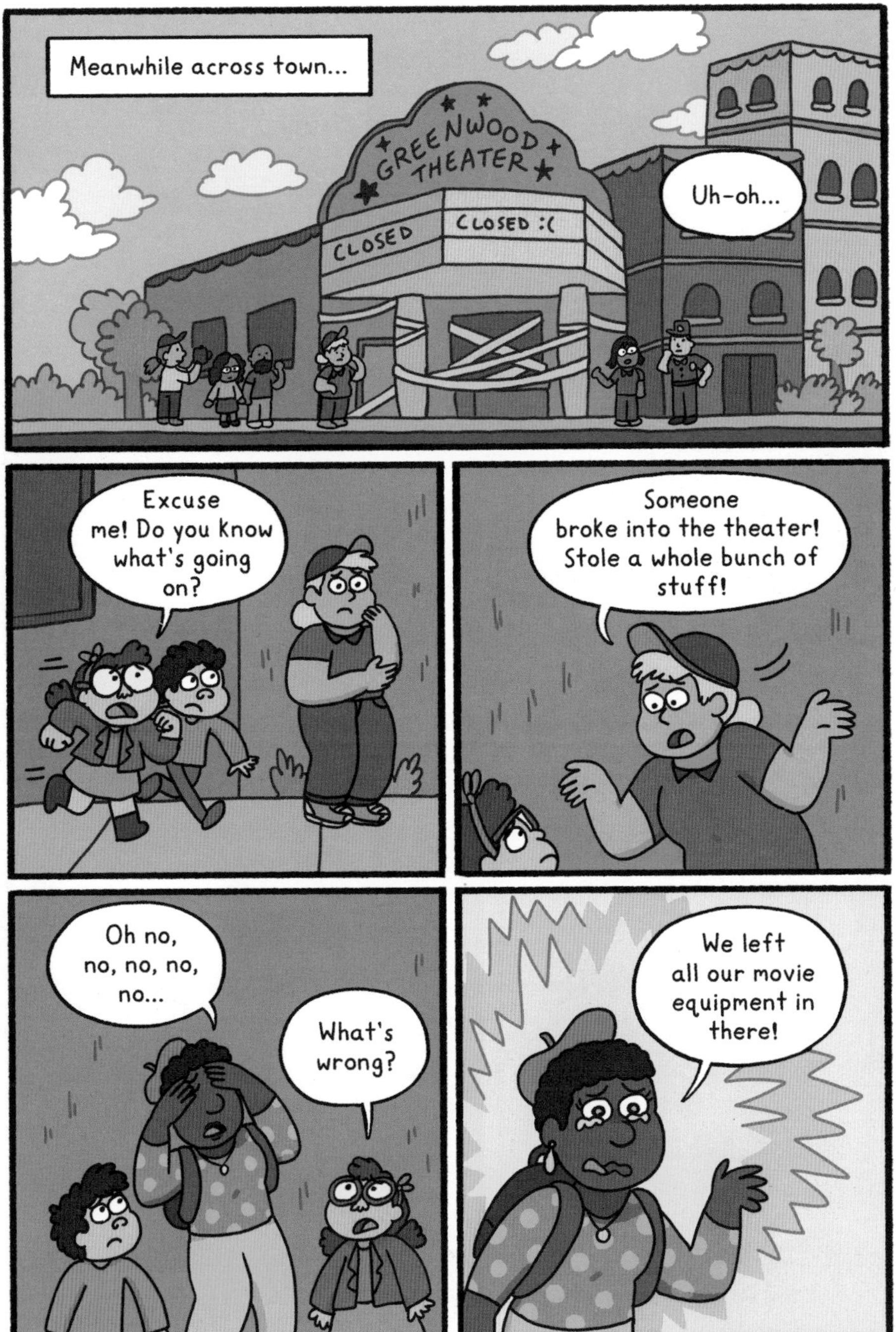

Meanwhile across town...
GREENWOOD THEATER
CLOSED
CLOSED :(
Uh-oh...
Excuse me! Do you know what's going on?
Someone broke into the theater! Stole a whole bunch of stuff!
Oh no, no, no, no, no...
What's wrong?
We left all our movie equipment in there!

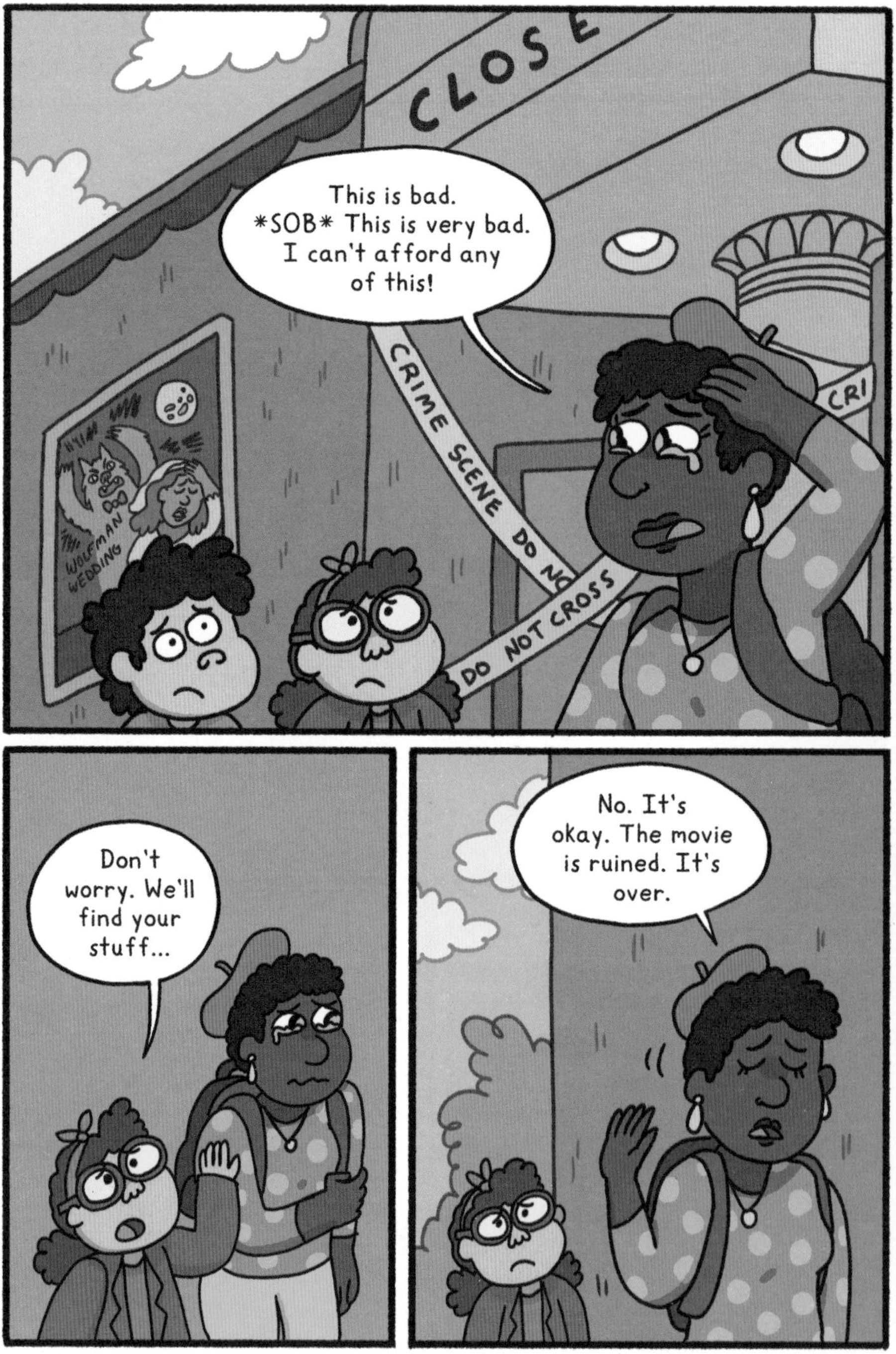
CLOSE
This is bad. *SOB* This is very bad. I can't afford any of this!
CRIME SCENE DO NO
DO NOT CROSS
CRI
WOLFMAN WEDDING
Don't worry. We'll find your stuff...
No. It's okay. The movie is ruined. It's over.

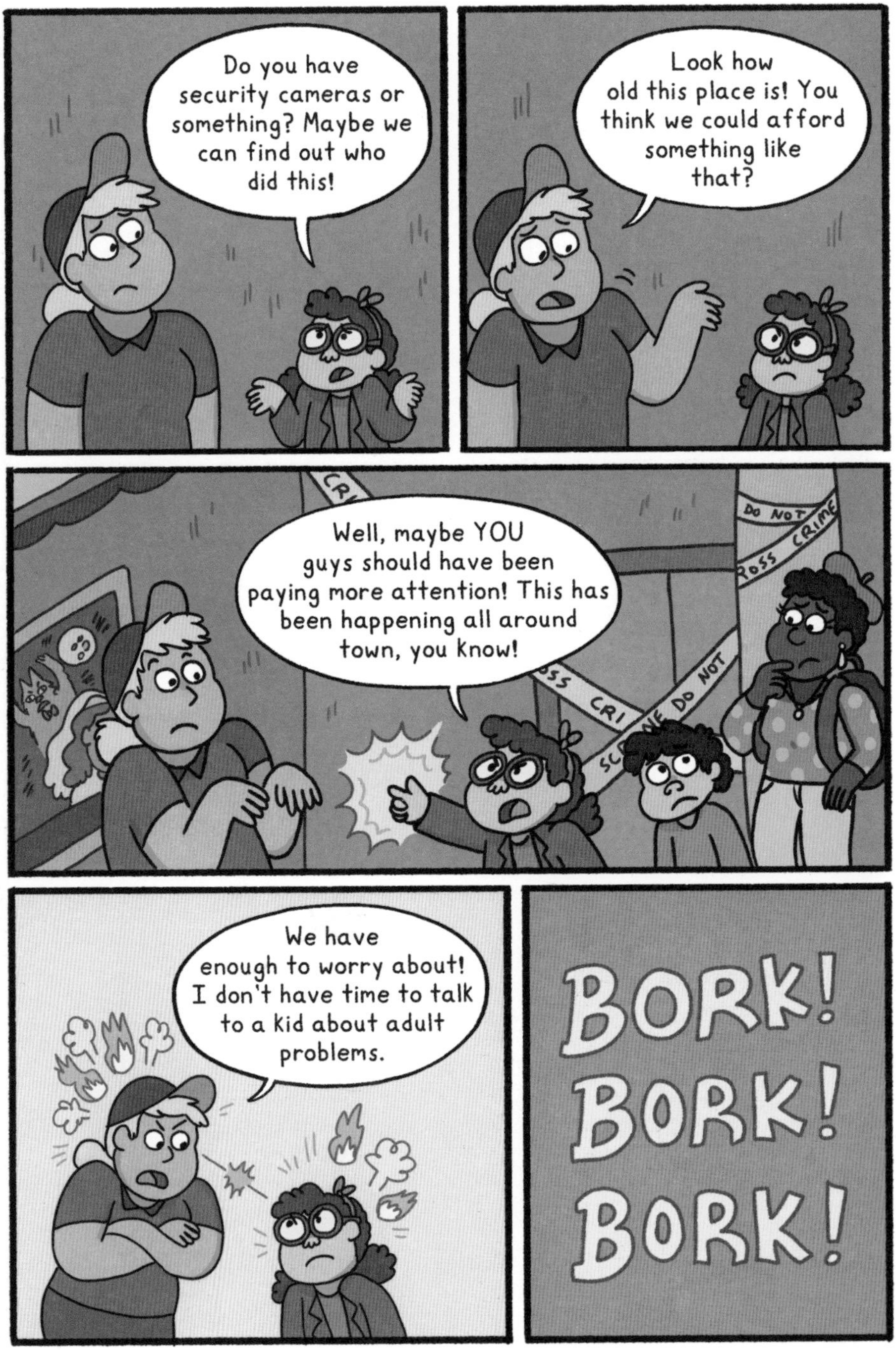
Do you have security cameras or something? Maybe we can find out who did this!
Look how old this place is! You think we could afford something like that?
Well, maybe YOU guys should have been paying more attention! This has been happening all around town, you know!
We have enough to worry about! I don't have time to talk to a kid about adult problems.
BORK! BORK! BORK!

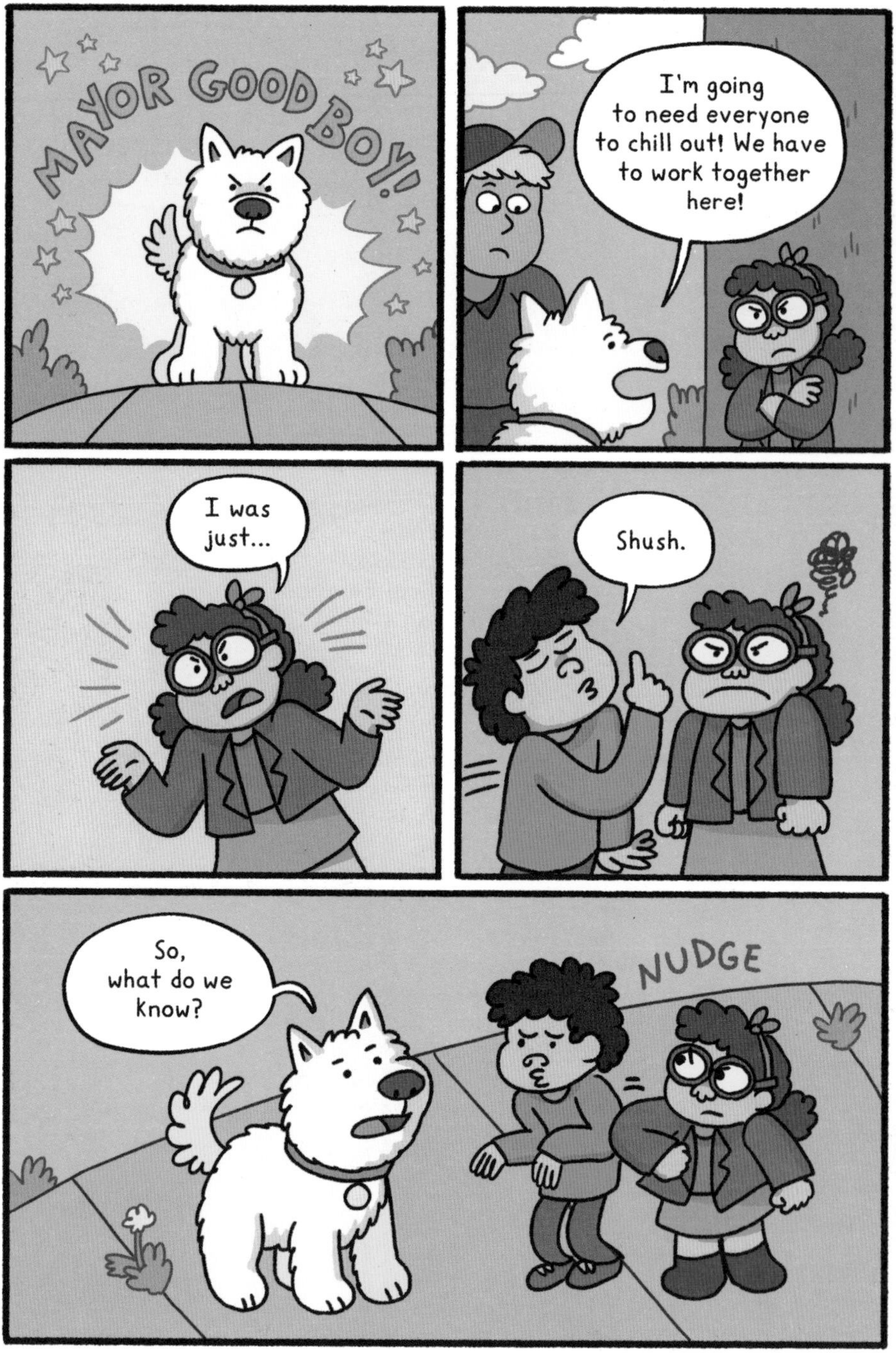

MAYOR GOOD BOY!!
I'm going to need everyone to chill out! We have to work together here!
I was just...
Shush.
So, what do we know?
NUDGE

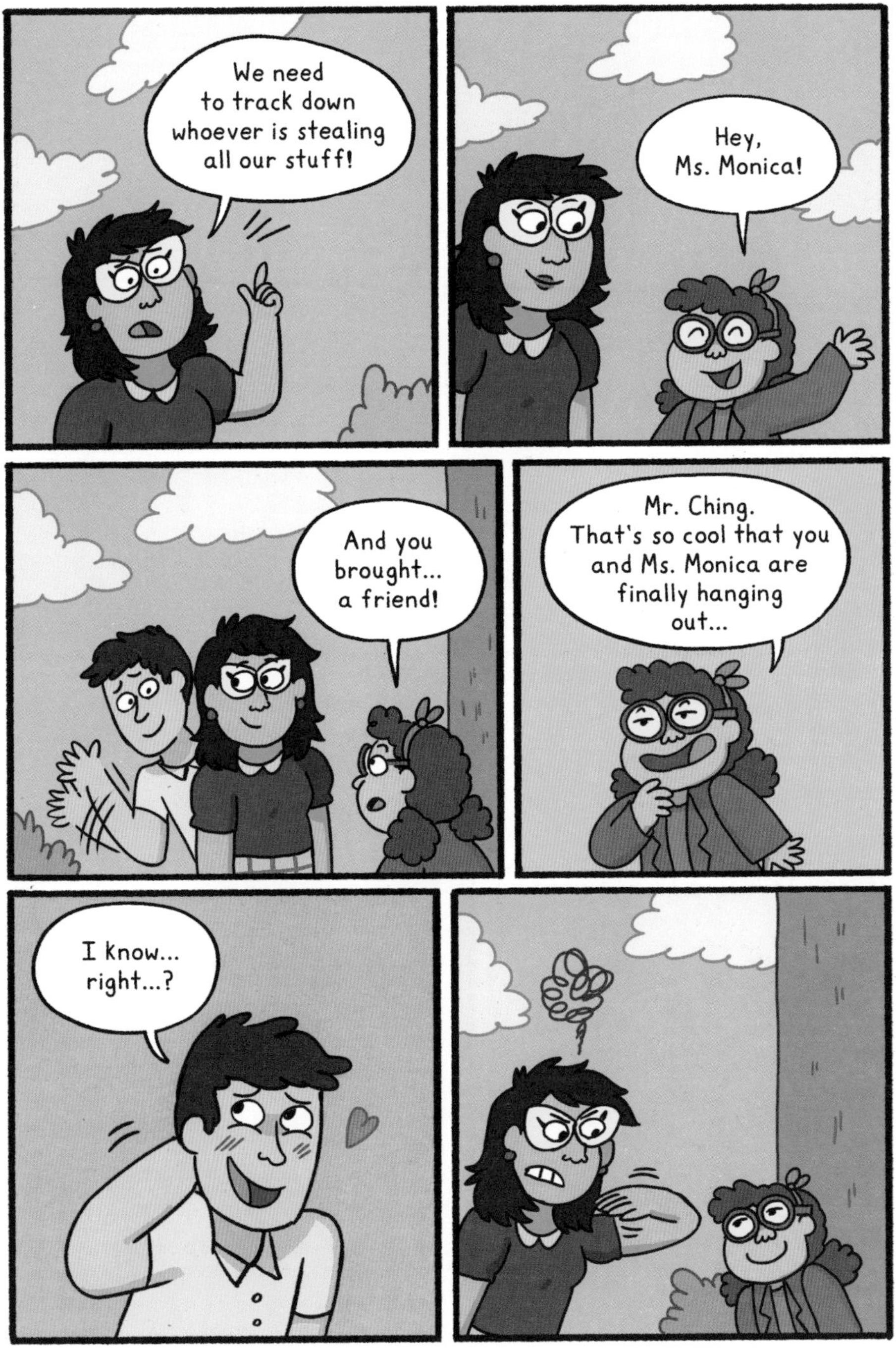
We need to track down whoever is stealing all our stuff!
Hey, Ms. Monica!
And you brought... a friend!
Mr. Ching. That's so cool that you and Ms. Monica are finally hanging out...
I know... right...?

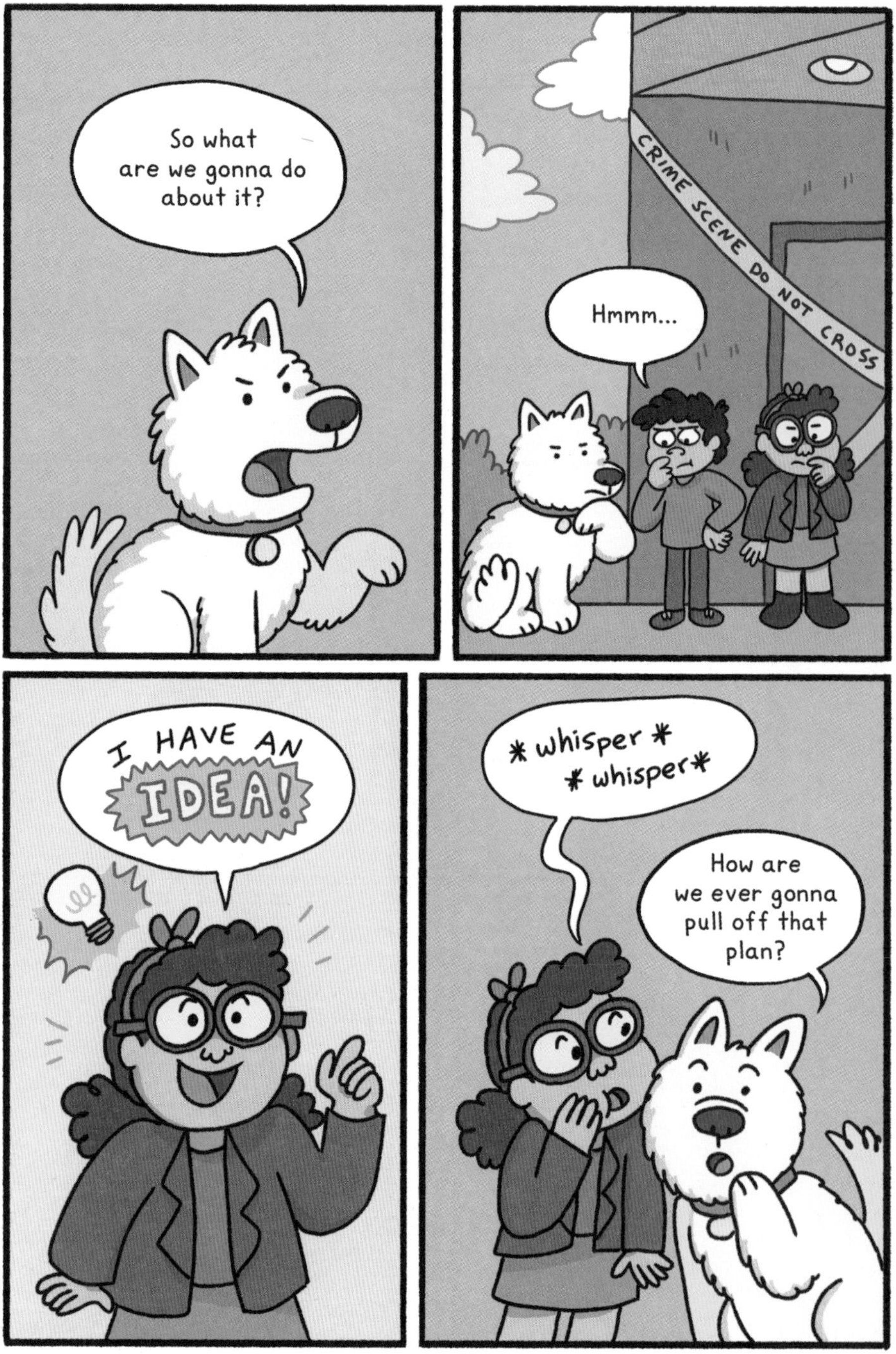
So what are we gonna do about it?
CRIME SCENE DO NOT CROSS
Hmmm...
I HAVE AN IDEA!
whisper *whisper*
How are we ever gonna pull off that plan?

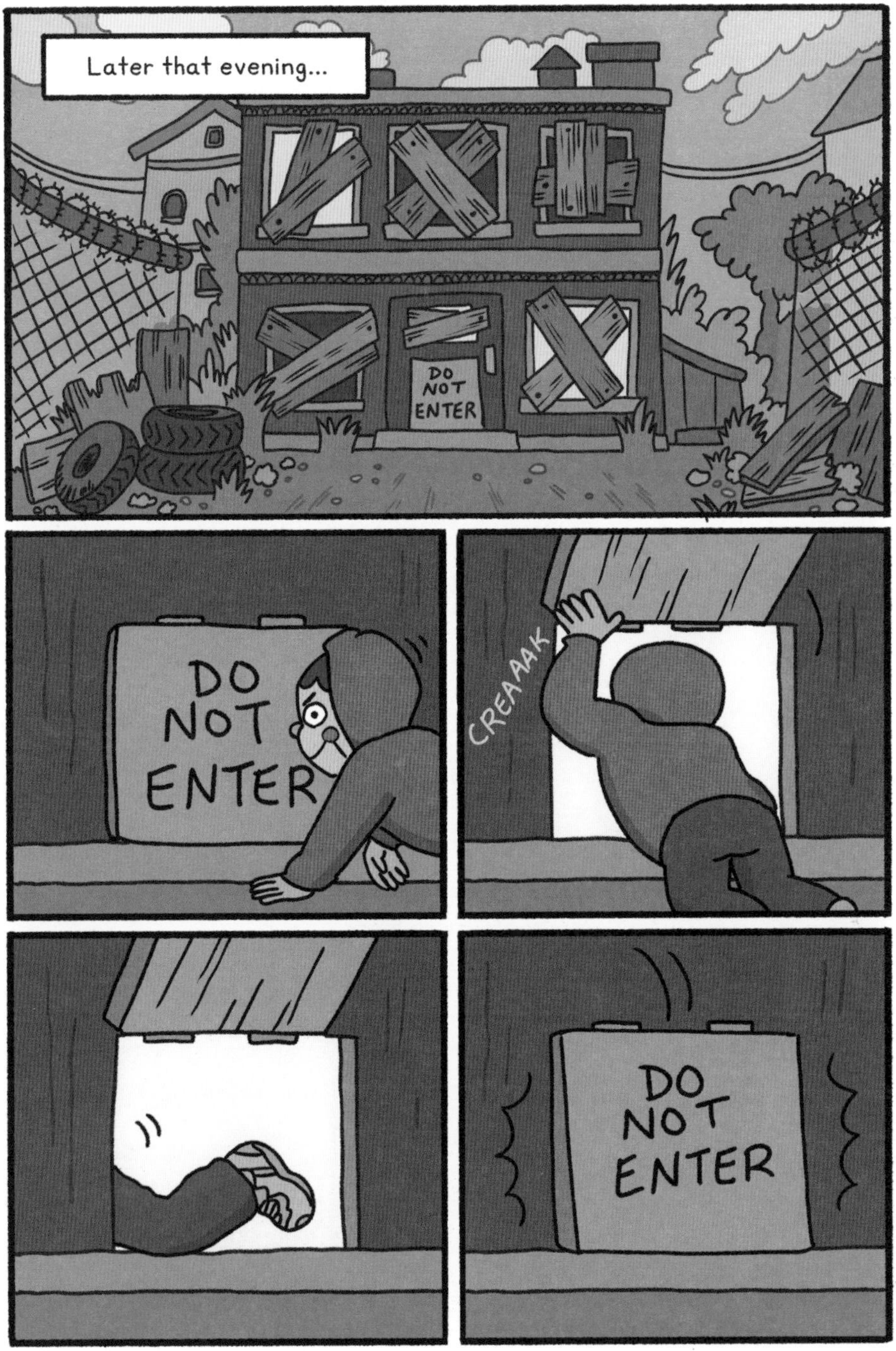
Later that evening...
DO NOT ENTER
DO NOT ENTER
CREAAAK
DO NOT ENTER

DON'T MOVE!

Whoa, whoa! Relax! It's just me!

See?

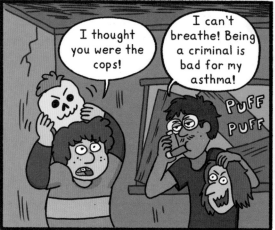

I thought you were the cops!

I can't breathe! Being a criminal is bad for my asthma!

PUFF PUFF

We've stolen enough stuff, right?

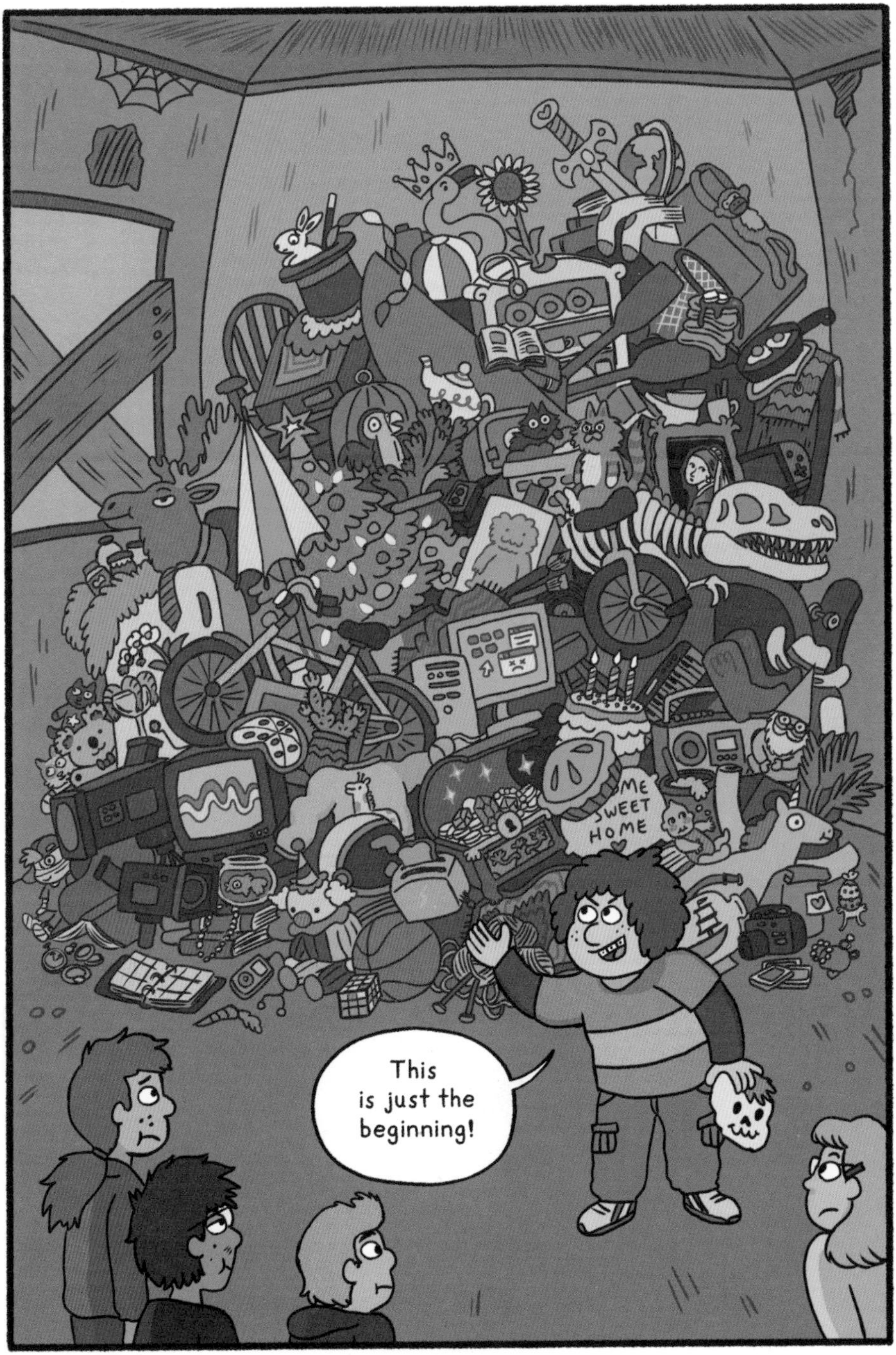
ME
SWEET
HOME
This is just the beginning!

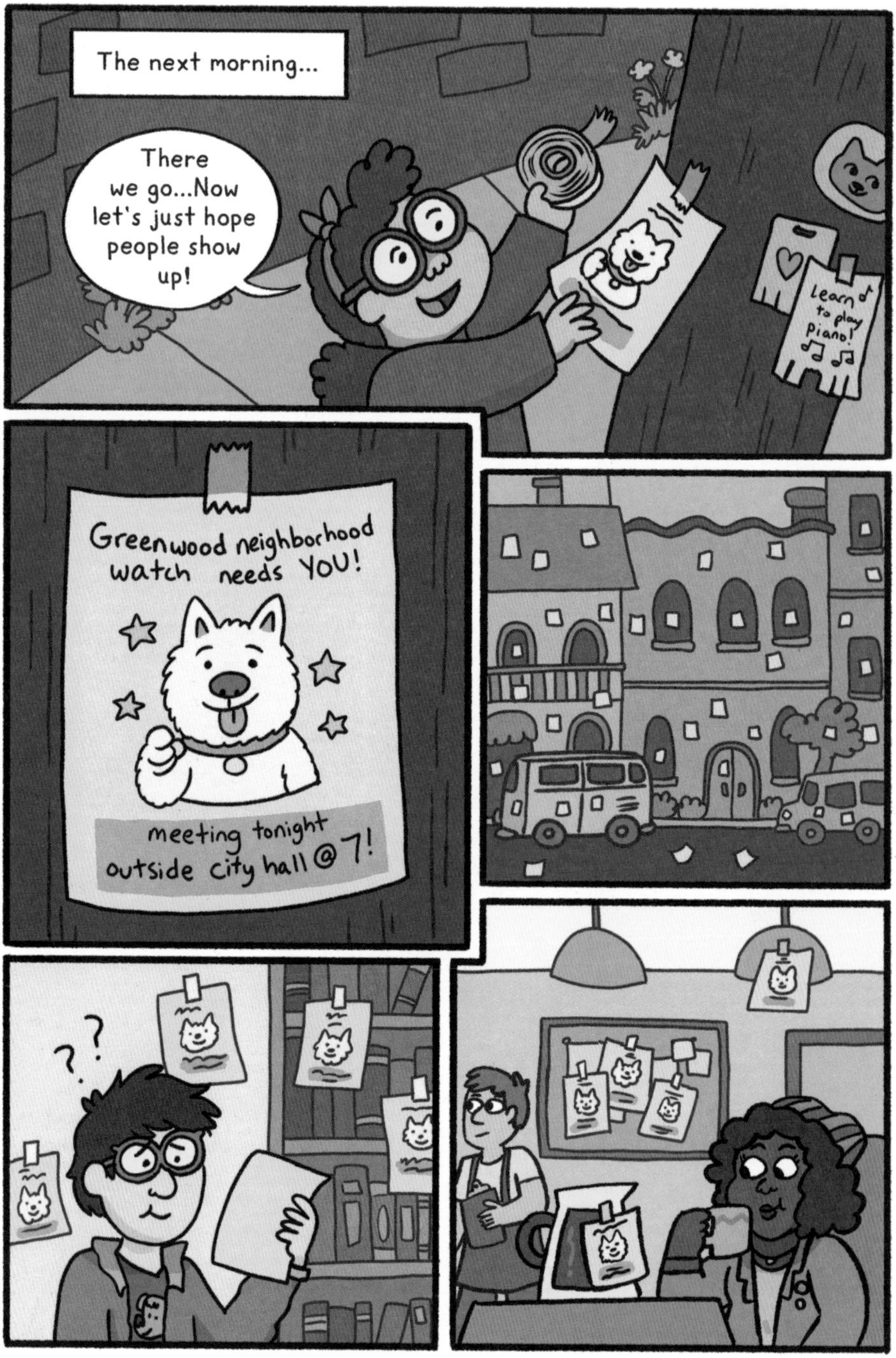
The next morning...
There we go...Now let's just hope people show up!
Learn to play piano!
Greenwood neighborhood watch needs YOU!
meeting tonight outside city hall @ 7!
? ?

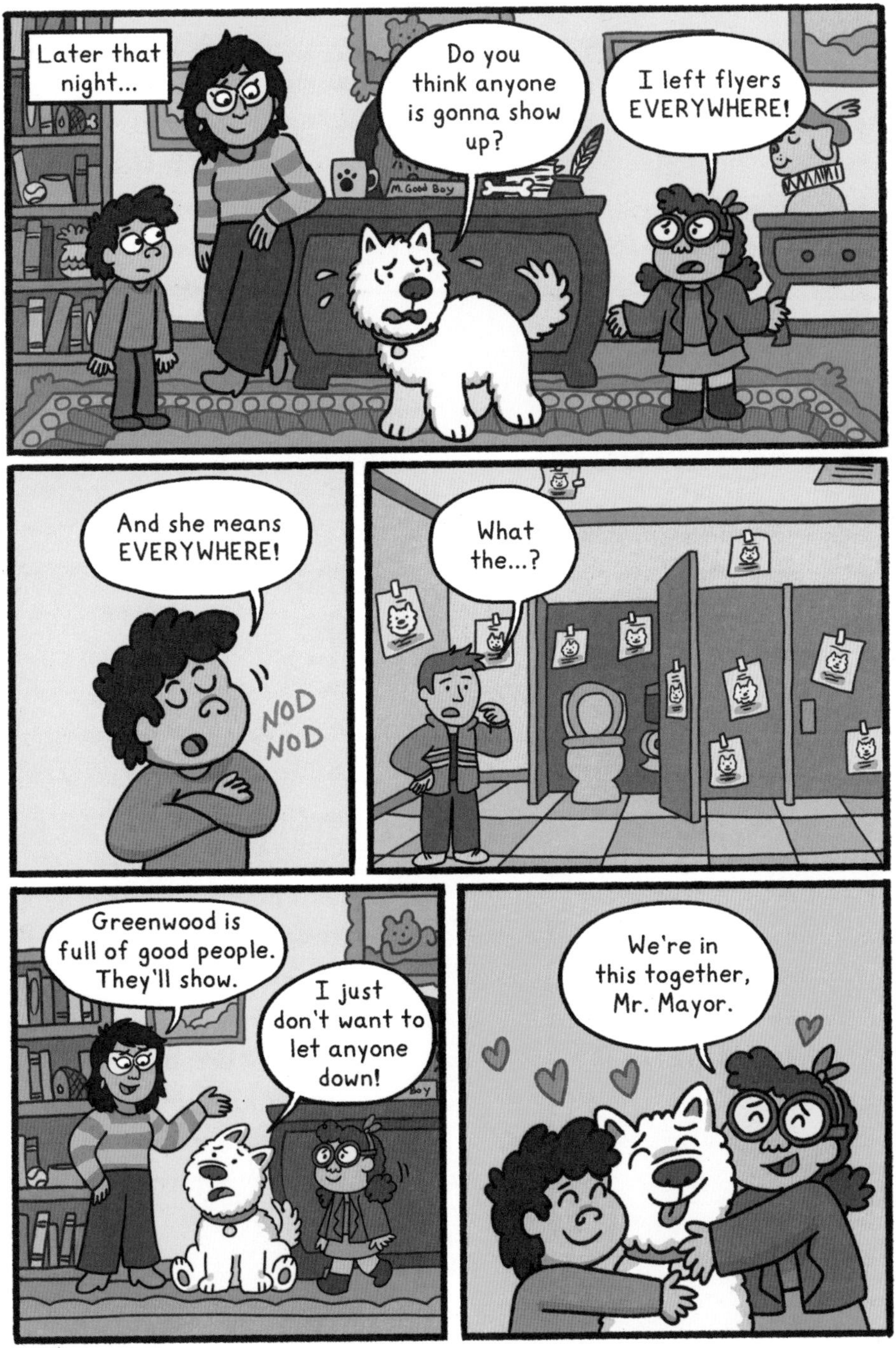
Later that night...
Do you think anyone is gonna show up?
I left flyers EVERYWHERE!
M. Good Boy
And she means EVERYWHERE!
NOD NOD
What the...?
Greenwood is full of good people. They'll show.
I just don't want to let anyone down!
We're in this together, Mr. Mayor.

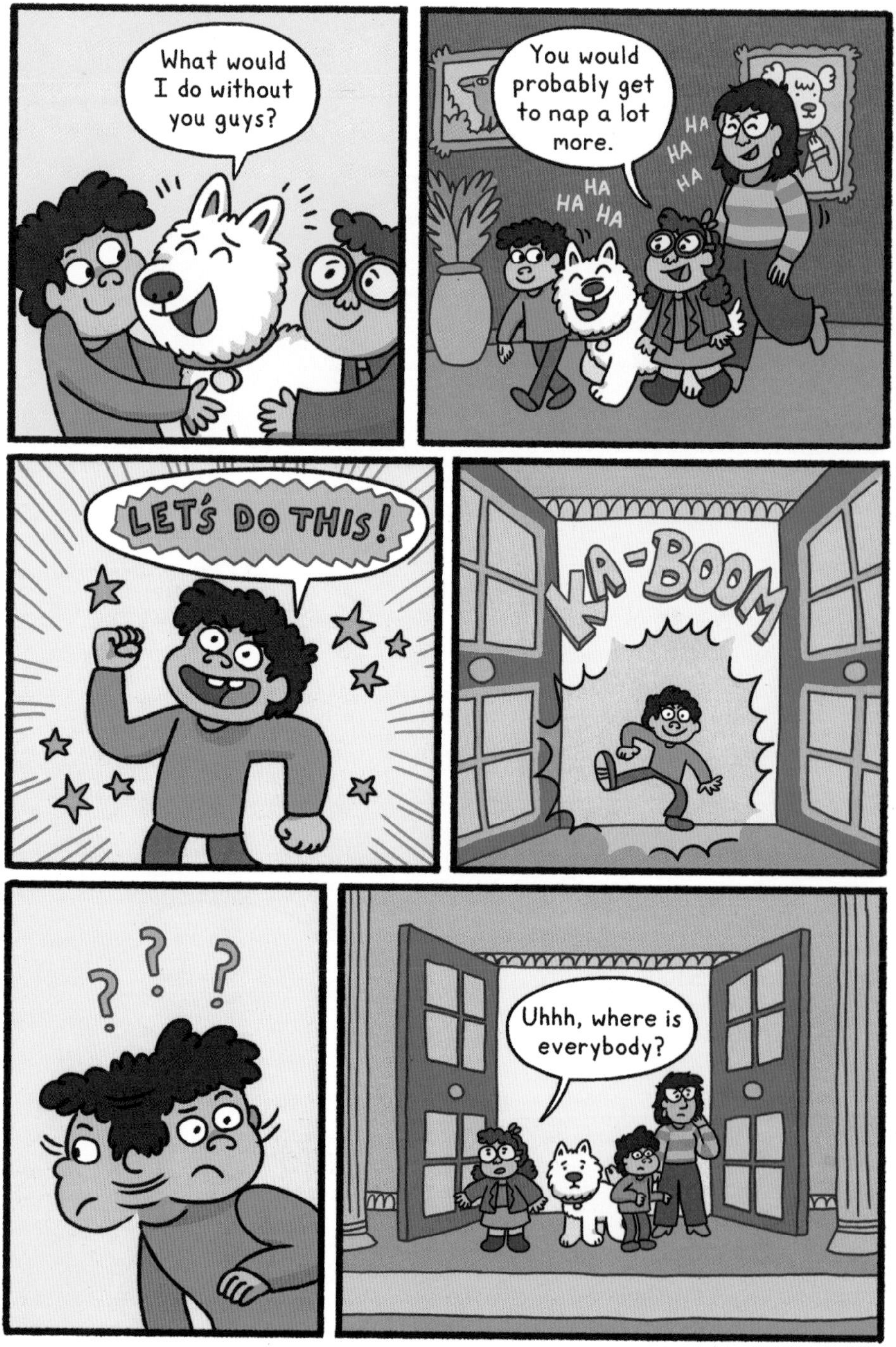
What would I do without you guys?
You would probably get to nap a lot more.
HA HA HA
HA HA HA
LET'S DO THIS!
KA-BOOM
? ? ?
Uhhh, where is everybody?

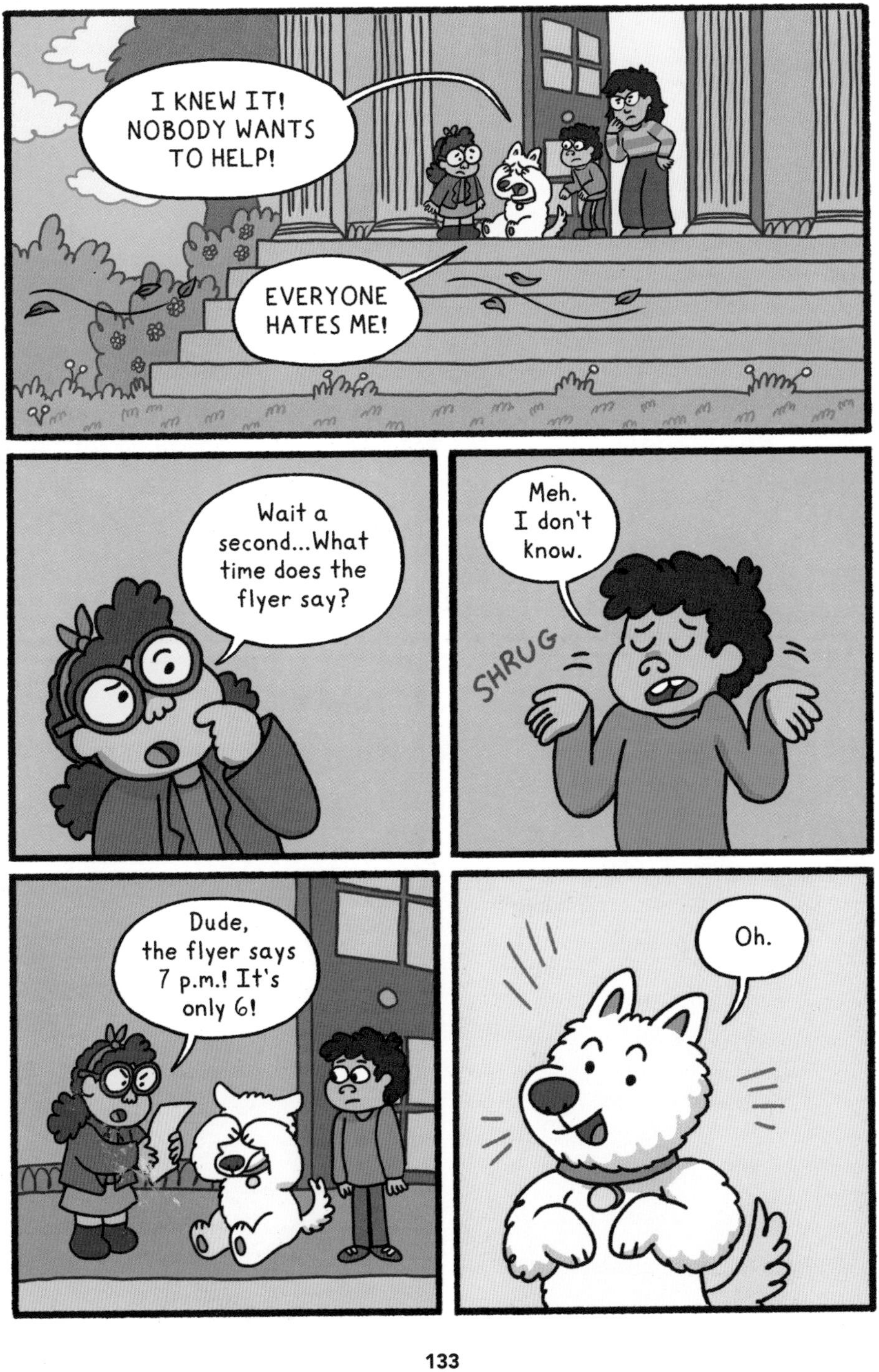
I KNEW IT! NOBODY WANTS TO HELP!
EVERYONE HATES ME!
Wait a second...What time does the flyer say?
Meh. I don't know.
SHRUG
Dude, the flyer says 7 p.m.! It's only 6!
Oh.

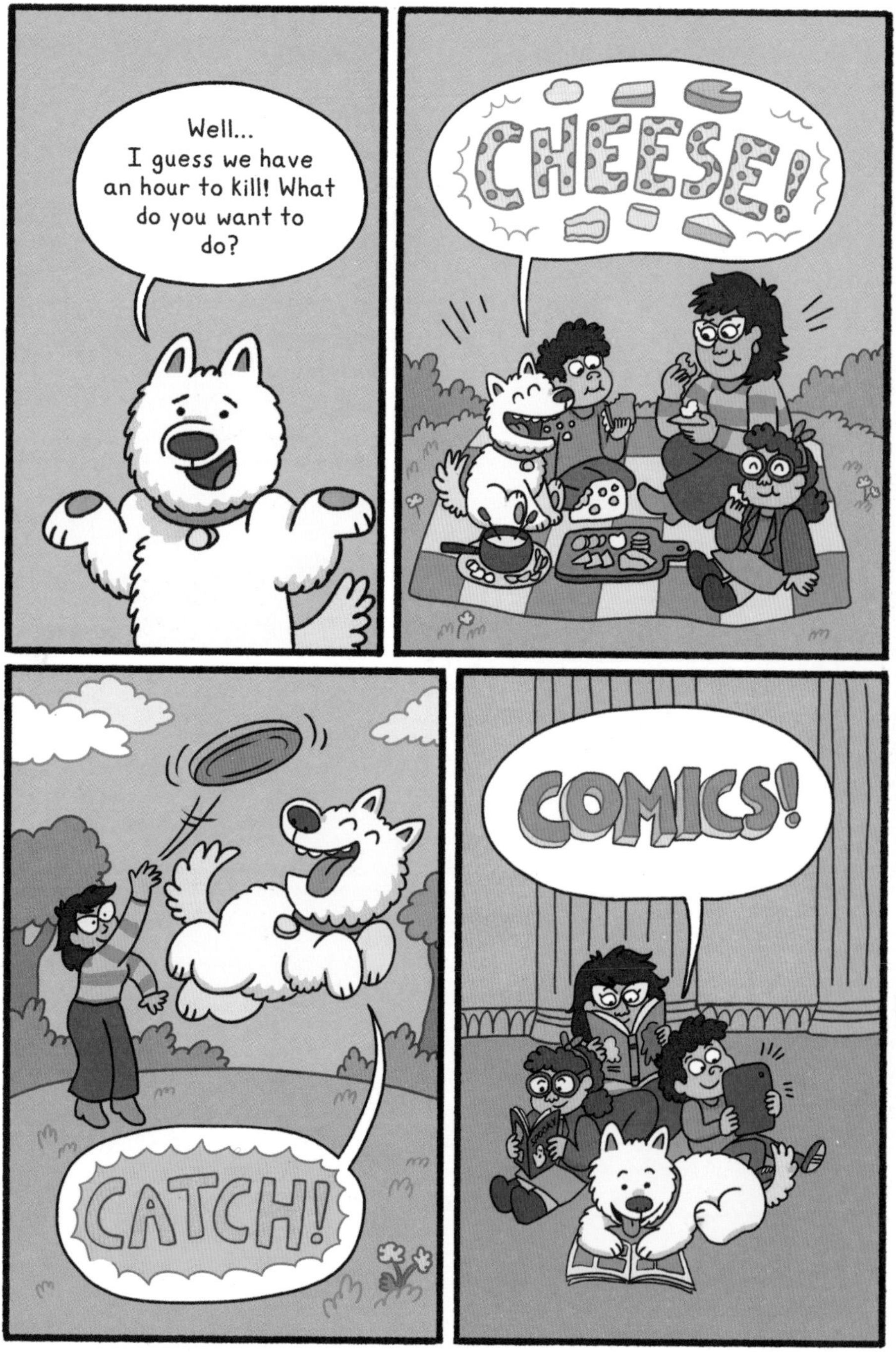
Well...
I guess we have
an hour to kill! What
do you want to
do?
CHEESE!
CATCH!
COMICS!

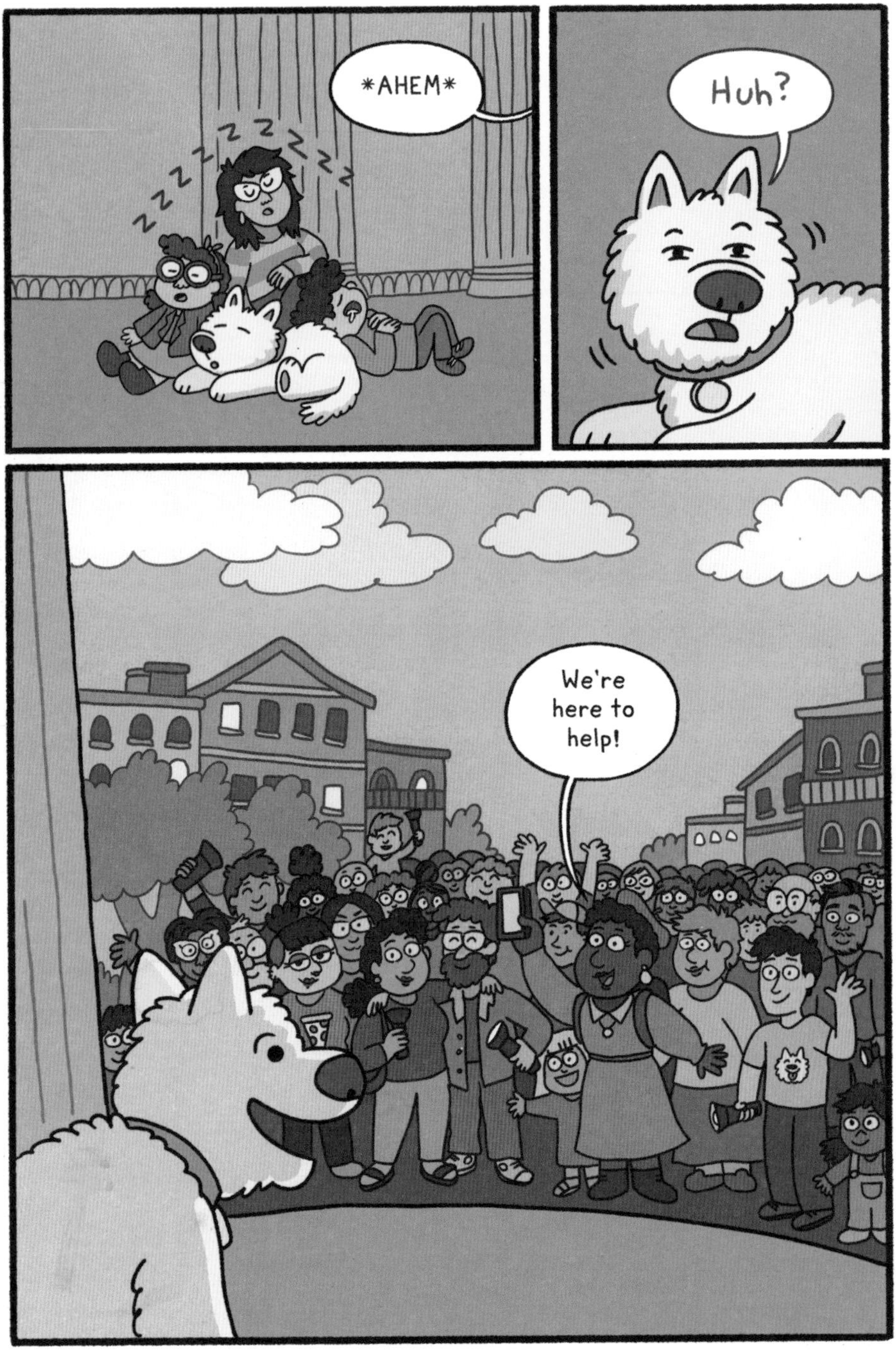
AHEM
Huh?
We're here to help!

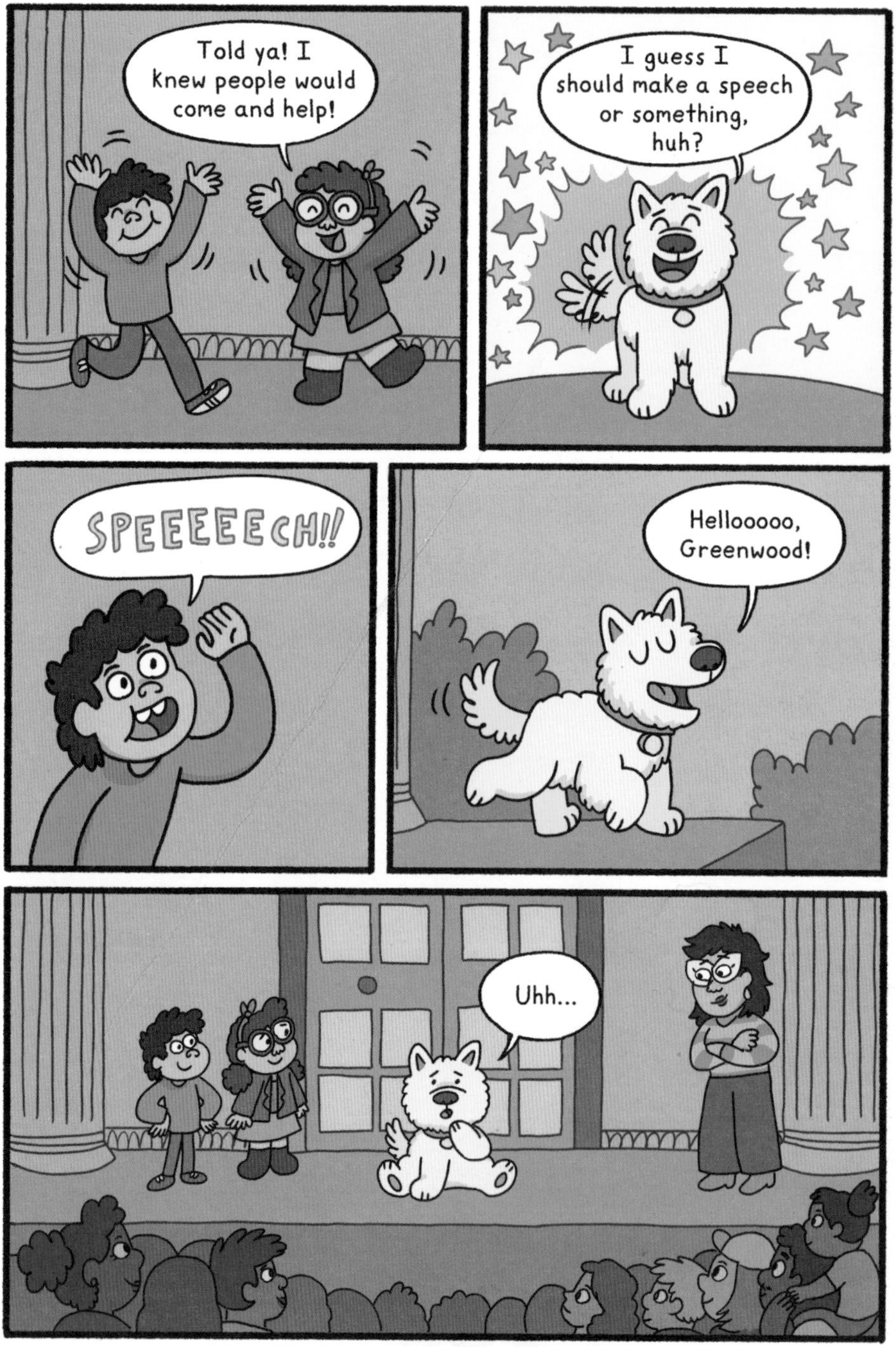
Told ya! I knew people would come and help!
I guess I should make a speech or something, huh?
SPEEEEEECH!!
Hellooooo, Greenwood!
Uhh...

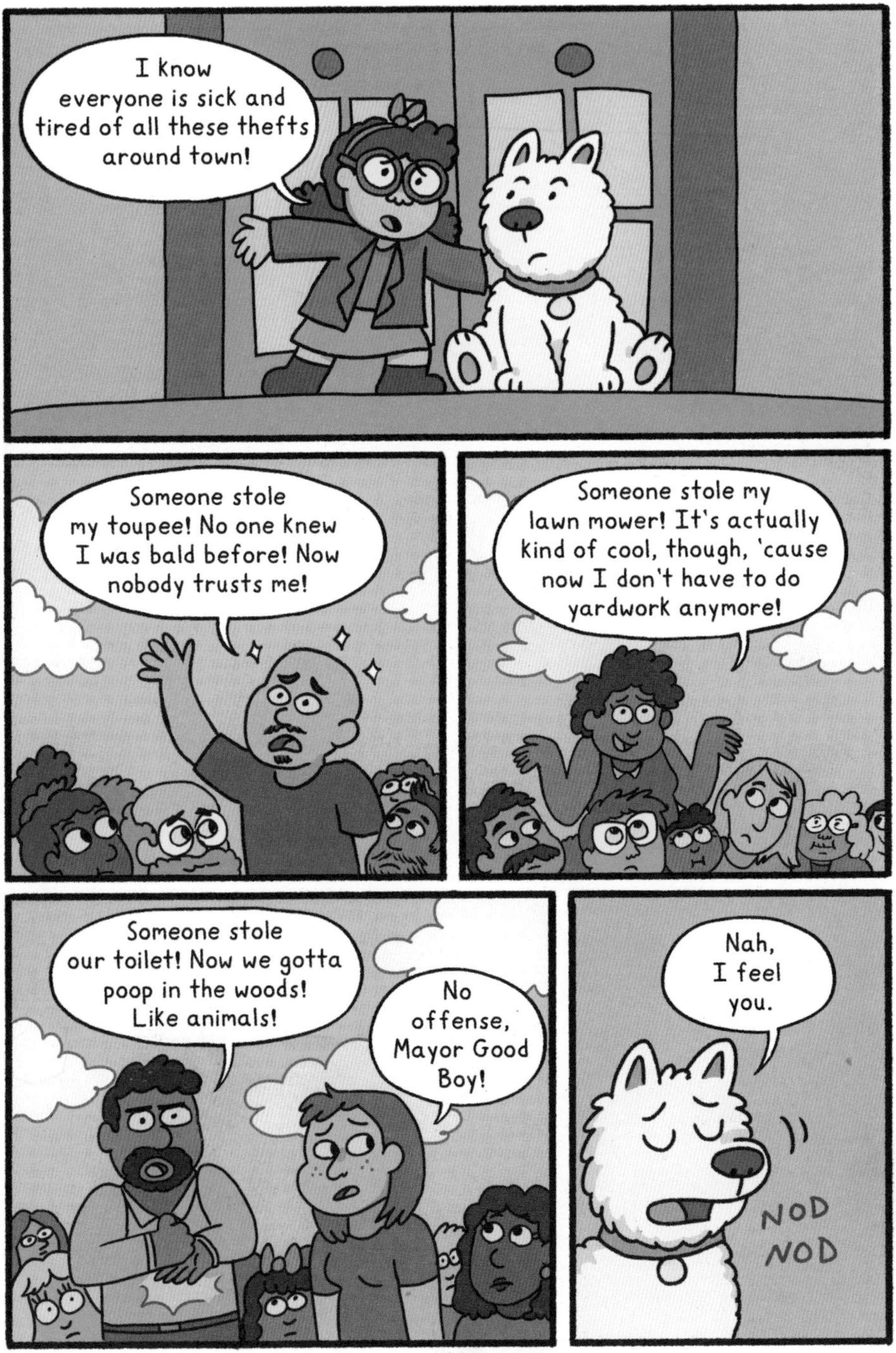
I know everyone is sick and tired of all these thefts around town!
Someone stole my toupee! No one knew I was bald before! Now nobody trusts me!
Someone stole my lawn mower! It's actually kind of cool, though, 'cause now I don't have to do yardwork anymore!
Someone stole our toilet! Now we gotta poop in the woods! Like animals!
No offense, Mayor Good Boy!
Nah, I feel you.
NOD NOD

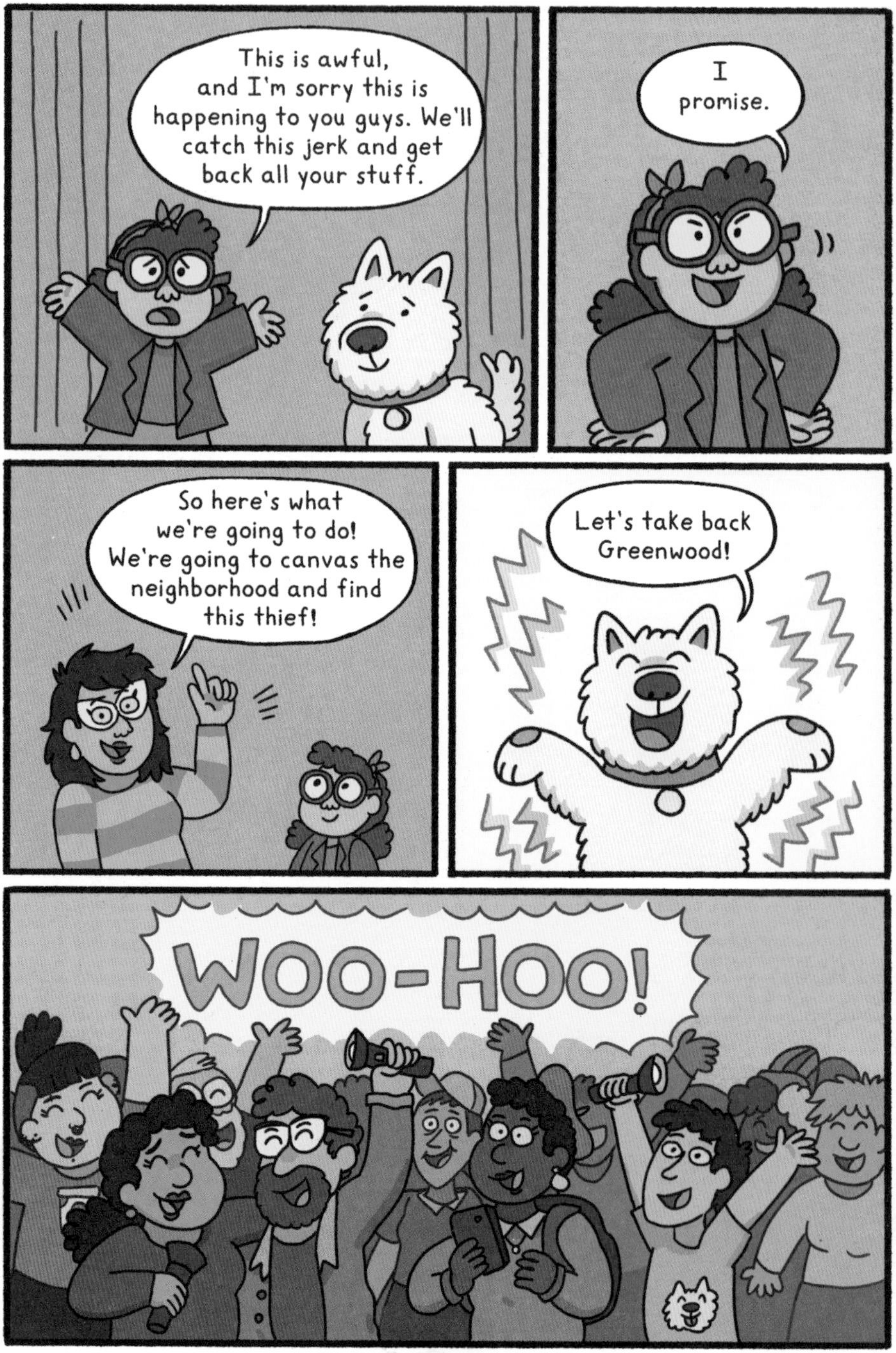

This is awful, and I'm sorry this is happening to you guys. We'll catch this jerk and get back all your stuff.
I promise.
So here's what we're going to do! We're going to canvas the neighborhood and find this thief!
Let's take back Greenwood!
WOO-HOO!

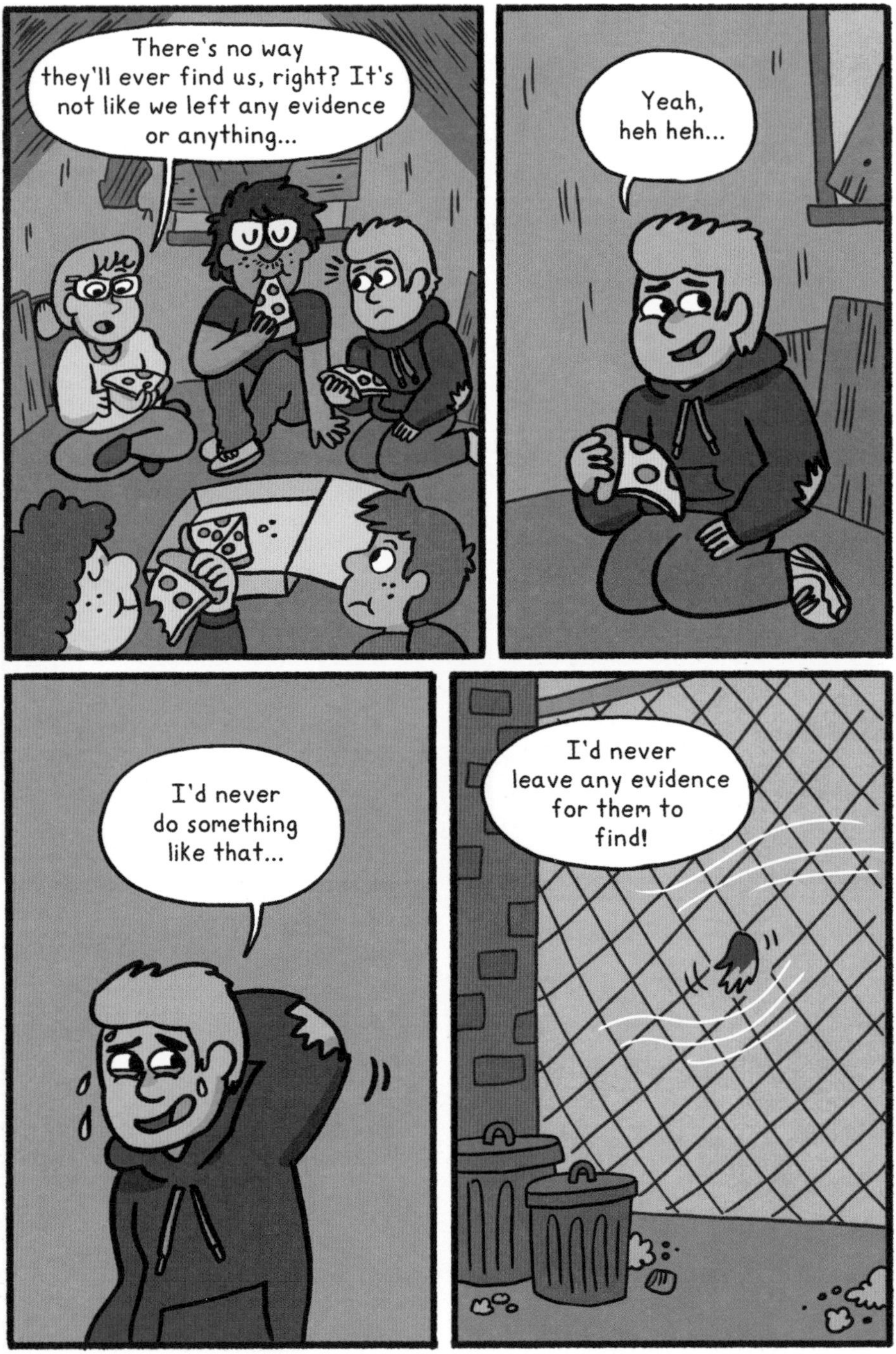
There's no way they'll ever find us, right? It's not like we left any evidence or anything...
Yeah, heh heh...
I'd never do something like that...
I'd never leave any evidence for them to find!

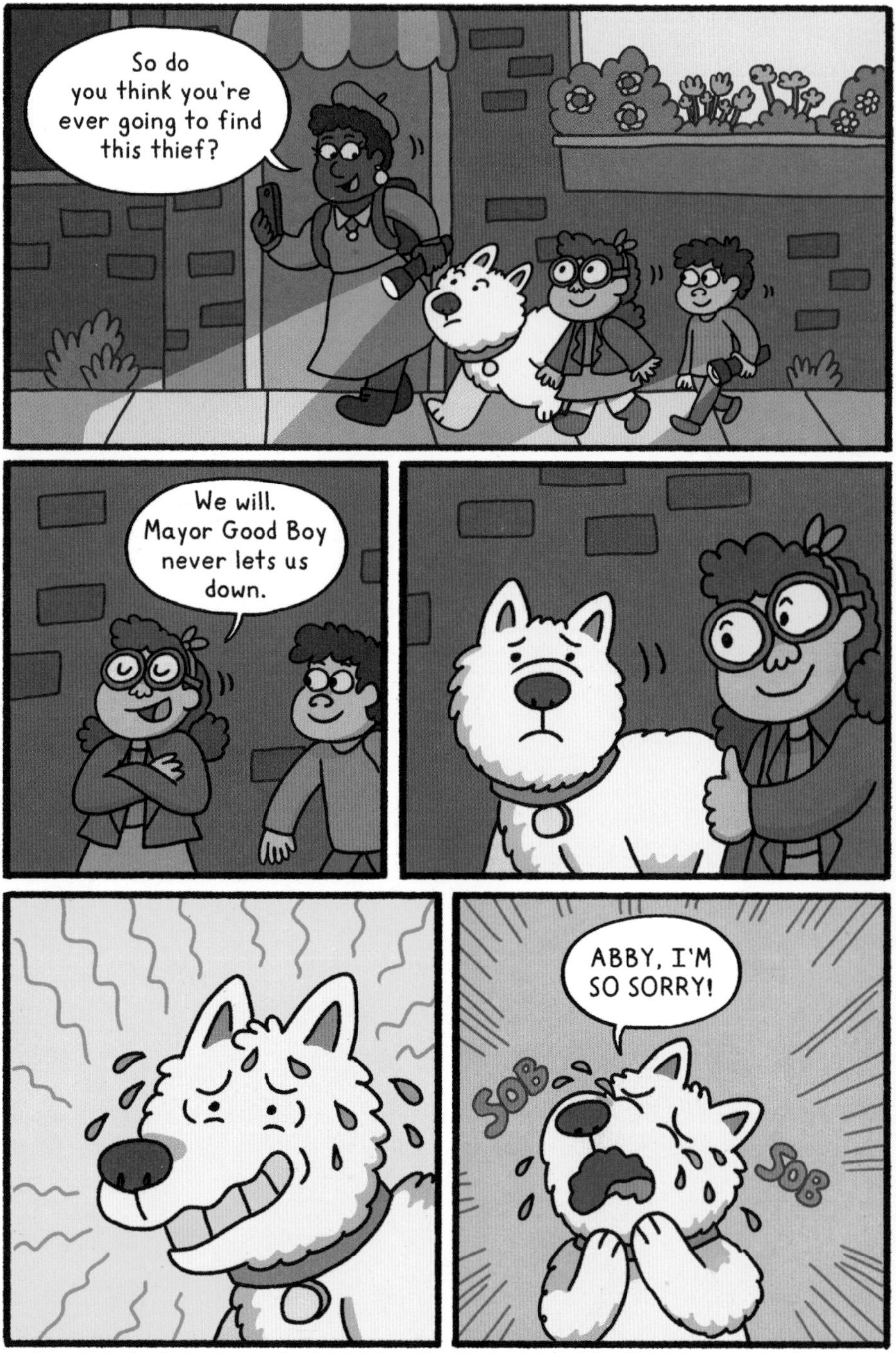
So do you think you're ever going to find this thief?
We will. Mayor Good Boy never lets us down.
ABBY, I'M SO SORRY!
SOB
SOB

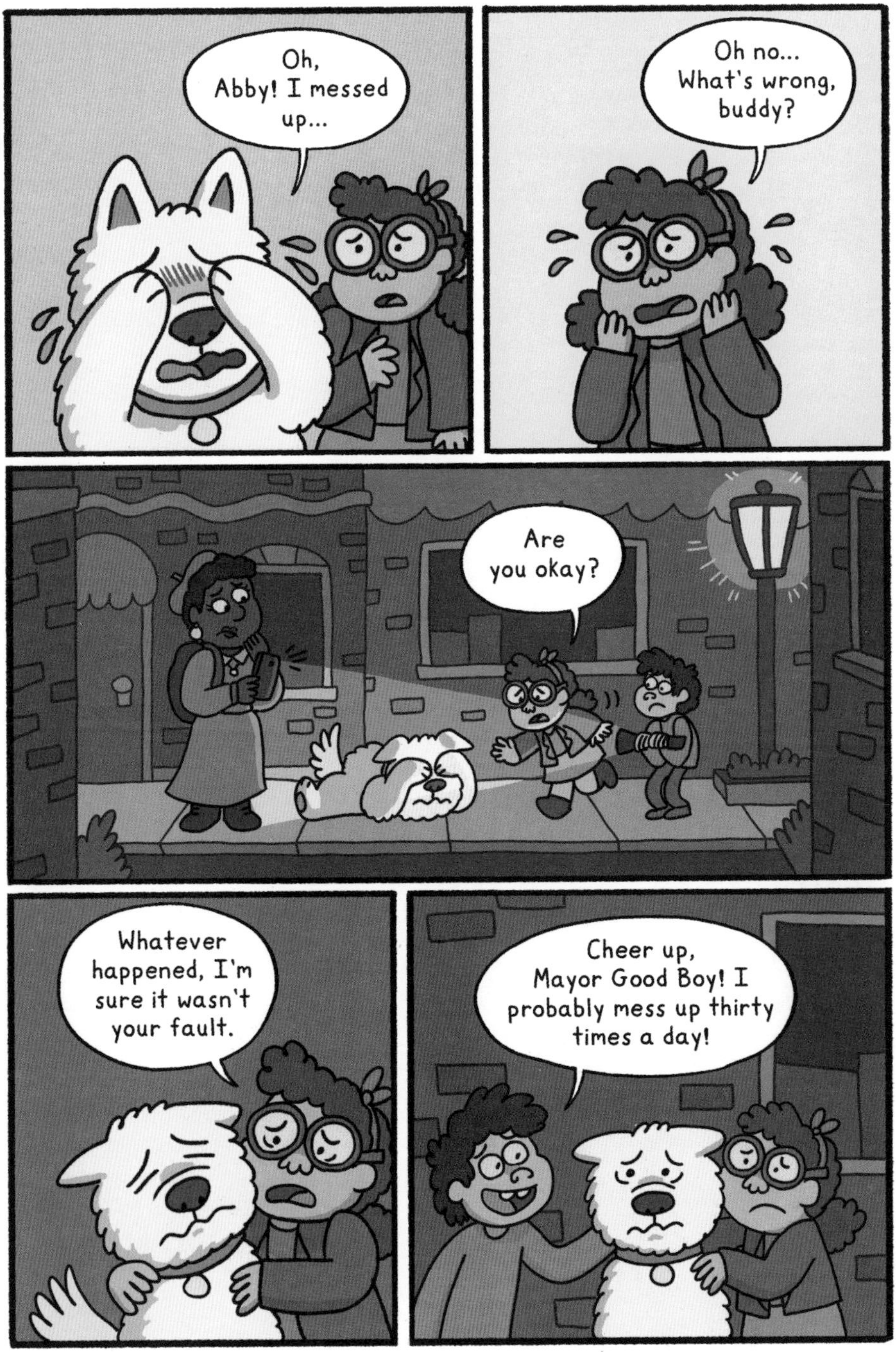
Oh, Abby! I messed up...
Oh no... What's wrong, buddy?
Are you okay?
Whatever happened, I'm sure it wasn't your fault.
Cheer up, Mayor Good Boy! I probably mess up thirty times a day!

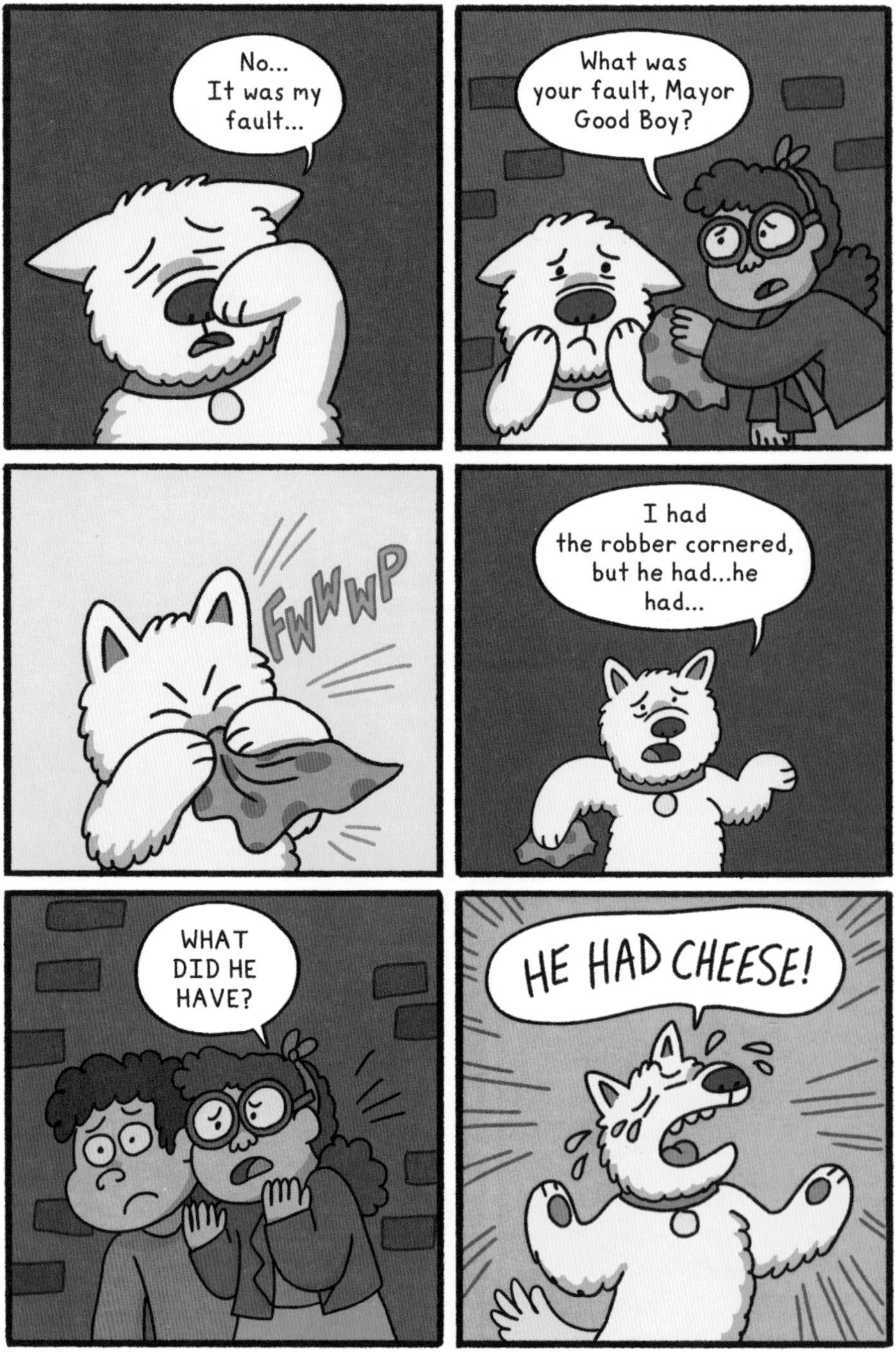
No...
It was my fault...
What was your fault, Mayor Good Boy?
FWWWP
I had the robber cornered, but he had...he had...
WHAT DID HE HAVE?
HE HAD CHEESE!

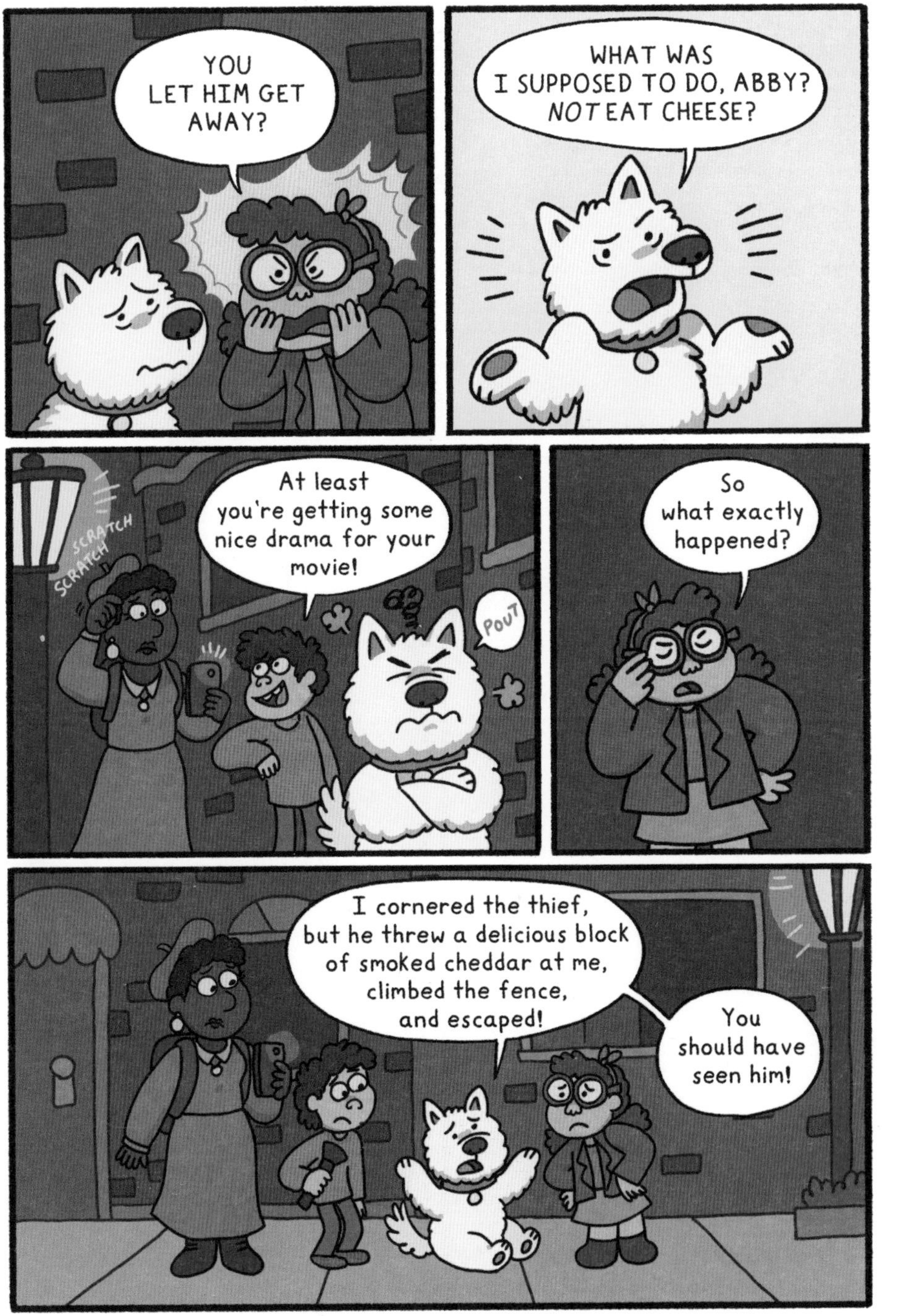
YOU LET HIM GET AWAY?
WHAT WAS I SUPPOSED TO DO, ABBY? *NOT* EAT CHEESE?
SCRATCH SCRATCH
At least you're getting some nice drama for your movie!
POUT
So what exactly happened?
I cornered the thief, but he threw a delicious block of smoked cheddar at me, climbed the fence, and escaped!
You should have seen him!

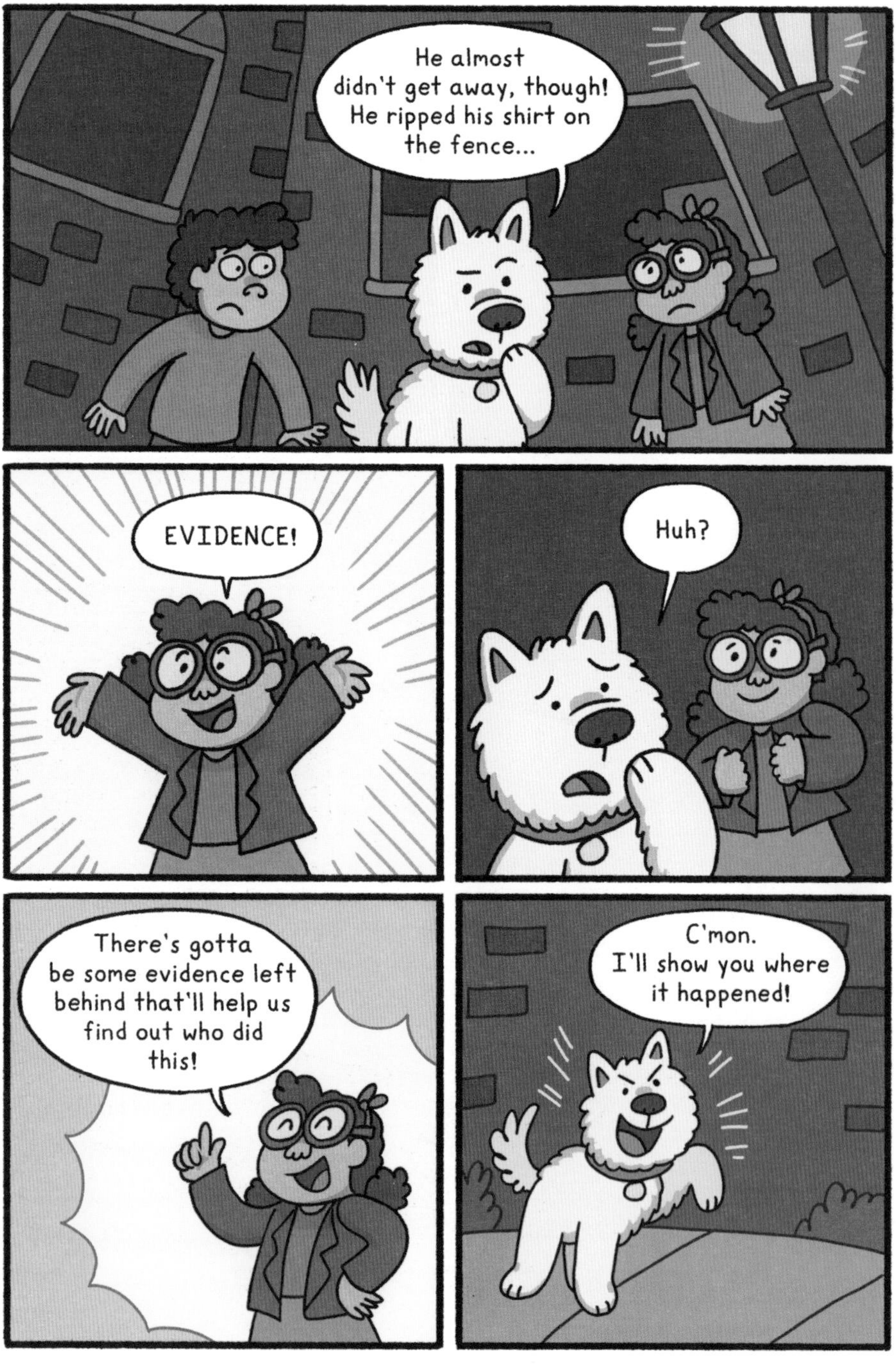
He almost didn't get away, though! He ripped his shirt on the fence...
EVIDENCE!
Huh?
There's gotta be some evidence left behind that'll help us find out who did this!
C'mon. I'll show you where it happened!

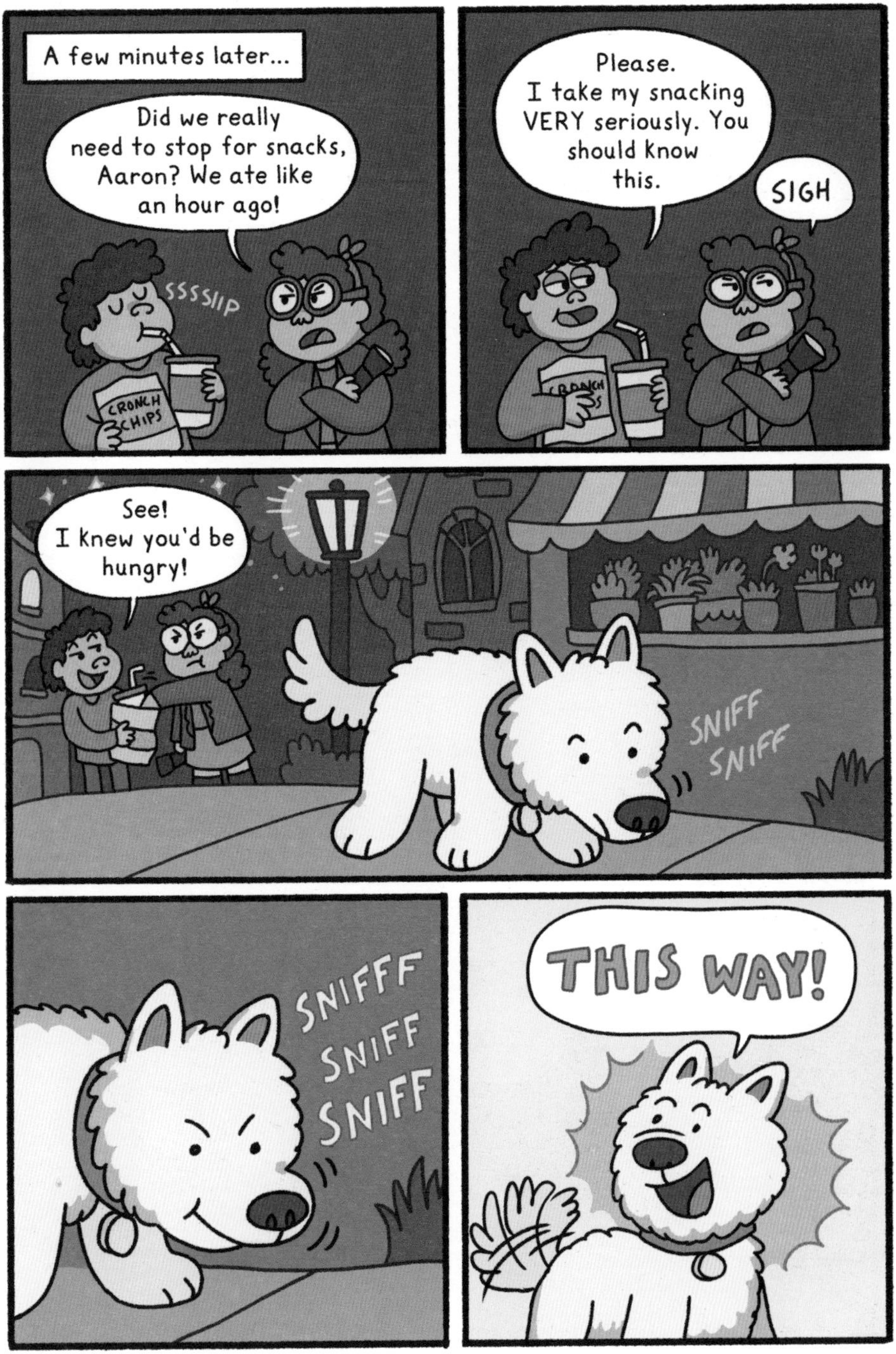
A few minutes later...
Did we really need to stop for snacks, Aaron? We ate like an hour ago!
SSSSSIIP
CRONCH CHIPS
Please. I take my snacking VERY seriously. You should know this.
SIGH
See! I knew you'd be hungry!
SNIFF SNIFF
SNIFFF SNIFF SNIFF
THIS WAY!

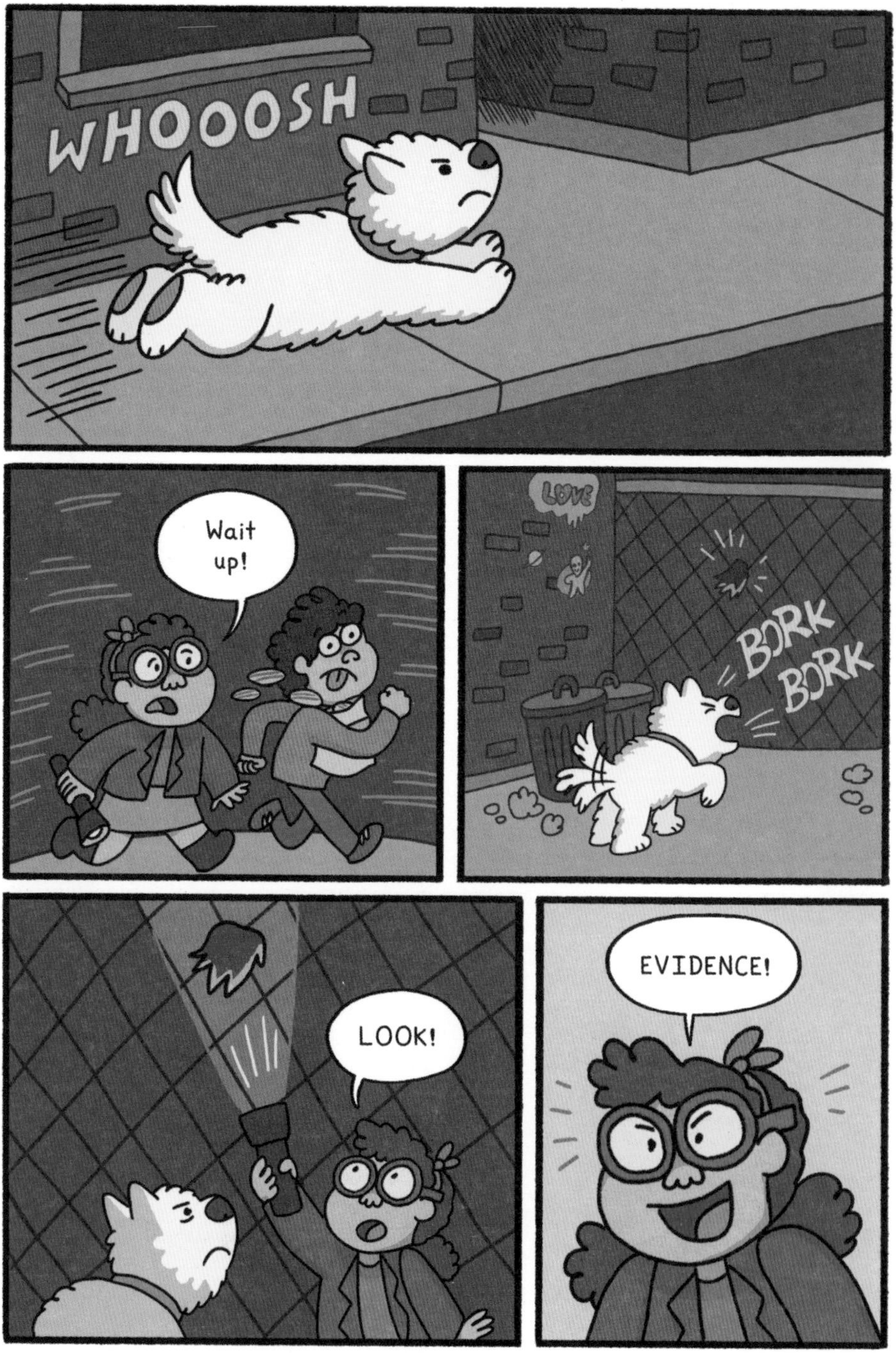
WHOOOSH
Wait up!
LOVE
BORK
BORK
LOOK!
EVIDENCE!

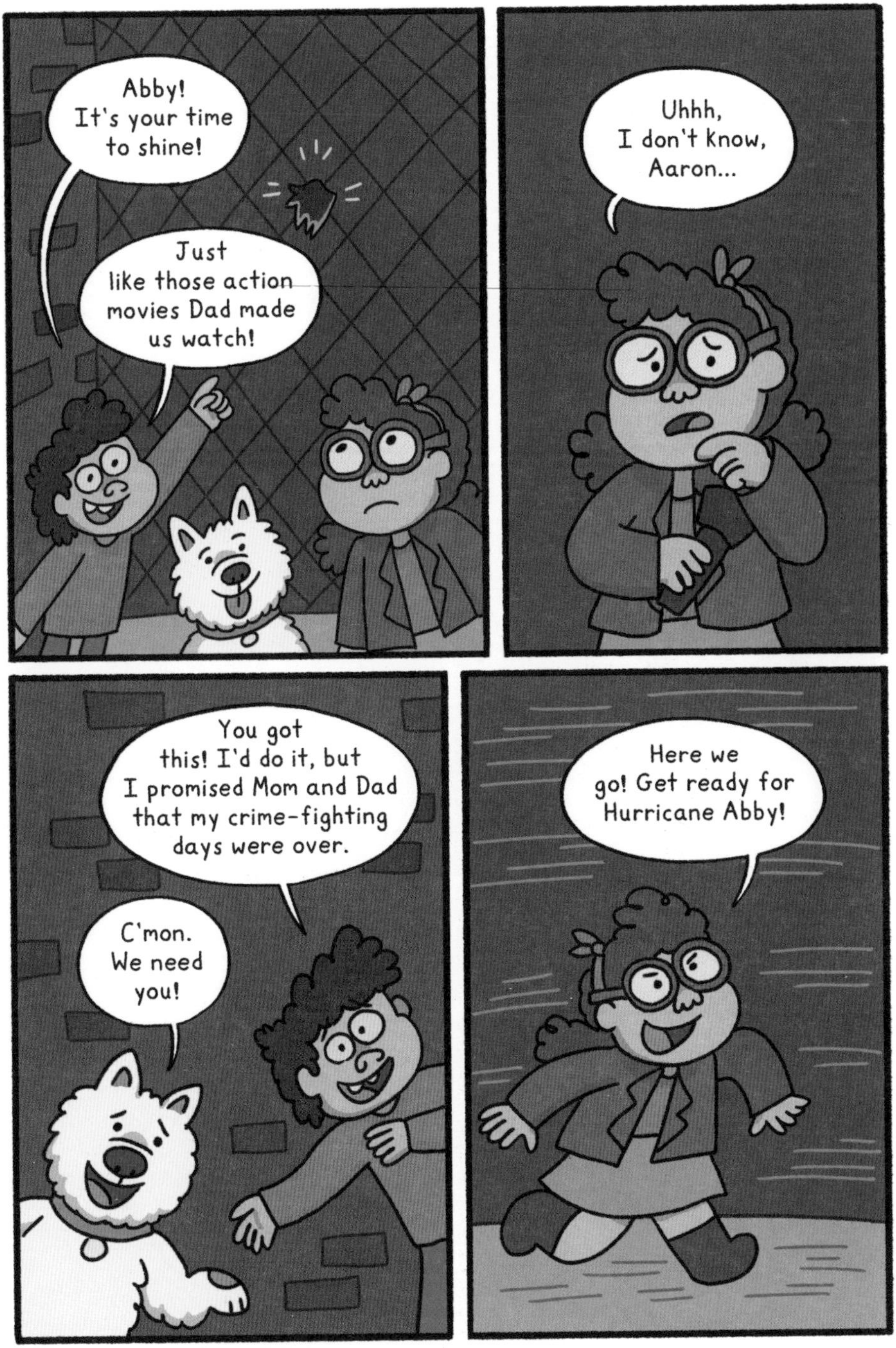
Abby! It's your time to shine!
Just like those action movies Dad made us watch!
Uhhh, I don't know, Aaron...
You got this! I'd do it, but I promised Mom and Dad that my crime-fighting days were over.
C'mon. We need you!
Here we go! Get ready for Hurricane Abby!

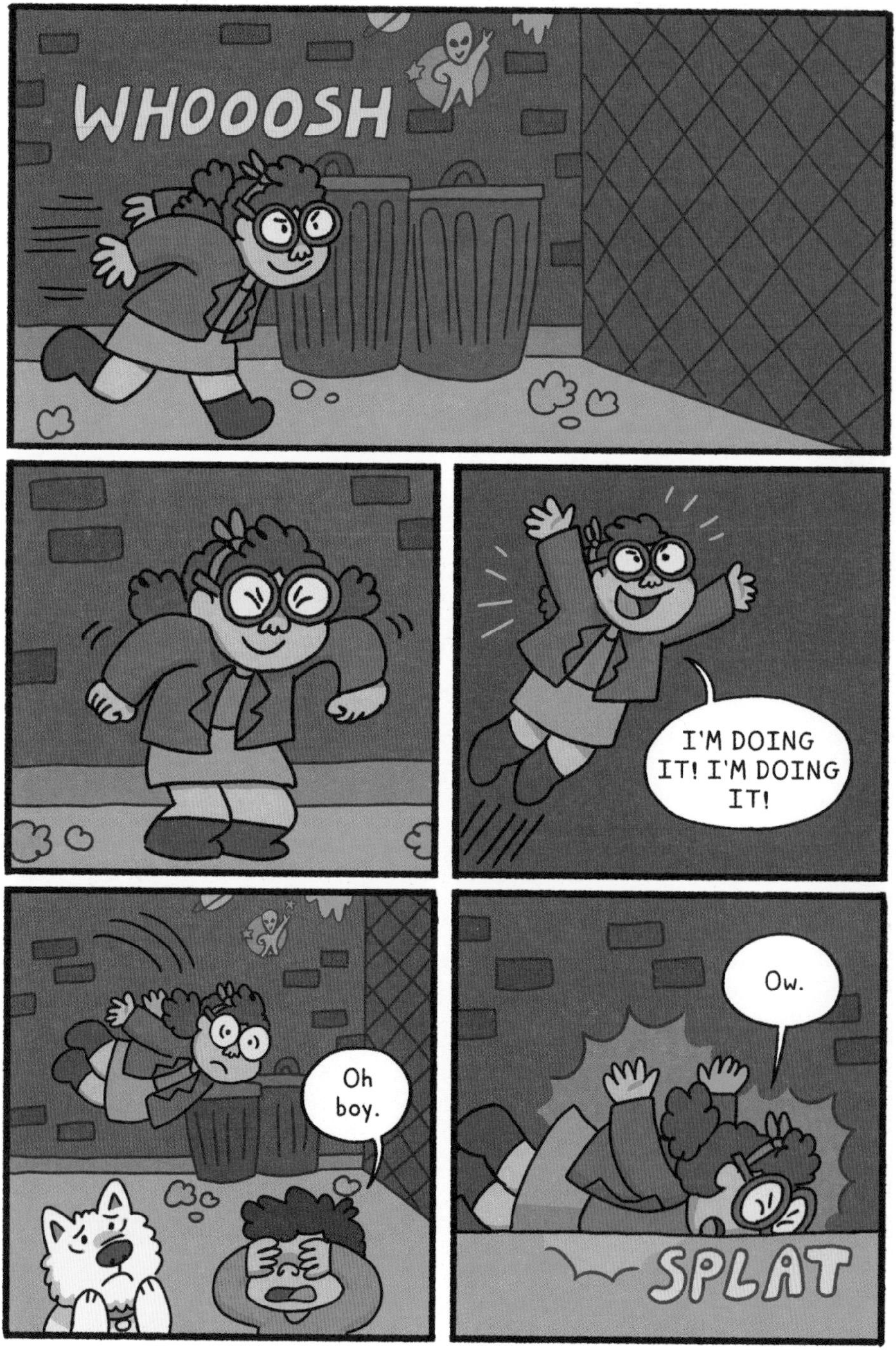
WHOOOSH
I'M DOING IT! I'M DOING IT!
Oh boy.
Ow.
SPLAT

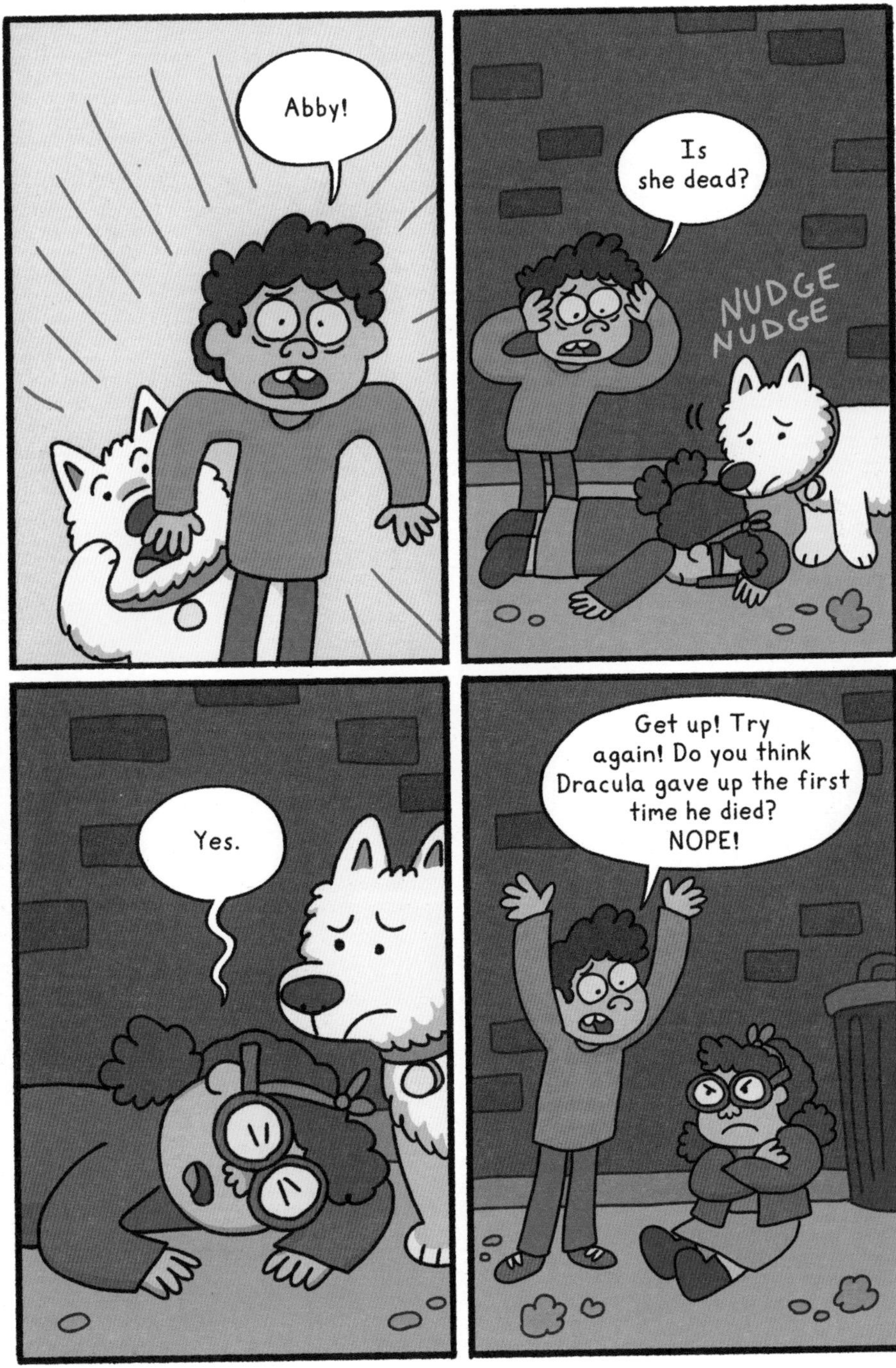
Abby!
Is she dead?
NUDGE NUDGE
Yes.
Get up! Try again! Do you think Dracula gave up the first time he died? NOPE!

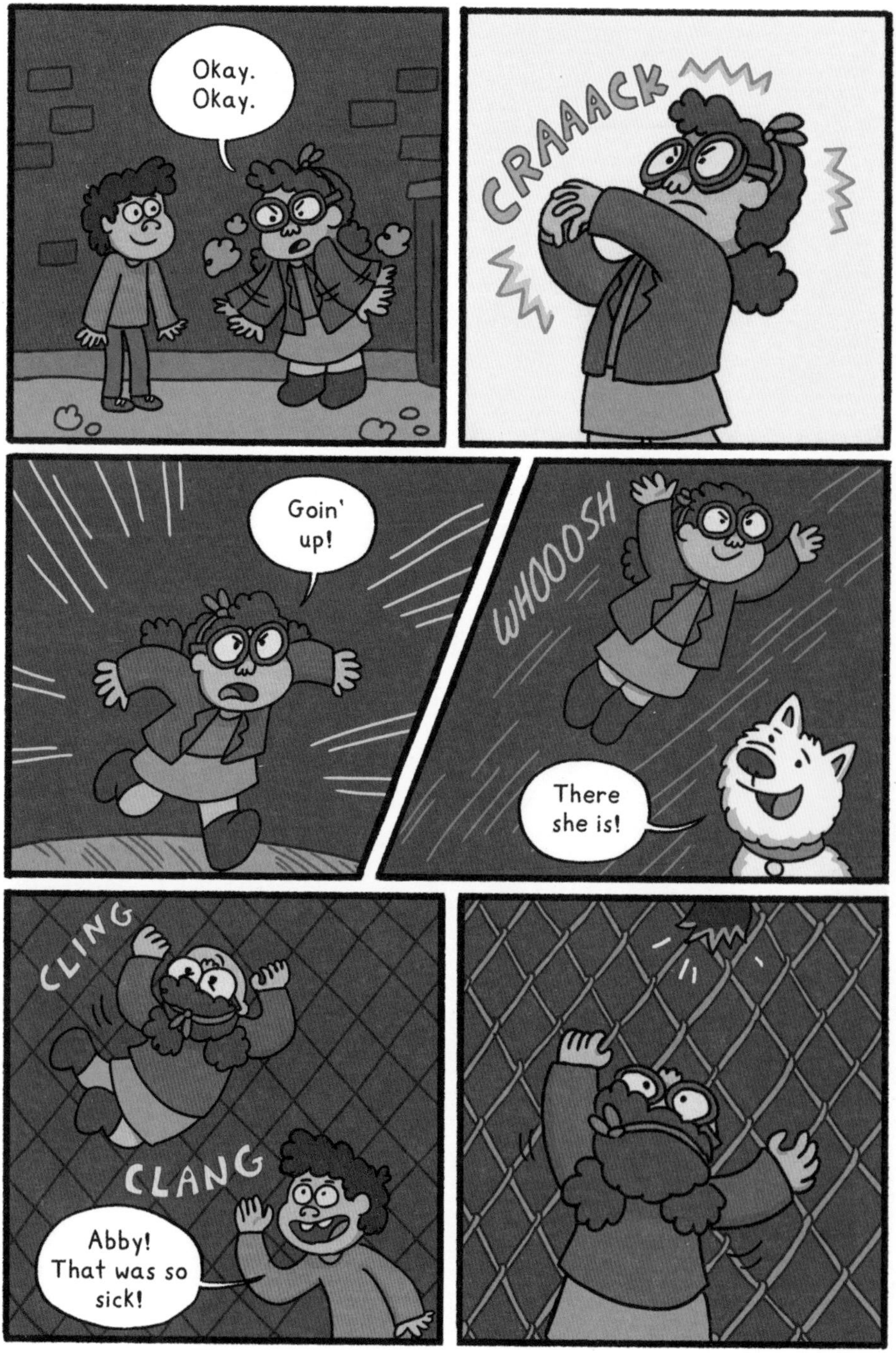
Okay.
Okay.
CRAAACK
Goin' up!
WHOOOSH
There she is!
CLING
CLANG
Abby! That was so sick!

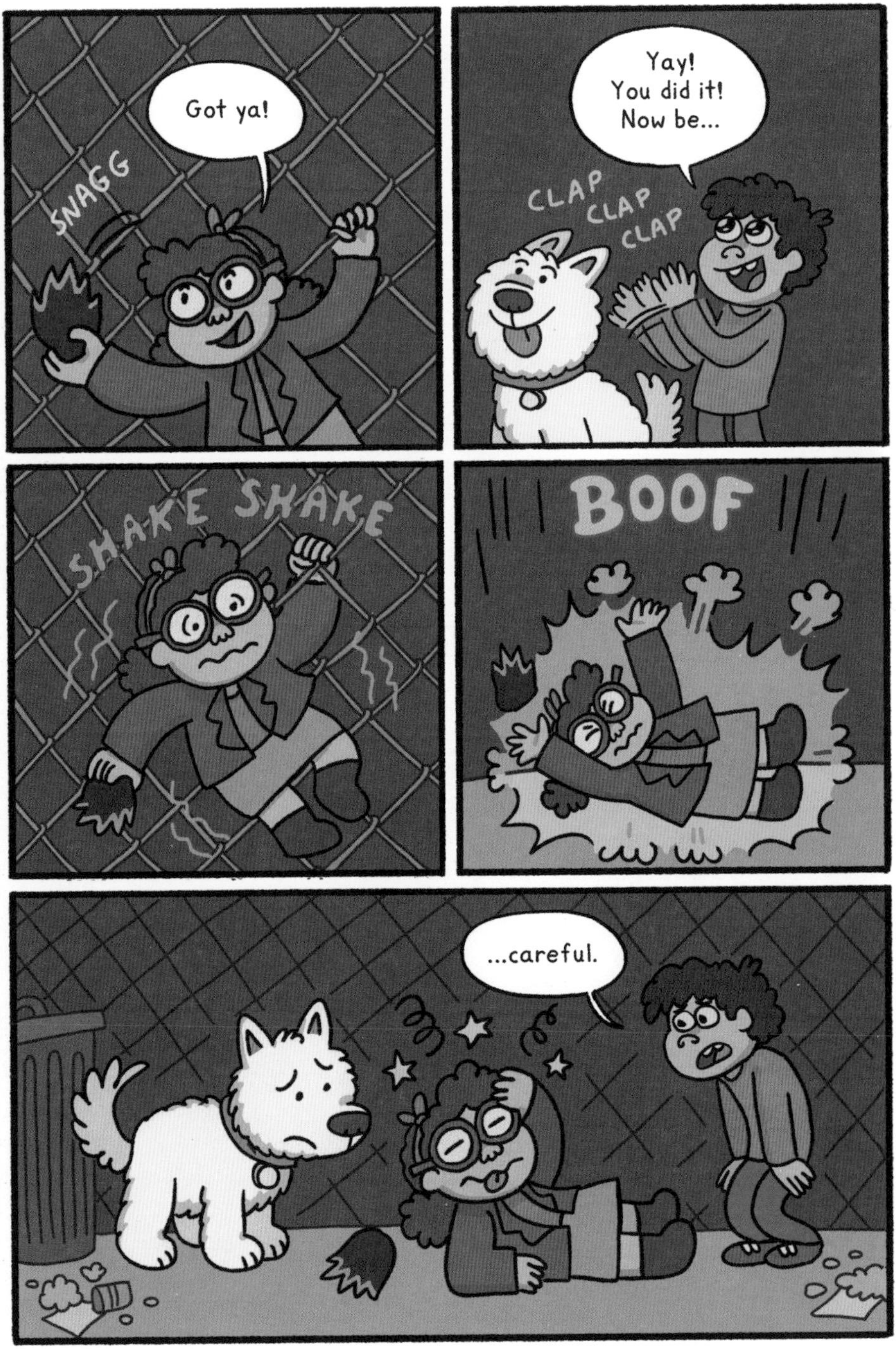

Got ya!
SNAGG
Yay!
You did it!
Now be...
CLAP
CLAP
CLAP
SHAKE SHAKE
BOOF
...careful.

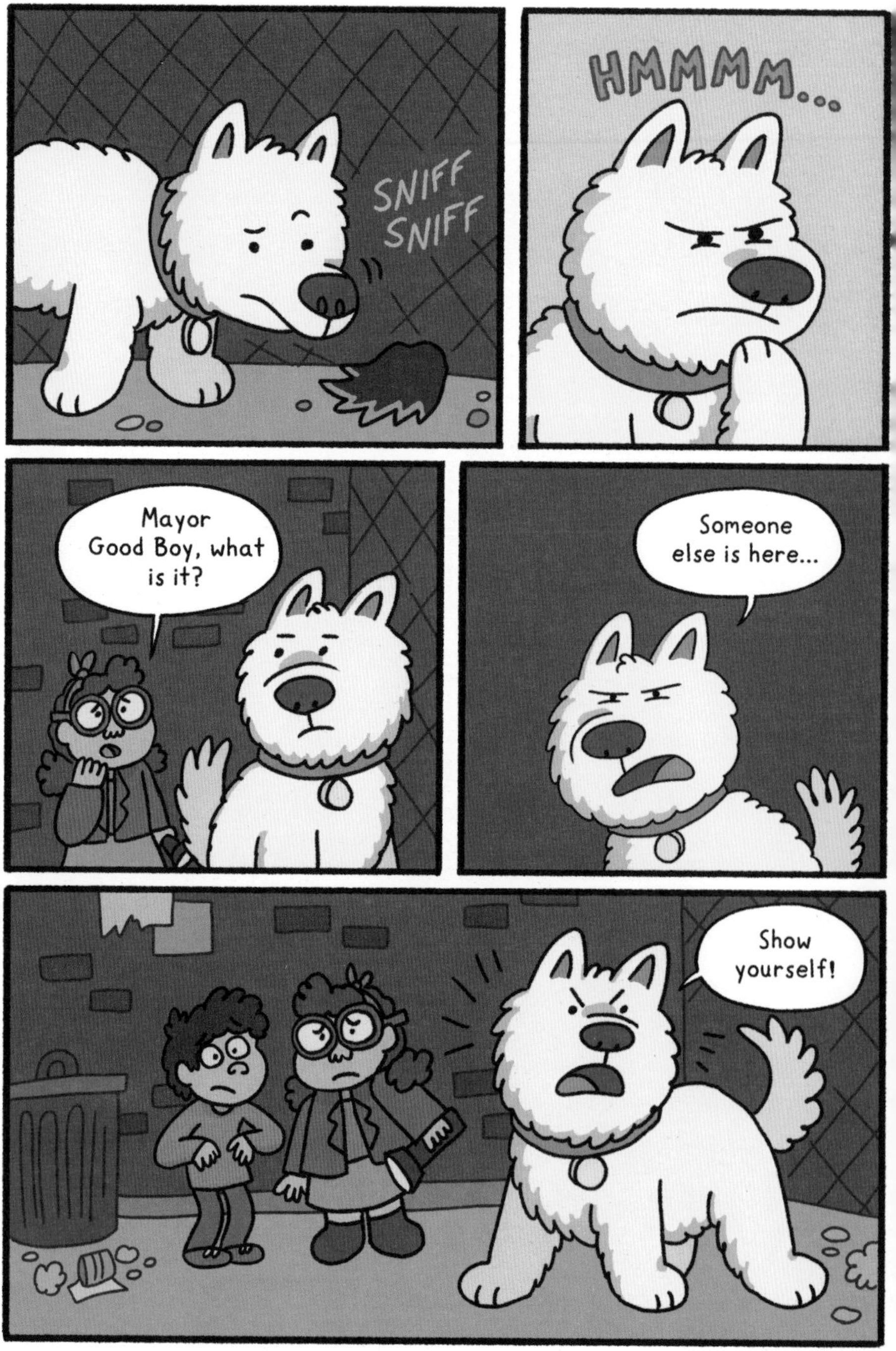
SNIFF
SNIFF
HMMMM...
Mayor Good Boy, what is it?
Someone else is here...
Show yourself!

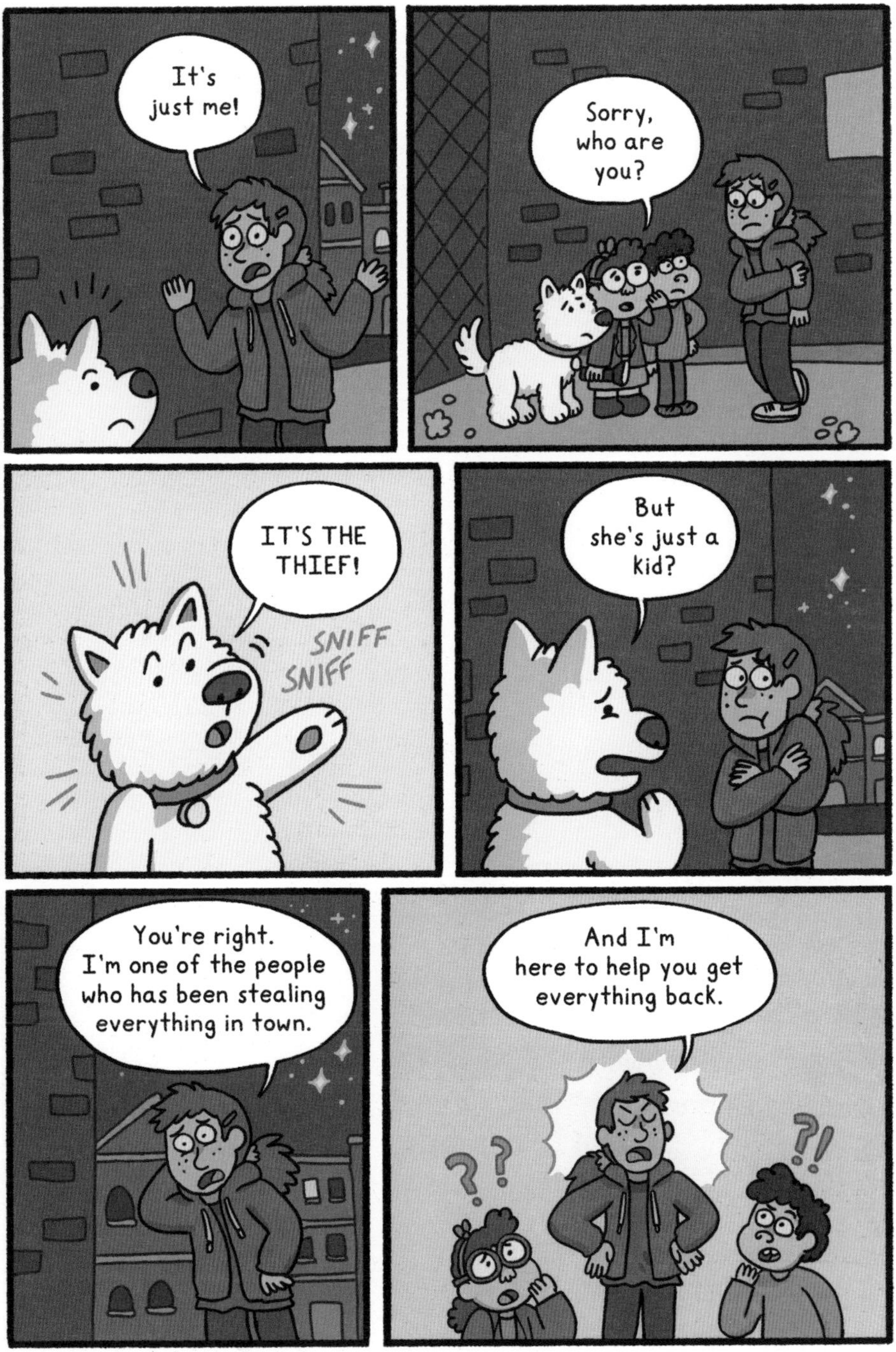
It's just me!
Sorry, who are you?
IT'S THE THIEF!
SNIFF SNIFF
But she's just a kid?
You're right. I'm one of the people who has been stealing everything in town.
And I'm here to help you get everything back.
?!

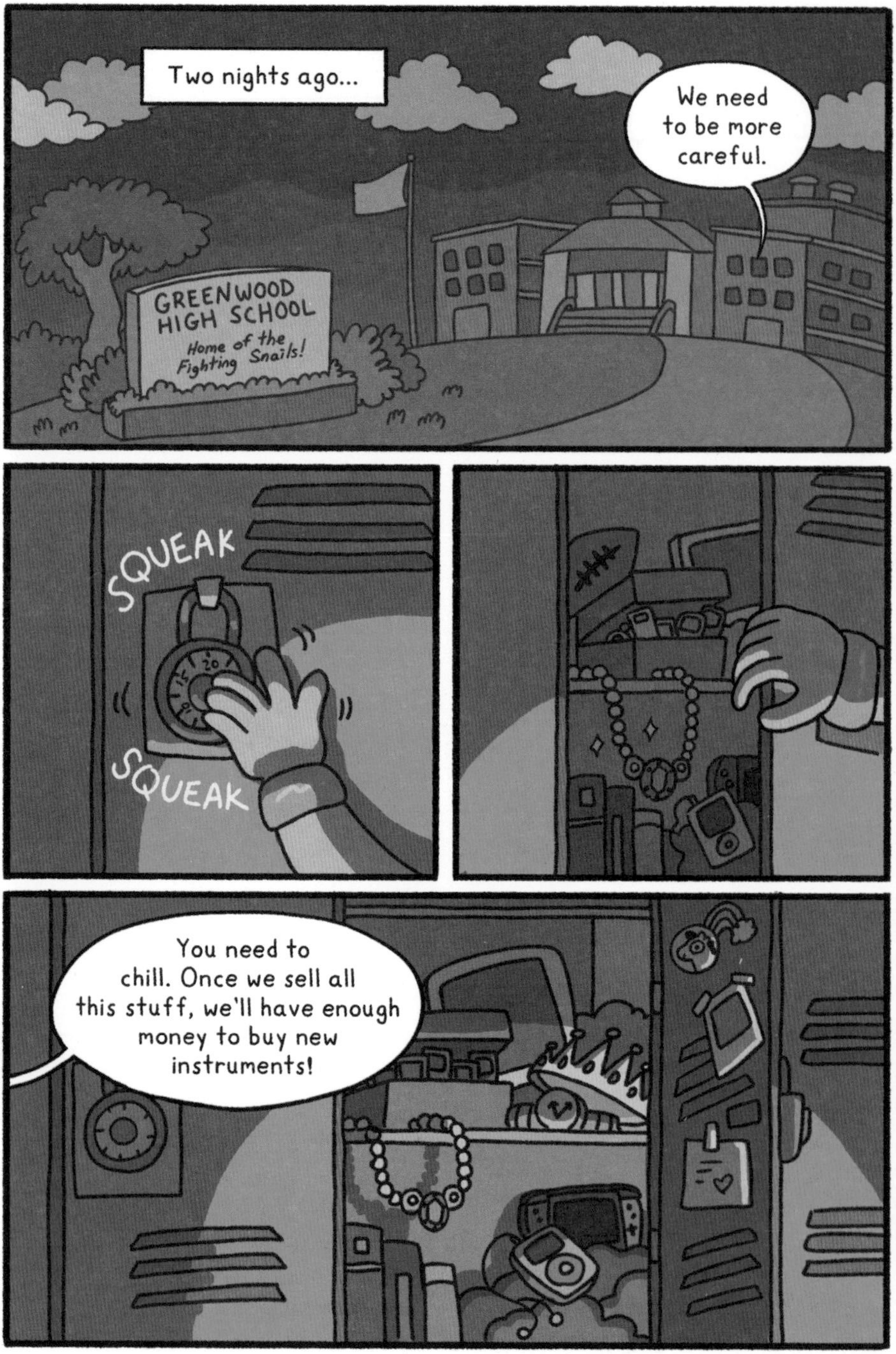
Two nights ago...
We need to be more careful.
GREENWOOD HIGH SCHOOL
Home of the Fighting Snails!
SQUEAK
SQUEAK
You need to chill. Once we sell all this stuff, we'll have enough money to buy new instruments!

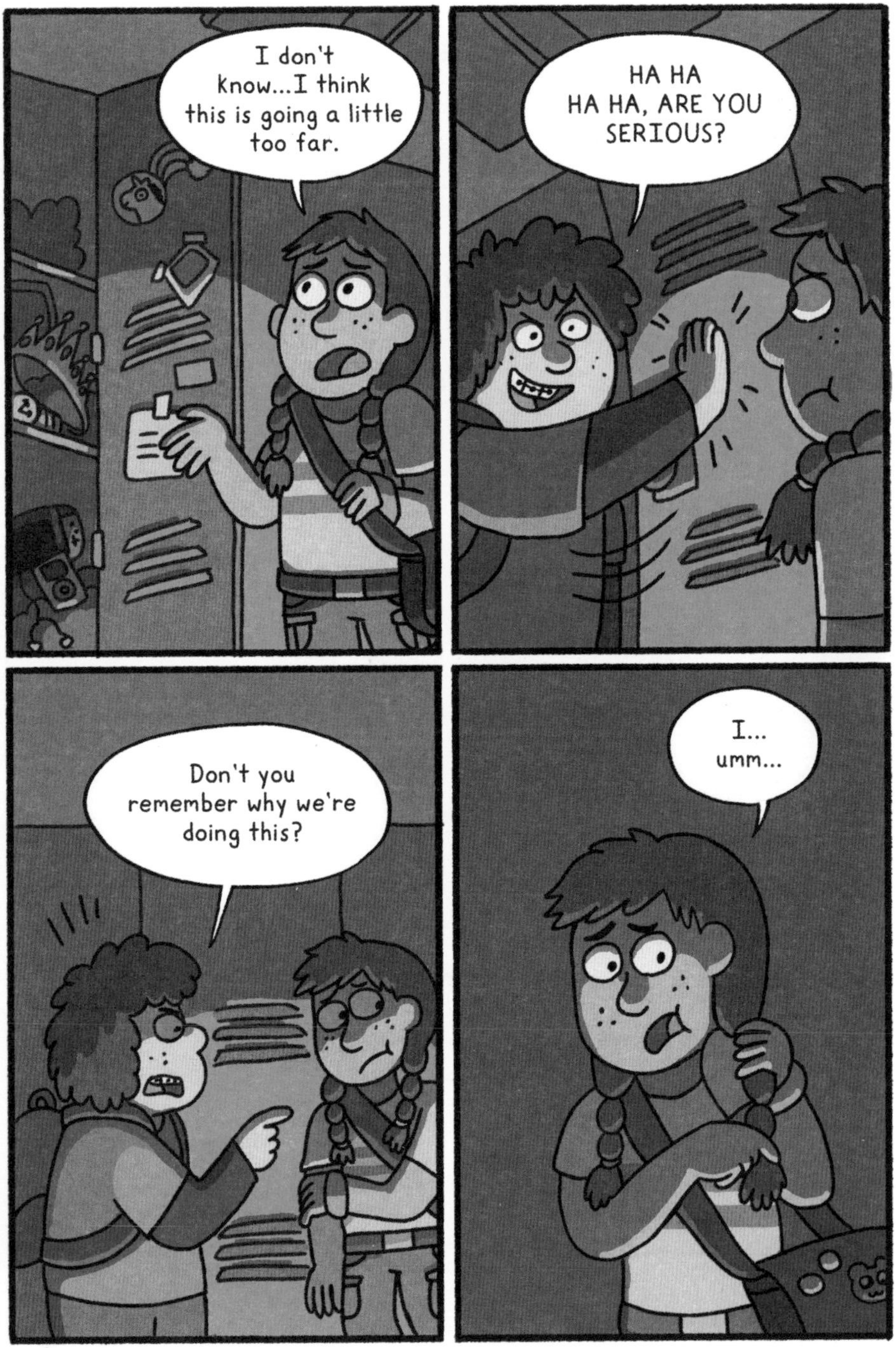
I don't know...I think this is going a little too far.
HA HA HA HA, ARE YOU SERIOUS?
Don't you remember why we're doing this?
I... umm...

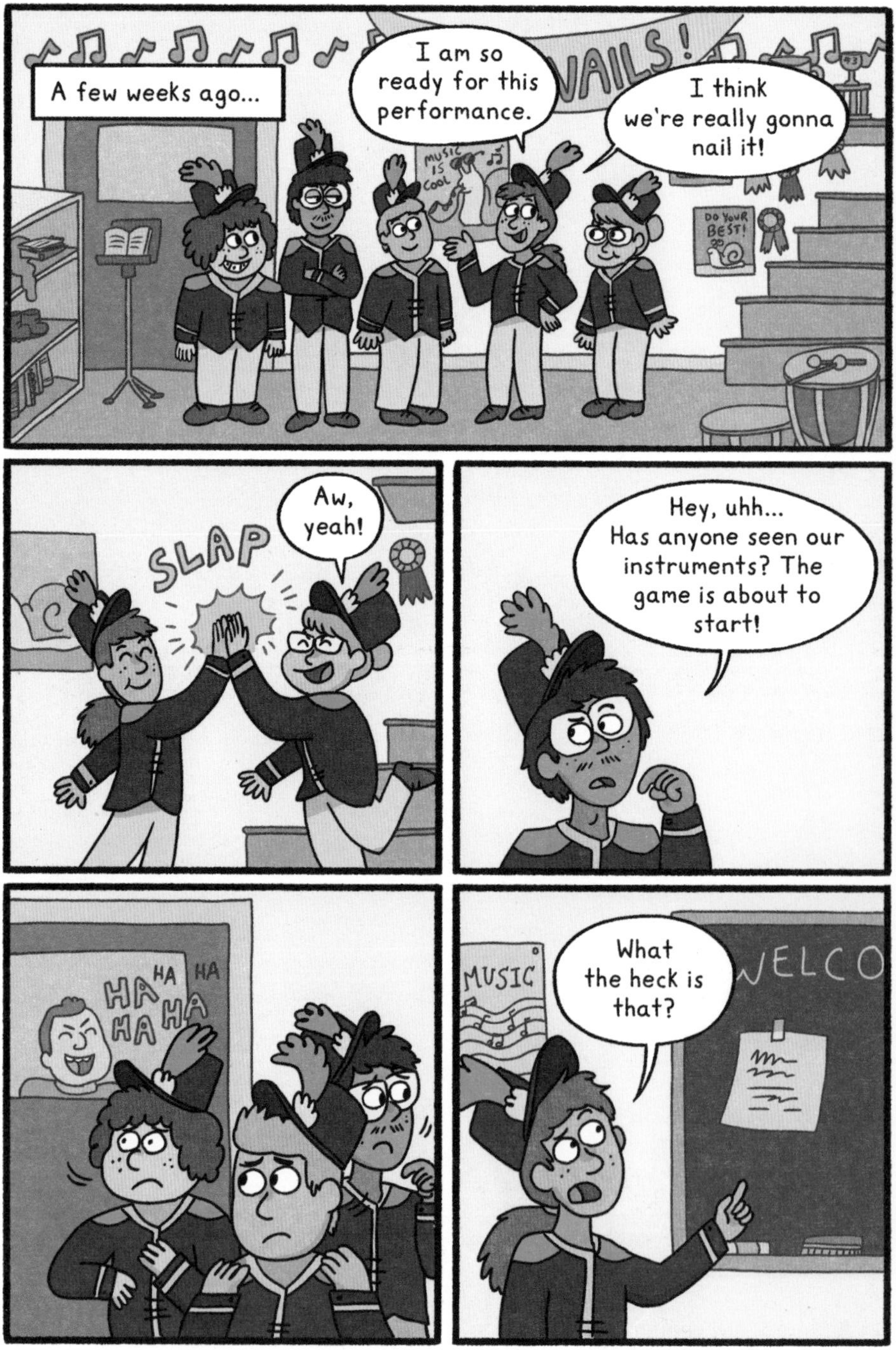
A few weeks ago...
I am so ready for this performance.
I think we're really gonna nail it!
MUSIC IS COOL
DO YOUR BEST!
SLAP
Aw, yeah!
Hey, uhh... Has anyone seen our instruments? The game is about to start!
HA HA HA HA HA HA
MUSIC
What the heck is that?
WELCO

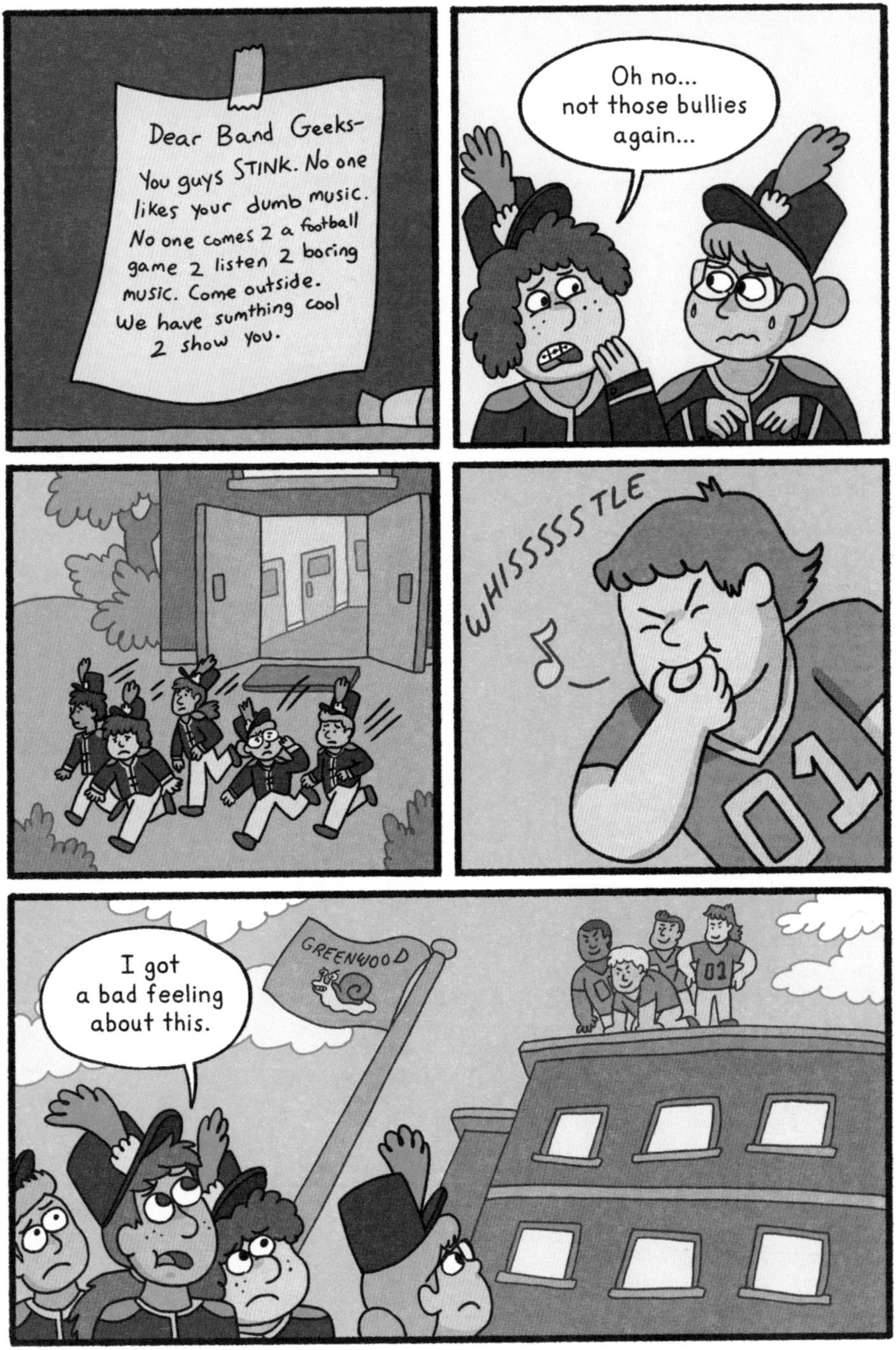
Dear Band Geeks-
You guys STINK. No one likes your dumb music. No one comes 2 a football game 2 listen 2 boring music. Come outside. We have sumthing cool 2 show you.
Oh no... not those bullies again...
WHISSSSSTLE
GREENWOOD
01
I got a bad feeling about this.

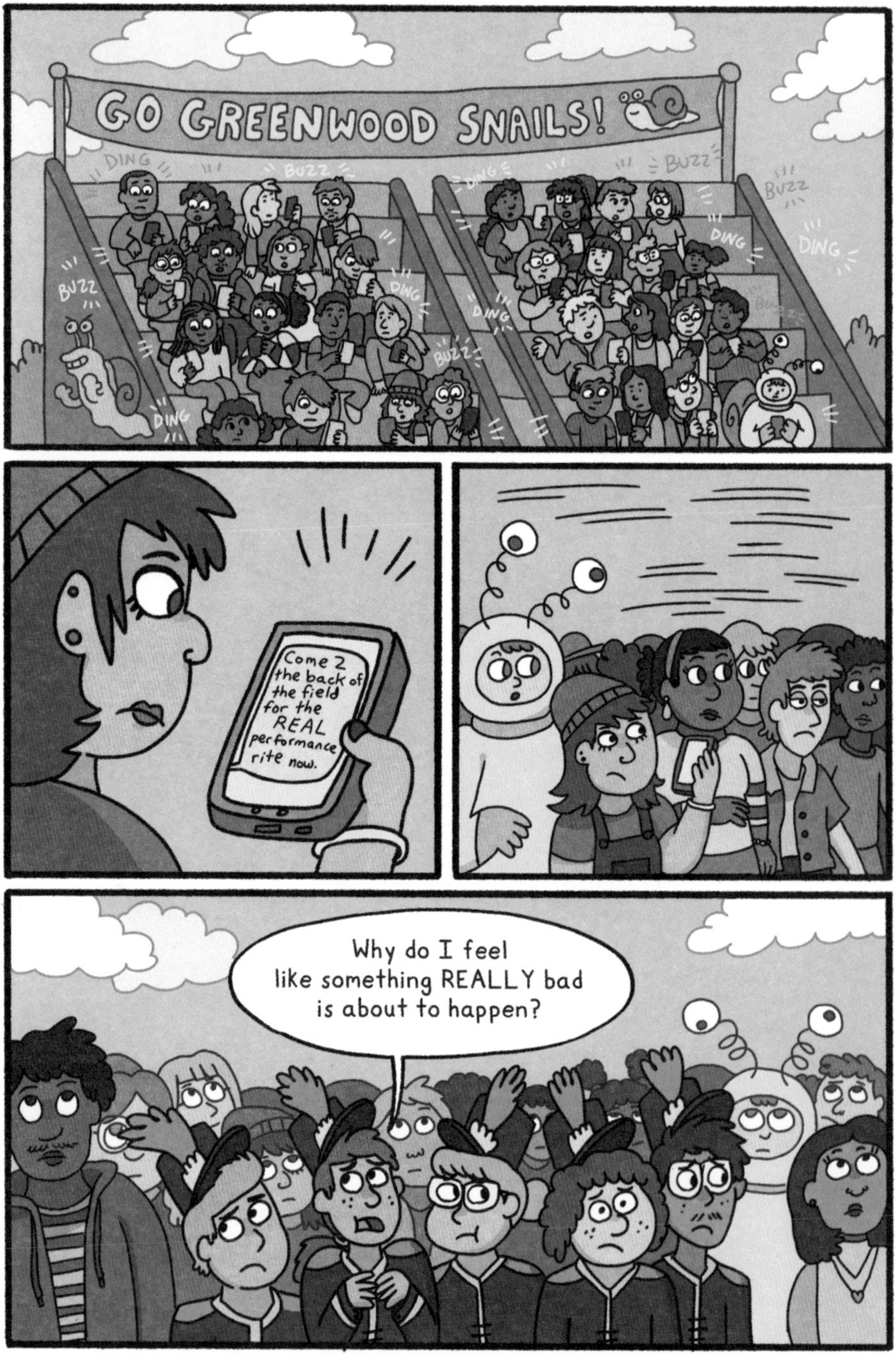
GO GREENWOOD SNAILS!
DING
BUZZ
DING
BUZZ
DING
BUZZ
DING
DING
DING
DING
BUZZ
DING
Come 2 the back of the field for the REAL performance rite now.
Why do I feel like something REALLY bad is about to happen?

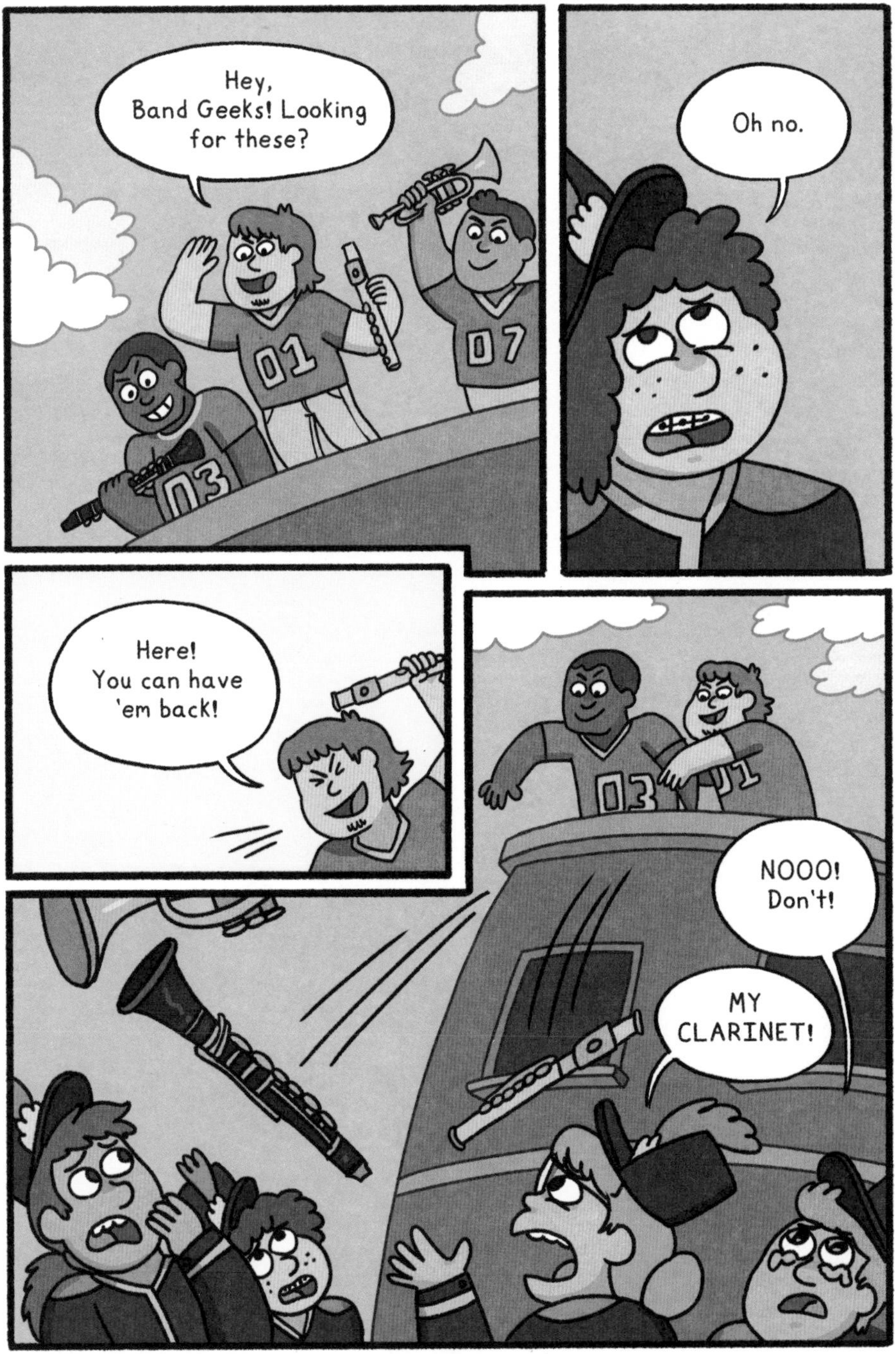
Hey, Band Geeks! Looking for these?
Oh no.
Here! You can have 'em back!
NOOO! Don't!
MY CLARINET!

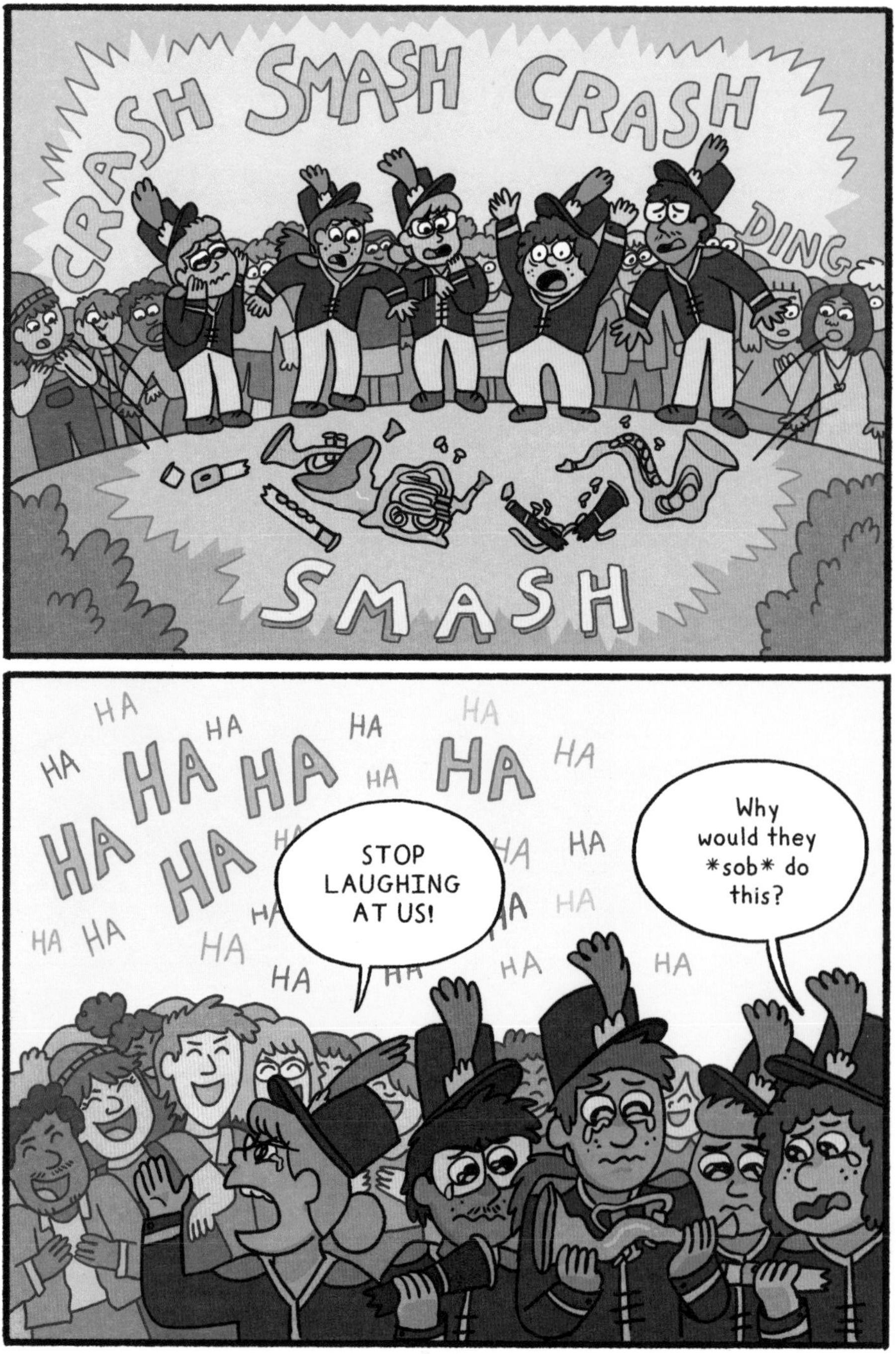
CRASH SMASH CRASH
DING
SMASH
HA HA HA HA HA HA HA HA HA HA HA HA HA HA
STOP LAUGHING AT US!
Why would they *sob* do this?

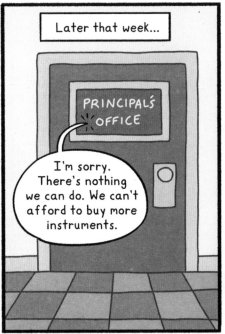

Later that week...

PRINCIPAL'S OFFICE

I'm sorry. There's nothing we can do. We can't afford to buy more instruments.

Believe me... I'm sorry this happened, but those instruments cost a LOT of money. Unless you have a way of paying for all of that.

PRINCIPAL

You can't be serious?

I'm sorry, but it's out of my hands.

HANG IN THERE

PRINCIPAL

MUSIC IS ALL WE HAVE! YOU CAN'T DO THIS! YOU CAN'T TAKE THAT AWAY FROM US!

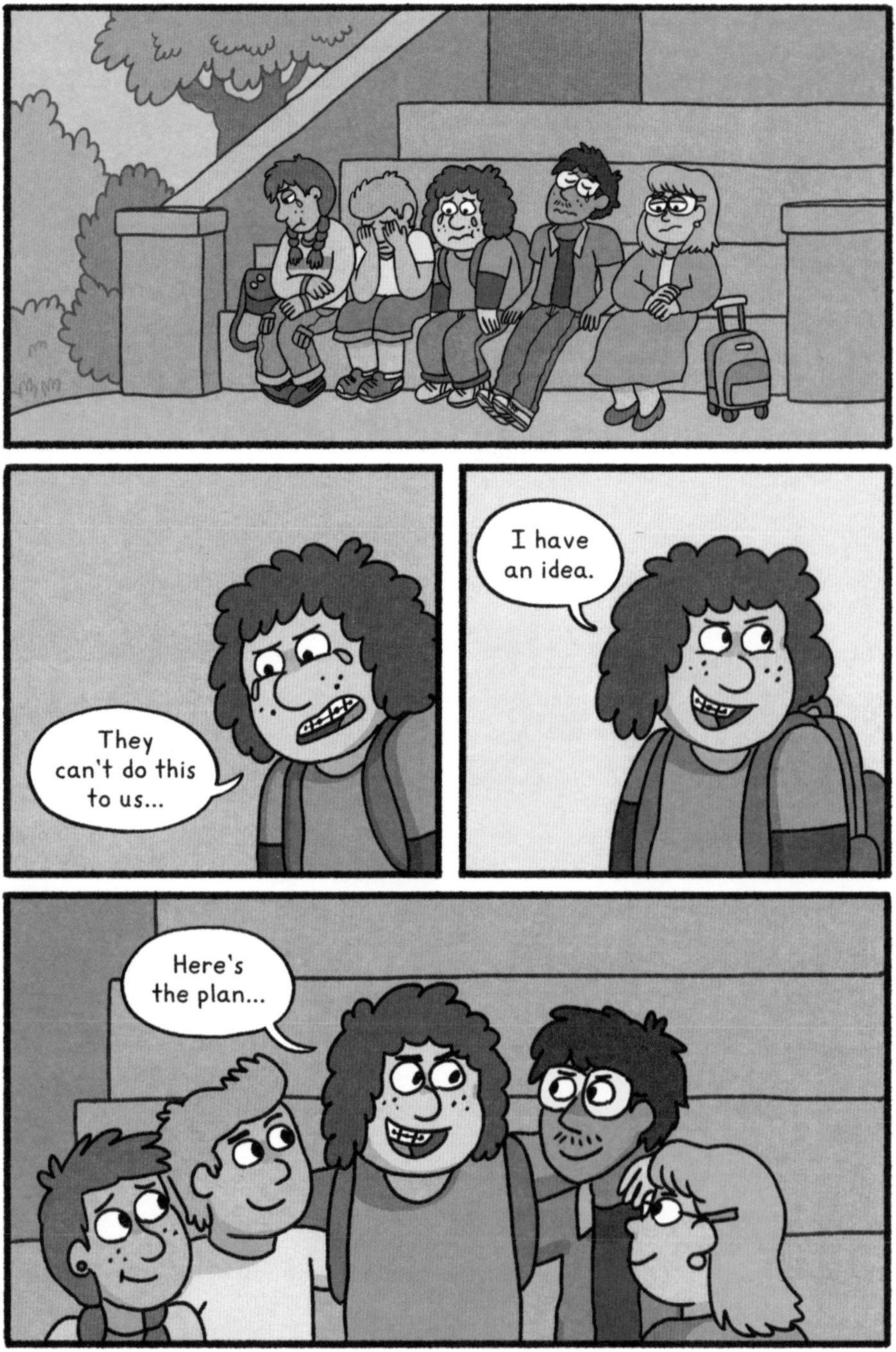
They can't do this to us...
I have an idea.
Here's the plan...

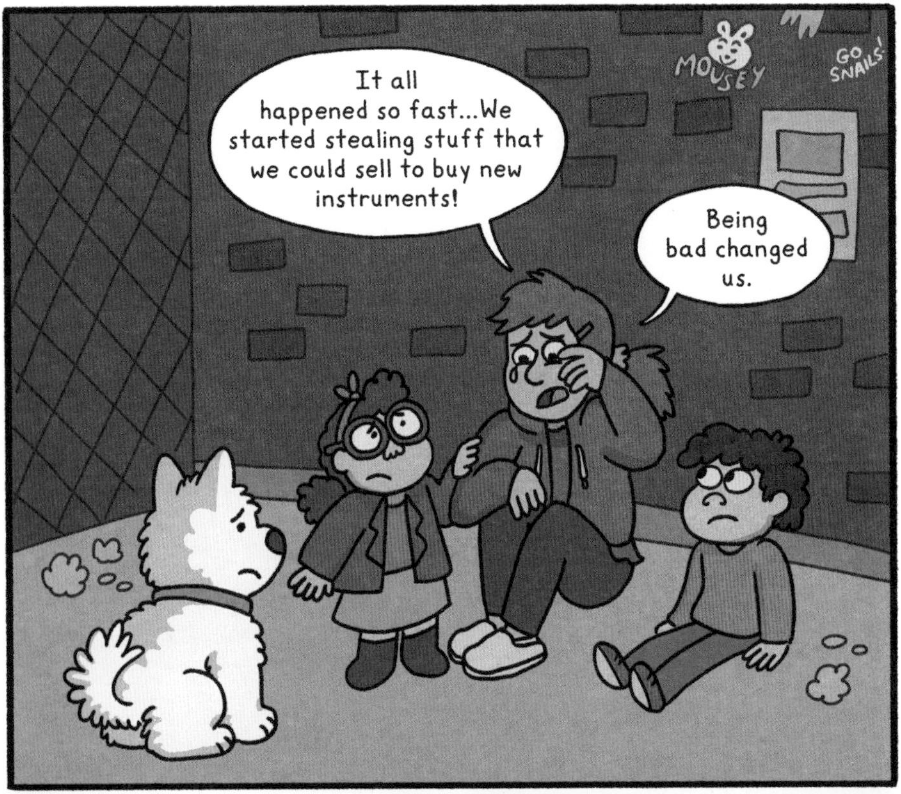
MOUSEY
GO SNAILS!
It all happened so fast...We started stealing stuff that we could sell to buy new instruments!
Being bad changed us.

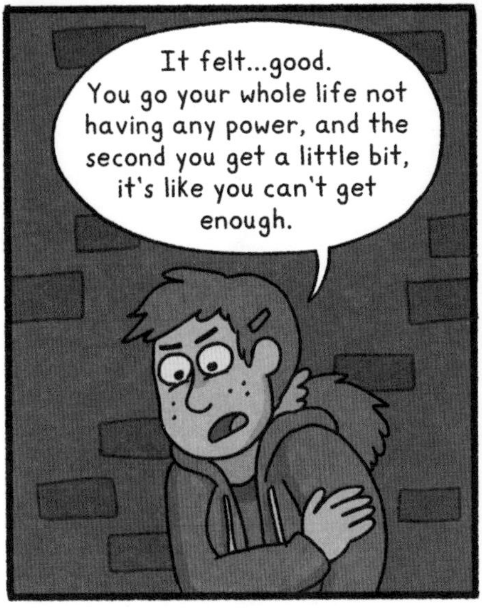
It felt...good. You go your whole life not having any power, and the second you get a little bit, it's like you can't get enough.

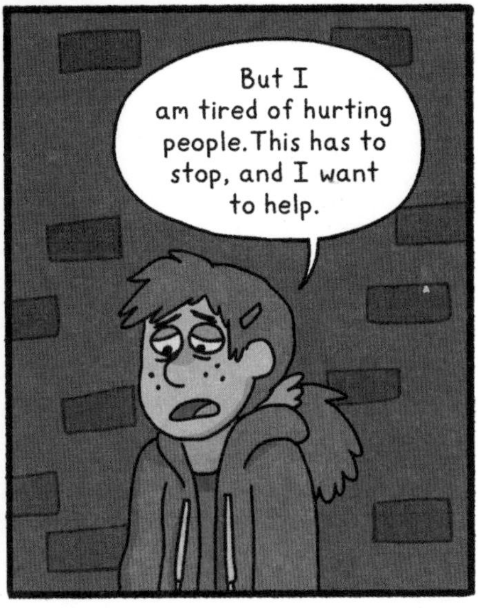
But I am tired of hurting people. This has to stop, and I want to help.

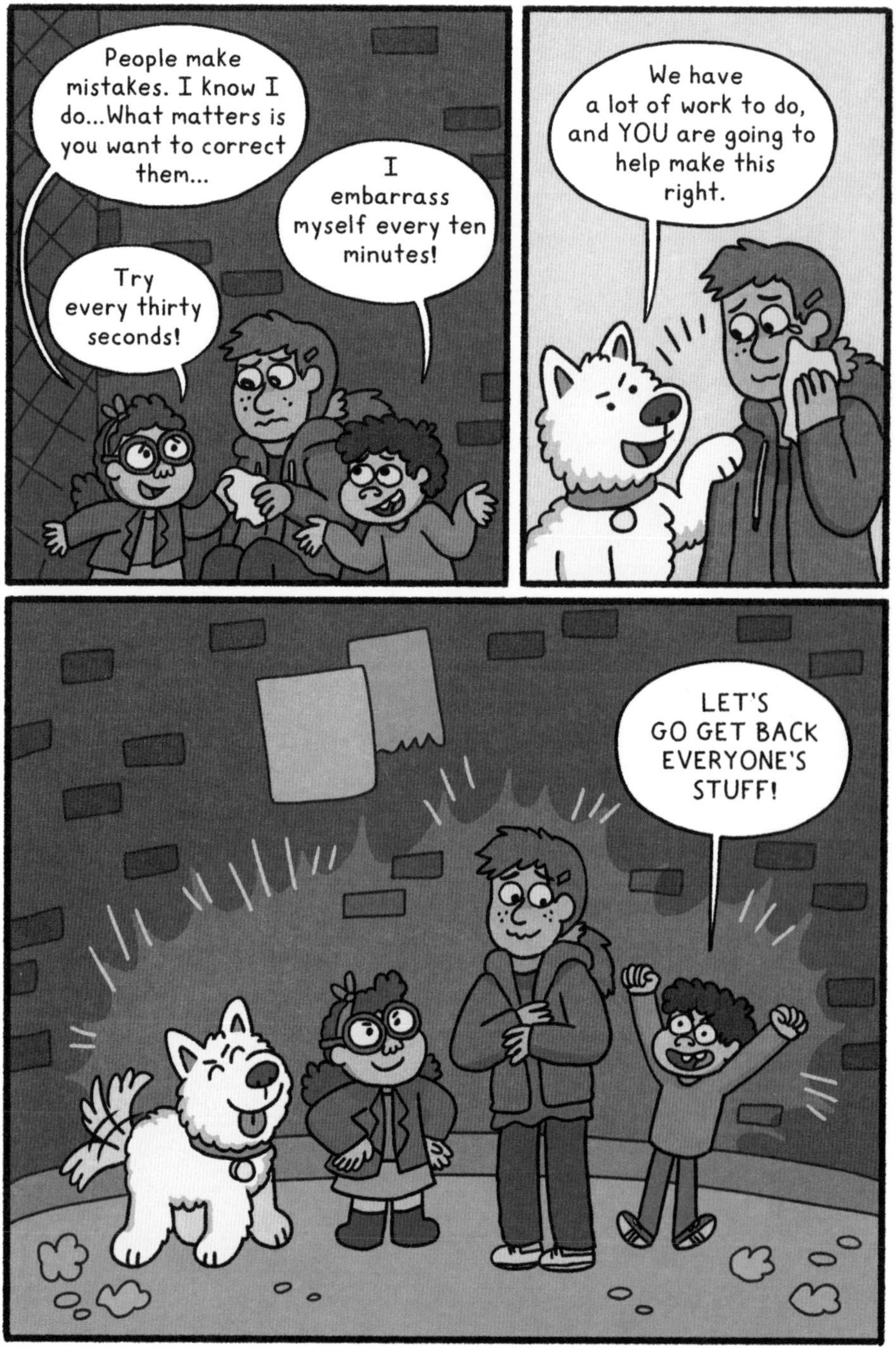
People make mistakes. I know I do...What matters is you want to correct them...
Try every thirty seconds!
I embarrass myself every ten minutes!
We have a lot of work to do, and YOU are going to help make this right.
LET'S GO GET BACK EVERYONE'S STUFF!

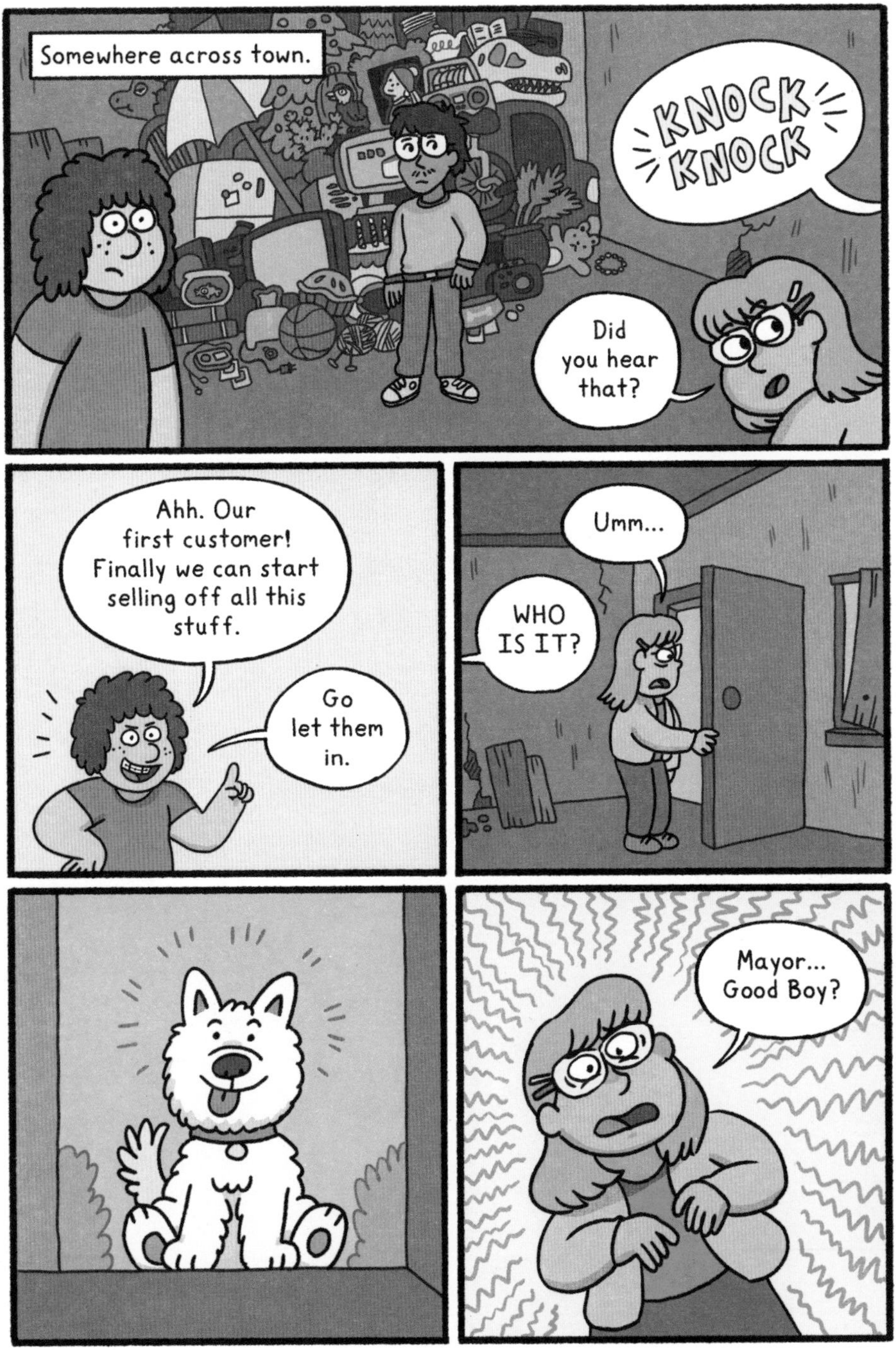
Somewhere across town.
KNOCK KNOCK
Did you hear that?
Ahh. Our first customer! Finally we can start selling off all this stuff.
Go let them in.
Umm...
WHO IS IT?
Mayor... Good Boy?

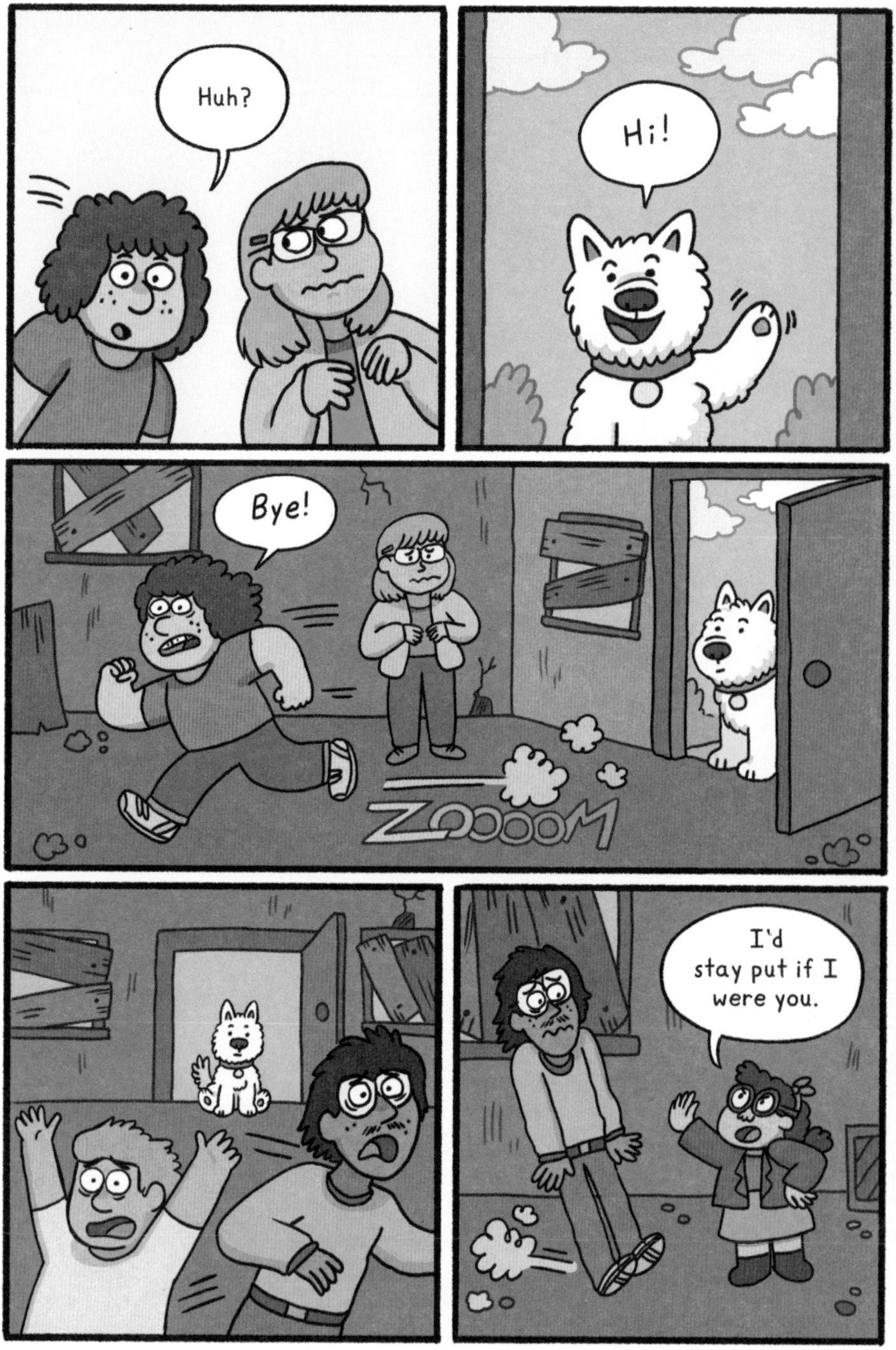
Huh?
Hi!
Bye!
ZOOOOM
I'd stay put if I were you.

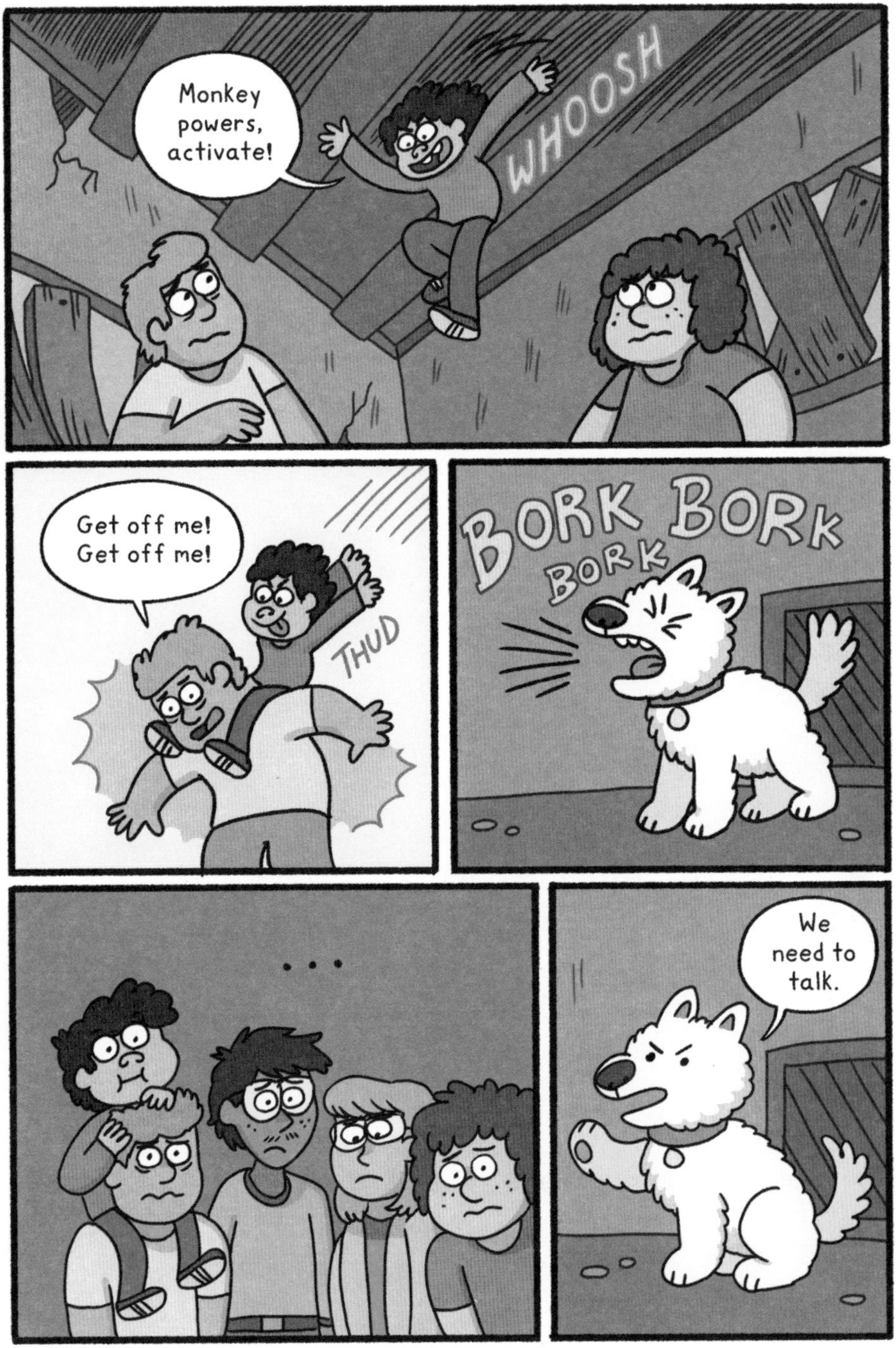
Monkey powers, activate!
WHOOSH
Get off me! Get off me!
THUD
BORK BORK
BORK
...
We need to talk.

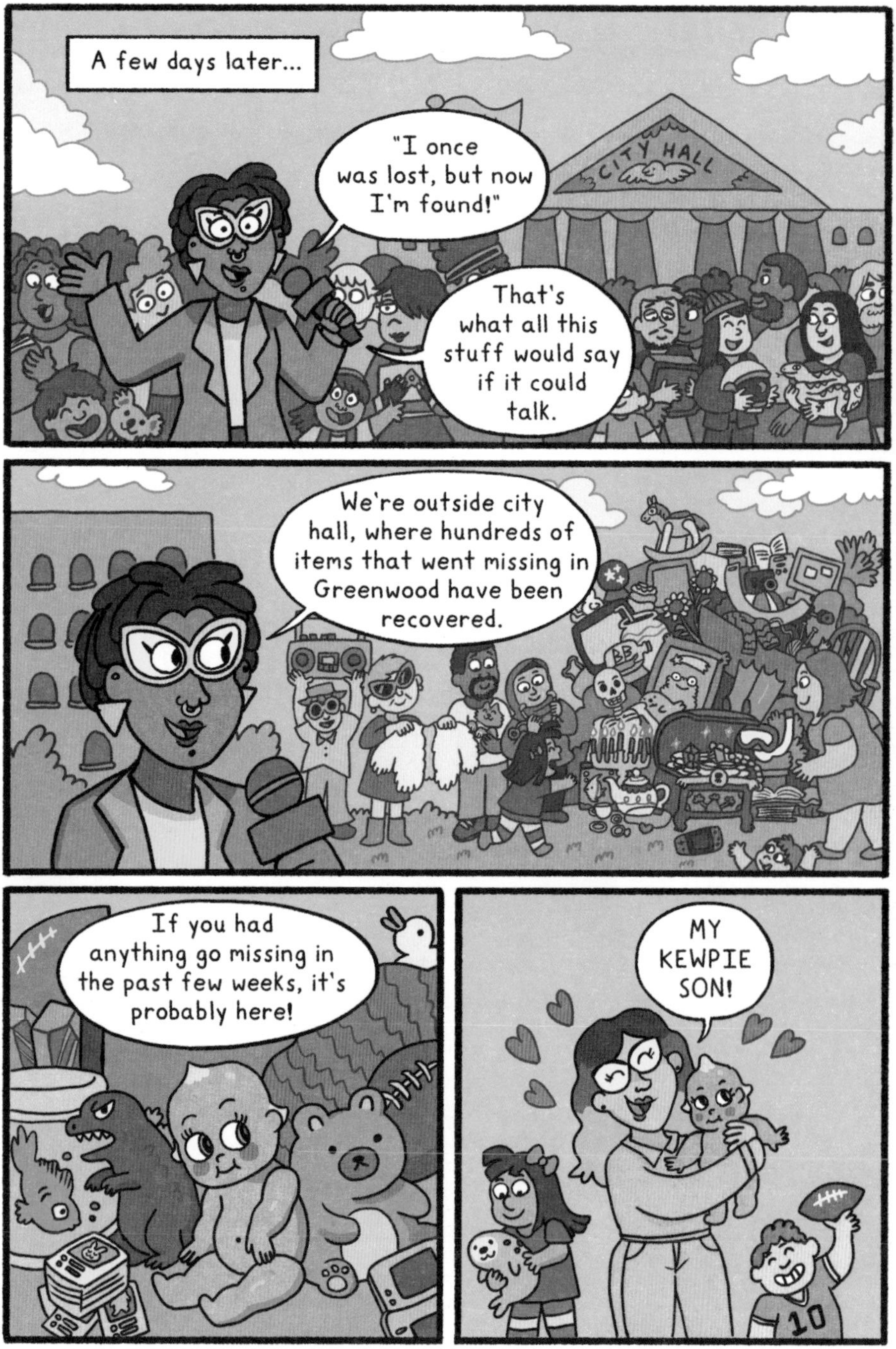
A few days later...
"I once was lost, but now I'm found!"
That's what all this stuff would say if it could talk.
CITY HALL
We're outside city hall, where hundreds of items that went missing in Greenwood have been recovered.
If you had anything go missing in the past few weeks, it's probably here!
MY KEWPIE SON!

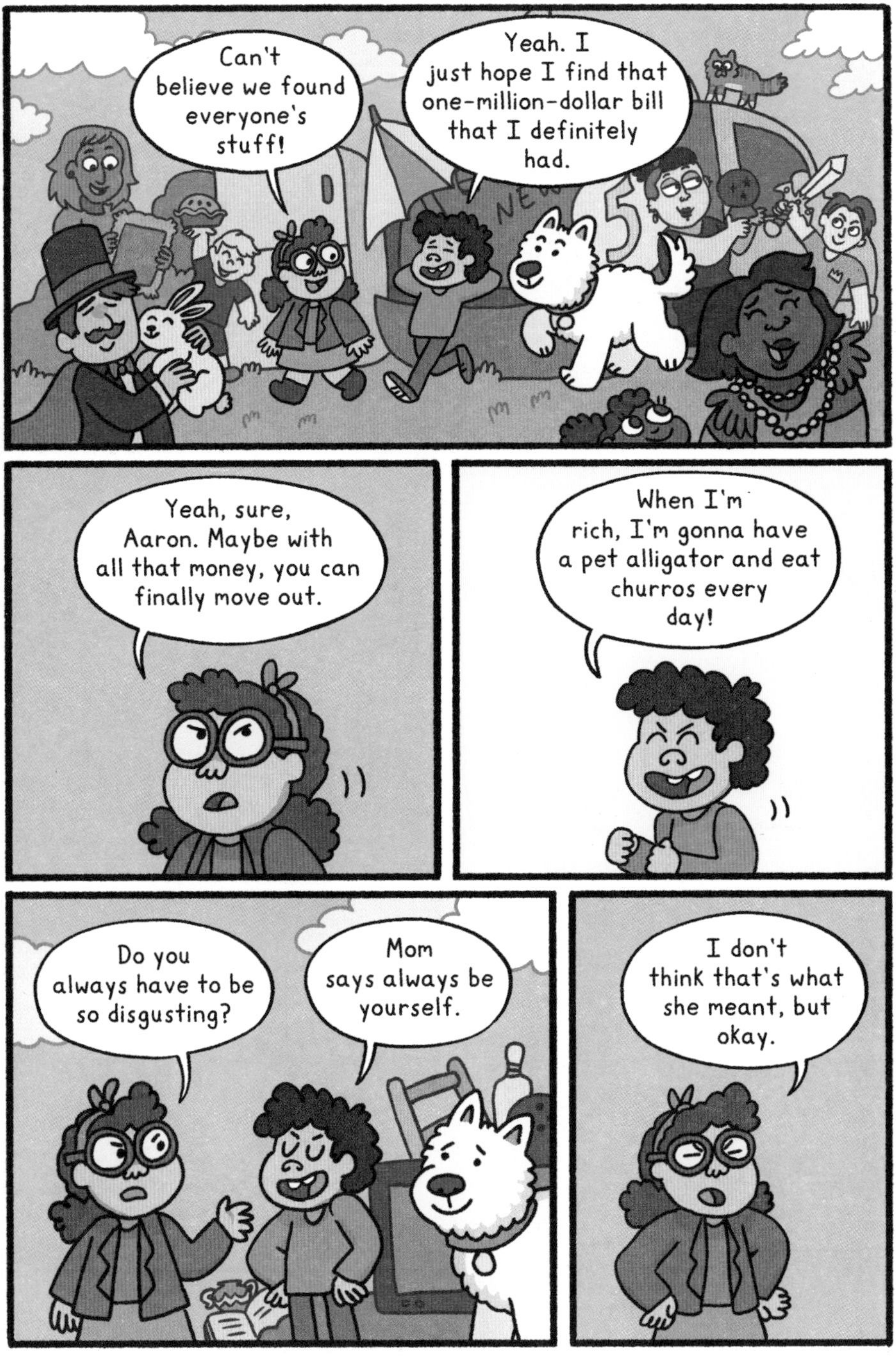
Can't believe we found everyone's stuff!
Yeah. I just hope I find that one-million-dollar bill that I definitely had.
Yeah, sure, Aaron. Maybe with all that money, you can finally move out.
When I'm rich, I'm gonna have a pet alligator and eat churros every day!
Do you always have to be so disgusting?
Mom says always be yourself.
I don't think that's what she meant, but okay.

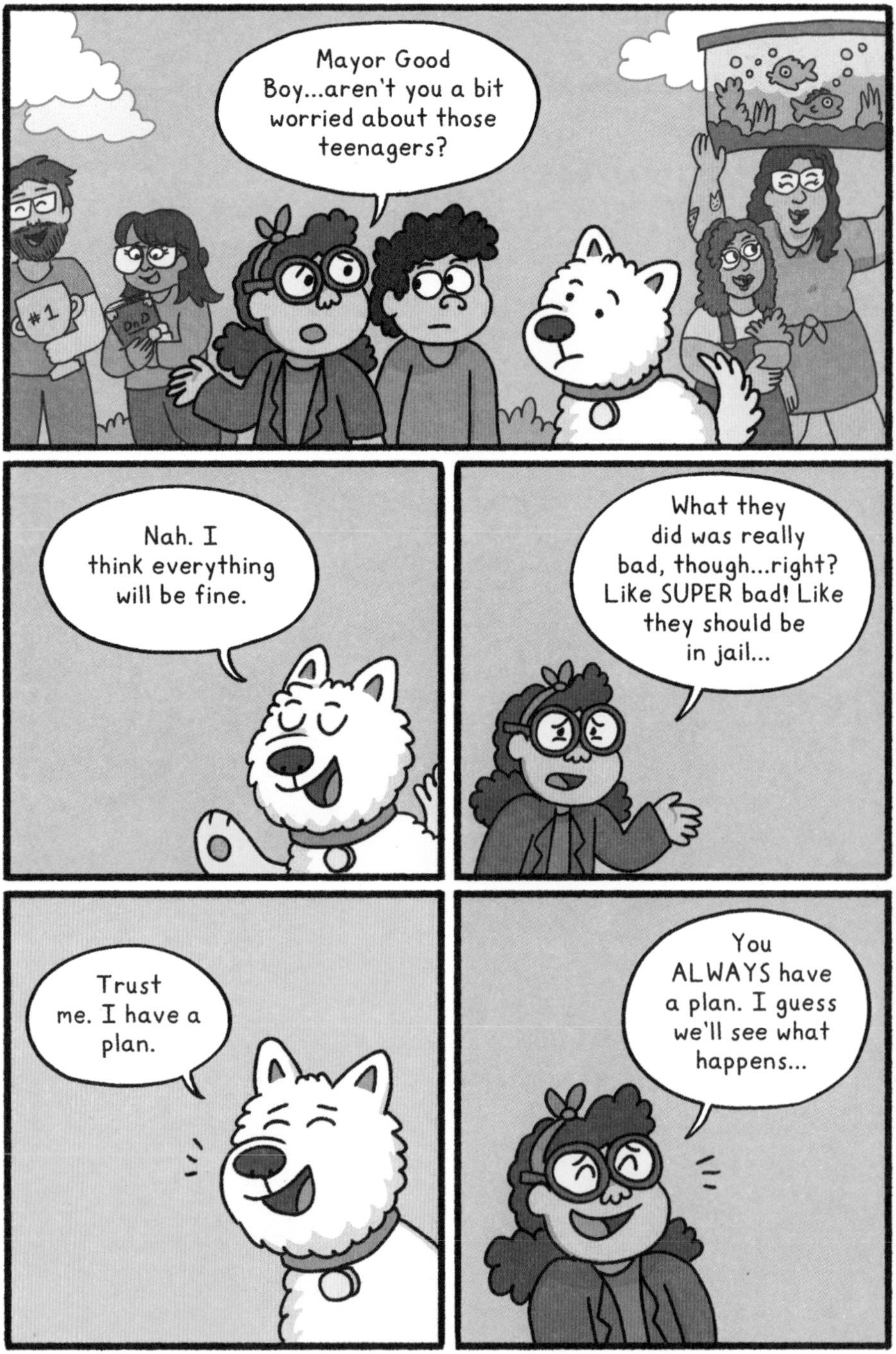
Mayor Good Boy...aren't you a bit worried about those teenagers?
Nah. I think everything will be fine.
What they did was really bad, though...right? Like SUPER bad! Like they should be in jail...
Trust me. I have a plan.
You ALWAYS have a plan. I guess we'll see what happens...

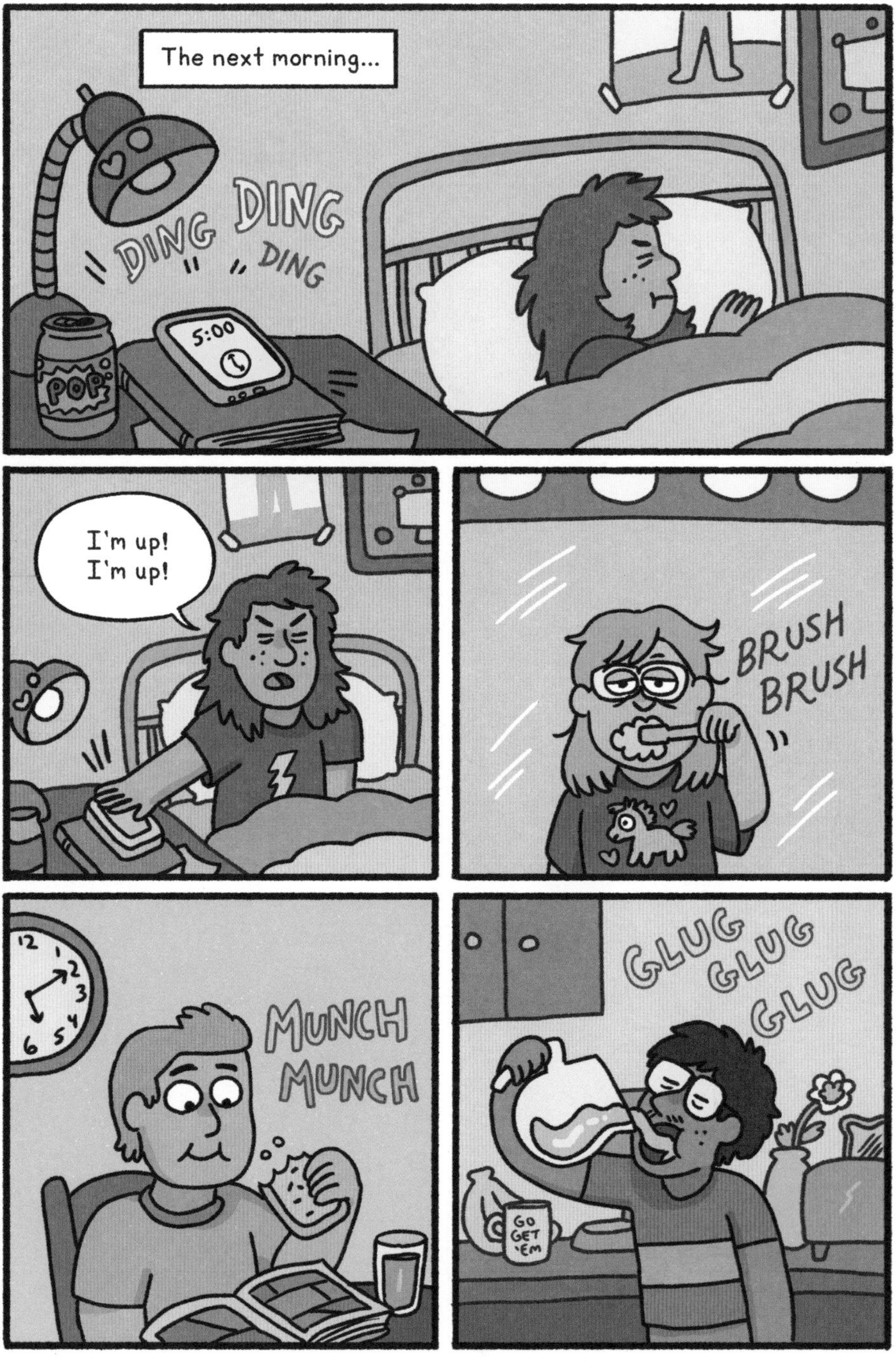
The next morning...
DING DING DING DING
5:00
POP
I'm up! I'm up!
BRUSH BRUSH
MUNCH MUNCH
GLUG GLUG GLUG
GO GET 'EM

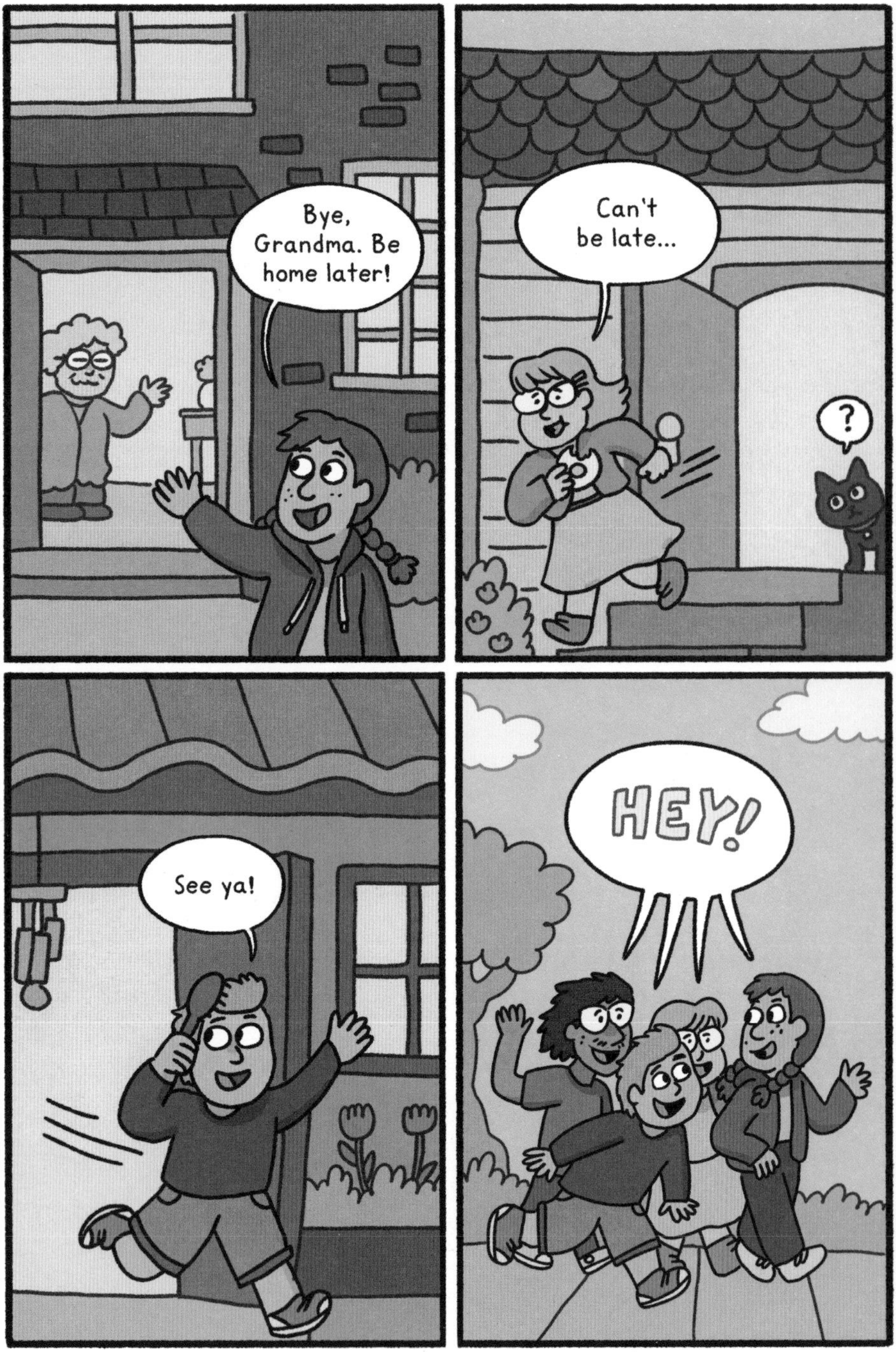
Bye, Grandma. Be home later!
Can't be late...
?
See ya!
HEY!

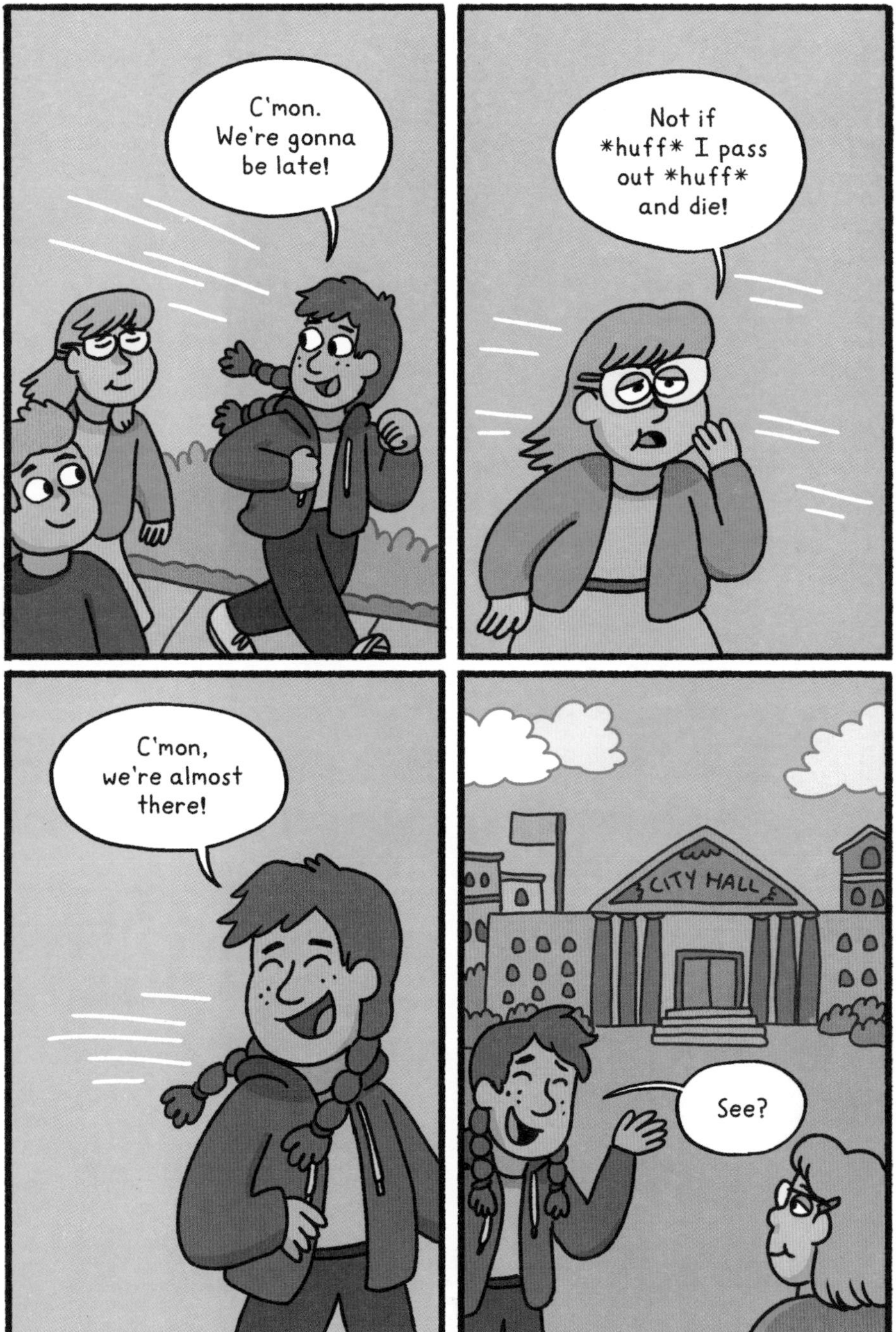
C'mon. We're gonna be late!
Not if *huff* I pass out *huff* and die!
C'mon, we're almost there!
CITY HALL
See?

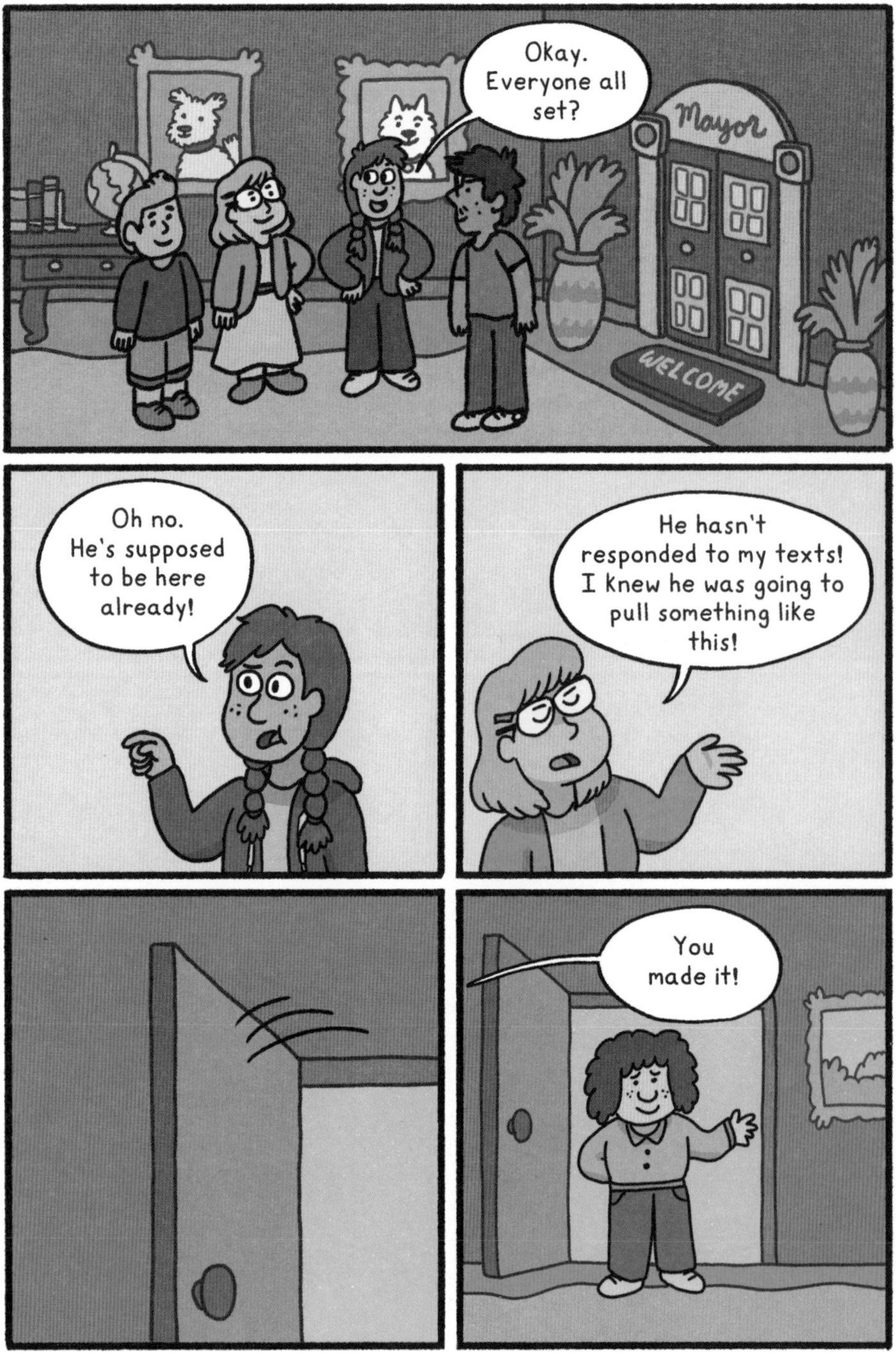
Okay. Everyone all set?
Mayor
WELCOME
Oh no. He's supposed to be here already!
He hasn't responded to my texts! I knew he was going to pull something like this!
You made it!

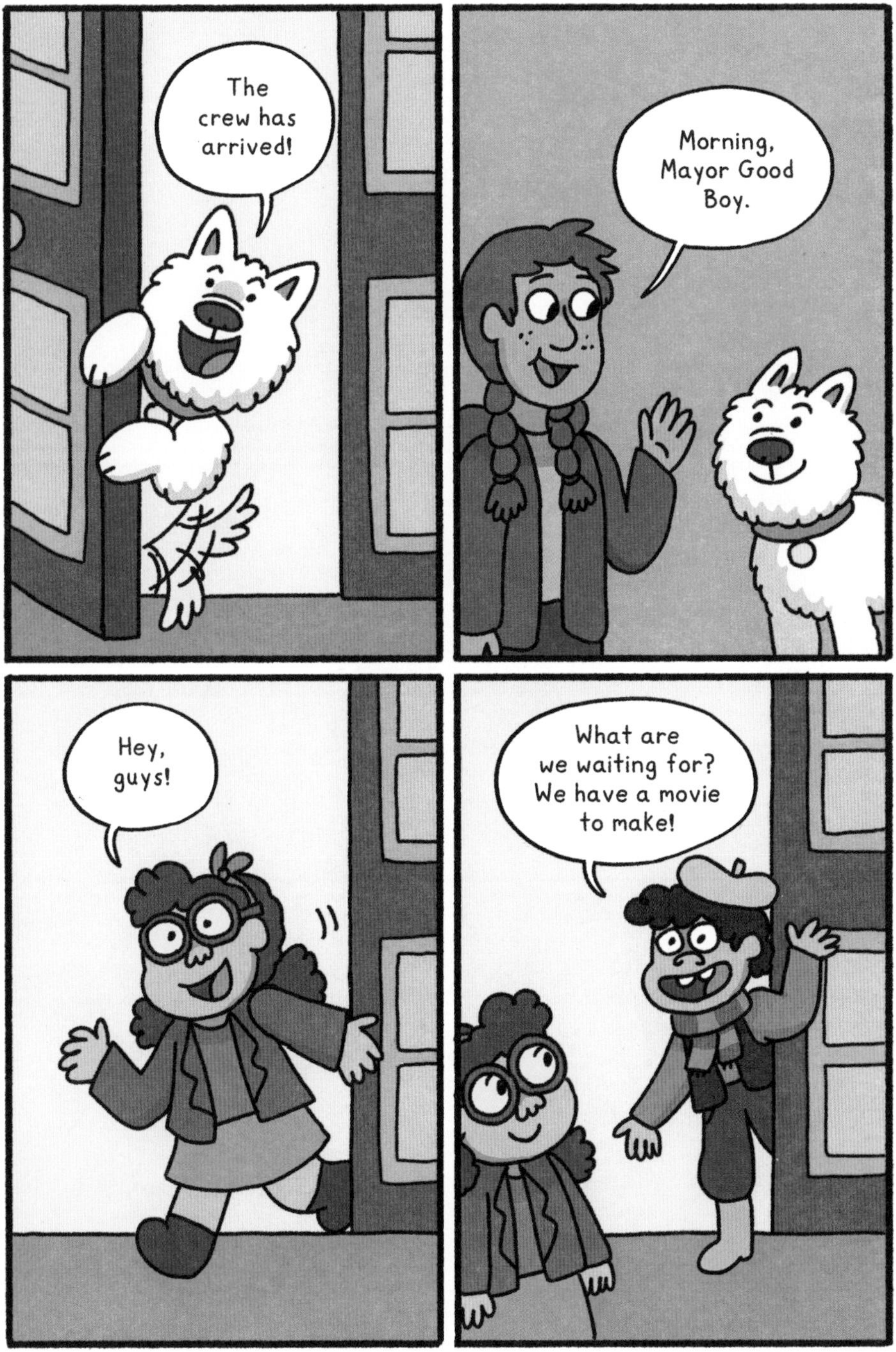
The crew has arrived!
Morning, Mayor Good Boy.
Hey, guys!
What are we waiting for? We have a movie to make!

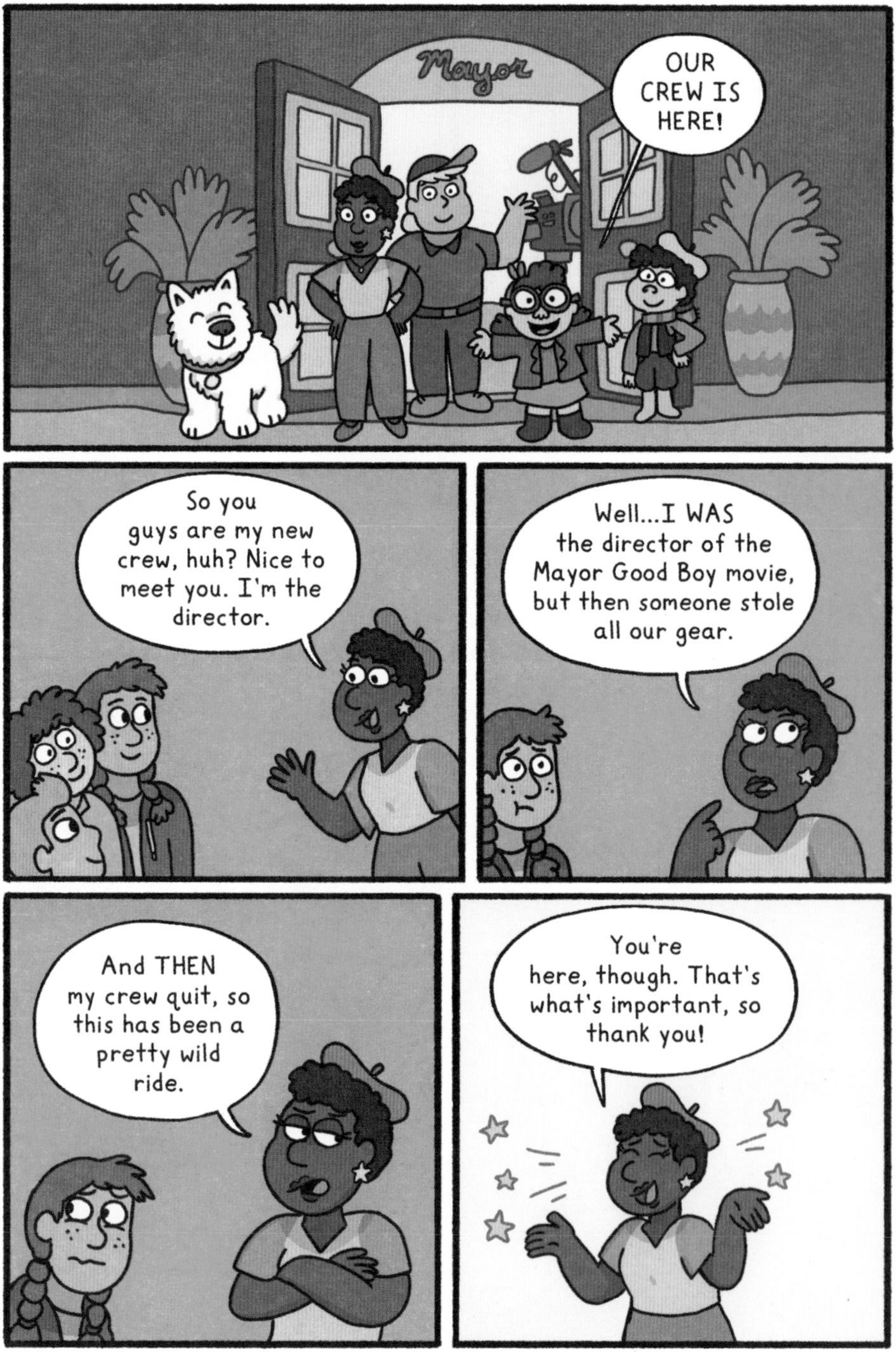
Mayor
OUR CREW IS HERE!
So you guys are my new crew, huh? Nice to meet you. I'm the director.
Well...I WAS the director of the Mayor Good Boy movie, but then someone stole all our gear.
And THEN my crew quit, so this has been a pretty wild ride.
You're here, though. That's what's important, so thank you!

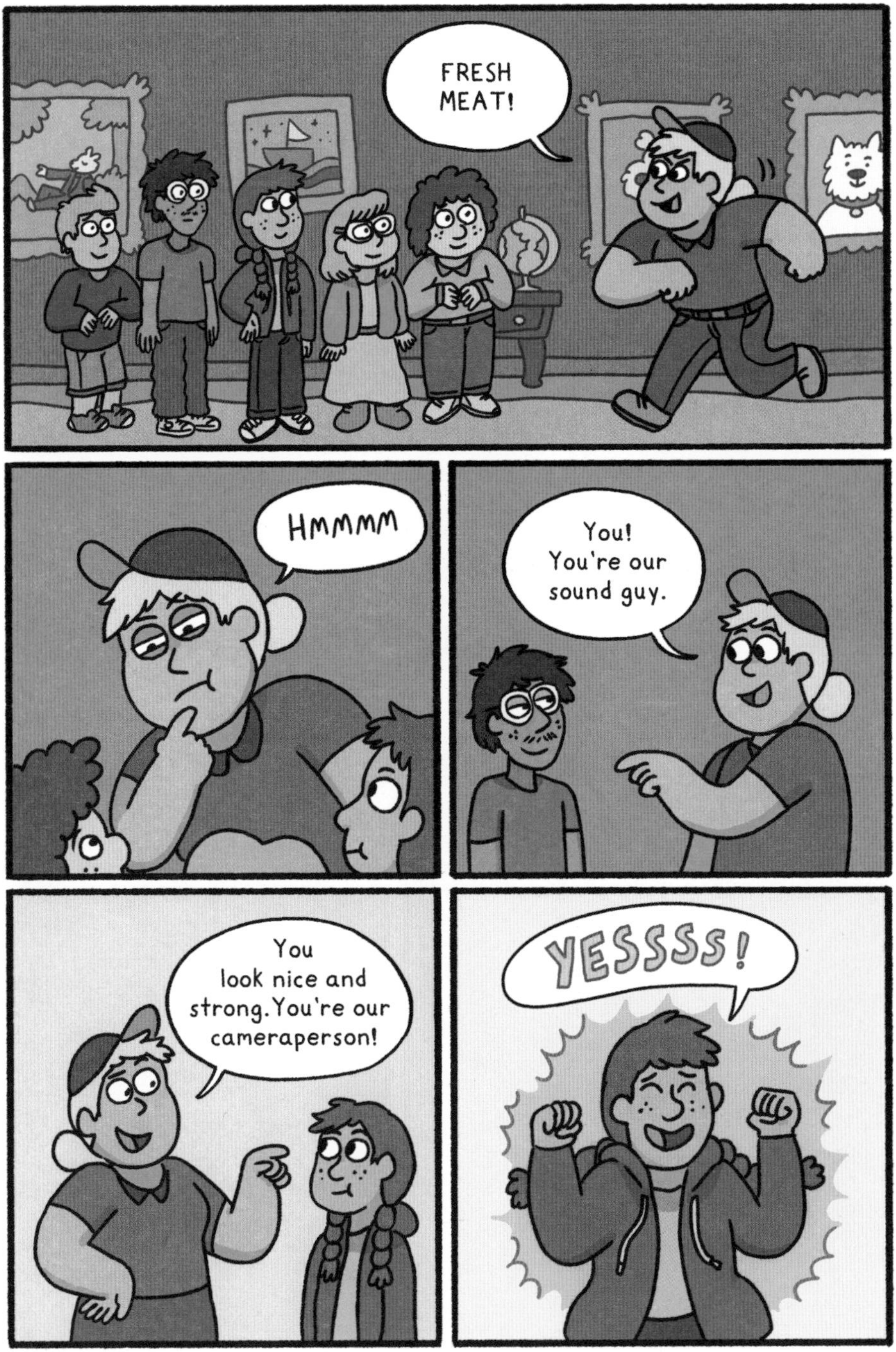
FRESH MEAT!
HMMMM
You! You're our sound guy.
You look nice and strong. You're our cameraperson!
YESSSS!

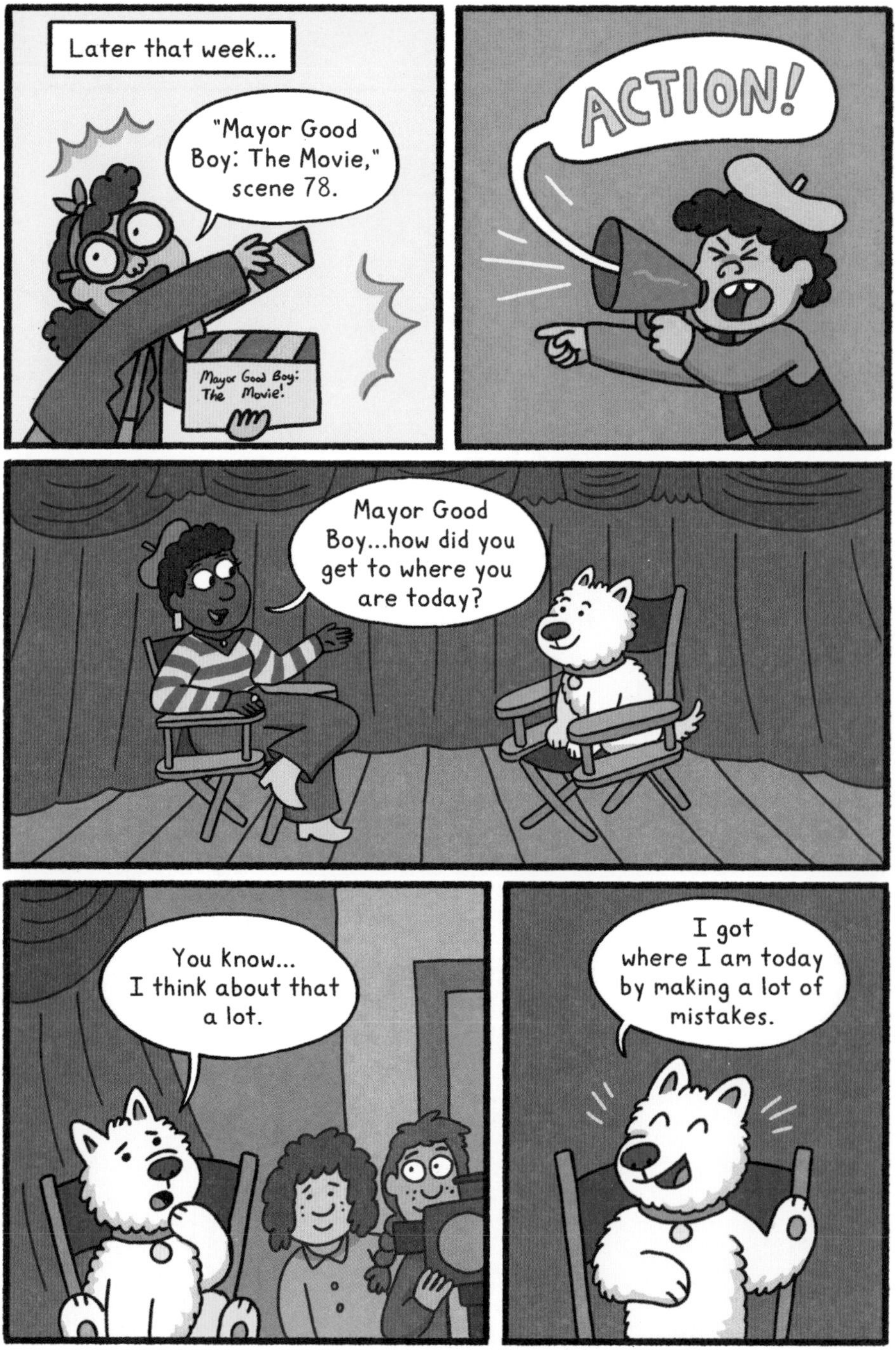
Later that week...
"Mayor Good Boy: The Movie," scene 78.
Mayor Good Boy: The Movie!
ACTION!
Mayor Good Boy...how did you get to where you are today?
You know... I think about that a lot.
I got where I am today by making a lot of mistakes.

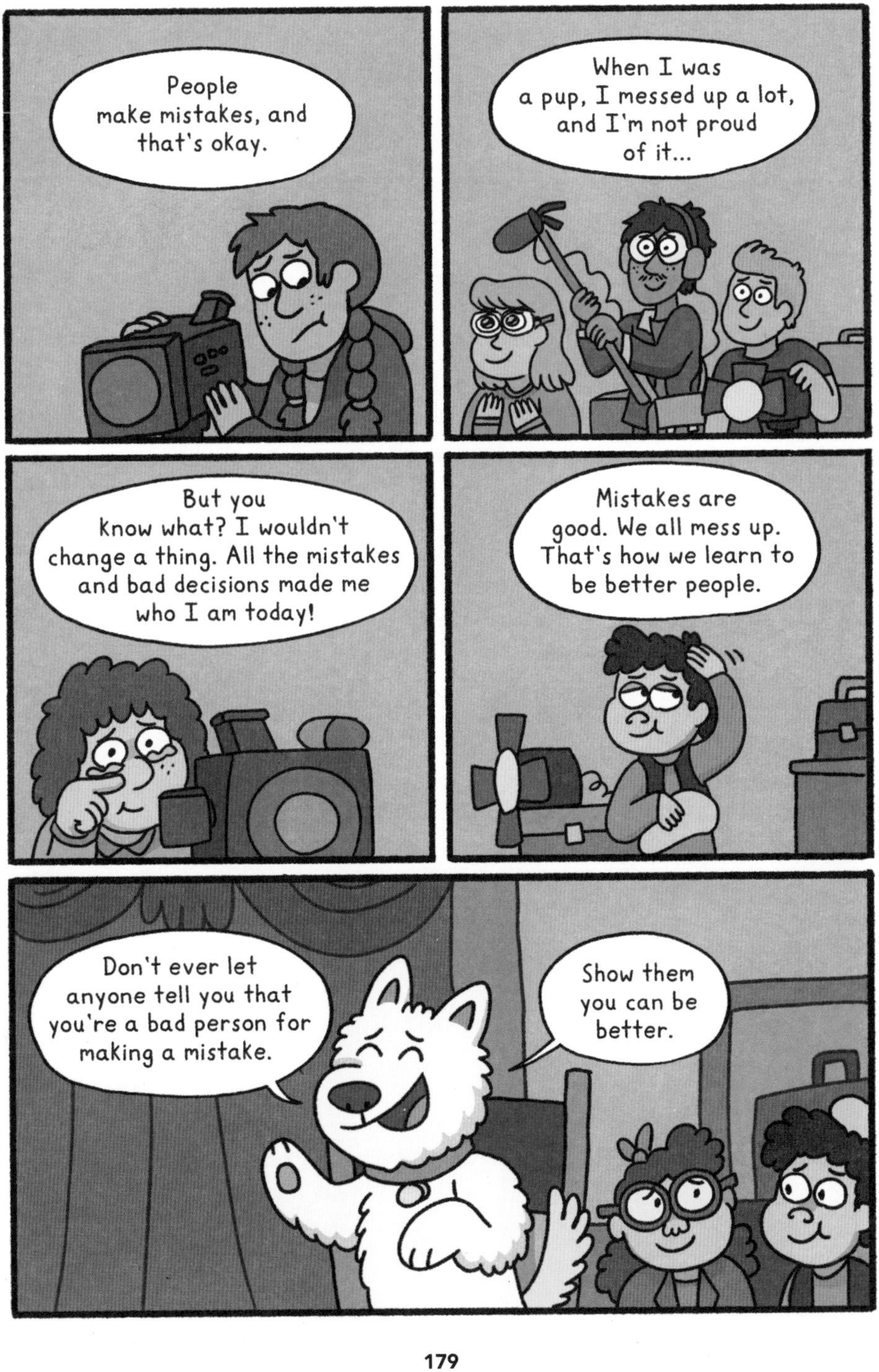
People make mistakes, and that's okay.
When I was a pup, I messed up a lot, and I'm not proud of it...
But you know what? I wouldn't change a thing. All the mistakes and bad decisions made me who I am today!
Mistakes are good. We all mess up. That's how we learn to be better people.
Don't ever let anyone tell you that you're a bad person for making a mistake.
Show them you can be better.

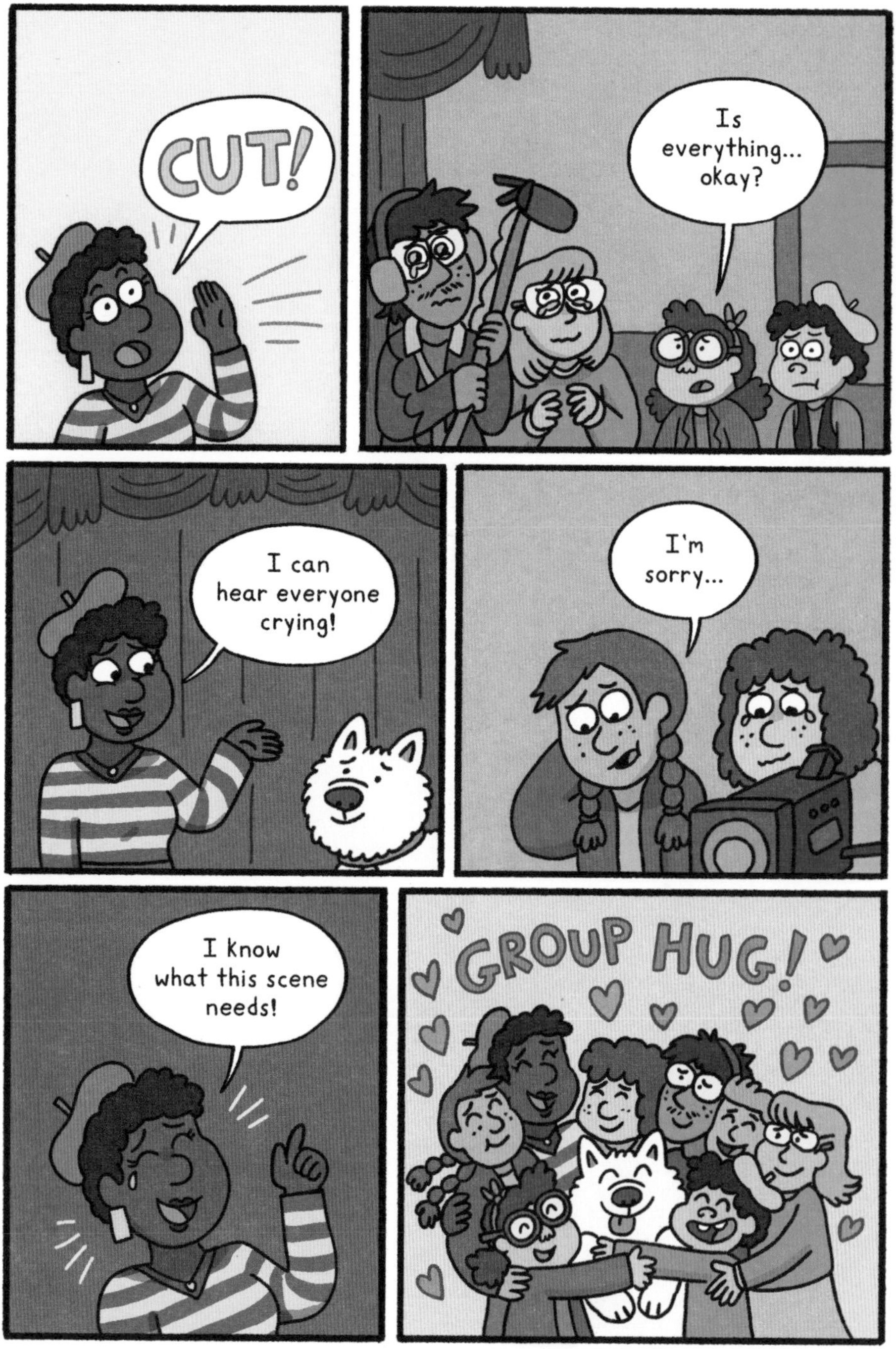
CUT!
Is everything... okay?
I can hear everyone crying!
I'm sorry...
I know what this scene needs!
GROUP HUG!

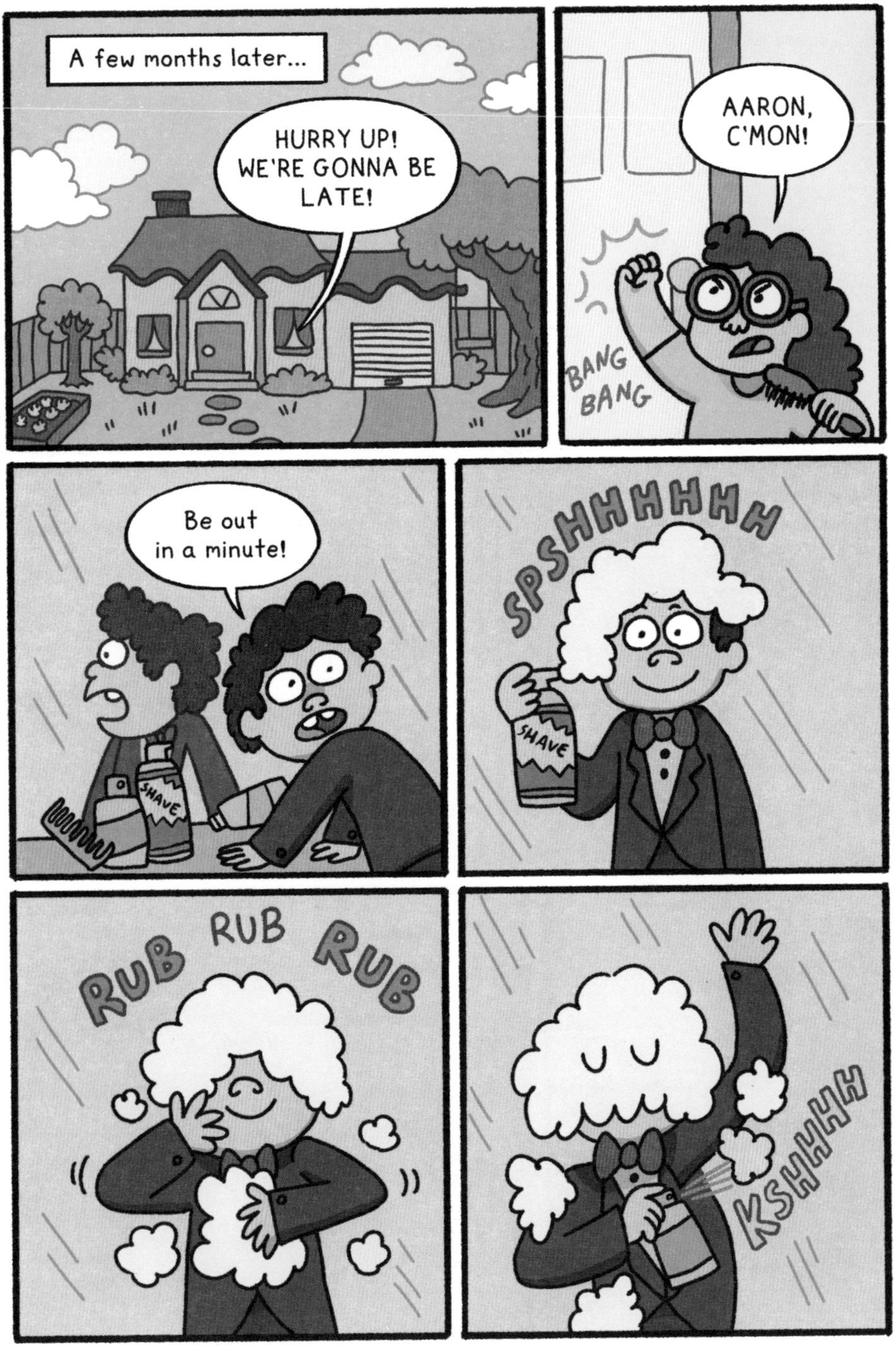
A few months later...
HURRY UP! WE'RE GONNA BE LATE!
AARON, C'MON!
BANG BANG
Be out in a minute!
SHAVE
SPSHHHHHHH
SHAVE
RUB RUB RUB
KSHHHHH

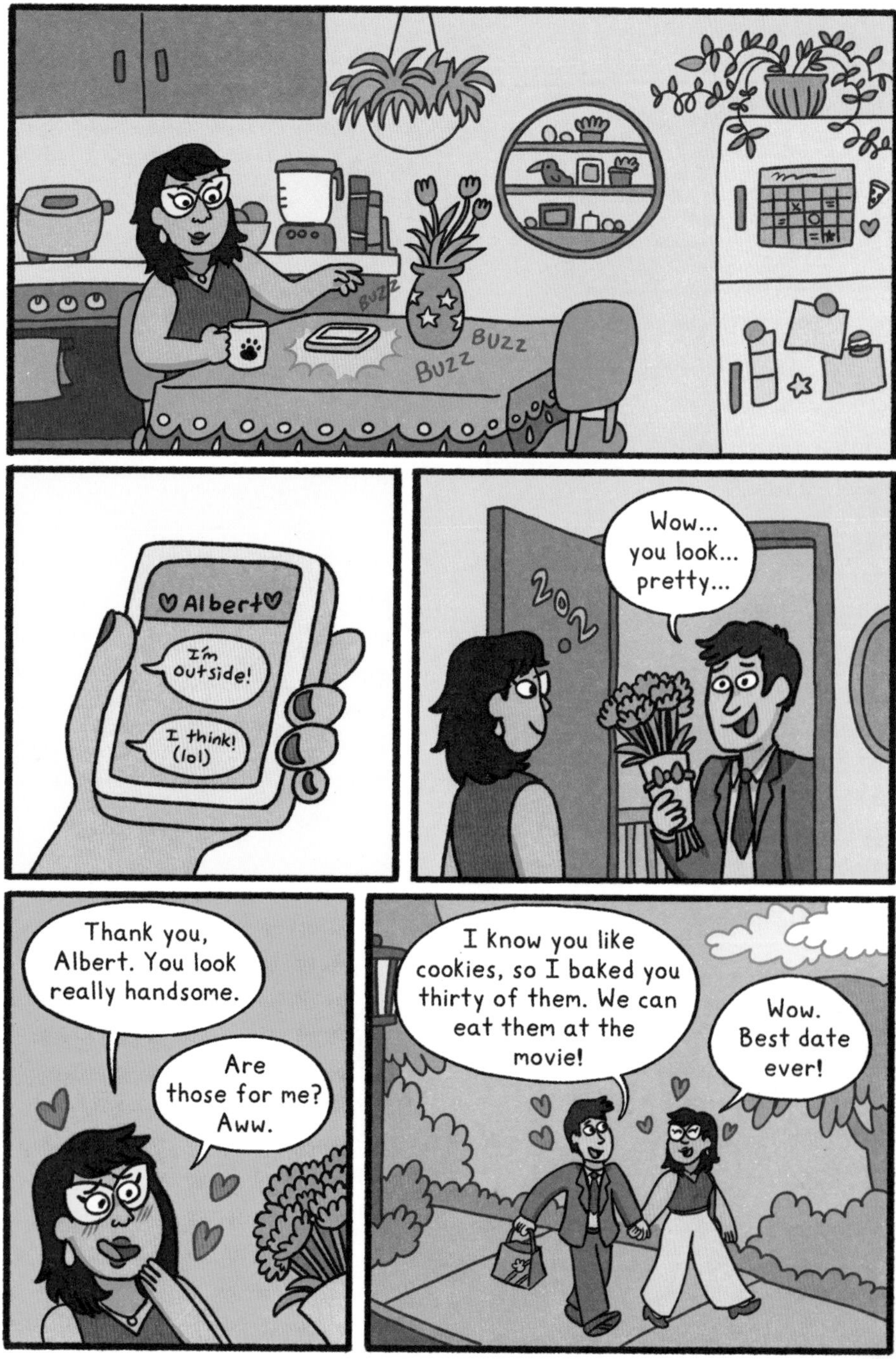
BUZZ
BUZZ
BUZZ
♡Albert♡
I'm outside!
I think! (lol)
202
Wow... you look... pretty...
Thank you, Albert. You look really handsome.
Are those for me? Aww.
I know you like cookies, so I baked you thirty of them. We can eat them at the movie!
Wow. Best date ever!

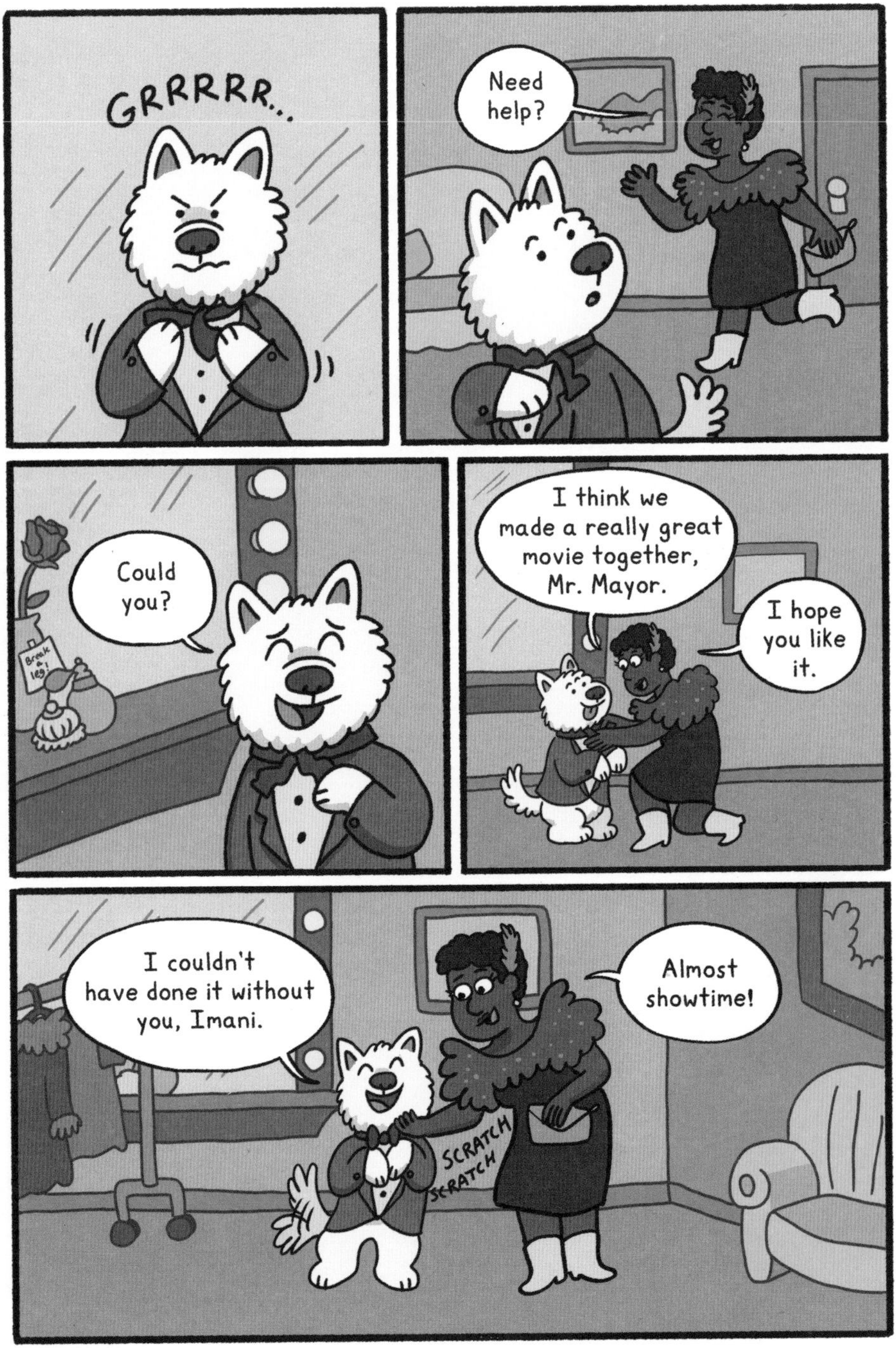
GRRRRR...
Need help?
Could you?
Break a leg!
I think we made a really great movie together, Mr. Mayor.
I hope you like it.
I couldn't have done it without you, Imani.
Almost showtime!
SCRATCH
SCRATCH

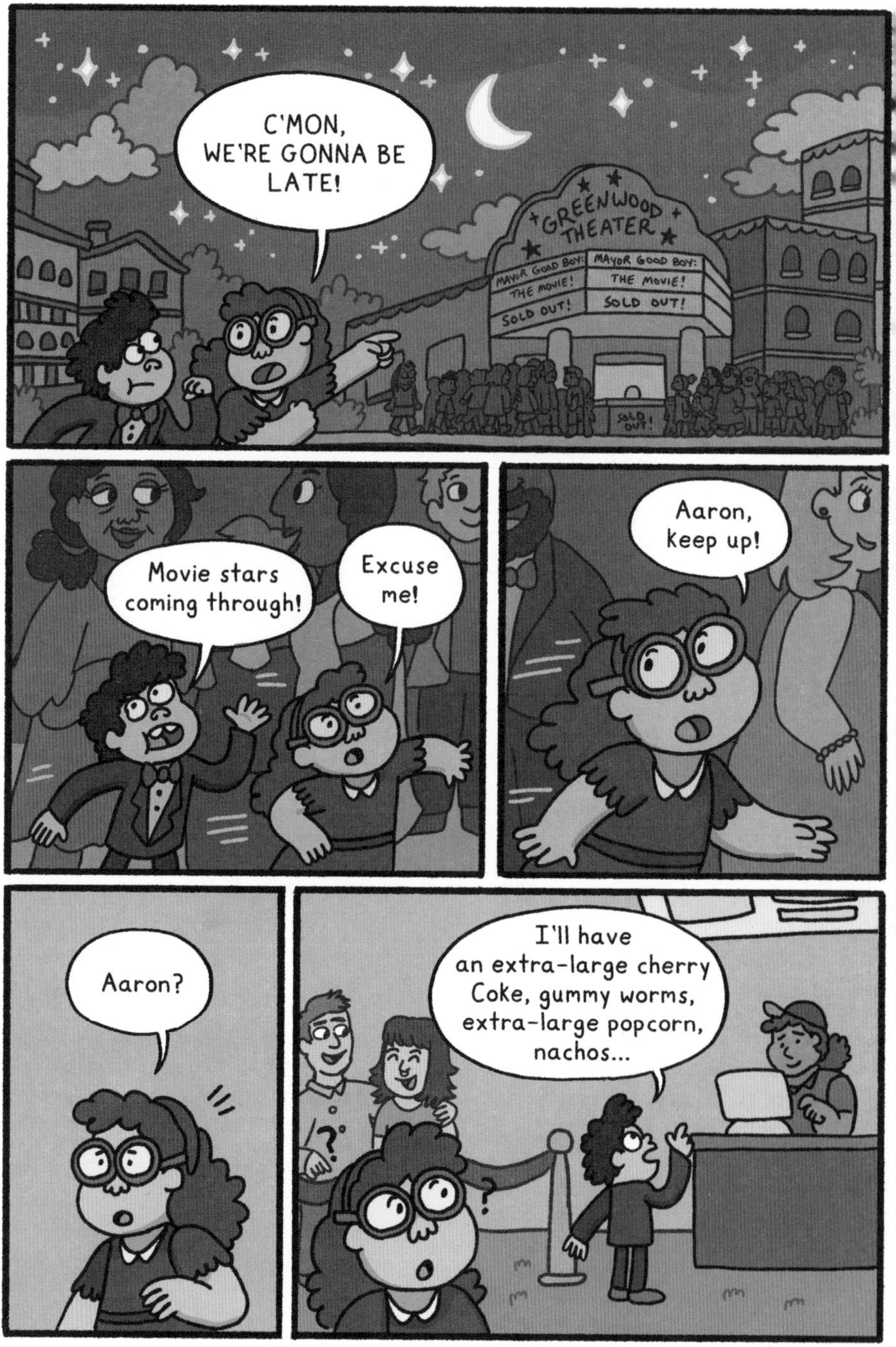
C'MON, WE'RE GONNA BE LATE!
GREENWOOD THEATER
MAYOR GOOD BOY: THE MOVIE! SOLD OUT!
MAYOR GOOD BOY: THE MOVIE! SOLD OUT!
SOLD OUT!
Movie stars coming through!
Excuse me!
Aaron, keep up!
Aaron?
I'll have an extra-large cherry Coke, gummy worms, extra-large popcorn, nachos...

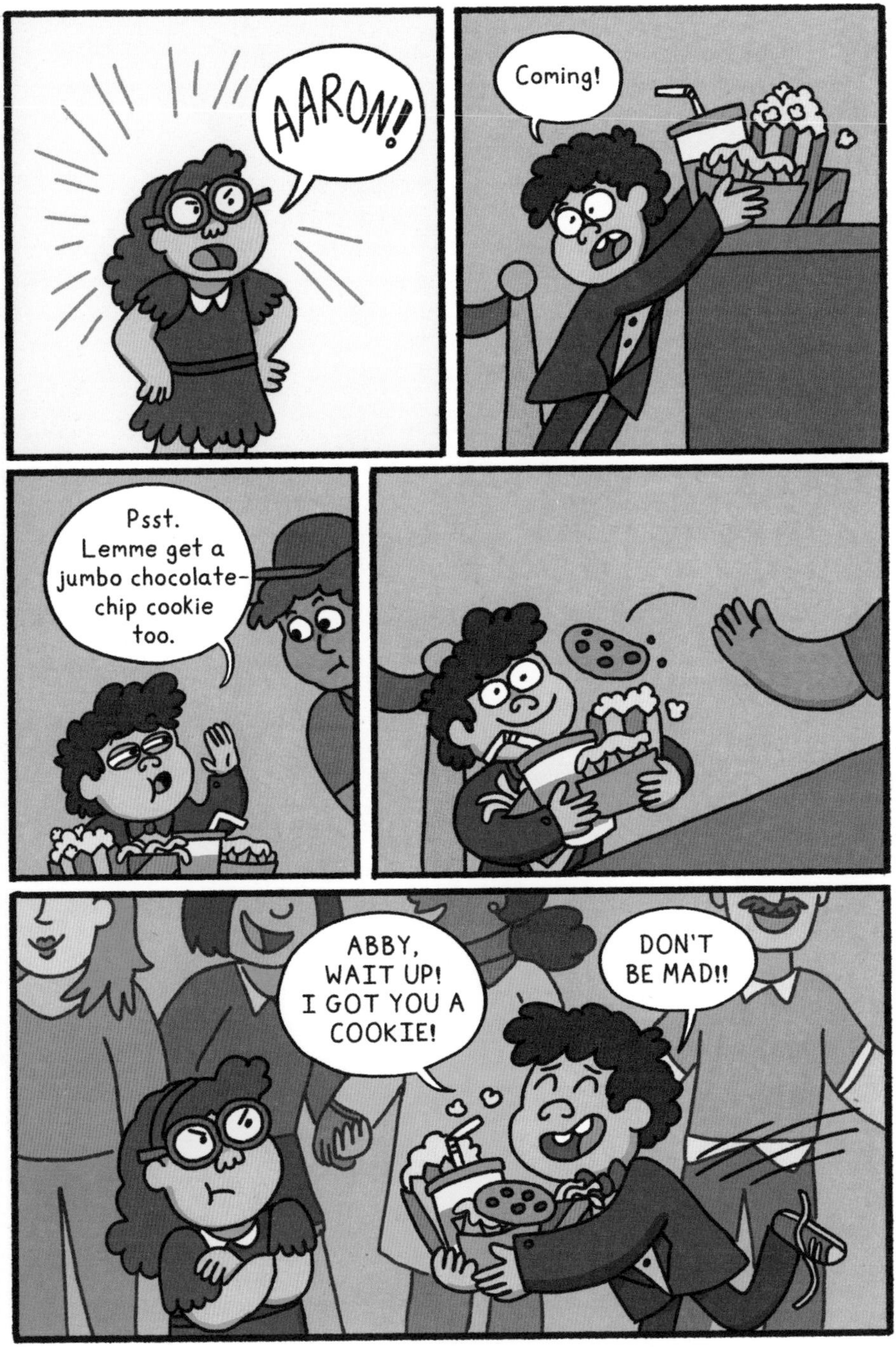
AARON!
Coming!
Psst. Lemme get a jumbo chocolate-chip cookie too.
ABBY, WAIT UP! I GOT YOU A COOKIE!
DON'T BE MAD!!

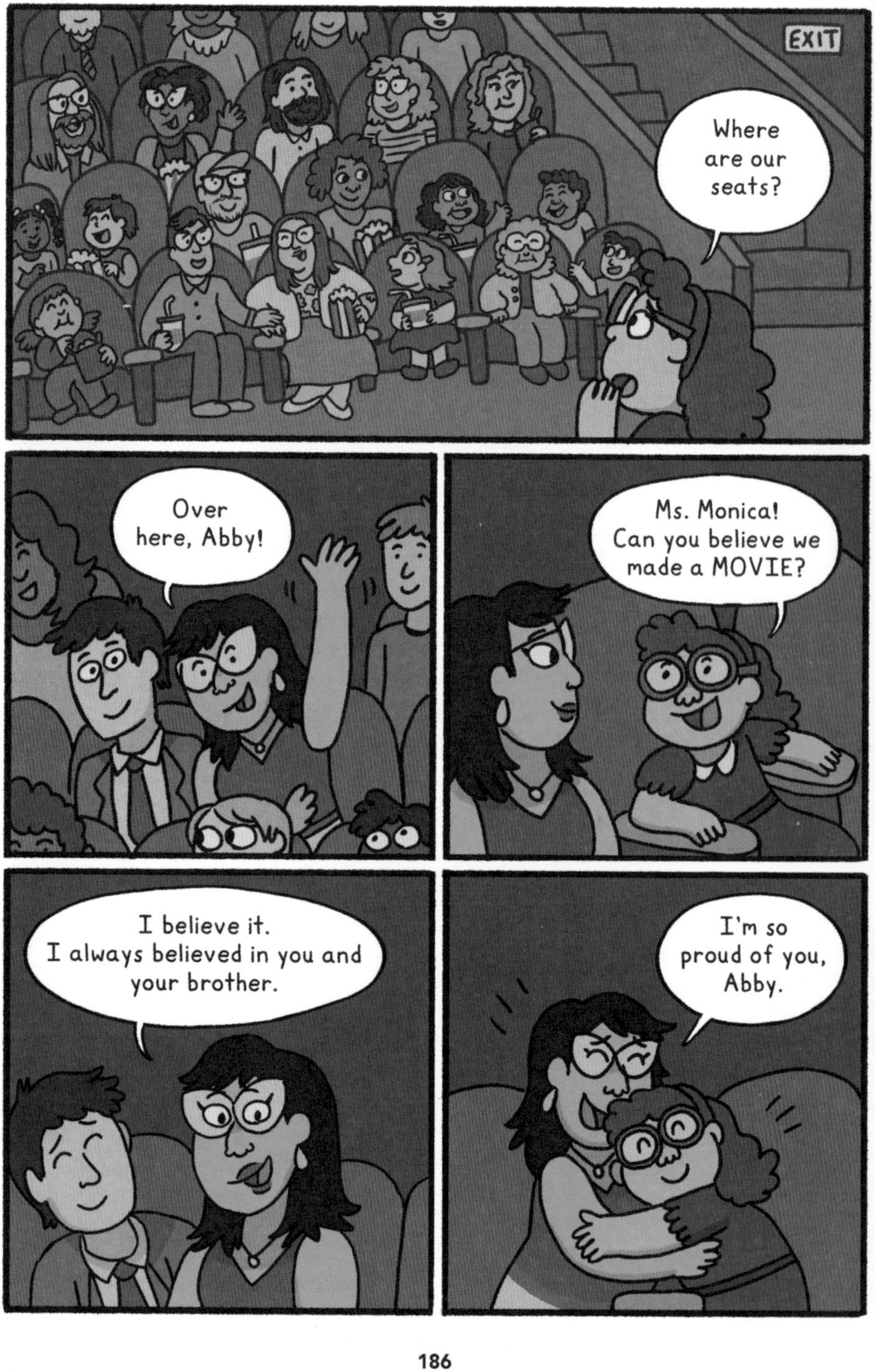
EXIT
Where are our seats?
Over here, Abby!
Ms. Monica! Can you believe we made a MOVIE?
I believe it. I always believed in you and your brother.
I'm so proud of you, Abby.

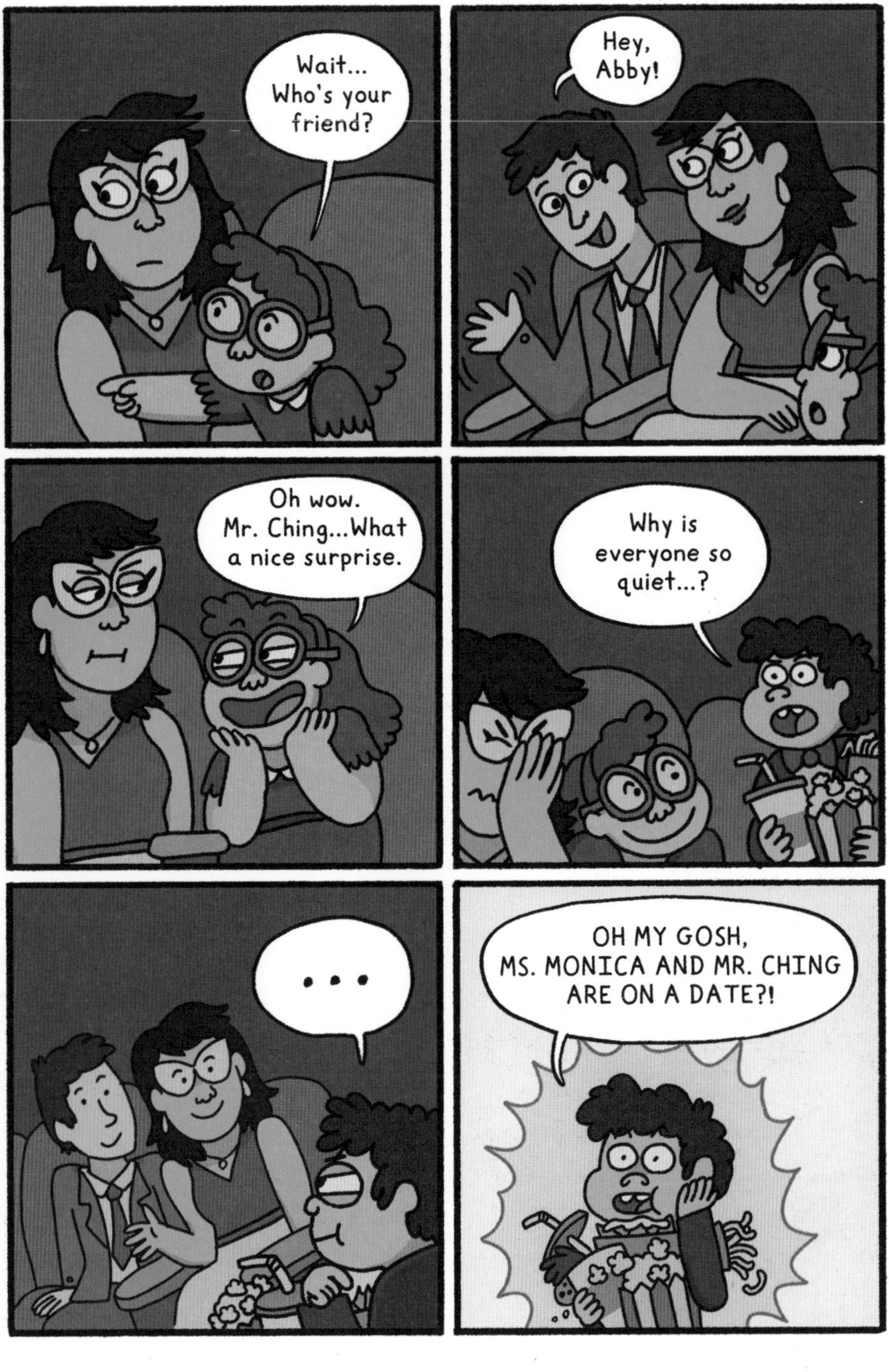
Wait... Who's your friend?
Hey, Abby!
Oh wow. Mr. Ching...What a nice surprise.
Why is everyone so quiet...?
...
OH MY GOSH, MS. MONICA AND MR. CHING ARE ON A DATE?!

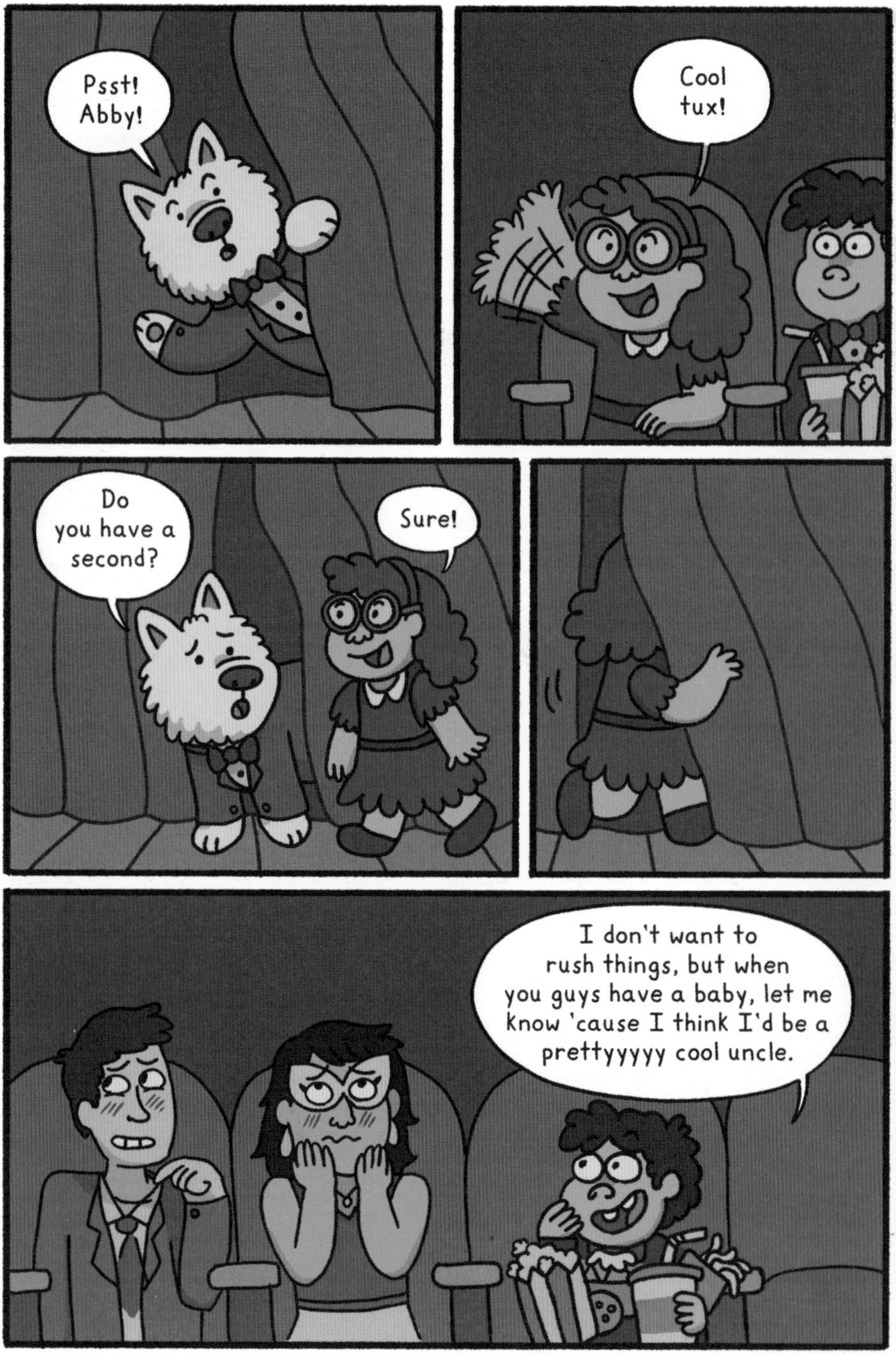
Psst! Abby!
Cool tux!
Do you have a second?
Sure!
I don't want to rush things, but when you guys have a baby, let me know 'cause I think I'd be a prettyyyyy cool uncle.

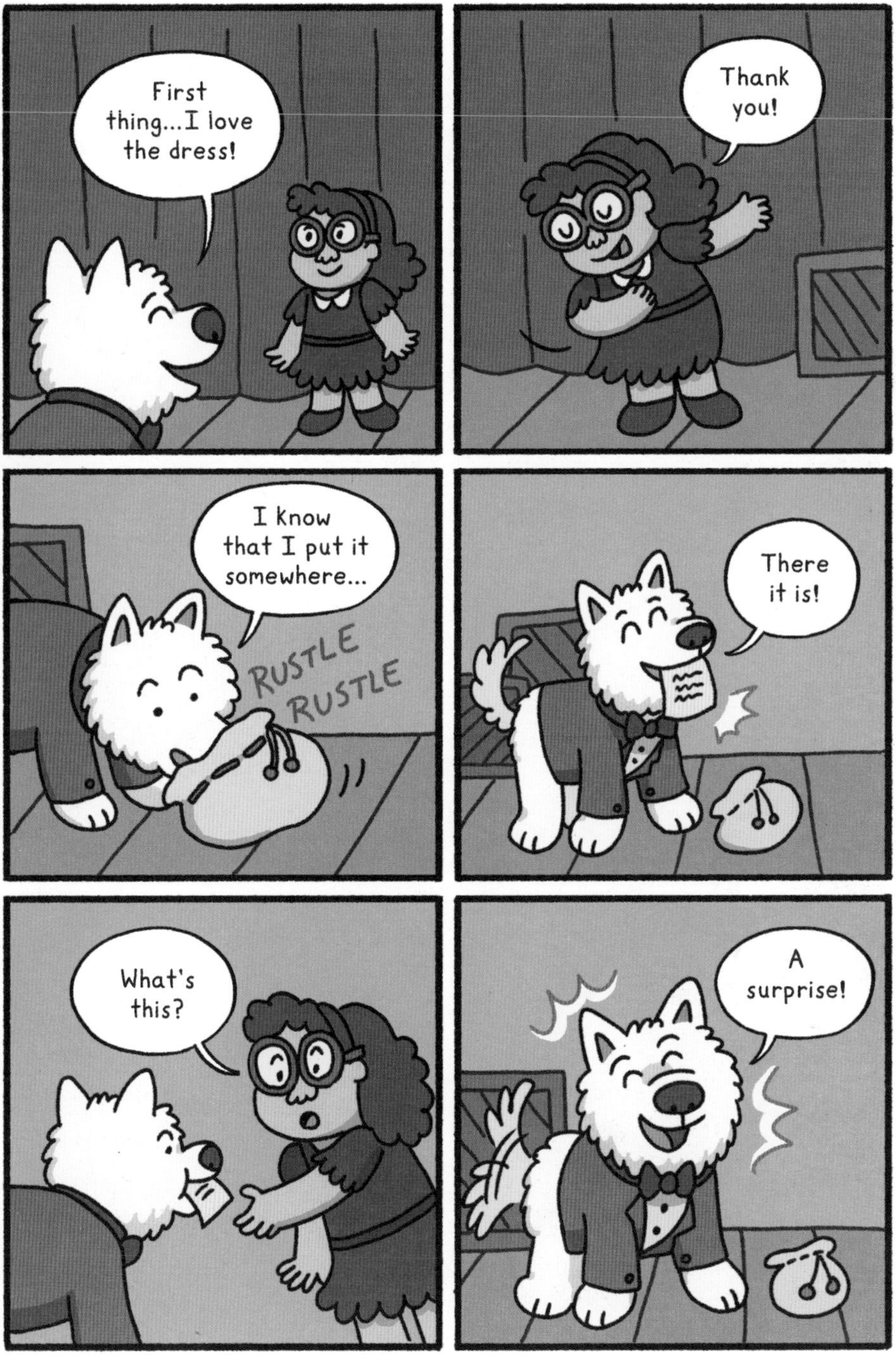
First thing...I love the dress!
Thank you!
I know that I put it somewhere...
RUSTLE RUSTLE
There it is!
What's this?
A surprise!

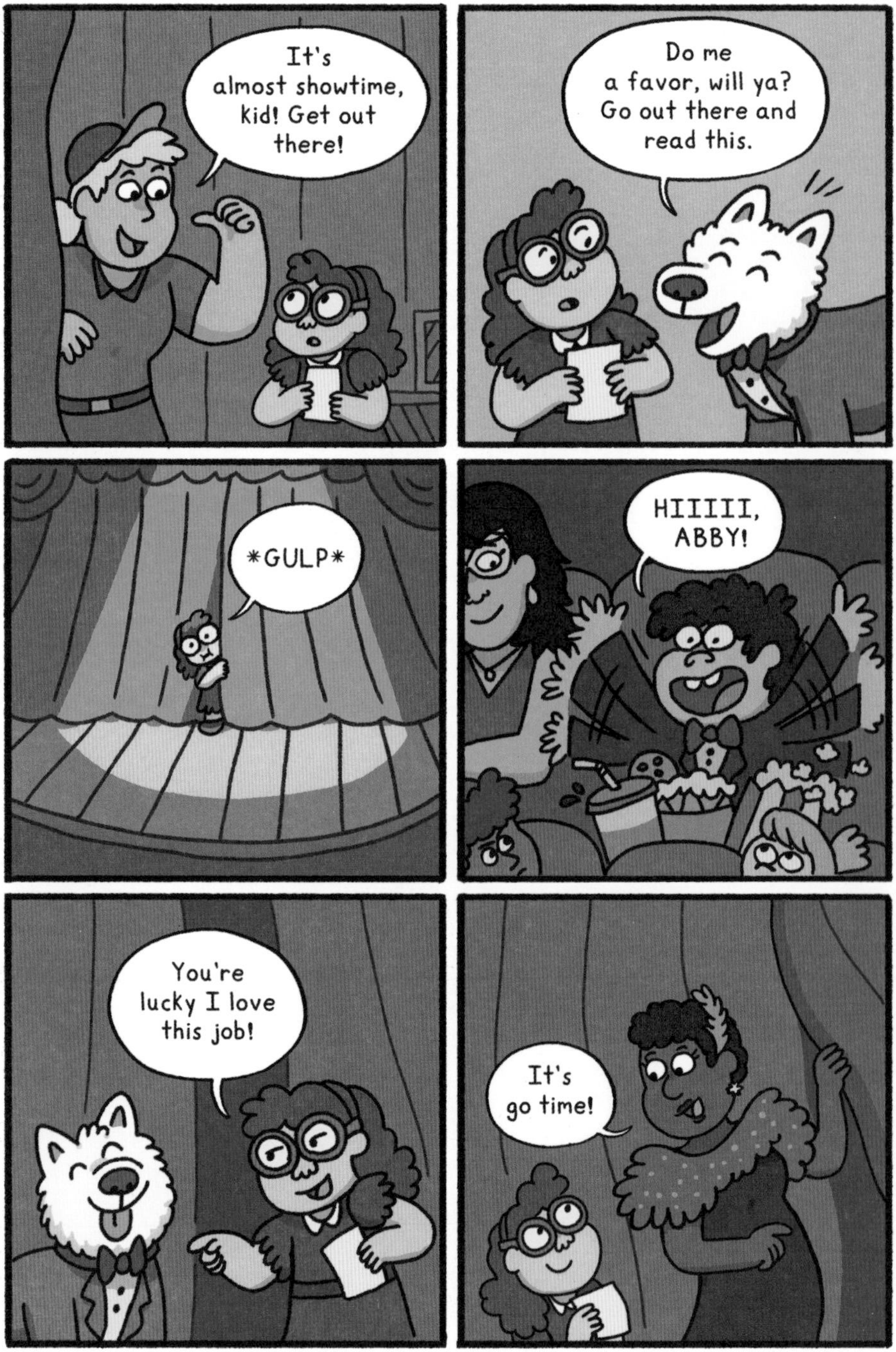
It's almost showtime, kid! Get out there!
Do me a favor, will ya? Go out there and read this.
GULP
HIIIII, ABBY!
You're lucky I love this job!
It's go time!

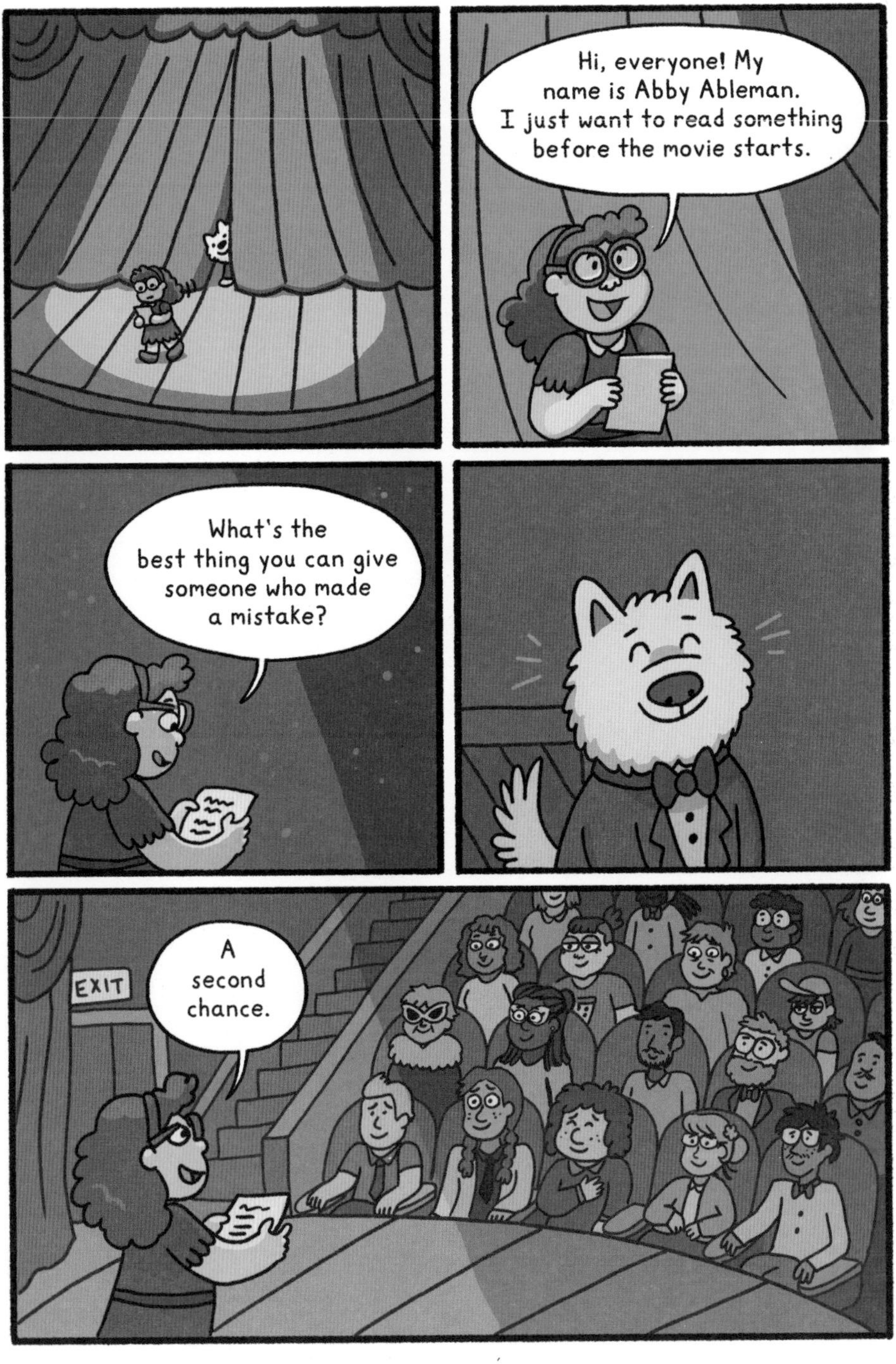
Hi, everyone! My name is Abby Ableman. I just want to read something before the movie starts.
What's the best thing you can give someone who made a mistake?
EXIT
A second chance.

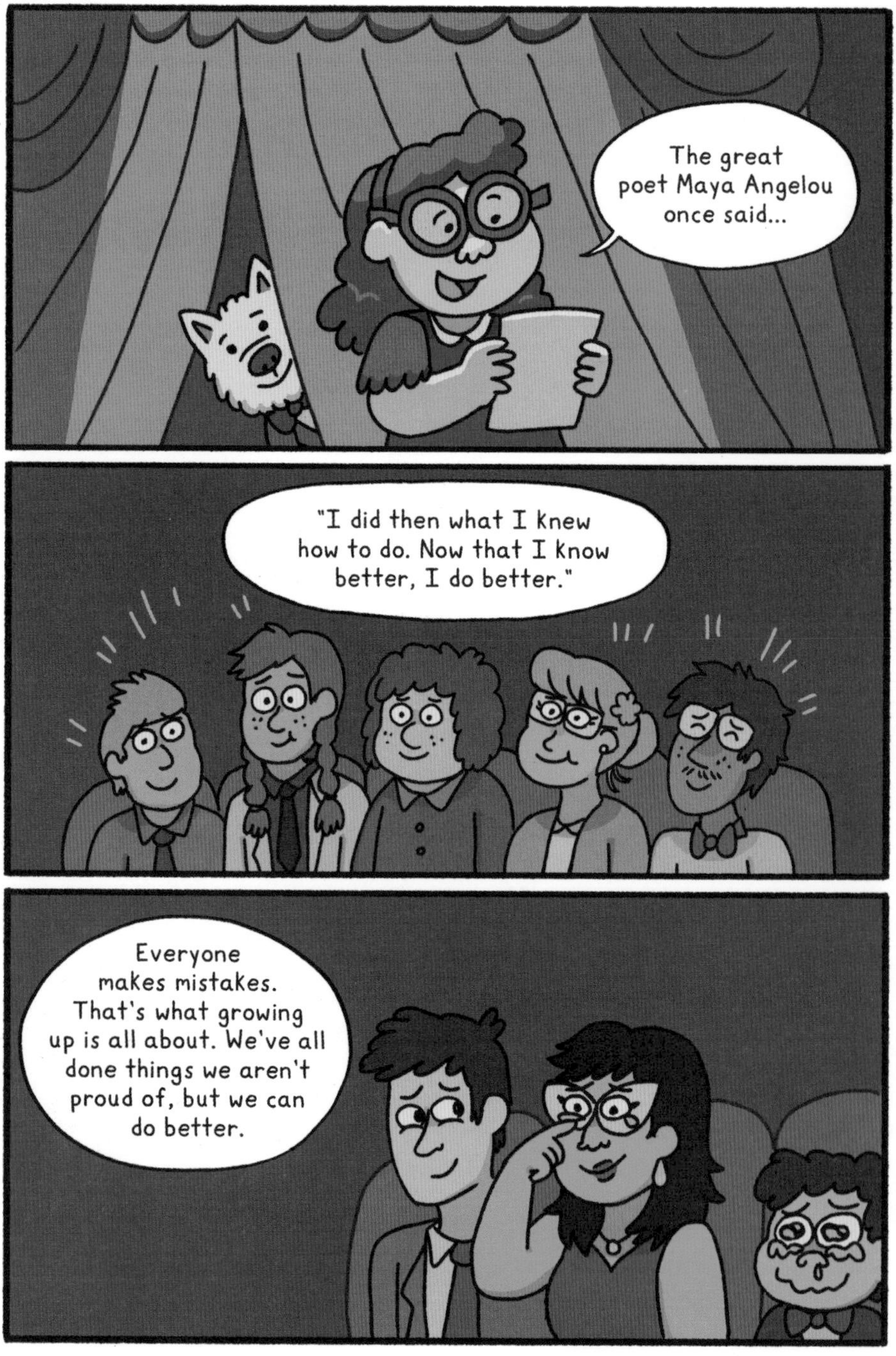
The great poet Maya Angelou once said...
"I did then what I knew how to do. Now that I know better, I do better."
Everyone makes mistakes. That's what growing up is all about. We've all done things we aren't proud of, but we can do better.

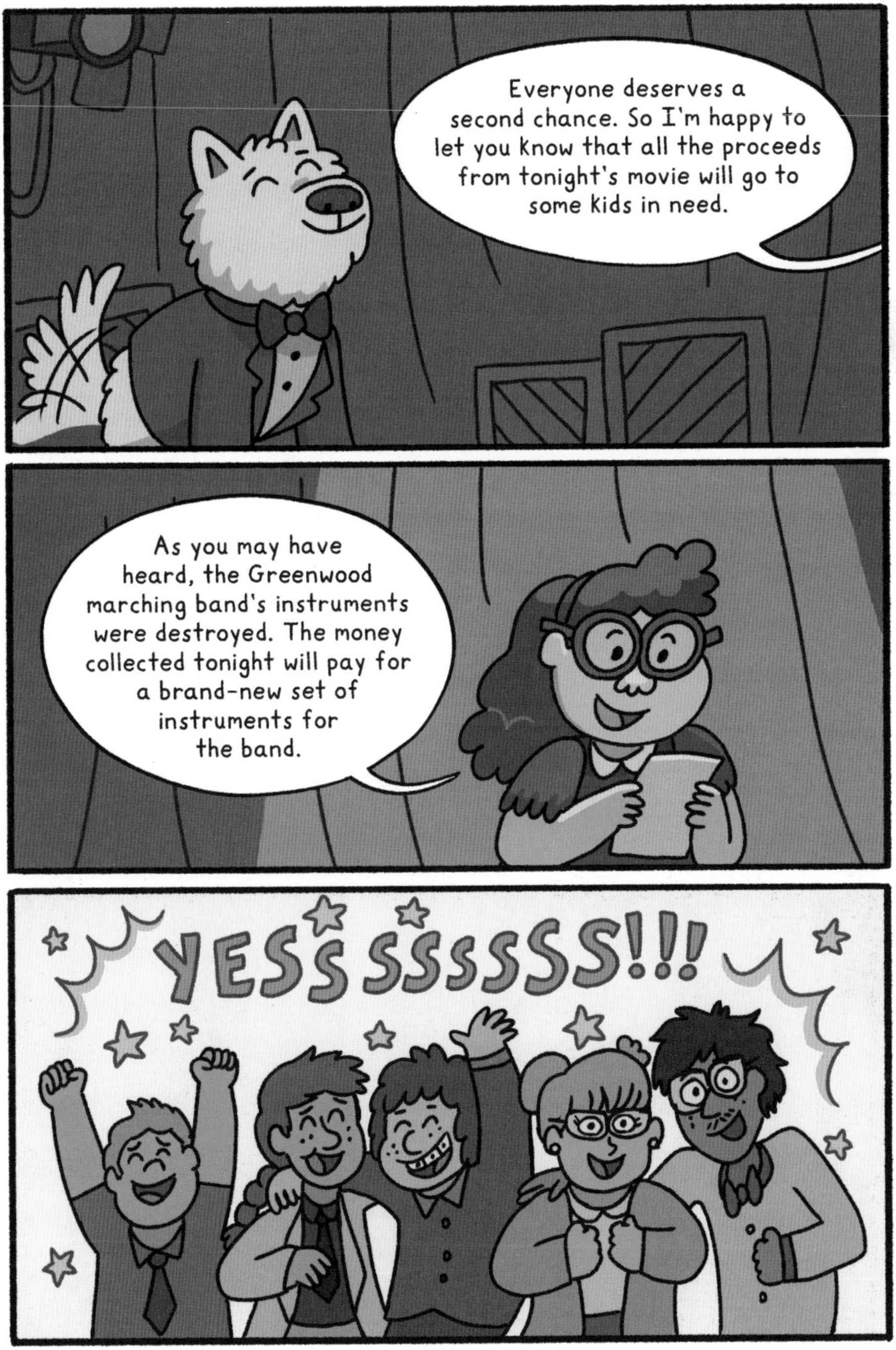
Everyone deserves a second chance. So I'm happy to let you know that all the proceeds from tonight's movie will go to some kids in need.
As you may have heard, the Greenwood marching band's instruments were destroyed. The money collected tonight will pay for a brand-new set of instruments for the band.
YESSSSSSSS!!!

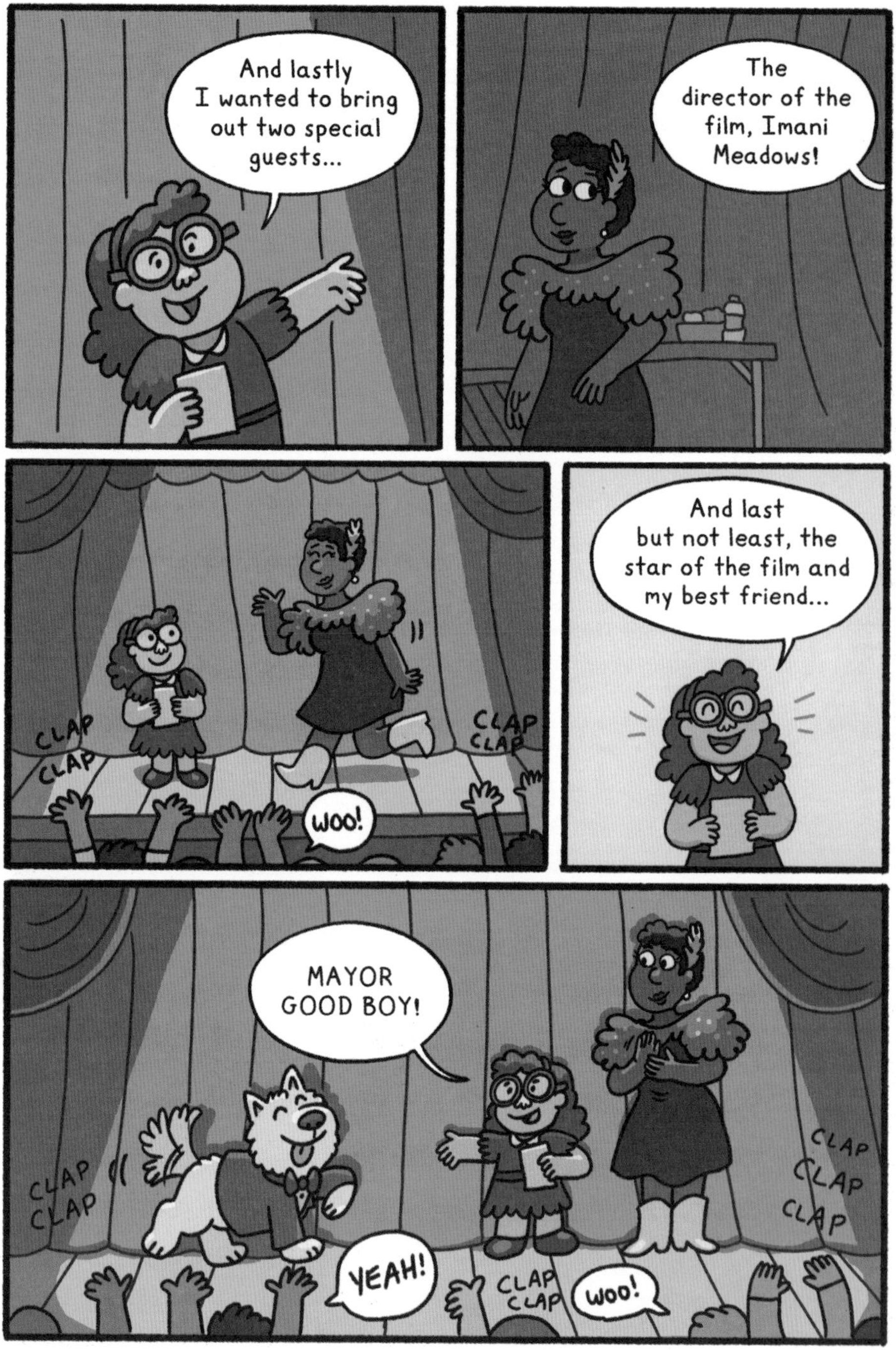
And lastly I wanted to bring out two special guests...
The director of the film, Imani Meadows!
CLAP
CLAP
CLAP
CLAP
WOO!
And last but not least, the star of the film and my best friend...
MAYOR GOOD BOY!
CLAP
CLAP
CLAP
CLAP
CLAP
YEAH!
CLAP
CLAP
WOO!

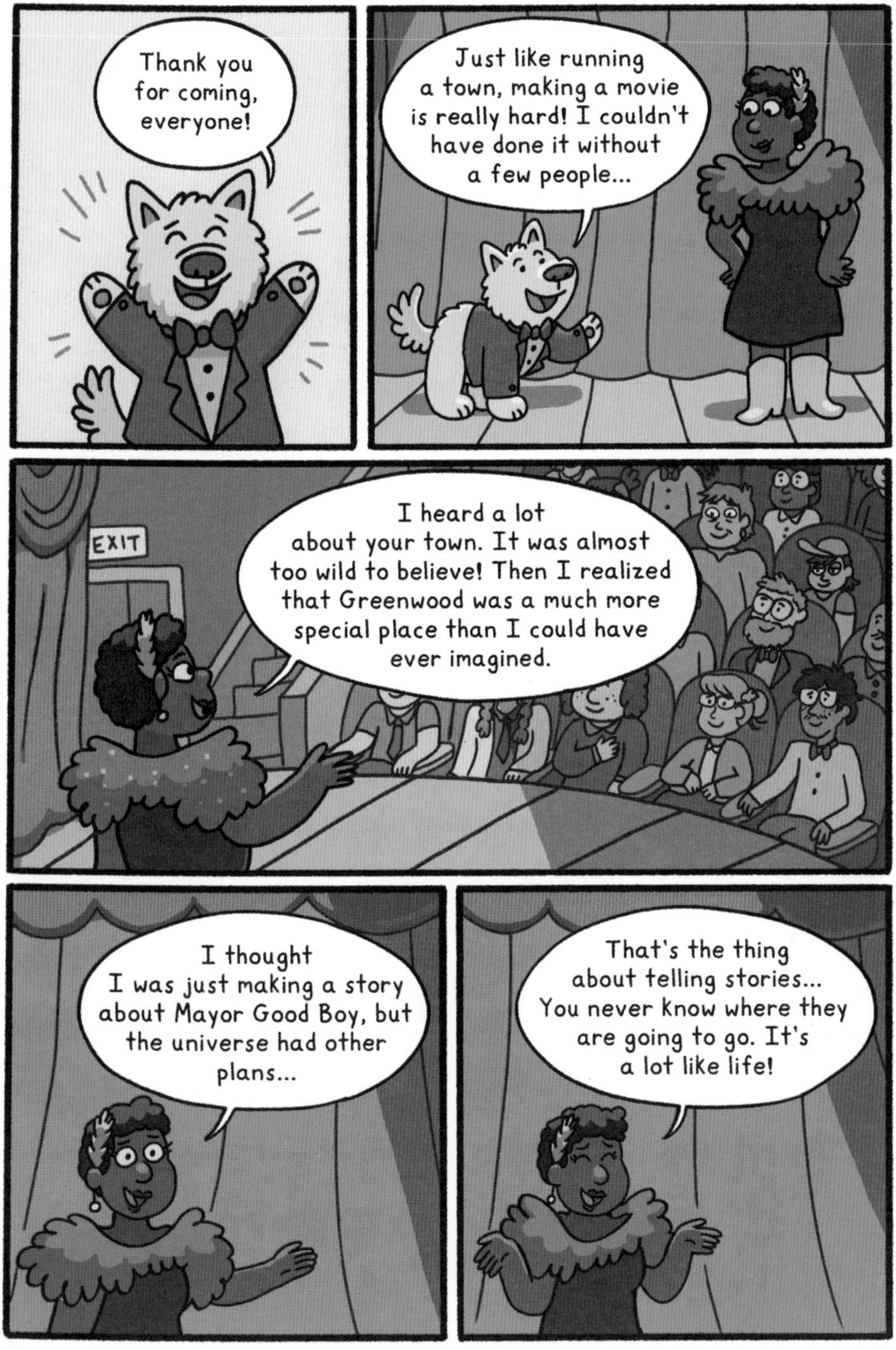
Thank you for coming, everyone!
Just like running a town, making a movie is really hard! I couldn't have done it without a few people...
EXIT
I heard a lot about your town. It was almost too wild to believe! Then I realized that Greenwood was a much more special place than I could have ever imagined.
I thought I was just making a story about Mayor Good Boy, but the universe had other plans...
That's the thing about telling stories... You never know where they are going to go. It's a lot like life!

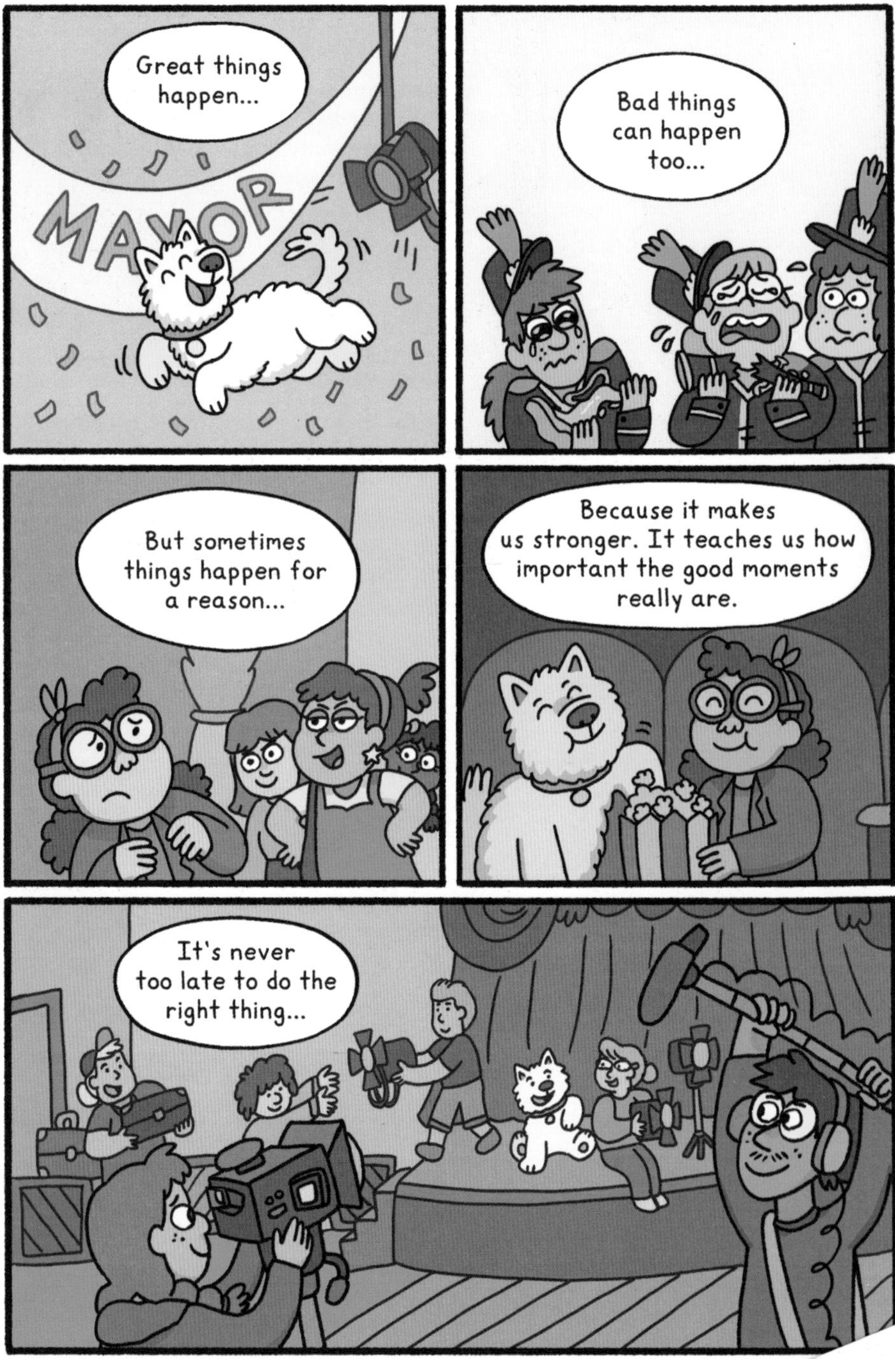

Great things happen...
MAYOR
Bad things can happen too...
But sometimes things happen for a reason...
Because it makes us stronger. It teaches us how important the good moments really are.
It's never too late to do the right thing...

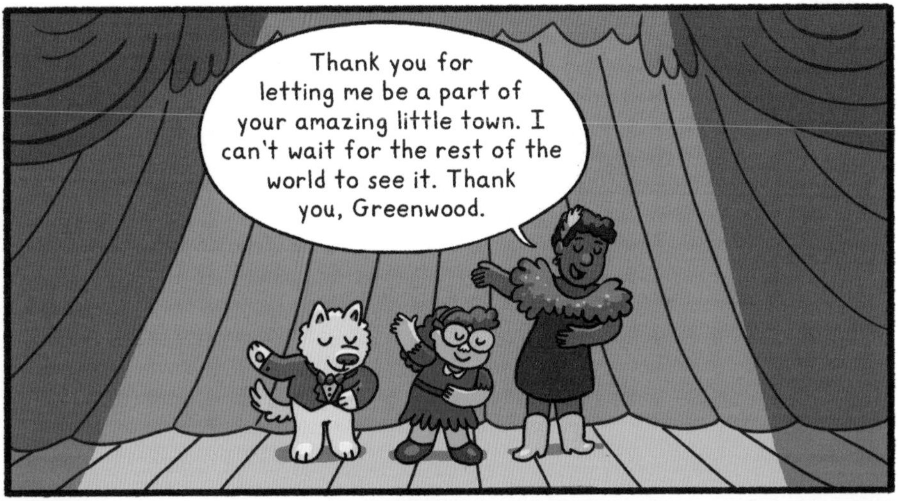
Thank you for letting me be a part of your amazing little town. I can't wait for the rest of the world to see it. Thank you, Greenwood.

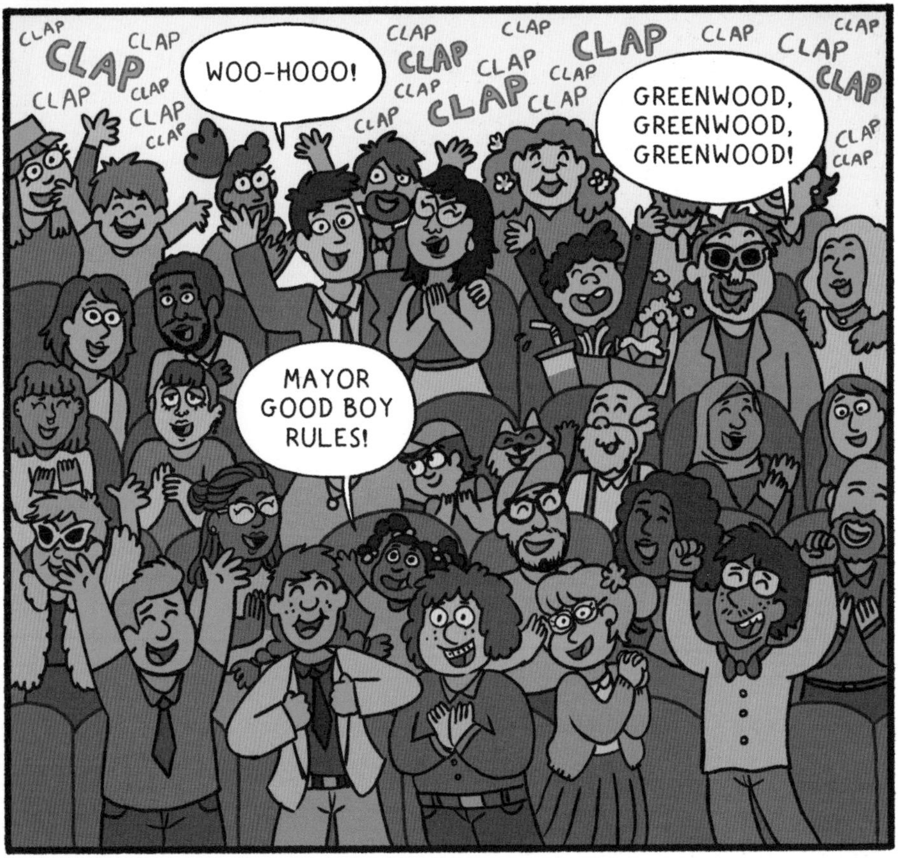
CLAP CLAP CLAP CLAP CLAP CLAP CLAP
WOO-HOOO!
CLAP CLAP CLAP CLAP CLAP CLAP CLAP CLAP CLAP CLAP CLAP CLAP
GREENWOOD, GREENWOOD, GREENWOOD!
MAYOR GOOD BOY RULES!

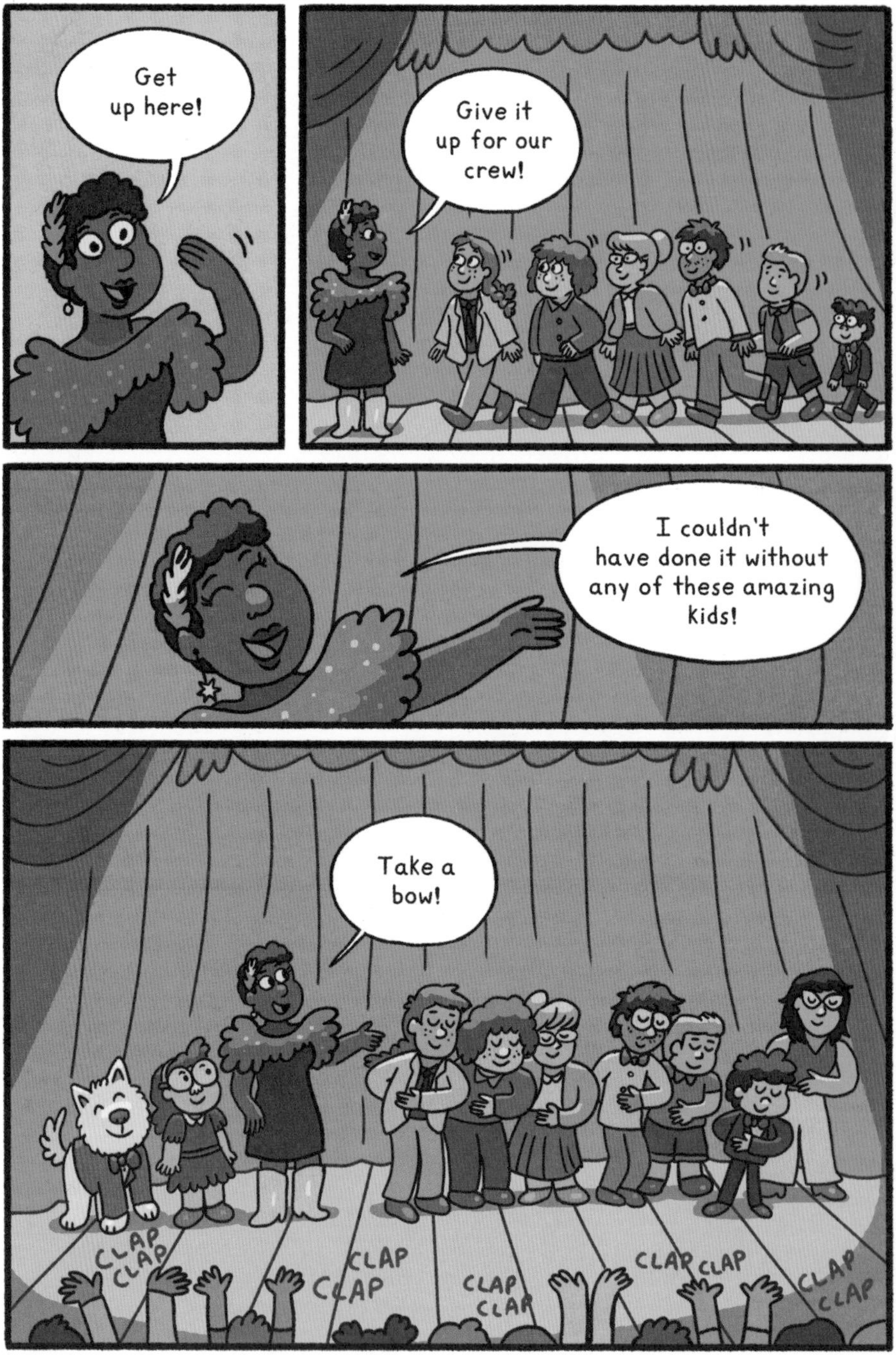
Get up here!
Give it up for our crew!
I couldn't have done it without any of these amazing kids!
Take a bow!
CLAP CLAP
CLAP CLAP
CLAP CLAP
CLAP CLAP
CLAP CLAP

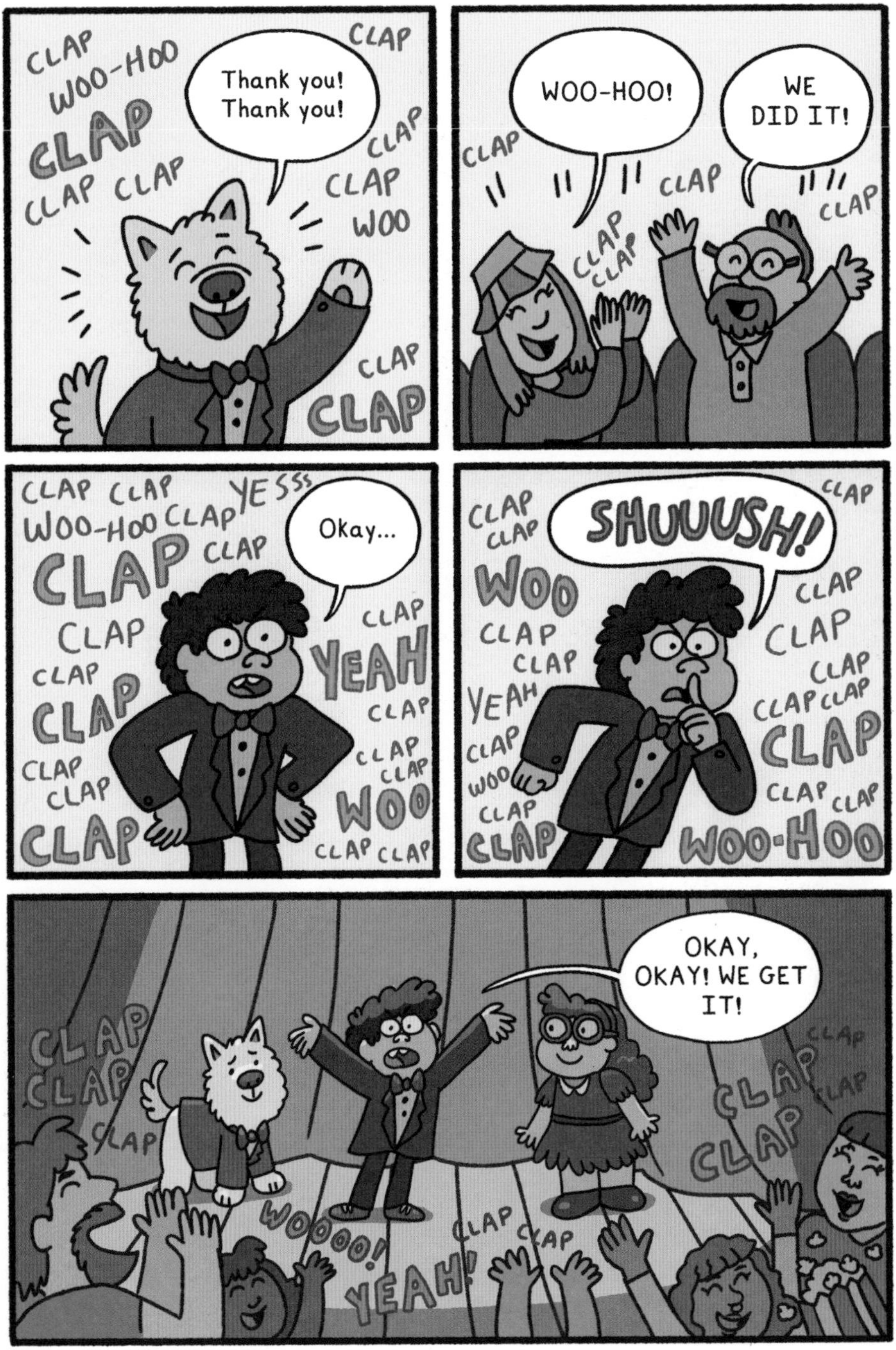
CLAP
WOO-HOO
CLAP
CLAP CLAP
CLAP
Thank you! Thank you!
CLAP
CLAP
WOO
CLAP
CLAP
WOO-HOO!
WE DID IT!
CLAP
CLAP
CLAP
CLAP CLAP
CLAP CLAP
WOO-HOO CLAP YESSS
CLAP CLAP
Okay...
CLAP
YEAH
CLAP
CLAP
CLAP CLAP
CLAP
WOO
CLAP CLAP
CLAP
SHUUUSH!
WOO
CLAP
CLAP
YEAH
CLAP
CLAP
WOO
CLAP
CLAP
WOO-HOO
OKAY, OKAY! WE GET IT!
CLAP
CLAP
CLAP
WOOOO!
YEAH!
CLAP
CLAP

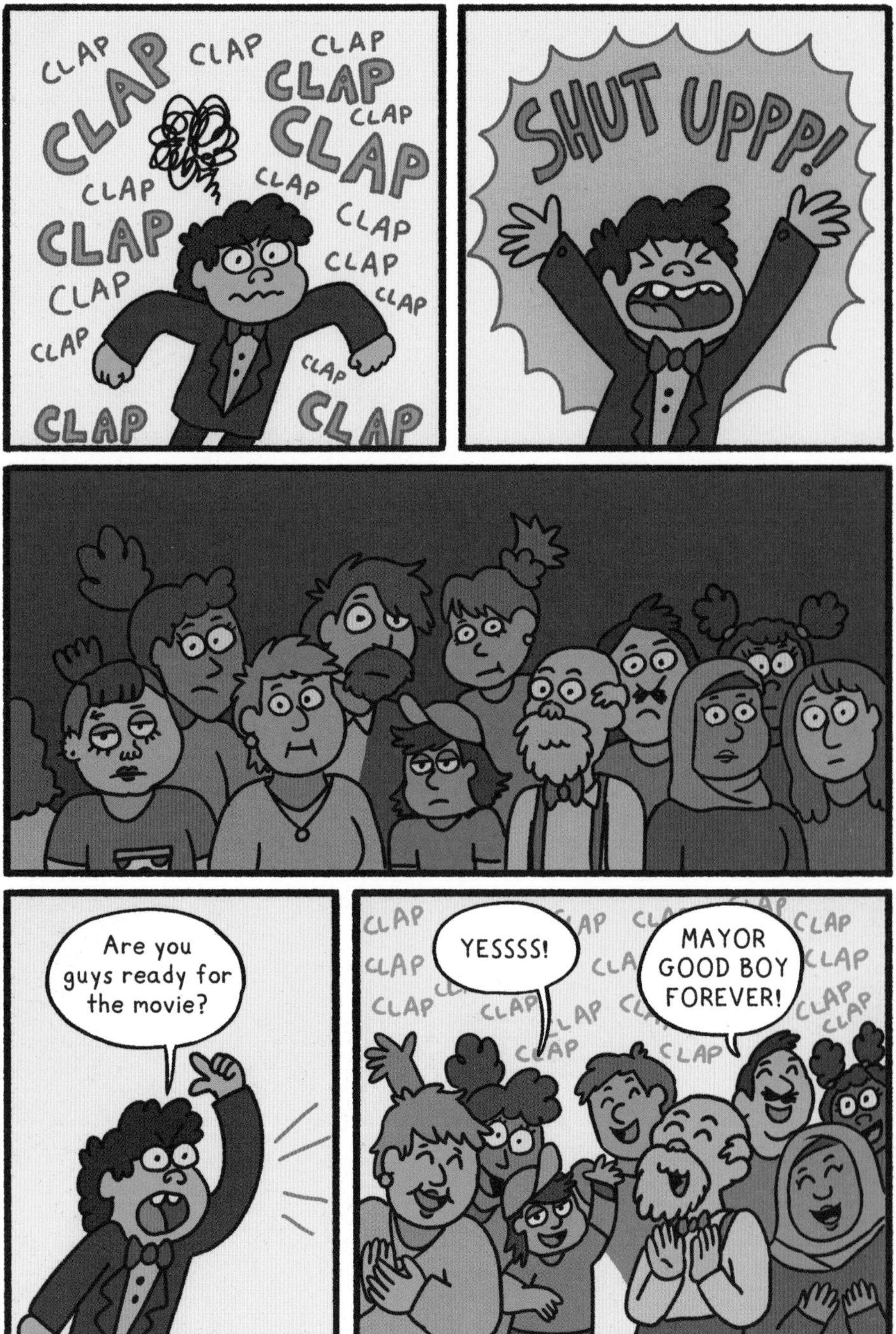
CLAP CLAP CLAP CLAP CLAP CLAP CLAP CLAP CLAP CLAP CLAP CLAP CLAP CLAP CLAP CLAP
SHUT UPPP!
Are you guys ready for the movie?
YESSSS!
MAYOR GOOD BOY FOREVER!

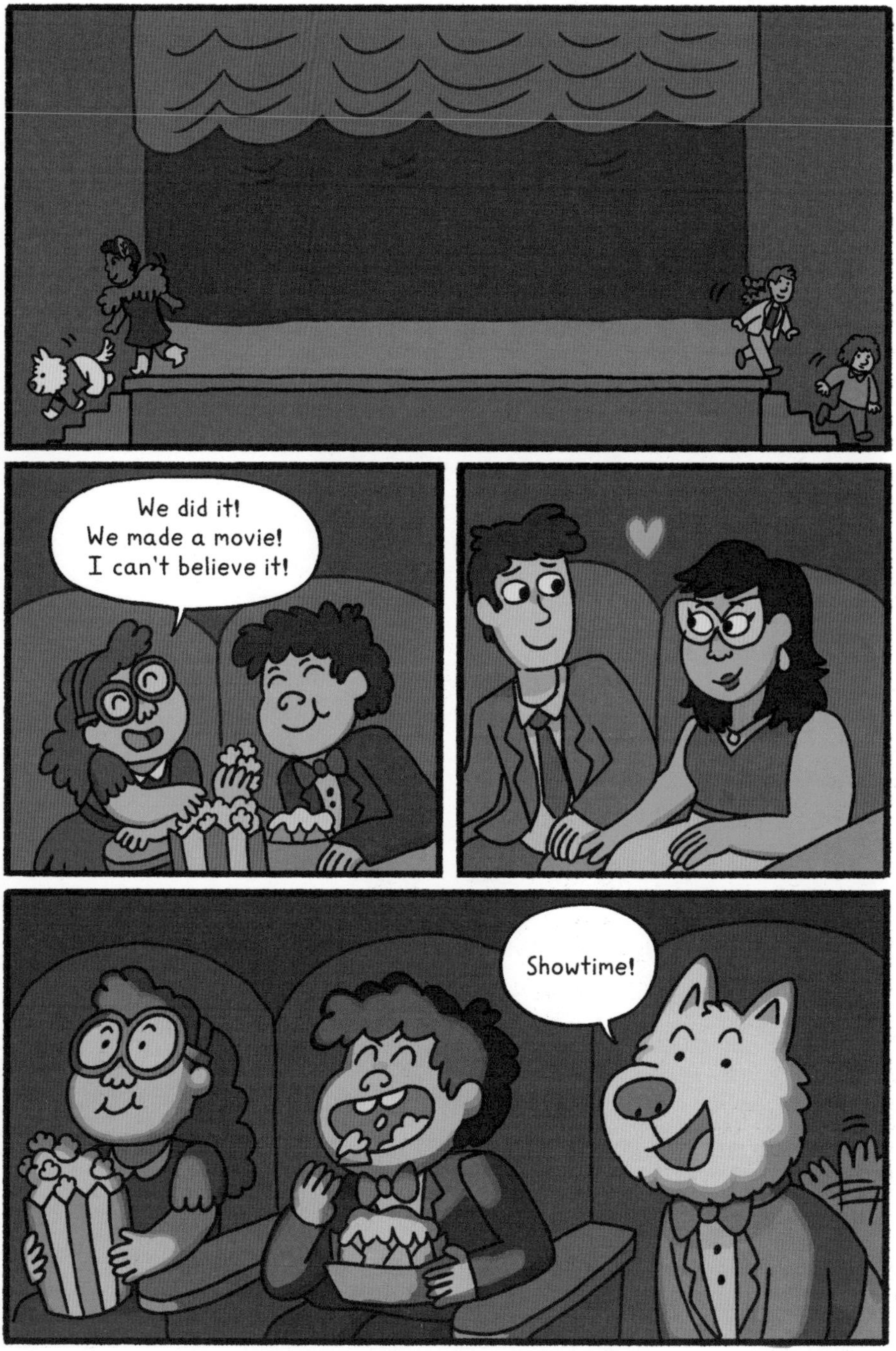
We did it!
We made a movie!
I can't believe it!
Showtime!

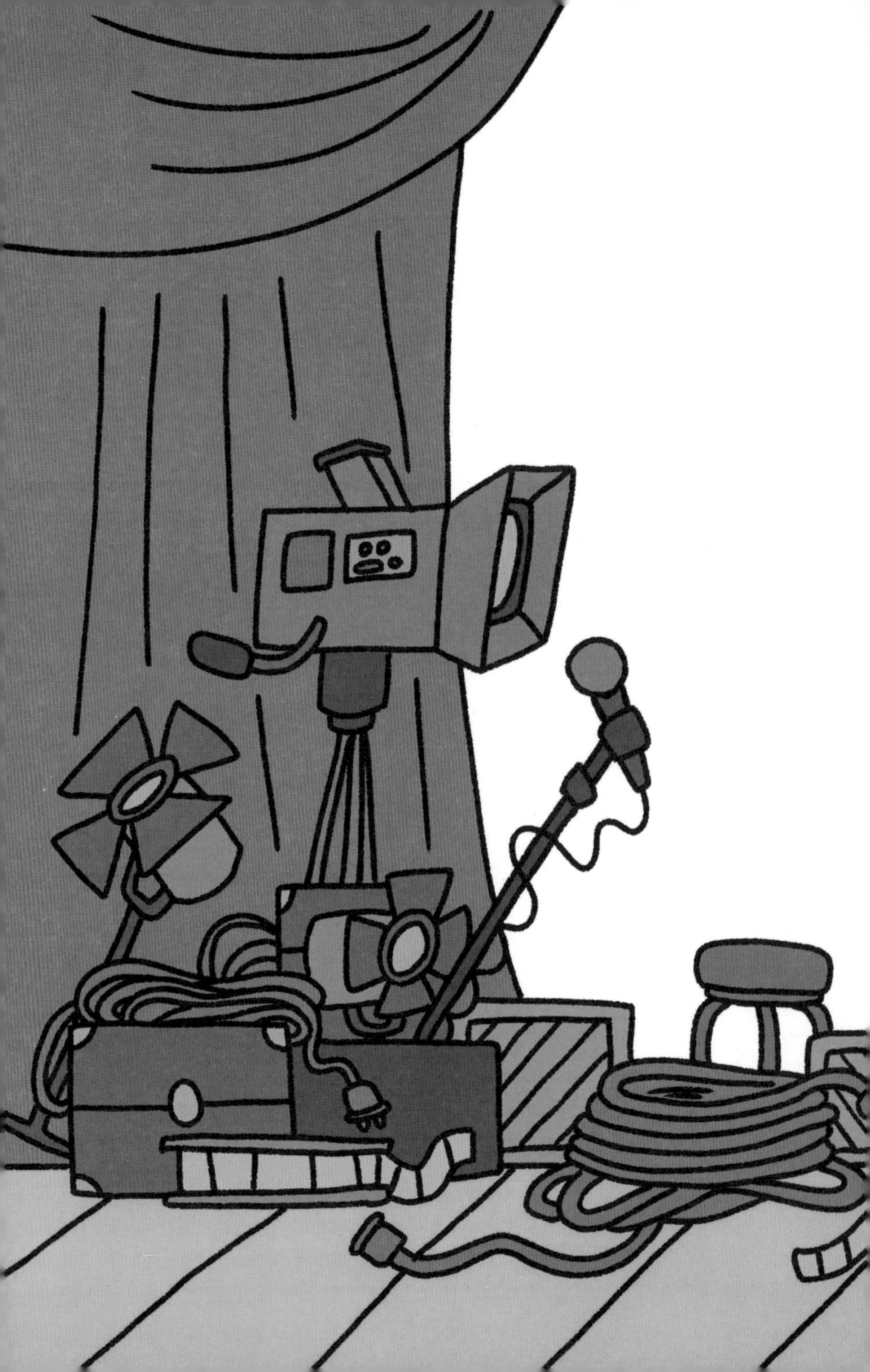

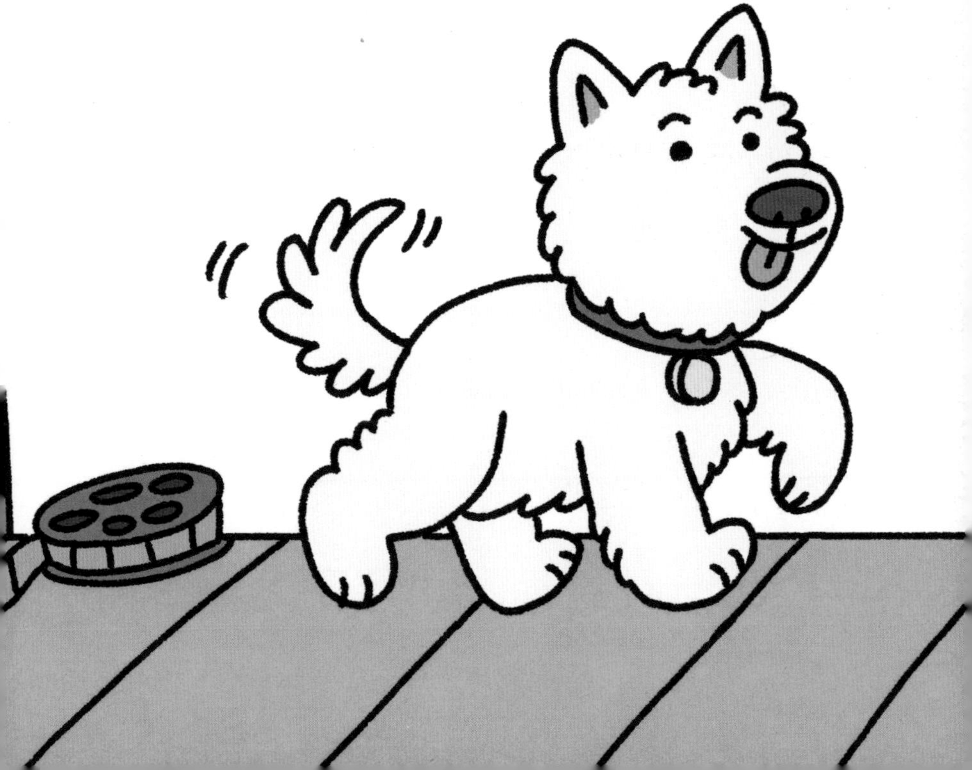

MEET the CAST!

Abby Ableman

Favorite Movie Snacks:
Popcorn, Cherry Cola,
Nachos, Churros

Favorite Movie Genres:
Anything with Vampires, Monsters,
Killer Dolls, Zombies, Aliens, Mummies,
and Other Spooky Stuff!

Aaron Ableman

Favorite Movie Snacks:
Orange Soda, Peanut Butter Cups,
Gummy Worms, Chocolate, Hot Dogs,
Ice Cream, Chips, Cookie Dough,
Cheese and Crackers

Favorite Movie Genres:
Dinosaur Movies! Kaiju Movies!
Cartoons! Action Movies!

Mayor Good Boy

Favorite Movie Snacks:
Cheddar Cheese, Brie Cheese,
Goat Cheese, Toscano Cheese,
Mozzarella Cheese!

Favorite Movie Genres:
Comedies, Action Movies,
Political Thrillers

Ms. Monica

Favorite Movie Snacks:
Pink Lemonade, Wasabi Peas,
Hot Chips, Soft Pretzels

Favorite Movie Genres:
Music Biopics, Indie Films,
'90s Romantic Comedies

Imani Meadows

Favorite Movie Snacks:
Root Beer, Sour Gummies,
Hot Dogs, Pizza

Favorite Movie Genres:
Documentaries, Music Videos,
Dramas, Adventure Movies

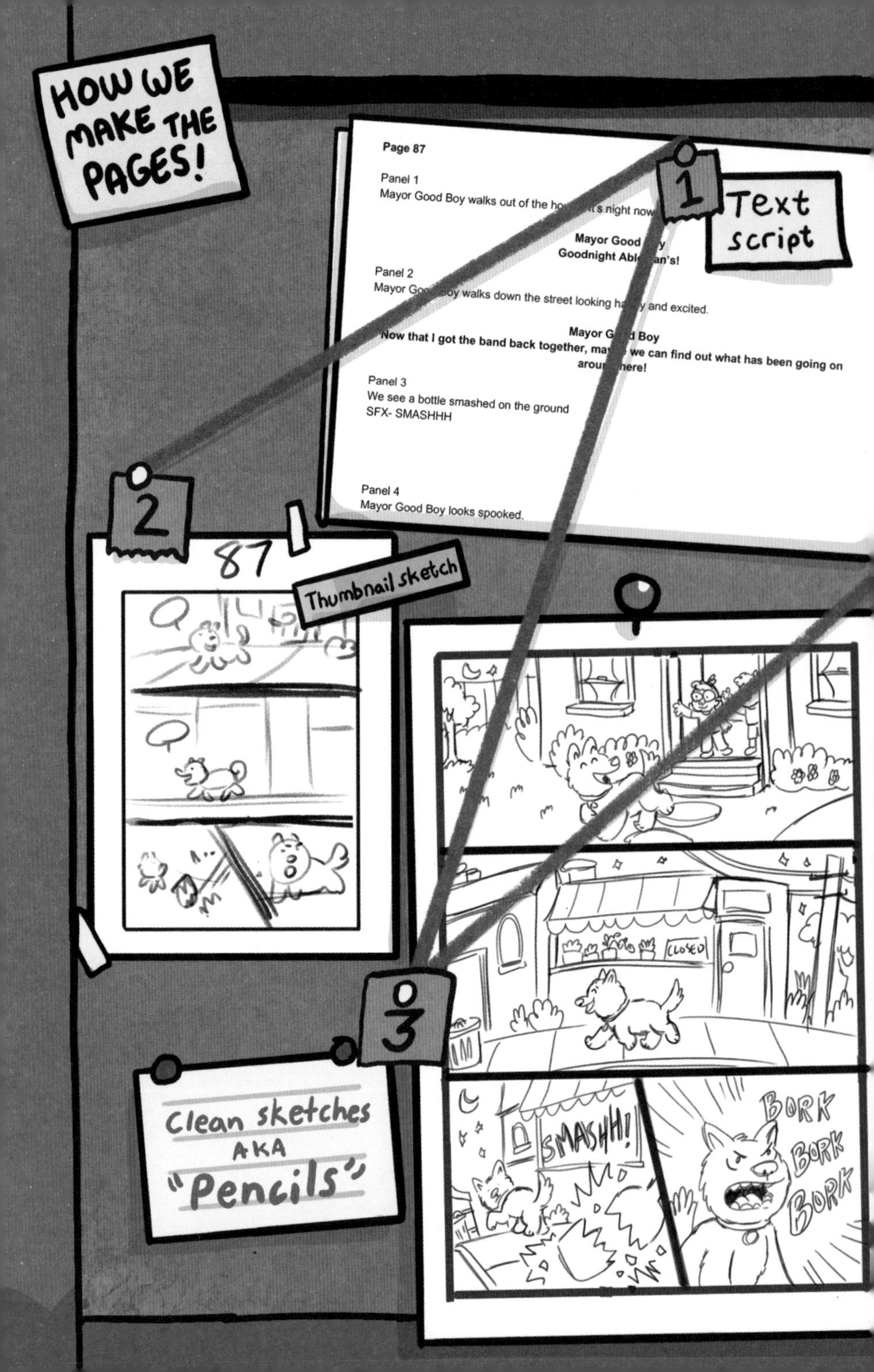

HOW WE MAKE THE PAGES!
1
Text script
Page 87
Panel 1
Mayor Good Boy walks out of the ho t's night now
Mayor Good y
Goodnight Able an's!
Panel 2
Mayor Go oy walks down the street looking ha y and excited.
Mayor G d Boy
Now that I got the band back together, ma we can find out what has been going on arou here!
Panel 3
We see a bottle smashed on the ground
SFX- SMASHHH
Panel 4
Mayor Good Boy looks spooked.
2
87
Thumbnail sketch
3
CLOSED
SMASHH!
BORK
BORK
BORK
Clean sketches AKA "Pencils"

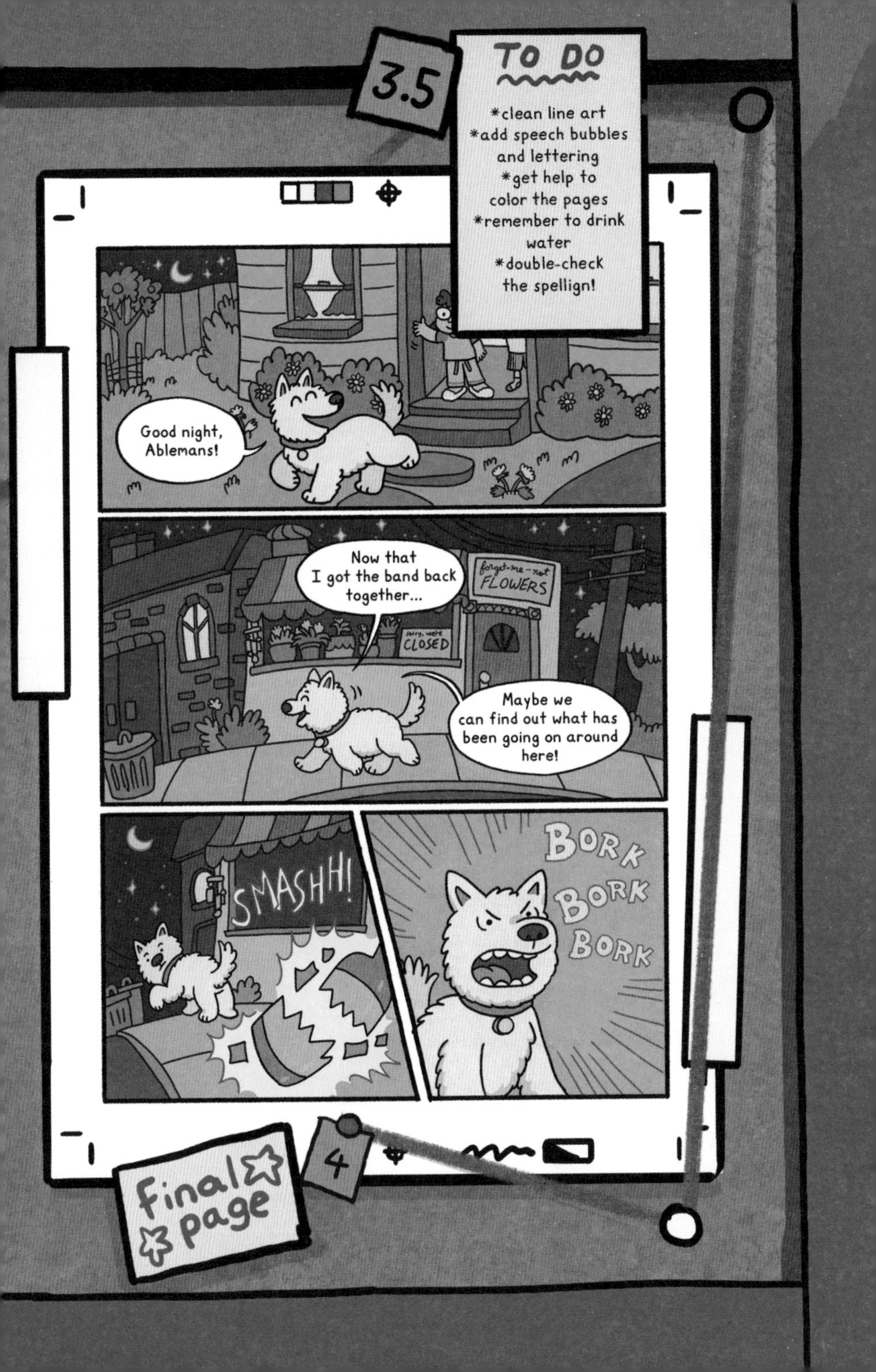

3.5
TO DO
*clean line art
*add speech bubbles and lettering
*get help to color the pages
*remember to drink water
*double-check the spellign!
Good night, Ablemans!
Now that I got the band back together...
forget-me-not FLOWERS
sorry, we're CLOSED
Maybe we can find out what has been going on around here!
SMASHH!
BORK
BORK
BORK
4
final page

Ms. Monica's Ultimate Peanut Butter and Banana Smoothie

Ingredients:

Make sure you have a grown-up's permission to use the blender!

-2 frozen bananas (Have an adult slice them for you.) 
-2 tablespoons of peanut butter
-2 cups of milk (You can use almond milk, oat milk, or soy too!)
-2 tablespoons of honey or brown sugar

Instructions:

1. Drop the frozen bananas into the blender.

2. Add the peanut butter and honey or brown sugar.

3. Add the milk.

4. Blend.

5. Pour into a glass.

6. YUM!

MAYOR GOOD BOY'S CHEESE POPCORN

Ingredients:

-6 cups of popped popcorn

-3 tablespoons of melted butter

-1/4 cup of cheddar cheese powder

Instructions:

1. Put popcorn in a large bowl. Drizzle melted butter over the popcorn and toss it to coat.

2. Sprinkle the cheese powder and shake the bowl to cover all the popcorn.

3. Enjoy!

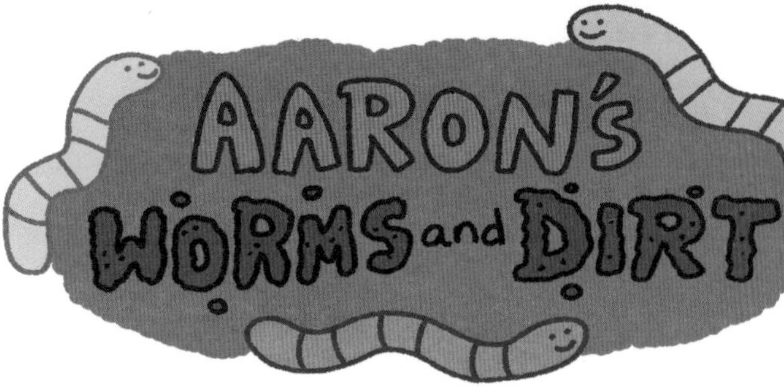
AARON'S
WORMS and DIRT

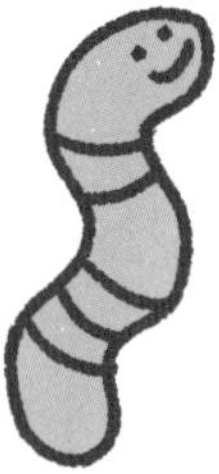

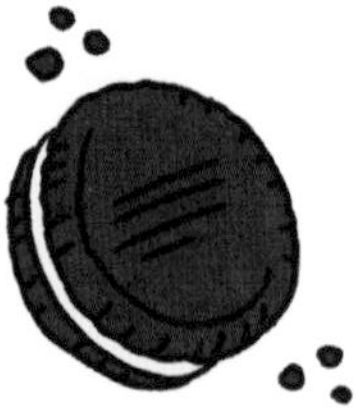

Ingredients:

- Prepackaged pudding cup
- Chocolate sandwich cookies
- Gummy worms

Instructions:

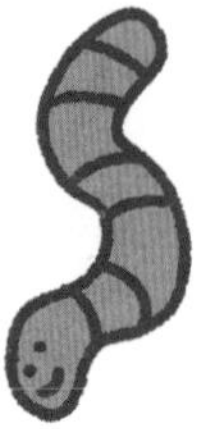

1. Put a few cookies in a ziplock bag, then crush them until they look like dirt.

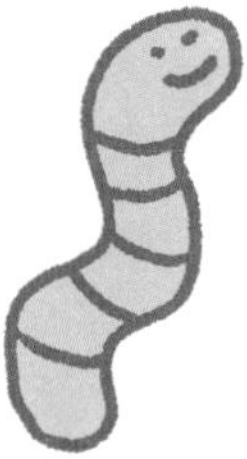

2. Sprinkle the cookie dirt into the pudding cup.

3. Drop some gummy worms into the pudding cup.

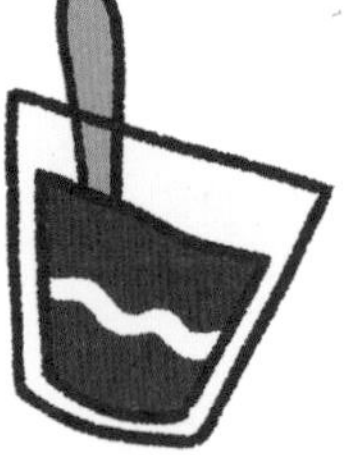

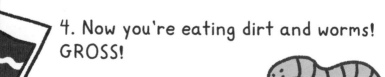

4. Now you're eating dirt and worms! GROSS!

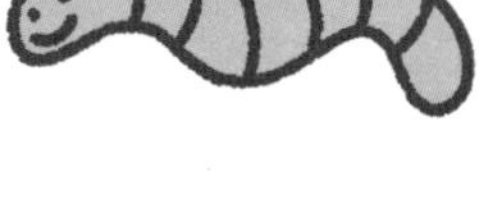

ABBY's ROOTBEER FLOAT

Ingredients:

-Vanilla ice cream

-Root beer

Instructions:

1. Drop one or two scoops of vanilla ice cream into a tall glass. Pour a little bit of root beer into the glass. Wait for the foam to rise to the top, then pour more root beer.

2. Use a straw or spoon. Eat up!

3. (Optional) Add a little chocolate syrup to make it a Brown Cow!

DAVE SCHEIDT is a writer from Chicago. When he's not writing comic books, he likes watching monster movies and eating snacks. He first started writing stories when he was ten years old and hasn't stopped since.

davescheidt.com

DAVE THANKS

I would first like to thank my family for all the years of support. My father, Thomas Scheidt, who was literally the first person on earth to read my stories and sacrificed everything to help me find my voice. My late mother, Elizabeth Scheidt, was one of the toughest people I have ever met. She had so much love to give even at the very end, and I miss her every day. To my brother, Eric, who filled my life with comic books and toys that shaped me and who supported my creativity since the very beginning. To my sister, Sarah, who has been with me during my darkest days and never gave up on me and made sure I turned out okay. I love you all deeply, and without you this book wouldn't exist.

I would also like to thank Natalie Djordjevic for always believing in me and for the thankless work you have done for my career. I would be lost without you, and I'm so glad to have you in my life. The amount of love and wisdom and laughs you bring is immeasurable. Love you forever and ever.

Thank you to everyone at Random House (Whitney, Gina, Patrick, Nicole) who believed in our little doggie and saw that his story was worth telling. I'd also like to thank Charlie Olsen, Scoot McMahon, Yehudi Mercado, Whitney Gardener, Joey Weiser, Kayla Miller, Steenz and Keya, Ryan, Carrie and Kirby Browne, Josephine M. Yales, Patrick Brower, Nick and Selene Idell, Art Baltazar, Franco Aureliani, Mitch Gerards, Jess Smart Smiley, Kenny Porter, Kris Erickson, Alejandro Rosado, John and Aneta Baran, Tim Beard, Tara Kurtzhals, Tara O'Connor, Andrea Colvin, Hazel Newlevant, Brandon Snider, Trevor Henderson, James Zespy, Shawna Gore, Eric Roesner, Raphael Espinoza, Mike Costa, Andrew Rostan, Rachel Roberts, Bethany Bryan, Elizabeth Brei, Brian Level, Andy Eschenbach, Liz Kozik, Steve Seeley, Jenny Frison, Brian Crowley, Sean Dove, Tony Blando, Jen Sabella, Robert Wilson IV, Tini Howard, Elio, Christopher Sebela, RJ Casey, and everyone and anyone who has supported me throughout the years.

I'd also like to thank each and every librarian, educator, and bookseller who is out there helping kids find themselves in the pages of a book. You are so important, and I'm so grateful to work in an industry with great people like you.

Last but not least, I would like to send all my love to Miranda Harmon. Without her incredibly sweet and beautiful cartooning, this book wouldn't exist. She has brought this book to life in a way I could have never imagined. I am in awe of her creativity, talent, and hard work, and it's been an honor creating this world with her.

MIRANDA HARMON

grew up in Florida and now lives in Los Angeles, where she works and takes care of several houseplants. She graduated from Goucher College and studied comics at the Sequential Artists Workshop. Even though she grew up with cats, she loves dogs too.

🐦 @MirandaMHarmon
mirandaharmon.com

MIRANDA THANKS

I have so many people to thank. I'd first like to thank my parents for being so supportive from the other side of the country. Thank you to Tom Hart, Leela Corman, Justine Mara Andersen, and everyone else at the Sequential Artists Workshop in Gainesville, Florida, for your patience and guidance. I might not be making books now if I hadn't been given use of the SAW Risograph machine for two years. Thank you, Eric Kubli, my loving and supportive partner, for making every day special. Thank you, Dave Scheidt, for coming to me with the brilliant idea for Mayor Good Boy, and for being a great collaborator and friend during the making of these books. A huge thank-you to Whitney Leopard, Danny Diaz, Gina Gagliano, Patrick Crotty, and Charlie Olsen for all your help making this series. I feel lucky to be a part of such a great team. Thank you, Lyle Lynde, for coloring this book and adding so much dimension to these pages. Thank you to all my friends I've met through comics, too many to name here, who have welcomed me into this industry and guided me for years. Thank you for all the memories at SPX and TCAF, for keeping in touch over long distances, for inspiring me, and for reminding me that comics are fun, and special, and worth it. Even though we see each other in person so rarely, you all have changed my life for the better just by being in it, even a little bit.

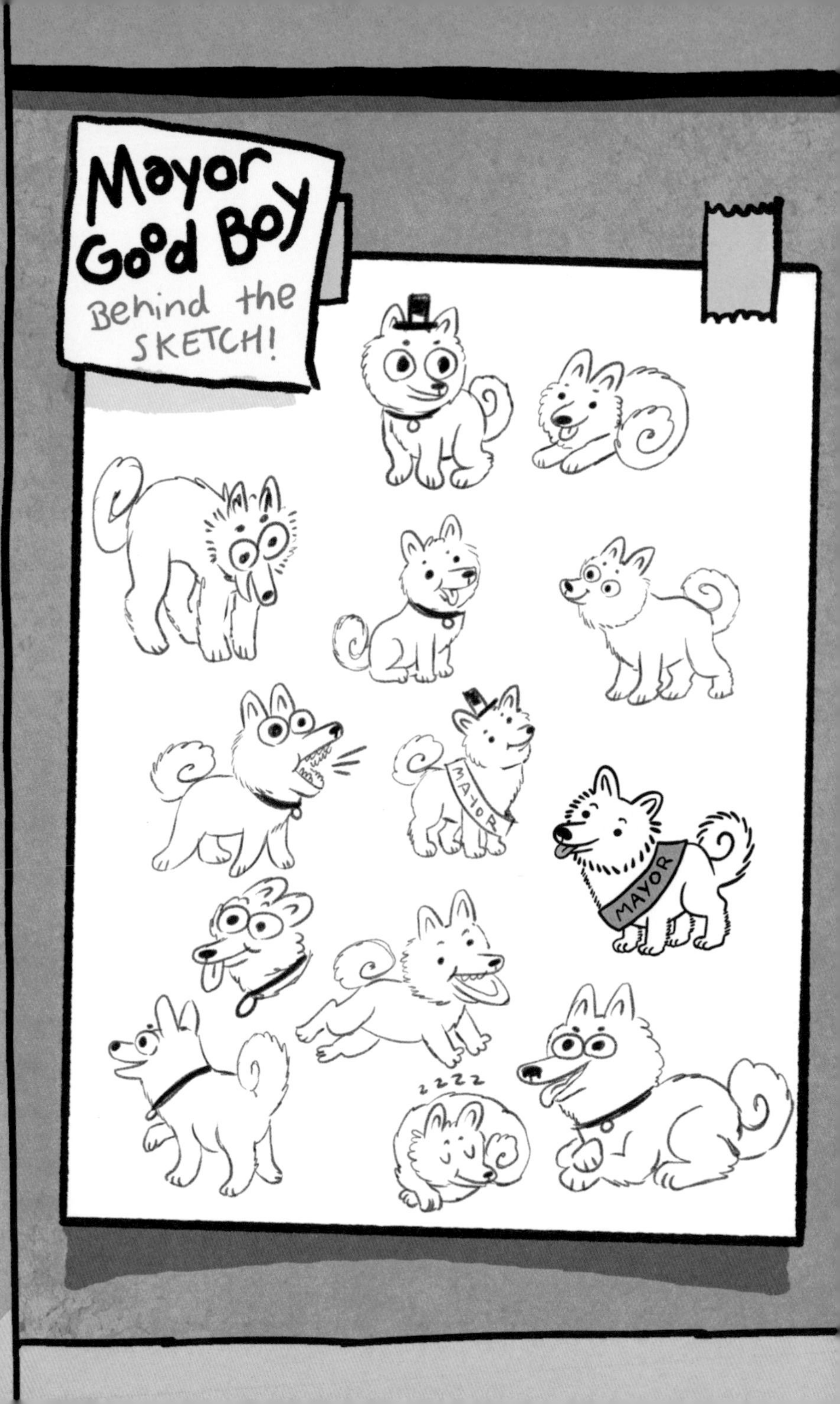

Mayor Good Boy
Behind the SKETCH!
MAYOR
MAYOR
zzzz

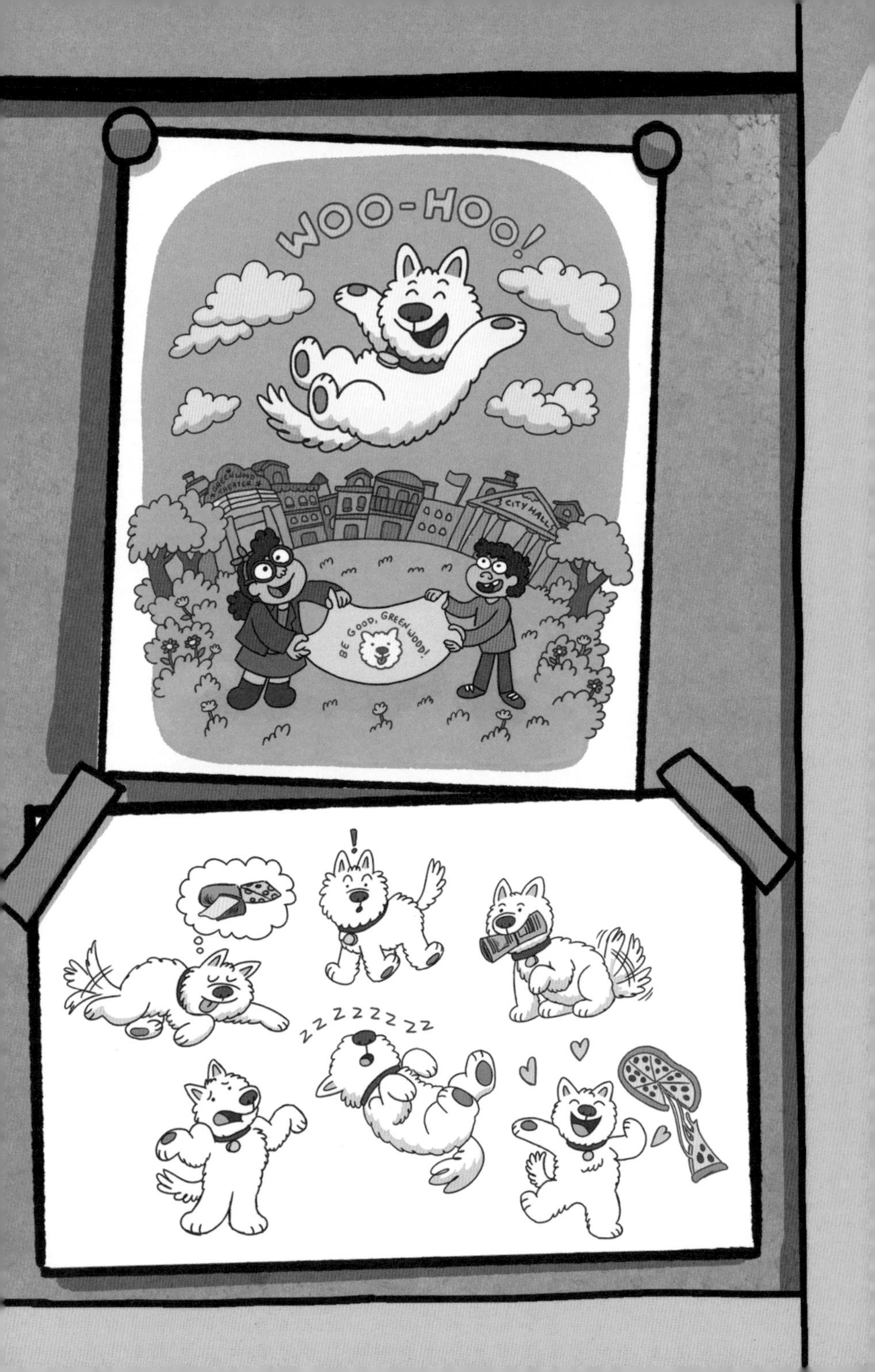
WOO-HOO!
GREENWOOD THEATER
CITY HALL
BE GOOD, GREENWOOD!

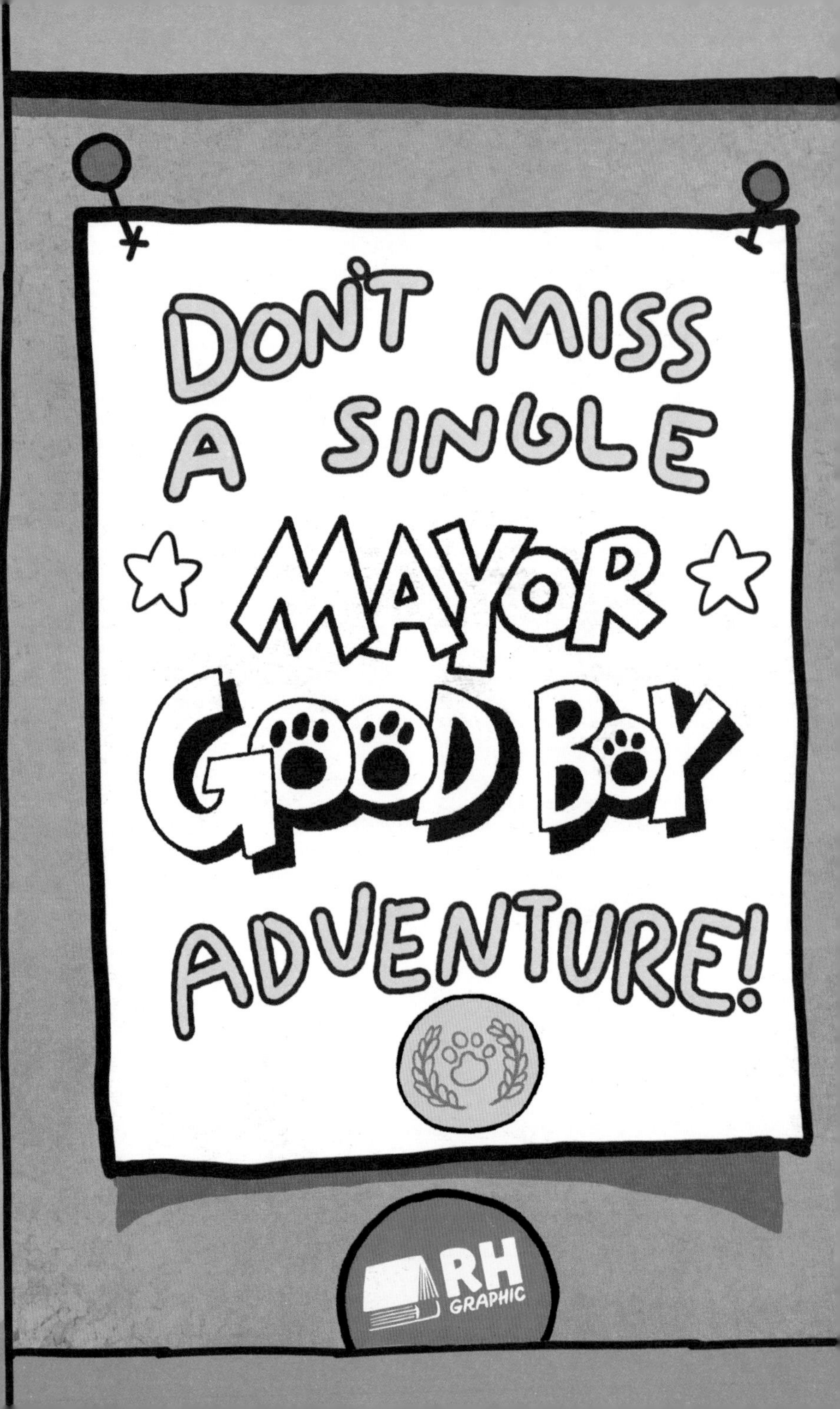
DON'T MISS A SINGLE
MAYOR GOOD BOY
ADVENTURE!
RH GRAPHIC

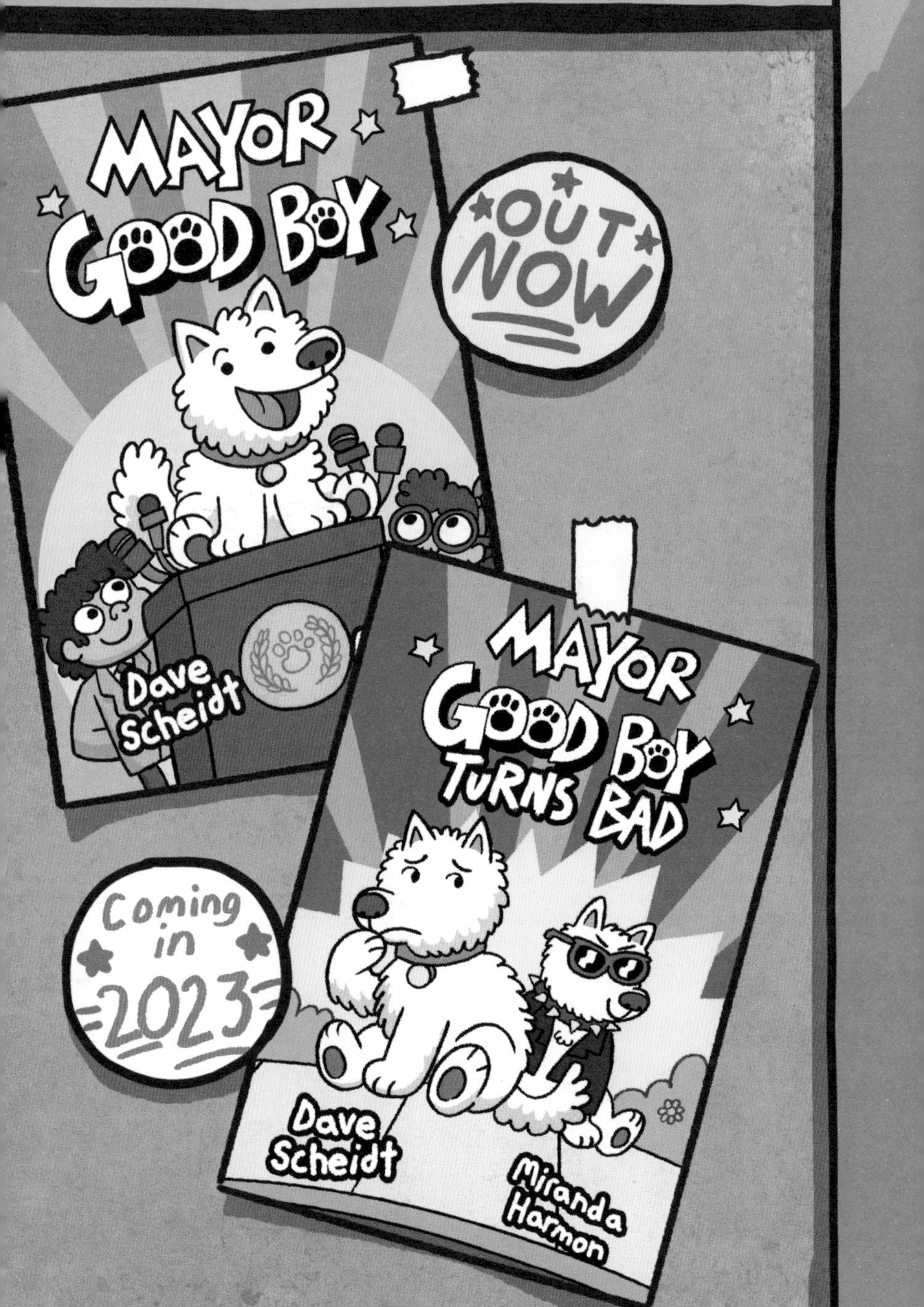
MAYOR GOOD BOY
Dave Scheidt
OUT NOW
MAYOR GOOD BOY TURNS BAD
Dave Scheidt
Miranda Harmon
Coming in 2023

FIND YOUR VOICE

WITH ONE OF THESE EXCITING GRAPHIC NOVELS

CHAD SELL
DOODLEVILLE
THE CARDBOARD KINGDOM
CHAD SELL
THE CARDBOARD KINGDOM
ROAR OF THE BEAST
CHAD SELL
LUCY KNISLEY
STEPPING STONES
JUST ROLL WITH IT
VERONICA AGARWAL & LEE DURFEY-LAVOIE
TURTLE IN PARADISE
The Graphic Novel
JENNIFER L. HOLM
SAVANNA GANUCHEAU
KATIE THE CATSITTER
Colleen AF Venable
Stephanie Yue

PRESENTED BY RH GRAPHIC

@RHKIDSGRAPHIC

A GRAPHIC NOVEL ON EVERY BOOKSHELF

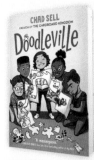

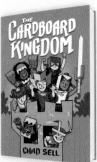

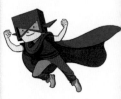

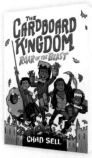

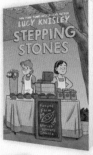

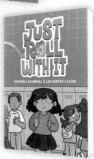

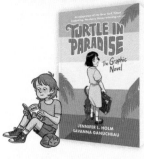

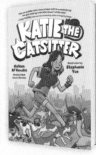

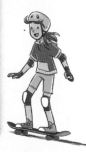